FOR KING AND COUNTRY

FOR KING AND COUNTRY

Kate Sedley

This title first published in Great Britain 2006 by
SEVERN HOUSE PUBLISHERS LTD of
9–15 High Street, Sutton, Surrey SM1 1DF.
First published in Great Britain in 1980 under
the title *The Lofty Banners* by *Brenda Clarke*.
This title first published in the USA 2006 by
SEVERN HOUSE PUBLISHERS INC of
595 Madison Avenue, New York, N.Y. 10022.

British Library Cataloguing in Publication Data

Sedley, Kate
  For king and country
  1.   Great Britain - History - Civil War, 1642-1649 - Fiction
  2.   Love stories
  I.   Title
  823.9'14 [F]

  ISBN-13: 978-0-7278-6406-2
  ISBN-10: 0-7278-6406-8

All Severn House titles are printed on acid-free paper.

Printed and bound in Great Britain by
MPG Books Ltd., Bodmin, Cornwall.

Trail all your pikes, dispirit every drum,
March in slow procession from afar,
Ye silent, ye dejected men of war!
Be still the hautboys and the flute be dumb!
Display no more, in vain, the lofty banner.
For see, where on the bier before ye lies
The pale, the fall'n, th' untimely sacrifice
To your mistaken shrine, to your false idol, Honour.

Anne, Countess of Winchelsea, 1661–1720

PART ONE
1642-1645

The trumpet's loud clangour
Excites us to arms
With shrill notes of anger
And mortal alarms . . .

John Dryden, 1631-1700

CHAPTER ONE

"Is it much farther?" she asked, as a cold wind cut her face and flattened her skirts against her legs which felt as though they had turned to water.

The weary, foot-slogging miles stretched endlessly behind her; the wastes of Dartmoor, where they had missed their way; the grey huddle of Exeter, where there had been no shelter; Taunton, where they had had their pockets picked and she had lost the only remembrance of her mother left to her, the thin gold chain and rubbed silver-gilt locket. She recalled rides in carts amongst verminous hay, or cheek-by-jowl with pigs destined for the nearest market. She thought of the rain and the whip of March winds; of lofts and barns and fire-bright hearths, when people had asked them in.

Her father said: "A mile or so to the Redcliffe Gate. We shall be there before sundown." His figure sagged with weariness and there was a film of sweat along his cheekbones. His head felt light, a reminder that he had not long risen from his sick-bed.

The shadows of early April were beginning to lengthen as father and daughter descended the rolling downs towards the village of Bedminster. Away to their left lay the deep, blue cleft of the Avon Gorge and the thin snake-like coil of the river.

"Is Bristol a big place? Bigger than Exeter?" the girl wanted to know, and her father nodded, too tired to speak. "Bigger than Plymouth?" she persisted, the largest town she had ever seen before they set out on this journey.

"It's the second city in the kingdom, though I doubt we'll see much of it if Mistress Hazard has already arranged for our passage."

"I still don't see why we had to come all this way. If we must go to America, why couldn't we have taken ship from Plymouth?"

Charles Pengelly sighed. He knew very well that Lilias did not want to leave England; that her repetition of this question was really the objection she was too fond of him to voice out loud.

"We could not embark from Plymouth," he told her patiently for at least the tenth time, "because the King's men are too watchful there, and because we had no one to whom we could turn for help. But in Bristol, Mistress Hazard will not only feed and shelter us while we wait, but she also has many friends among the ship owners and ships' masters who will be willing to smuggle us secretly on board."

"Stowaways!" Lilias exclaimed scornfully, with all the contempt for secrecy which was part of being sixteen years old.

"Very well, stowaways," Charles Pengelly agreed resignedly. "But as long as King Charles decrees it illegal to emigrate to New England, we have no other choice." He drew his cloak more firmly about him so that Lilias could not hear his teeth chattering.

"We could have stayed in Cornwall," Lilias pointed out, as the last of the Bedminster houses disappeared, like wraiths, in the dusk.

"And be forced all our lives to worship as the King would have us worship? According to the rites of the Church of England? Never! That's not the freedom that our forefathers fought for; that Sir John Eliot died in the Tower for; that Prynne had his ears lopped off for."

Lilias was still rebellious. "You said yourself that things might be different, now that we have a Parliament again, after all these years."

"Perhaps." Charles Pengelly was racked by coughing. A light drizzle was starting to fall. "But this will be a completely new beginning for us. Massachusetts! Think

10

of it, Lilias! And my old friend John Winthrop has promised us his aid."

Lilias made no reply, remembering the little Cornish village where she had been brought up; the wild call of the sea-birds and the sharp, salt smell of the sea; the crash of waves on the endlessly stretching beaches, and the tiny wind-battered church, high on its cliff, where her father had once been curate. Her childhood years had been happy, safe, loved and secure with her parents. But after her mother's death, eight years ago, things had changed. Or, rather, her father had changed, renouncing his living, joining the Separatists, relying on other people's charity while he travelled about north Cornwall, preaching the Word of the Lord.

But Lilias loved her father and would not wittingly do or say anything to make him unhappy. They had always been close. From him she had learned to read and write and received a grounding in arithmetic. "Education is wasted on a girl," her mother used to protest, but Charles Pengelly had only laughed. He had laughed a lot in those days, as happy a man, declared his parishioners, as you would meet in a month of Sundays. But that, too, had changed with his conversion, and his friends had dropped away one by one. Lilias, however, would not allow a word to be said against him, not even when they had been reduced to the direst poverty, not even when her father had decided that they must leave all that they held most dear and make a new life in Massachusetts.

They should have left Cornwall two months ago, but as they were about to set out, plague had struck the village. It had been unexpected in February, being mainly a summer pestilence; but the cold weather, in its turn, had been largely responsible for the unusually low number of deaths. Lilias and Charles Pengelly had been two of half a dozen or more who had made a complete recovery.

At least, Lilias had made a complete recovery, but her father had never fully regained his strength. Doctor

11

Tregarron had warned him not to make the exhausting journey on foot from Plymouth to Bristol, but Charles Pengelly was chafing at the delay, anxious to go before his daughter's obvious unhappiness preyed on his conscience and persuaded him to change his mind. But on this April afternoon, as they trudged past the grey pile of St Mary Redcliffe, he felt at the end of his tether.

★　　★　　★

The front parlour of Dorothy Hazard's house in Broad Street was crowded to suffocation, all eyes turned towards Parson Pennill, who, with arms upraised, was addressing his spellbound congregation.

"Are we not," he demanded of his listeners, "the Chosen People of God?" There was an ecstatic murmur of assent. "Are we not the descendants of the lost tribes of Israel?" There was a general nodding of heads. "Have we not made a new Covenant with God, even as Moses did on Mount Sinai?" There was a full-throated chorus of "Alleluiah!"

Parson Pennill cleared his throat and continued: "For centuries, this country was in thrall to the Scarlet Woman of Rome. Then came Luther and Calvin to show us the light. But now, once again, evil men seek to corrupt us; wish to lead us back into the paths of Rome with their profane images, their vestments and their hierarchy of bishops and archbishops. They wish us to believe in that most shocking of all heresies, transubstantiation!" His audience groaned. "But," cried Parson Pennill, rolling his eyes heavenwards, "God will not be mocked! He has given His Chosen People a new Promised Land! A new Zion! A new Eden! A New England!"

Dorothy Hazard, seated in the front row, inclined her head in agreement. Everything about her, from her severe black dress with its unadorned white collar, to her thin unsmiling lips proclaimed the Puritan. Two years

12

earlier, she had embraced Separatism, even though her husband, the Reverend Matthew Hazard, still continued with his duties as a vicar of the Anglican Church. The couple agreed to differ, although the Reverend Hazard's narrow interpretation of the Scriptures left him more in sympathy with the Dissenters than with his fellow clergy.

Parson Pennill's sermon was drawing to its close when one of the many urchins who hung around the Corn Market, making a precarious living by running messages, pushed his way into the crowded room and whispered in Dorothy Hazard's ear. She nodded, waited for the final "Amen" to bring the meeting to an end, then turned to her friend, Regina Stillgo.

"They have arrived. Make my excuses to Parson Pennill. Explain why I couldn't stay."

Regina clutched her arm. "Be careful, Dorothy," she begged.

"I'm always careful."

"You're always lucky," corrected Regina. "That's different. Make sure you're not seen by any of the Watch."

"Pooh! Half the Watch of this city are thorough-going Dissenters. They'd turn a blind eye to anything I did."

"And half of them are not. There are still enough King's men in Bristol to have you inside the Bridewell if they so much as got a whiff of what's going on."

Dorothy was amused. "I'm deeply touched by your concern, Regina—particularly as you are not even a Dissenter and only come to these meetings to oblige me. But I am quite capable of looking after myself. Now, don't forget to make my apologies to Parson Pennill. I know he'll understand."

It was bitterly cold as she made her way up Broad Street to where two figures huddled for protection in the ee of the ancient High Cross.

"Mr Pengelly? Mr Charles Pengelly?"

"Your servant, ma'am. My daughter, Lilias."

13

Dorothy acknowledged Lilias briefly. "Follow me, please, and do nothing to attract attention to yourselves."

Curfew had not yet been rung, but there were few people about as the three figures walked quickly for several yards along Corn Street, then slipped between high hedges into the garden of St Ewen's Rectory. Half an hour later, Charles and Lilias Pengelly were eating their way through a plain but substantial supper in one of the rectory's upper rooms.

Dorothy looked searchingly down into the street before drawing the much darned and patched brocaded curtains.

"I don't think anyone saw us come in, but I can't be too careful. We don't want the authorities to get wind of what I'm doing."

She came back to the table, taking stock of her guests, summing them up with her small, shrewd eyes. The man, she thought, looked extremely unwell, emaciated by illness and starvation. It was hard on an Anglican clergyman who gave up his living to become one of the True Believers. This one was too much of a gentleman, too finely bred, to support himself in other ways. He would be incapable of earning his livelihood by the sweat of his brow. He had been a handsome man once, but now the skin was pulled tightly over the bones of the face, giving him a cadaverous appearance. The hair, too, which had been very dark, was liberally streaked with grey.

Dorothy turned her attention to the girl, now seen plainly for the first time in the light of the candles, and received a shock. She was unprepared for such a beauty. A cloud of almost midnight-black hair surrounded a pointed face in which the eyes seemed even bluer than they were, in contrast to the delicate skin. The nose was small and straight, the lips red and softly curving. But there was character there as well, indicated by the stubborn set of the chin and the direct, no-nonsense

14

gaze. Dorothy hoped grimly that the men of Massachusetts were ready for the havoc that this girl would create amongst them.

She sat down at the table while they finished their meal, noting how the father pushed his food almost untasted around his plate, while the daughter ate with the hearty appetite of the young and healthy. She made desultory small-talk about their journey.

"They say that Dartmoor is very bad now; that you can't cross it without being robbed. And the roads! The public highways around Bristol are in a disgusting state. I have written complaining to the King."

Her efforts, however, met with small response. Finally, the man asked abruptly: "You have managed to book us a passage?"

"Yes. On the *Talisman*. She leaves the Backs in three days' time. The master, Simon Reddy, is completely reliable and has carried many similar passengers before. But you will have to stay battened down below decks until the ship clears English waters."

Charles Pengelly nodded, taken with another fit of coughing. He fished a leather purse from the body-belt around his waist and pushed it towards Dorothy Hazard.

"Take the passage money from that," he croaked, as soon as he could speak; and Dorothy knew that the little hoard of gold represented Heaven-knew-what of deprivation and discomfort; the unbelievable sacrifices so many of her "customers" made in order to get to New England.

She apologised for the smallness of the fire. "We dare not make too much smoke or it might provoke attention. I live in Broad Street with my husband, and the rectory is only used as a temporary shelter for people such as yourselves." She wiped some dust from the tabletop with a grimace of disapproval. "I wasn't sure that you would come. I thought that all this talk of war might have made you change your minds."

15

"Why?" Charles Pengelly pushed aside his plate. He looked exhausted. "It makes no difference to me. Besides, I can't believe it will really happen."

"Well," Dorothy said, "the King is at Oxford because London has shut its gates against him. You know, of course, that he tried to arrest Pym and four other Members of Parliament in January? Yes ... But did you know that the Queen's in Holland? She went there, ostensibly, for Princess Mary's wedding to Prince William, but they say that she's really selling the Crown Jewels to the Dutch Jews. And what can that be for, except armaments?" She regarded Charles Pengelly straitly. "It will be a glorious struggle if it happens. A chance to make a new England."

"There is already a New England," the man answered, smiling thinly, "and that is where I intend going."

Dorothy rose. "I didn't mean to try to change your mind. I'll leave you, then. As you can see, a bed has been made up in the corner there. The kitchen is on the lower floor, where your daughter can wash the dishes. The privy is at the bottom of the garden, but be careful not to be seen. Someone will come in every day with food." She glanced around to make sure that nothing had been forgotten, then wished them both a brief "Good-night".

When she had gone, her heels rapping on the dusty stairs, the outer door closing behind her with a final click, Lilias collected up the dirty dishes and descended to the kitchen. It was small and dank, with a rusty pump in one corner and the same smell of decay which permeated the rest of the little-used rectory. The wind had risen, blowing across the house-tops from the river Frome, shrieking among the chimney-pots and rattling all the shutters like the teeth in an old man's head. Lilias felt an acute sense of loss. Tears welled up behind her half-closed lids.

Determinedly she blinked them away and returned to the upper room with the mugs and dishes. In spite of a

16

feeble remonstrance from her father, she put another log on the fire.

"You can't freeze to death, father, whatever that woman says. Look at you! You can barely stop your teeth from chattering." She spoke brusquely to cover her anxiety. Her father's face looked waxen and he seemed to be finding it difficult to breathe. "Get into bed," she ordered, and turned to look for their packs which had been dumped at the other end of the room. "I'll get your old flannel night-shirt and wrap it around your feet."

Charles Pengelly shook his head. "First, we must say our prayers."

"Father—" she began, then shrugged and gave in. She knew he would never settle until he had prayed. Dutifully she knelt beside him on the floor.

"Lord, we thank Thee most humbly for the comfort of Thy presence on our journey and for our safe arrival here in Bristol. We also thank Thee for the new start which Thou wilt vouchsafe to us in that New England beyond the seas, where all men may worship according to their consciences. Give us the strength to perform Thy will at all times and to withstand the forces of evil which walk abroad in our midst." Charles Pengelly was forced to break off as he was shaken with another' spasm of coughing, and it was Lilias who repeated the Lord's Prayer in the ancient Cornish tongue that she had learned at her mother's knee.

"Agan Tasn'y us yn nef, Benygys re bo dha Hanow . . ."

Then she helped her father undress and climb into the big, rickety four-poster bed on which clean lavender-scented sheets had been laid. Presently she joined him, snuggling for warmth and comfort into the soft goose-feather mattress, as a flurry of rain drummed with ghostly fingers against the leaded panes of the windows. Charles Pengelly groped with a skeletal hand until he found one of hers, and she noticed how dry and hot it felt.

17

"You'll like America, Lilias," he said, willing her through the stuffy darkness of the drawn bed-curtains to agree with him. "We'll have our own home. Governor Winthrop and I were at Cambridge together and he won't let us starve. I'll be someone of importance again; an accepted preacher, not an outcast because I don't see fit to worship God in the way that the King and the bishops tell me to do."

She heard the pleading note in his voice and squeezed his hand. It had been like this for a long time now; as though she were the parent and he the child in need of reassurance.

"That's all right, father," she told him gently. "I'm sure I shall like Massachusetts when once we're settled."

But every nerve in her body screamed that it was a lie; that she was already engulfed in a wave of homesickness that made her feel as if she were drowning. She stared into the blackness, at the little patch of colour where the fire could dimly be seen through the threadbare material of the curtains. She listened to the wind as it howled along the canyons of the Bristol streets and moaned around the arches and niches of the High Cross. She listened, too, to the heavy, almost stertorous breathing of her father . . .

How long she had been asleep she did not know, but suddenly she was wide awake, filled with a sense of foreboding. Something was wrong, but what? She sat up in bed. The darkness was total for the fire had long since gone out. The wind, too, had dropped and she was blanketed by a deafening silence . . .

With hands that shook so much that she could barely strike a spark from the tinder-box, Lilias managed at last to light a candle. And by the pale aureole of its unsteady flame, she turned, with pounding heart, to peer at the unnaturally still form of her father.

*　　*　　*

18

"But why me?" asked Regina Stillgo plaintively. "Why do you want me to offer this young woman a home?"

"She can't travel to Massachusetts on her own," said Dorothy Hazard briskly. "A young girl alone in a shipload of men; it wouldn't be right and proper. And there are no relatives in Cornwall, so there is no point in sending her back there. She will have to stay in Bristol until I can find another family willing to let her travel with them to America ... No. On second thoughts, I'll write first to Governor Winthrop, who seems to have been a friend of the father's. Simon Reddy can carry the letter for me on the *Talisman*. Meantime, the girl will have to stay here. I shall be prepared, of course, to find something towards her keep, and there is the money her father left me to pay for their passage. And she can make herself useful by helping you and Hannah about the house."

"But why here?" persisted Regina indignantly. "Why can't she stay with you?"

"My dear Regina, I'm much too busy, what with my own flock and helping Matthew to run the parish. No, no! And you'll find her of such great help, especially now that Hannah is near her time. And that little charity orphan of yours—what's her name? Mollie? Mollie Hanks?—she's worse than useless."

"Oh, I wouldn't say that," Regina demurred. It was just like Dorothy, she reflected bitterly, to ask a favour and then make it sound as if she were doing you the good turn. She was so dominating, and Regina was never able to resist people with stronger personalities than her own. Unfortunately, what Dorothy said in this case happened to be true. She and her daughter, Hannah, were indifferent housekeepers, while Mollie Hanks was positively feather-brained. "All the same, I shall have to ask Richard," she said.

Dorothy accepted this with a regal inclination of her

head. Number eleven Broad Street was not strictly speaking Regina's house, although she presided over it in her haphazard fashion. It belonged to her son-in-law, Richard Pride, who had invited Regina to make her home with them when he had married Hannah. With far greater reluctance, he had also extended the invitation to Regina's nephew, who had lived with his aunt and cousin since he had been orphaned at the age of fifteen. Richard Pride, sober, conscientious, possessor of a strong Puritan sense of duty, had had few illusions as to the nature of the young man he was taking under his roof. And he had made it clear from the outset that none of the hard-earned Pride fortune was to be squandered on Barnaby Colefax.

"What you do with your own money," he had told his mother-in-law austerely, "is up to you. But, if you let him, that boy will be the ruin of you yet."

Regina had secretly acknowledged that Richard might be right, but she had been born into a more rumbustious age than the present, when men had been less unhealthily concerned with the state of their souls. She was fond of her nephew in spite of, or perhaps because of, his shortcomings. She took a less gloomy view of his future than did Richard.

"Where is Richard?" demanded Mistress Hazard, sensing the absence of masculine presence in the quiet little Broad Street house. There was no need to enquire where Barnaby was. He would be frequenting one of Bristol's dozen or so inns and taverns.

"He has ridden to Westovers to see the Earl." Regina's voice held a touch of pride, even though it was no longer fashionable to admire the aristocracy. It was something for her son-in-law to be on speaking terms with an Earl. Plain, ungainly Hannah had done well for herself, even though she was a Stillgo, when she captured one of Bristol's leading citizens.

Dorothy was unimpressed. "The Earl of Chelwood!"

she snorted. "That man of sin! They say there isn't a brothel in Bristol or London that he hadn't been in before he reached the age of fourteen. What has Richard gone to see him about, anyway?"

"The soap monopoly," Regina answered vaguely, uncertain what a monopoly really was. "I think he wants the Earl to use his influence with the King."

"What's the use of that?" Dorothy was scathing. "If Charles Stuart could be influenced we shouldn't be standing on the brink of war. The man's a fool! And a dangerous fool, at that."

"Oh hush!" begged Regina, pressing a hand to her palpitating heart. "Someone might hear you. You might end up like poor Prynne, without any ears."

"I'd like to see them try to lop mine off! Now, Regina, may I take it that if Richard agrees, you'll house this Lilias Pengelly for me?"

"I—I suppose so. What is she like?"

"Capable," said Dorothy, "and, I should say, strong-willed. You won't have to put up with any nonsense."

"I should think not, indeed," agreed Regina firmly; she who had never been firm with anyone in her life. "But I really meant, what's she like to look at?"

Dorothy decided that there was nothing to be gained by prevarication.

"Pretty. In fact, extremely pretty. To be honest, it would not be exaggerating too much to call her beautiful. At least, she will be in a year or two. Poor little soul," she added hastily, making a belated bid for Regina's sympathy on Lilias' behalf, "it's a great tragedy, being orphaned at sixteen."

"Beautiful?" Regina breathed apprehensively.

"If you are worried about Richard," Dorothy declared, "he's far too sensible and devoted a husband to have his head turned by a superficial attribute such as beauty."

"That shows just how little you know about men," her

21

friend retorted with asperity. "But I wasn't thinking of Richard."

"Not Barnaby?" Dorothy was incredulous. "Then that, my dear Regina, shows just how little you know about your nephew. Or admit to knowing, at any rate."

"What do you mean?" cried Regina, flushing deeply. "Just because Barnaby shows no present thought of marrying, that doesn't mean that he's . . . well . . . you know . . . Really, Dorothy! Nice women don't talk about such things."

"They may not talk about them, but they know about them, all the same. Particularly nice women! For Heaven's sake! Barnaby is twenty-three years old, passably good-looking, well-breeched, thanks to the industry of your late brother—and spends all his time in the company of that young Phineas Leach. There are plenty of good Bristol girls—girls with something put by in their stockings for a rainy day—who would be willing enough to have him. But he has never, to my knowledge, fancied one of them. No, my dear, I don't think you need worry about Master Barnaby where Lilias Pengelly is concerned."

"You're very unkind." Regina stood up and shook out her skirts. "However, as I feel sorry for the girl, I'll ask Richard about her. But you'd better bring her here for me to have a look at first.

★   ★   ★

"And what's your name, my dear?"

"Lilias Pengelly, if you please, ma'am."

Lilias bobbed a curtsey, returning the stare of two pairs of curious eyes as steadily as she could. Her own were red with weeping.

"Your father's death must have been a great shock to you," Regina said, moved by compassion.

Lilias made no answer. Shock and grief had numbed her senses. She did not want, at present, to talk about

22

Charles Pengelly.

"Can you cook?" It was Hannah who now spoke for the first time. Eight months pregnant, a plain, dour girl, she had ranged herself behind her mother's chair, although it was she who was the rightful mistress of the house.

"Yes, ma'am."

"Sew?"

"Yes, ma'am."

The cool monosyllables rang with truth. Indeed, the girl's whole attitude somehow inspired Regina with confidence. It was true that Lilias Pengelly was exceptionally pretty; but in spite of what she had said to Dorothy, Regina did not really think her son-in-law susceptible to feminine charms. As for Barnaby—the less she thought about her nephew and women, the better for her peace of mind. And it would be nice to have a fresh face about the house, if only for a while. It would be even nicer to have a fresh mind to provide new distractions during the long, dismal evenings between now and the lighter nights of summer. Regina sighed. She could not disguise from herself, partial as she was, that her daughter could be a tedious companion. Hannah had always been sober-minded, taking after the gentleman frequently referred to by Regina as "your poor, dear Papa." And since Hannah had abandoned the family church of St Nicholas and joined the Separatist movement, she had, reflected her mother, become just the tiniest bit boring. Moreover, they could do with some extra help; some small, additional parade of the Pride household's consequence now that Richard had got himself elected to Parliament. Her son-in-law was now a man of national, as well as local, affairs.

The street door banged and, a moment later, Barnaby Colefax lounged into the room. He was, Lilias judged, peeping at him beneath her lashes, in his early twenties, with a mild, slightly vacuous expression, but with the

23

same hint of stubbornness around the mouth and in the eyes which was so plainly visible in Hannah. He was whistling tunelessly under his breath and it was obvious that he had been drinking.

He bent to kiss his aunt, and would cheerfully have done the same by his cousin, but Hannah virtuously turned away.

"Wine is a mocker; strong drink is raging," she quoted. "Proverbs, chapter twenty, verse one."

Barnaby gave his high-pitched crow of laughter. *"Drink no longer water, but take a little wine for thy stomach's sake.* Timothy, one, chapter five, verse twenty-three. It's no good, coz, I can always beat you at that game. My mother was nearly as pious as you."

"Hold your tongue, Barnaby," Regina ordered. "Can't you see that we have a visitor?"

Barnaby's blood-shot eyes rolled in Lilias' direction. The whistle died a protracted death and his first cursory glance slid into a stare. He did not, as a general rule, like women, but there was something different about this girl. She was, for a start, quite the prettiest creature he had ever seen; and then there was a kind of calm strength about her which, for him, at least, made an instant appeal. His feelings surprised him. He had listened to his friends boasting of their conquests in the brothels of the quayside and the Backs, and felt nothing but abhorrence. Now, for the first time in his life, he was drawn towards a woman.

Regina was explaining to him the reason for Lilias' presence and he experienced a sudden glow of pleasure at the thought that this girl might be here, eating, breathing, sleeping under the same roof as himself.

"We shall naturally have to hear what Richard says," his aunt concluded; and Barnaby found himself hoping desperately that Cousin Hannah's husband would agree.

CHAPTER TWO

"My dear Pride, you overrate my influence with the King."

Priam Lithgow, fifth Earl of Chelwood, sat behind his desk in the library at Westovers, his impatience and anger ill-concealed. Behind him, the leaded windows, framed in their swags of rich red velvet, let in the afternoon light. And beyond the windows lay the formal gardens—laid out in Queen Elizabeth's time—the outhouses, bakery and byre, and the magnificent sweep of pasturage rolling down from Lansdown in the direction of Bath. Westovers had been built, and extended, over the last one hundred and thirty years, ever since Priam's great-great-grandfather had won himself an earldom on the blood-stained battlefield of Flodden. Today, it was a splendid and imposing sight.

Richard Pride repeated stolidly: "You have influence with the King, my lord, if only you'd choose to use it."

The Earl's thin nostrils flared. The lids closed over the grey eyes, hooding them like a hawk's.

"And why should I choose to use it? What are Bristol lives and Bristol trade to me? The soap monopoly!" The lids flew up and the Earl leaned forward, staring ferociously at Richard. "This country is teetering on the brink of civil war. The King is virtually in exile at Oxford, prevented from entering his own capital. And by whom is he prevented? By Pym and Hampden! By Cromwell and Vane! By you and all the rest of the Parliament at Westminster!"

The two men glared at each other in mutual dislike. Each represented everything that the other most abominated. For the Earl, Richard Pride stood for trade, religious dissent, the arrest and imprisonment of

Archbishop Laud, the trial and execution, the previous year, of his friend, the pro-Irish Earl of Strafford. For Richard, the Earl of Chelwood personified the abuse of aristocratic privilege, the Romanising of the English Church, the threat of Irish Catholic troops in England and, above all, the slow erosion of trade, particularly Bristol trade.

"Look, my lord"—Richard's tone was abrasive—"things'll get no better between Crown and Parliament while unemployment lasts. Bristol jobs are being forfeited because of the injustice of these monopolies. We had a fair trade going with Virginia, my lord, which has all been lost. Furthermore, Governor Winthrop of Massachusetts had agreed to take a consignment of our soap." A triumph, that, if only the Earl could be brought to see it, for the thrifty ladies of Massachusetts usually made their own.

The Earl's eyes blazed. "Winthrop! Don't mention that canting Puritan to me! Damn all colonials, that's what I say."

Richard remembered that it had been Sir Henry Vane the younger, a former governor of the Massachusetts Bay Colony, who had provided the evidence which had finally condemned Strafford to death. And it was Hugh Peters, co-founder of Harvard College and former minister at Salem, who had been most active in stirring up hatred against the ex-lord-lieutenant of Ireland. Undoubtedly, it had been unwise to mention the American colonists. He tried another tack.

"My lord, the state of Bristol trade can affect the whole of the West Country. And that means your prosperity also, my lord."

Priam curled his lip. "Money-grubbing! Trade! That's all you Bristol merchants ever think of." He smiled mirthlessly. "But you know the old saying, I'm sure: 'Scratch a Bristolian and you find a Jew.'"

Richard reached for his hat, the plain, steeple-crowned

hat which had become as much a badge of the anti-royalist faction as the defiantly pudding-basin cropped hair.

"I can see when I'm wasting my time, my lord. I could have saved us both this meeting, so I'll wish you good-day." He moved ponderously towards the door, where he delivered his parting shot. "We'll be seeing one another again one of these days, I daresay—at the opposite ends of a sword or a gun!" And he went out, shutting the library door with studied care behind him.

The Earl closed his eyes. The encounter had disturbed him more than he would have thought possible. His head ached and great suns of red and yellow rolled up inside his tightly clenched lids. Dear God! What was happening to the world when men such as Laud and Strafford could be brought low by men like Richard Pride?

He felt a cool hand on his forehead and looked up. His wife, Magdalen, was bending over him, her delicate features puzzled and concerned. He lay back, pillowing his head against her breast, listening to the steady beating of her heart.

"You're upset," she said, in that remote, cool way of hers which masked her almost overwhelming devotion to him.

"Yes."

"By such a man as that?" Her scorn, like everything else about her, had in it an element of ice.

"'Such men' may soon be our masters if we don't draw our swords and fight for our lives."

But he did not really want to discuss the matter now. He shifted in her embrace, reaching up and pulling her down to him. His hands closed over her breasts, his lips sought hers, eager, demanding.

Magdalen tugged herself free, cheeks aflame. "For Heaven's sake, my lord," she protested faintly. "Not at this time of day!"

"What's wrong with this time of day? Do you think

loving is only for the night?"

"One of the servants might come in, might see us . . ." Her voice tailed off as if unable to speak of a situation too embarrassing to contemplate.

"You think it might upset him?"

"It would upset me." She looked at him pleadingly, begging him to understand.

Priam understood only too well. He watched her, grim-faced, as she fluttered about the room, aware, as so often in the past, that his sudden passion had unnerved her.

Passion! His thin lips trembled in self-mockery. She was too young, too sheltered, too prudish ever to know what true passion was. It was ironic that out of all her many suitors her heart should have betrayed her into caring for him. Magdalen had no idea of his real character, which had sent him in search of the pleasures of the Bristol and Southwark brothels before he had passed his fourteenth birthday. There was still something very virginal about Magdalen, for all their five years of marriage and the two children she had borne him. At twenty, she had very little knowledge of either men or the world, and imagined that the chaste love-making in which they indulged was the height of sexual passion.

Unawakened! That was the word that Priam had thought of when he had first seen her six years ago, standing demurely beside her parents, waiting to be presented to the Queen. And in his conceit, he had imagined that it was he who could awaken her; he, the practised lecher with the innocent, unawakened maid! Instead, he had, in the beginning, terrified her, until he had learned to keep his emotions under control.

Most men envied him. Within weeks of bringing Magdalen to court, Sir Amery Prestcott had received more offers for his daughter's hand than he had either the time or the inclination to deal with. To his alarm, the King had even proposed a match with one of his

28

nephews, one of the pauper Palatines—Rupert, Carl or Maurice—living in exile with their mother at The Hague. The profligate Lord George Goring had thrown lures in Magdalen's way, and Sir John Suckling had written some highly improper verses in praise of her milk-white breasts . . .

It had been a relief, therefore, to both Sir Amery and his wife when their daughter had fallen in love with the Earl of Chelwood, a man of standing and substantial fortune. His reputation where women were concerned was not altogether blameless.

"But then, whose is?" Sir Amery had demanded large-mindedly, and with a backward glance over his own broad shoulder. "A man in his twenties must have sampled some of the pleasures of life."

So, in the spring of 1637, Magdalen Prestcott had become the Countess of Chelwood. It had been the marriage of two aristocratic families, two great estates, two large fortunes. And, to cap it all, the lady had a real sweetness of disposition which must make her the perfect wife. The Earl was a lucky dog; everyone said so. Everyone except one or two of his most intimate friends.

*   *   *

Richard Pride rode home through the softly glimmering landscape, watching the shadows gather and the grasses blacken in their path. From a long way off came the faint ululating cry of an owl.

He felt tired and was glad to be almost home. He was not truly cut out for the hurly-burly of politics, but he was a devoted adherent of the Parliamentary cause, and felt it to be his duty to serve his fellow citizens whenever and however he could.

He was against the King on political rather than religious grounds. Although Hannah went her own way and he did not prevent her, he was not a Dissenter from the Church of England. He still worshipped with Regina at St Nicholas'. His quarrel with the Crown was financial. Supplies of bullion from the New World had reduced the value of money, and the Stuart kings had been forced to look for additional sources of revenue. The ancient custom of purveyance had been resurrected, with its taxes on groceries and wines. Mayor Whitson had fought it in the reign of King James and had been threatened with action by the Board of Green Cloth for his pains.

The system of monopolies had also been revived, by which, in return for a handsome cash payment, the monarch would grant his favourites sole right to trade in certain commodities. Monopolies on tobacco-pipes, starch and soap had all be granted to hastily formed London companies; and Bristolians, who had manufactured these articles for generations, had been forbidden to produce them under threat of heavy fines. Thirty Bristol soap-makers had been imprisoned and strictly penalised for ignoring the royal ban.

But, like the Earl, Richard did not want to think of his problems just at present. As he jogged through Lawford's Gate and along the market towards the castle, he felt a sudden surge of happiness. He could not say what caused it; perhaps the evening star hanging low over the castle keep; perhaps a heightened sense of awareness of being on his own home ground. But whatever the reason, as he skirted the sun-flecked torrent of Countess Weir, he felt more contented than he had done for a very long time. His instinct, some echo from the primeval past, told him that something important was about to happen in his life.

But all that greeted him as he walked wearily in through the kitchen door, having stabled his horse in Tower Lane, was the sight of Hannah's small, set face and the sound of her voice lifted in altercation with her mother. His heart sank. However great the crises piling up in the outside world, the domestic crisis still had the

30

greater power to dismay him.

Hannah turned and saw him. Without preamble, she began: "I had been saving the rest of the rabbit stew for your supper and now it appears that Barnaby has eaten it. Mother said he could. I have told her it is not her place to give such orders in this house. I wish you would speak to her, Richard, and make that plain. And over this other matter of the girl, only you have the right to make the final decision. Mother should not go making promises to Mistress Hazard before obtaining your permission. However, there is the beef pudding that you can have, that is if Mollie has warmed it up, which I don't suppose she has. She is quite the stupidest girl I have ever met."

Mollie Hanks, a thin-faced girl with a watery, belligerent eye, promptly threw her apron over her head and burst into tears. Regina subsided on to a stool near the fire, flustered and defensive.

"I'm sure I never meant to do anything you wouldn't like, dear Richard, but you know how Dorothy is . . . She can be so forceful. But truly, I never intended to usurp your authority, and I do assure you I know my place. The girl can be sent back to Dorothy's at once . . ."

"Hannah!" Richard caught his wife by her thin shoulders and gave her a shake. "The beef pudding will do as well as the rabbit stew; and as for this girl, whoever she is, I have no idea what you are talking about. I'm tired and hungry and I should appreciate a little peace and quiet in my own home."

Hannah, in her turn, was reduced to tears. "How can you be so horrid to me?" she sobbed, as Richard strove to preserve his calm.

Into this lachrymose scene strolled Barnaby, demanding to know if his spare shirt had been washed, stepping on the cat, who clawed and spat, and generally adding to the confusion. Mollie Hanks had by now recovered herself sufficiently to start an aimless clattering, banging plates on the table, overturning a pan and hitting her head on one of the strings of onions which were suspended, with bunches of dried herbs, from the ceiling. All Richard's former peace of mind was shattered.

Lilias, who had been left in the front parlour, was aware of the growing din. Cautiously she edged her way towards it, along a narrow passageway at the foot of the twisting stairs, to a room which, judging from the homely smells of cooking, must lead to the stone-flagged kitchen. Carefully she eased the door ajar.

It opened on a scene of chaos which, to her, was an almost personal affront. From her earliest years, she had had a strong dislike of mismanagement and disorder. Even in the most impoverished days of her father's ministry, she had endeavoured to keep things neat and clean. By instinct now, she went forward and led the weeping Hannah to a chair, picked up the fallen pan from the floor, straightened the plates and moved to the charcoal table, where the beef pudding was cooking among the embers. She spooned a generous helping into a dish, motioned Richard to be seated, and, finally, giving ear to Barnaby's complaints, handed him a clean shirt which was drying on a chair near the fire.

It was only then that she saw them all staring at her, mouths agape, and became conscious of what she had done. Horrified by her own temerity, she blurted: "I— I'm sorry!" and stumbled back to the parlour, now in total darkness, except for the criss-crossing of moonlight patterning the polished floor. Her father had always warned her that she was too managing. And at the thought of her father, now lying stiff and cold in St Ewen's Rectory, she once more fought down the tears.

In the kitchen, the stupefied silence was followed by a babel of voices as Hannah and Regina and Mollie Hanks all recovered their breath.

"Who would have believed it?" fumed Hannah. "In my own house! A perfect stranger . . ."

Barnaby whooped with laughter. "It was a treat to

watch your face, my dear coz. Anyone who can reduce order out of your chaos is worth her weight in gold."

"You horrid creature! Richard! You heard what he said? Am I to be spoken to under my own roof with such a lack of respect? Richard! Say something to him this instant!"

"I am waiting," her husband answered, dangerously calm, "for someone to say something to me. I think an explanation is due. I assume that that was the girl you have both been talking about. Who is she, and what is she doing here? One at a time!" he thundered, as Hannah and Regina both began speaking at once. "Mother-in-law, as this seems to be your doing, perhaps you had better explain."

Hannah retired to a stool and sulked while Regina falteringly told her story. She was a little in awe of her son-in-law. But when he had heard her out, all Richard said was: "Winthrop, eh? You say the father was a friend of John Winthrop's?"

"So Dorothy says."

"So he will possibly take an interest in the daughter ... I might," he added, more to himself than to his listeners, "get that soap concession after all ... Besides, as Barnaby so rightly says, anyone who can improve the running of this household will prove a treasure, however long or short a time she stays."

A few moments later, Lilias heard a heavy tread in the passage. The door opened and Richard Pride came in. It was too dark for her to see his face, so she was unaware of the faint line of bewilderment which furrowed his brow. Richard himself was unaware of it, battling with the strange and disturbing emotion which had gripped him on first seeing Lilias. He cleared his throat and said awkwardly: "My mother-in-law has explained your unhappy situation, Mistress Pengelly. You are welcome to remain with us for as long as you like."

★   ★   ★

The White Lion in Broad Street was crowded, as it always was in the afternoons, the bright June sunshine from the open door spilling across the sanded floor. Barnaby Colefax had to blink several times to clear his vision after the glare outside, before forcing his way between the overflowing tables to where his friends waited for him in the further corner.

"You're late," accused Tom Burley, a sour-faced youth whose boast it was that he had slept with every whore in Bristol.

And: "You're late. Where have you been?" demanded Phineas Leach in plaintive echo.

"Christ! What does it matter? I'm here now, ain't I?"

Tom Burley, clearing a shred of meat from between his teeth, looked spitefully at Phineas and grinned. "I daresay he's been chasing the beautiful Lilias Pengelly."

Barnaby coloured painfully. "That girl's hot for me, if you want to know. She'd eat me alive if I'd let her."

Tom Burley shifted uncomfortably on his bench. Something he had eaten for his dinner was beginning to disagree with him. He could feel those sharp little stabs of pain which he so often experienced after food.

"Fancies you, does she, Barney?" he asked in a voice which made his friend suddenly wary.

"Don't they all?"

"I don't know. So you keep telling us."

"And what is that supposed to mean?" Barnaby gave one of his bragging laughs which, irritatingly, broke in the middle.

A familiar dull weight had settled over Tom Burley's chest, and the bad temper which always accompanied it urged him on to the picking of a quarrel.

"Going to lay the lovely Lilias then are you, Barney? Why don't you just be honest for once and admit that you really fancy Phineas here?"

"Jesus!" breathed Phineas Leach, his frightened gaze flickering from Barnaby to Tom.

34

"My God," muttered Barnaby, rising slowly to his feet and reaching blindly for Tom Burley's scrawny throat. "My God, if I didn't think you were drunk, I'd swing for you, Tom."

His voice had risen to a roar, bringing the landlord anxiously through from the tap-room, while, all around them, heads were starting to turn in their direction.

Tom Burley, too, was on his feet, evading Barnaby's clutching hands.

"I ain't drunk, Barney Colefax. The day you bring me proof that you've slept with a woman, I'll admit publicly that I've been wrong about you."

Barnaby stared at him, eyes dilated, then his fists flailed the air, vainly trying to contact Tom Burley's chin. Tom side-stepped, but knocked against the edge of the table, which went over with a crashing of pewter tankards, the ale streaming away between the cracks in the boards.

"Get the Watch," hissed the landlord to one of the tapsters, while his customers shouted gleefully: "A mill!" They were already clearing a space for the two combatants and laying bets on the probable winner.

But then, suddenly, to the disgust of the spectators and the relief of the landlord, Barnaby turned and lurched unsteadily for the door.

"I'll show you!" he shouted at Tom Burley over his shoulder. "I'll show you!" And he staggered out into the sunlight.

*　　*　　*

Six weeks after she went to live with the Prides, Lilias helped to deliver Hannah's baby: a boy, christened Eliot. It was three weeks after that, at the end of a hot June day, that Barnaby Colefax tried to seduce her.

Lilias was lying in bed in the tiny attic which she shared with Mollie Hanks. But Mollie was suffering from a heavy summer cold and had asked for permission to sleep downstairs. The shapes of the meagre furniture, so familiar by day, seemed oddly menacing at night, and Lilias missed the friendly rhythm of Mollie Hanks' snores. She envied her the cooler atmosphere of the stone-flagged kitchen.

The house was still. The shadows broke up and reformed as she drifted towards the edge of sleep, seeing in her dreams the mistily smiling face of her father. The first agony of grief had burned itself out, leaving her apprehensive of an unknown future. Mistress Hazard had not yet received a reply from Governor Winthrop, and meanwhile the days spun past in a meaningless and purposeless procession . . .

Suddenly, Lilias was wide awake, as she had been on that night when her father died, every nerve taut in her trembling body. She could have sworn that she had heard the creak of the attic stairs. And the next moment, her suspicions were confirmed as there came the unmistakable lifting of the latch. She sat up in bed and had just managed to light her candle when Barnaby slid stealthily into the room. Lilias saw the pale glimmer of his naked body as the loose gown he was wearing fell open. She eased herself as far as she could to the other side of the bed.

"What do you want?" she asked foolishly, as though she did not know perfectly well.

He made no answer, but leant across and slipped his hand inside the neck of her shift. Furiously she pushed it away.

"You'd better go, now, Mr Colefax, before I let everyone know that you are here. Your cousins and aunt would not be pleased."

"You wouldn't do that." His tone was almost pleading. She sensed in him some need, other than the obvious one.

"Perhaps not." Lilias was bemused by her own emotions, by the excitement which had welled up in her

36

at that glimpse of his naked body. She wanted him to take her in his arms. But upbringing and education triumphed over her natural inclinations, and, with a wriggle like an eel, she was out of bed, standing with her back pressed against the farther wall. Her night-rail shone whitely through the darkness. "All the same, please go," she said firmly. "If you do, I promise I'll tell no one."

For answer, Barnaby came round the bed, his slippered feet shuffling softly on the uncarpeted boards. He pulled her to him and felt the momentary pliancy of her body as it touched his own, and smelled the faint herbal scent of her hair. A sense of her abundant femininity rose and washed over him, then receded, leaving him sweating and shaken. He released her abruptly, fighting down the nausea that always possessed him whenever he tried to make love to a woman.

It was not true! God in Heaven, it was not true! Not that dreadful thing that Tom Burley had imputed to him in the White Lion this afternoon. He refused to believe it. He denied it utterly! Barnaby turned and lunged for Lilias again.

From the floor below, came the staccato wail of little Eliot. This was followed by two thumps on the floor as first Hannah and then Richard crawled sleepily out of bed to attend to their son. Lilias gave Barnaby a push which sent him staggering, and ran out on to the tiny landing.

"Do you need any help, Mistress Pride?" she called down the attic stairs. "Is there anything that I can do?"

Richard emerged on to the lower landing. In the light of his candle he could see Lilias in nothing but her shift, and hastily lowered the flame.

"The child only needs feeding," he said in his rather terse way. "Go back to bed."

Lilias crept two stairs lower. "It's very hot. If Mistress Pride would like it, I'll fetch her a cold drink from the kitchen."

Richard grunted assent. "But first, for pity's sake, go and put something on."

Lilias thought of Barnaby still lurking in the darkness somewhere behind her, and resolutely shook her head. "I'm all right," she insisted, descending the last three stairs.

"You're indecent," Richard answered with unwonted violence. Then he added brusquely: "Wait here."

He disappeared inside the room he shared with Hannah and came out a moment or two later with one of his heavy frieze coats.

"Here," he said, "put this round you."

He swung it round her shoulders and, at the slight contact with her, began to tremble. What was there, he wondered, about this girl that he found so unusually disturbing? He watched the dark head, gleaming like black silk as it rose out of the collar of the all-enveloping coat, vanish round the bend of the lower stairs. Then, slowly, he rejoined Hannah.

"Do you think Eliot's teething?" she asked, peering at the contorted little face so close to hers.

"No. He's too young." Richard climbed wearily back into bed, feeling suddenly old, as though he had never lived. "Feed him. That's all he wants."

Hannah put the groping mouth to her breast. "Are you still worried about the money?"

"A little," he agreed, seizing on the excuse she had unwittingly given him. "But perhaps when Dorothy hears from Massachusetts, I might get their concession for the soap. Things would be better then."

"You'd be fined by the authorities if they ever found out."

"Heavily. But it's a chance worth taking. Meantime, however, both William Penn and Robert Cann have offered me a loan if I should need it. And there are other good Bristol men who would be willing enough to invest money, just to tide us over. Now, finish feeding the child

38

before Lilias brings us that drink. Then, for Heaven's sake, let us get some sleep."

When Lilias returned to the attic half an hour later it was empty. Barnaby had gone. Thankfully, yet with a faint feeling of surprise, she closed and bolted the door.

*　　*　　*

Barnaby stared up at the shadow patterns on his ceiling. He had pushed the bed-curtains back as far as they would go. He felt alternatively hot and freezing.

It was not true! It was not true! The phrase spiralled round and round inside his head until it no longer had any meaning; just a jumble of words which he kept repeating as some sort of charm. On the edge of his consciousness, faces mocked and gibbered, taunting him with nameless horrors behind censorious, upraised hands. He saw people laughing at him behind his back. Words, horrible words, bubbled and boiled inside his brain. He felt as though he had been stripped naked and his shame exposed to the world.

He sat up in bed, hugging his knees, his mind still bolting from the truth. It was true that he had never yet slept with a woman, but what of that? He did not believe half the stories that Tom Burley told. Men always exaggerated their sexual prowess. He was not old, not really: only twenty-three. What he really needed was a woman of his own. All rumours would be stifled if he were to marry. Yes, that was it. What he really needed was a wife.

The idea, born of the moment, seemed like a revelation. An inspiration! He would marry Lilias Pengelly. Why not? He conjured up a picture of her: the midnight-black hair; the blue eyes fringed by thick, dark lashes; the delicate curve of cheek and breast; the skin, whiter than many a so-called lady could boast; the proud set of the head and the slender line of the throat. With such a wife a man would have no need to prove himself: Lilias would say everything and more that needed saying.

Confidence surged through him, fresh and tingling. No one could prevent his marrying Lilias, portionless though she was. He was of age; not even his aunt could stop him, and anyway, he had always been able to twist Regina round his thumb. He lay down to sleep. It would be, he thought, like Ahasuerus and Esther; like Cophetua and the beggar-maid.

★ ★ ★

"Marry me! Marry me!"

Barnaby had caught her at the foot of the stairs, in the dark corner beside the parlour door, pinioning her back against the panelling, so that the bevelling bit into her flesh.

Lilias put up a hand to ward him off as he again repeated his astonishing proposal, with which he had been bombarding her for the past few days. He caught her hand and pressed it to his lips, a gallant little gesture somehow out of keeping with his character and therefore strangely pathetic. And when Barnaby clasped his fingers over hers, Lilias did not at once withdraw her hand.

"Why won't you marry me?" he asked. "Give me one good reason."

"I don't love you," she answered steadily.

"You would—given time."

Again, the sad little qualification proved unexpectedly moving. She sighed and rubbed his cheek, touched by a fleeting affection.

"Your aunt would never allow it. I have no money. It would be a poor way to repay your family's hospitality."

"It has nothing to do with my aunt. Nothing to do with any of them. My money is my own. I have more than enough for two."

Lilias hesitated. When Barnaby had first asked her to marry him three days ago, she had refused to take him seriously, treating the proposal as a preposterous joke.

40

But when she had at last realised that he was in earnest, the temptation to accept him had become overwhelming. She was not in love with him and doubted that she ever would be; but only that morning, Dorothy Hazard had informed her that another family of emigrants had moved into St Ewen's Rectory. She had every hope, she said, of persuading them to take Lilias to America.

But Lilias did not want to go to America, to settle in New England. She would much rather stay in old England and face the coming war; for everyone now said that war between King and Parliament was inevitable. (The city militia had already set to work strengthening Bristol's defences, fortifying the gates, cleaning rust from the portcullis and mounting the great towers of the castle with cannon.) Furthermore, Lilias had read many of her father's books and knew that life in the American colonies was often hard and bleak. She remembered the story of the settlers of Roanoke Island who had vanished one winter without trace.

Why, then, should she not seize this opportunity which had so miraculously presented itself to her? It offered her financial security and a place in society, and she was strong enough to cope with whatever disapproval it aroused. But what of happiness? She would have to take a chance on that.

She came to a decision and, leaning forward, kissed him on the mouth. "I'll marry you, Barnaby," she said.

CHAPTER THREE

On a hot morning very early in August, ex-Sheriff Robert Yeamans and his friend, George Boucher, rode through the gates of Westovers and up the winding carriage-drive to the door. It was, thought Yeamans sadly, as beautiful a day as he had ever seen, with the light hanging in layers across the distant hills; with the brooding stretch of Lansdown and the sun-splashed trunks of the trees; with the limitless horizons towards Bristol and Bath as fragile and crystalline as blown glass. Impossible to think that war was imminent, yet there had already been skirmishing around Shepton Mallet.

The house was in uproar. Servants scurried in and out, packing the Earl's clothes and military effects into the two travelling carriages which waited outside on the broad sweep of sunlit gravel. Horses were led round from the stables, sidling and champing at their bits. Voices were raised and there was a general air of urgency as the master of the house made ready to take his departure.

"Only just in time," George Boucher grunted, as they were shewn into the library, where, a few months earlier, Richard Pride had stood. "Another hour and we should have missed him."

Priam came into the room with his long, hasty stride and nodded curtly at the two men. He was annoyed at being disturbed at such a time, but knowing Yeamans and Boucher to be extremely loyal, he felt it necessary to spare them a few moments.

"Gentlemen! I'm busy, as you see. I leave almost at once to join His Majesty at Nottingham."

"So it is war then, my lord," Yeamans said sombrely. His delicate features, with the slightly turned-up nose and small, straggling, pointed beard, reminded the Earl of an earnest spaniel.

"Yes. It would seem that it can no longer be averted. God help us all." Priam seated himself at the desk. "May I take it that you two gentlemen have something you wish to tell me?"

A little girl ran in and Yeamans recognised Lady Cassandra Lithgow, the elder of the Earl's two daughters.

"Papa! Papa! May I keep this watch? Mama says you won't need it while you're fighting for the King." She dangled a golden sphere, set with diamonds, on the end of a silver-gilt chain.

"Cassie, I'm busy . . . Oh, yes, very well. But you must be careful with it. Put it away safely and keep it for me until I come home."

The hard face had softened as the Earl bent over the child, and he gave her one of his rare, sweet smiles. The romantically minded Yeamans, watching, thought that it was like the sun coming out from behind a cloud. Priam kissed his daughter, gave her a little pat and sent her back to her nurse.

"Now, gentlemen," he said.

"Bristol has declared for Parliament, my lord. We thought you ought to know. Not that it's a surprise to anyone, the temper of the town being what it is. His Majesty—God bless him!—sent the Marquis of Hertford and Sir Ferdinando Gorges to hold the city in his name, but Mayor Locke has refused them entry."

"On what authority?"

George Boucher rubbed his nose with the back of his hand and shifted from one foot to the other. "Well, the authority quoted was that of the King, my lord."

"How so?" the Earl demanded sharply.

Yeamans cleared his throat. The sunlight slanted through the windows and lay in pools of yellow and saffron on the floor.

"Unhappily, my lord, back in April, His Majesty

43

wrote a letter to the Mayor, forbidding him to let in soldiers of either persuasion. Which, at the time, was a sensible precaution. But now, the Mayor and the Mayor-elect, Richard Aldworth, are using it against the King for their own purpose."

"Although they'll let in the Parliamentary commander soon enough, I'll warrant," George Boucher put in viciously.

"What has happened to Hertford and Sir Ferdinando Gorges?"

"They've joined Sir Ralph Hopton—or so we heard—and have withdrawn towards Sherborne. Sir Ferdinando—do you know Sir Ferdinando, my lord?"

The Earl nodded. He knew the fiery Sir Ferdinando, founder of the County of Maine, only too well.

"Sir Ferdinando sent a very rude message to the City Fathers, my lord, saying that they ought to be scalped. Mind you, the City Fathers gave as good as they got." Yeamans' chest swelled a little. In spite of the difference in his political persuasions, he could not but be proud of his fellow citizens when they closed ranks against the despised outsiders.

"What did they say? Knowing the inhabitants of your fair city, Mr Yeamans, I'm sure it was something rude."

"They reminded him of his unfortunate law-suit against Lord Baltimore of Maryland. They said that anyone who could be worsted by an Irish Catholic peer was not fit, in any case, to have command over good Bristolians."

The Earl's lips twitched, but all he said was: "Thank you, gentlemen, for bringing me this news, especially on such a hot and tiring morning. If you will put yourselves in the hands of my housekeeper, she will see that you have refreshment before starting your journey back to Bristol. And now, if you'll excuse me . . . Ah, John! See that Mrs Trowbridge looks after the needs of these gentlemen before they leave." The Earl held out his

44

hand, first to Yeamans and then to Boucher. "It will not be long, I trust, before we meet again. You may rest assured that Bristol will be one of His Majesty's prime targets."

When the two men had been ushered out, Priam went in search of Magdalen, who was overseeing the packing of his musical instruments and books, all of which were to travel with him to Nottingham. She was wearing one of the pale colours which she loved so much, and which, with her white skin and very fair hair, made her look even more ethereal and remote.

"I don't know where all these things will go," she began distractedly, as soon as she saw him. "Both carriages are full already. Priam, *do* gentlemen have to take so much baggage on campaign? It seems excessively silly to me."

He caught her gesticulating hands and held them, two captive birds, against his heart. "Sweeting, we shan't be in the saddle all day long. There will be moments for leisure, I hope, as well. I travel light by comparison with someone like George Goring." He lowered his head and said urgently: "Send the servants away. I must have you to myself a while before I go."

Her eyes flew up to meet his, wide with sudden apprehension. A delicate colour suffused her cheeks and she struggled to free her hands.

"But we are in the middle of crating your books—"

"Send them away," he repeated, and his voice grew hard. "I probably shan't be seeing you for months."

Magdalen flinched as she always did when he spoke to her like that, and he immediately began to feel guilty. He felt even guiltier an hour later, as he lay beside her in their ornate, brocaded bed and watched her softly crying. The sensation angered him and made him brutal. He forced her head round to look at him.

"You'll be free of me now, my dear," he said grimly, "for a while, at least. And, who knows, I might even be

45

killed. Then you could sleep in your neat, virginal cot without the necessity for any more of these shameful fumblings between the sheets."

She twisted away from him and he could feel the painful shaking of her body. "Don't say such hateful things. I love you. I love you more than life itself." It was his turn to flinch; the naked emotionalism of words always set his teeth on edge. "I adore you. I worship you," Magdalen went on, unaware of the affect she was having. "But I can't ... in broad daylight ... it seems so ... "

"Abandoned?" Priam swung himself out of bed and began to get dressed. But his anger was already draining from him. He felt empty, as he so often did after making love to Magdalen.

"I'm sorry!" she exclaimed desperately, in a cry which was wrung from the heart.

He threw his shirt back on the chair and sat down on the edge of the bed, drawing her to him.

"No, I'm the one who should apologise. I shouldn't have forced you against your will." He felt the slackening of tension as she sighed and nestled closer, saw the relief in her eyes as she returned his kisses, happy in the kind of affection that she could understand. She should have married a gentleman in every sense of the word. His only pretensions to gentleness were on account of his birth. His instincts, as he knew only too well, were really those of the gutter. As tenderly as he could, he released himself from her hold.

★   ★   ★

"Oh, miss, you look lovely." Mollie Hanks stooped to straighten the hem of Lilias' white dress and gave a final twitch to the simple garland of flowers set on the cloud of dark hair.

Lilias, looking at herself in the hand-mirror which Mollie held up, thought she looked pinched and worn. If

46

she did, it was hardly surprising after the gale of opposition which had blown about her head for the last two months; tears from Regina, threats from Hannah, downright disapproval from Dorothy Hazard. Only Richard Pride had stood her friend. But, like all gales, it had eventually blown itself out, leaving the calm of resigned acceptance in its wake.

"She'll at least make him a good wife," Regina had consoled herself and Hannah. "She can cook and sew, which a lot of these girls with money can't do. And Richard has said that they can stay here, so she'll be able to help you with Eliot. I'm not saying that I wouldn't have preferred Barnaby to marry one of the Canns or the Treadles or some other nice girl with money—well, perhaps not Susannah Winyates: she has a cast in one eye—but things could have been very much worse."

And Dorothy Hazard, who had also been present, had finally conceded: "She's a girl with a sound Christian upbringing and I suppose you can't ask fairer than that. At least she isn't one of these fly-by-nights, decked out in ribbon and lace and with a bodice cut low enough to show all she's got. You can be thankful for small mercies, Regina. What's more, I don't think Barnaby would have married anyone else. Lilias Pengelly might make a man of him yet."

And so, slowly, acceptance if not approval had been won, even from the grudging Hannah.

"Do I really look all right, Mollie?" Lilias asked, peering at her dim reflection.

"Oh, yes, miss," Mollie breathed ecstatically. "You look a regular queen."

Lilias laughed, shaking out the folds of her white dress, part of her wedding present from Barnaby. Then, carefully, she descended the stairs, leaving the attic behind her for the very last time. Tonight, she thought with a tingle of excitement, she would be sharing her husband's room.

Richard, who had agreed to give the bride away, was waiting for her in the passage, his thickset body clothed soberly in his Sunday-best. As Lilias descended the last few stairs, he glanced up—and was shaken by such a surge of emotion that it knocked the breath from his body. As she laid her hand on his proffered arm, her touch seemed to scorch his flesh. What was he doing, letting her marry Barnaby?

He said with an intensity which made her blink in surprise: "Are you sure about this, Lilias? Are you sure that you want to go through with this marriage?"

"Why . . . yes."

He heard the note of hesitation and pressed again. "It's not too late, if you wish to withdraw. Better embarrassment or unpleasantness now than a lifetime of regrets."

"What should I regret?" Lilias had the feeling that Richard was trying to tell her something, something that, deep down, she already knew; something that everyone knew, but which they carefully avoided putting into words.

And this time was no exception. Richard shied away from her question, patting her hand and muttering: "Nothing . . . nothing . . . But—" Again he hesitated, looking uncomfortable, then blurted out: "But if you ever need me, you have only to say. Be assured that I shall always stand your friend."

Lilias smiled at him and he felt his stomach muscles contract. His longing for her at that moment was like a physical pain. It was as well that she should be married, another man's wife. He could not have answered for the consequences, had she continued to live under his roof a single woman.

"You're very kind, Mr Pride."

"Richard. You must call me Richard now that you are to become a member of the family." At least he would have the pleasure of hearing his name on her lips.

"Richard, then . . . I think we should go, Richard, or

48

we shall be late. Everyone will be waiting. Barnaby might think that I've changed my mind."

St Nicholas' Church was crowded, although the actual bridal party was small: Regina, Hannah and Regina's widowed sister, Lucinda Codrington, who had come from Abbot's Leigh. Curiosity had brought most of the spectators, but there was a sprinkling of Barnaby's drinking companions and one or two of his closer friends, Phineas Leach amongst them.

"A good Bristol fortune being thrown to the winds," grumbled Alderman Cann's wife in an undertone to her husband. "A pity you couldn't have talked some sense into one of your own daughters, sir, and persuaded her to marry Barnaby Colefax. Upon my word, if I'd known he was hanging out for a wife, I'd have done something about it, I can tell you."

"Hush, woman," groaned the harassed alderman, who had endured enough curtain-lectures on this subject. His only consolation was that he was in the company of many of his friends.

The service was short. There were no hymns, out of deference to the Prides' Separatist connections. Hannah and Dorothy Hazard had stated roundly that if there was singing, they would not come. Afterwards, the family, together with the Hazards, returned to Broad Street for the wedding breakfast.

"A decent, sober, Christian wedding," Dorothy observed to her husband, as, later, they walked the few steps to their own front door. "I think that perhaps it has been all for the best. That girl might make something of Barnaby Colefax yet."

But in the little bedroom above the front parlour, Barnaby lay unmoving beside his wife. His hands felt icy, yet sweat was pouring down his body and the familiar waves of nausea washed him from head to foot. Lilias lay quietly, not daring to speak, her expectancy dissolving into a kind of resignation, as though, somehow, she had

49

always known that this night was doomed to failure. She choked back her disappointment and reached out to take Barnaby's hand . . .

He was out of bed, softly moaning, "I can't . . . I can't . . . " and gasping for breath like a man drowning. Suddenly he grabbed his bed-gown and ran for the door, his whole body shaken by retching.

★   ★   ★

The night was quiet at last, disturbed only by the groans of the injured and the dying. The light had drained away behind the crest of Edgehill and a faint moonshine was silvering the mist. The Earl of Chelwood, in his tent, heard the soft chink of harness as a horse moved, cropping the grass. Beyond the raised flap, he could see the camp fires studding the night like jewels.

He drew paper towards him, dipped his quill in the ink-horn, absently wiped blood from a small, untended cut on his forehead and wrote: "Edgehill, near Kineton, Warwickshire. By my hand this twenty-third day of October."

It was two months now since that wild and fateful day when King Charles had raised his standard at Nottingham Castle, only to have it blown down again in the teeth of the gale. A bad omen many had thought it, those who had hoped that the King might still come to terms with his Parliament. Priam had not been one of them. Nevertheless, looking back over the events of those weeks and of this indecisive day, he knew the horror of Englishman fighting Englishman. But he knew, too, the exhilaration, the exultation of the charge and the tingle of excitement pulsing in his veins. He relived the impetus of today's mad cavalry dash which had carried Prince. Rupert and his troops through the enemy lines and on to the Parliamentary baggage-waggons at Kineton.

And that, of course, had been the trouble, the reason why Edgehill, the first serious encounter of this hateful

50

war, had not meant total victory for the King. For Prince Rupert and his officers, including Priam, had been unable to prevent their men wasting valuable time while they ransacked the bulging provision carts. Had Rupert been able to shepherd his men back to the battlefield half an hour earlier, the final outcome might have been different. As it was, both sides were claiming victory.

Priam re-dipped his quill in the standish and once more set it to paper.

"My Heart," he wrote—and at once Magdalen's pale face swam towards him out of the dark. It was so vivid, it was almost real.

Why had he married her? He had not been in love: he had never been in love in his life. He had been flattered, he supposed, by being singled out by the most attractive woman at the English court. So many men had wooed Magdalen Prestcott, been smiled upon but never favoured. He had found it impossible to resist being the admiration and envy of his friends. It had been pleasant, too, to cut out men such as the arrogant Lord George Goring, who were so certain of their charm with the opposite sex. There had been other considerations, as well. Magdalen Prestcott had had money, birth and breeding; everything requisite to become the Countess of Chelwood. Moreover, she had made it plain from their very first meeting that she adored him. And what man, he asked himself cynically, could remain indifferent to that?

With a frustrated sigh, Priam returned yet again to his letter.

"My Heart, this day we engaged the enemy on the plain below Edgehill and Sir Edmund Verney was mortally wounded. The rebels were led by the arch-traitor, the Earl of Essex, who brought his coffin with him on to the field. This greatly heartened our men, as did Sir Jacob Astley's prayer: 'Lord, I shall be very busy this day and may forget Thee. But do not Thou forget

51

me.' I know you will consider this to be lamentably brief, but it was more to the point than the canting prayers and psalms which we had been forced to endure from the enemy lines all morning.

"Perhaps their commanders had in mind the recent encounter at Powick Bridge, when a company of their troopers under Sir Nathaniel Fiennes was routed by Prince Rupert. This victory, I am sorry to say, has done the Prince little service amongst those of our side who see him and his brother as having undue influence with the King. Lord Lindsey, our General-in-Chief, resigned his command because Rupert is to take orders direct from His Majesty. Lord Falkland, whom I love as a brother, but cannot agree with over this matter of the Prince, threatened to follow suit, and was with difficulty dissuaded. Digby, Goring and Wilmot also hate the Prince. They cannot, or will not, see that he is the ablest commander that we have. It is unfortunate that the elder brother, Prince Carl, should have thrown in his lot with the Parliament and now sits comfortably in London, an honoured guest of the rebels.

"Shortly before the start of the battle, a troop of the rebels rode out from their lines, fired their pistols into the ground, tore off their orange scarves and about faced into our own lines. Their leader, Sir Faithful Fortescue, told the Prince that they had been recruited by Essex for service in Ireland, so, as there were some Irishmen as well as English Catholics in their number, they had forsworn their allegiance to the Parliamentary cause.

"An hour since, while we were still gathering in our wounded, one of the Irishmen, a Captain Patrick O'Mara, came to see me and remind me that our fathers had been friends. I recall my father speaking of Sir Connor O'Mara, who was with him at Oxford, and had estates somewhere in the south of Ireland. They were close enough in their undergraduate days for my father to speak of this particular friend with affection, a thing he

52

did not often do, although they later lost touch with one another. Now here was the son, eager to make himself known as soon as he heard my name mentioned. Sir Connor, it seems, is also dead, but under what circumstances I had not, at that moment, time to enquire. (They had just carried Sir Edmund Verney's body from the field.) Later, when I asked further after Captain O'Mara, I learned that he had been sent on some errand by the Prince to the Army of the West, and the prospect of his immediate return was unlikely. Perhaps our paths will cross again, however, when I shall be able to discover more about him.

"My Heart, my thoughts are with you and our two little girls. Give them my dearest love and tell them to be good children. Remember me in your prayers. Your loving husband, Chelwood."

Priam scored his customary thick, black line beneath the signature, laid down his pen, kicked off his boots and threw himself thankfully on to the camp-bed which stood in a corner of his tent. Five minutes later, he was deeply and dreamlessly asleep.

★   ★   ★

Barnaby Colefax stared through the haze of wine and tobacco fumes at the great embossed rose on the ceiling. It seemed to be moving, heaving like some nebulous sea-monster beneath the waves. His eyes were glassy and ale trickled from the corner of his mouth down over his badly shaven chin. The white-aproned landlord of the Rose Tavern in Temple Street jogged Barnaby's elbow as he passed, hurrying to serve a group of gentlemen on the high-backed settles near the fire. The February wind, blowing across the Marsh and Redcliffe Back, brought with it a flurry of rain.

Barnaby was at that stage where, without being precisely drunk, his troubles seemed less than he had thought them. They dwindled, as though seen through the wrong end of a seaman's spy-glass, and took on more manageable proportions. But even the potency of the Rose Tavern's ale could not altogether disguise the fact that his marriage had been a disaster, that he could only bring himself to touch Lilias when he was three parts drunk.

"Silly bitch," he muttered to himself. "Her fault . . . silly bitch . . . 'Tisn't true what they say about me. 'Tisn't true . . . " His eyes oozed tears of self-pity which ran down his pale, thin cheeks. "'Tisn't true," he repeated again.

He stirred, and the embossed rose on the ceiling stirred with him. A tapster went by him again with yet more tankards of ale for the gentlemen by the fire. Barnaby peered at them hazily, recognising familiar Bristol faces; Robert Yeamans, George Boucher, his own neighbour, Henry Taylor of Broad Street, and Edward Dacre, plumber of St Michael's Hill. He recalled, vaguely, having seen them together in the Rose once or twice before, always huddled in the corner beside the hearth, heads inclined, voices lowered—plotting!

Barnaby stifled a drunken giggle, which turned into a fit of coughing. What would such sound, solid citizens be plotting? Yet the little gathering intrigued him, and he was not the only one. A certain Mr Clement Walker was standing beside his chair, also intent on the group by the fire.

"'Evening, Walker," Barnaby said, hauling himself unsteadily to his feet. He smiled fatuously. "I shee . . . see," he corrected himself carefully, "that you are intereshted, too. Seen 'em here before on sheveral— several occashions. Wish you a very goo'-night. We have Governor Fiennes dining with ush thish evening." And he wove a path towards the door.

Halfway there, he paused to turn and stare. "Phineas?" he queried unbelievingly.

The figure in the corner of the settle near the fire had

shrunk back, as though hoping to remain unseen. At Barnaby's greeting, however, Phineas Leach smiled uncertainly.

"Hullo Barney," he said.

"What . . . what you doin' here? Why didn't you tell me you were goin' to be here tonight?"

"I . . . " Phineas looked anxiously at his companions.

"Get rid of the drunken fool," hissed Yeamans, but, unfortunately, loud enough for Barnaby to hear.

"I am not drunk," he said with tremendous dignity. "Anyone who saysh sho ish a liar. Don' think a lot of your friendsh, Phineash, old fellow." A frown creased his brow. "Come to think of it, what you doing with 'em, anyway? Ain't your short. Old fogies, mosht of 'em,"

"Oh, go home and sleep it off, Barney," Phineas said, almost angrily.

Barnaby drew himself up. "If that'sh your attitude, I'll go. Better thingsh t' do. Goo'-night." And he continued his unsteady progress to the door. It swung wide for a moment on gaping blackness, then shut with a slam behind him.

Meantime, Colonel Nathaniel Fiennes, Major Langrish and Captain Clifton sat in Hannah Pride's front parlour, making it seem all at once a very masculine preserve. For the last few months, Richard had been in London on Parliament's business and the ladies were glad of fresh company. They were acquainted with Major Langrish and Captain Clifton, but Colonel Fiennes was something of an unknown quantity, having but recently replaced Colonel Essex as commander-in-chief of the Bristol garrison.

Regina was reliving with relish the scandal that had rocked the city for the past weeks.

"To think of Colonel Essex actually shooting one of his troopers! To kill the poor man simply because he asked for his pay! I was never more shocked in my life than when I heard."

"I am sure it was no surprise to me," declared Hannah. "Colonel Essex was an ungodly man. He gambled and swore and . . . and . . . " She hesitated, an unbecoming tide of red suffusing her high cheek-bones. She finished with a rush: "And he liked women."

"Now that," murmured Captain Clifton in Lilias' ear, "I can understand. I think it shows some spirit in a man. What do you say, Mrs Colefax?"

Lilias glanced into the light, opaque eyes and shifted her chair as far away from the captain as she could. She answered coolly: "I shouldn't let Colonel Fiennes hear you say so, or you, too, may find yourself a prisoner in Berkeley Castle."

"Fiennes!" The captain curled his lip. Taking advantage of the fact that they were a little out of earshot of the rest of the group, he went on: "After that disaster at Powick Bridge, he ought to have been court-martialled, not promoted." Clifton's hand, seemingly by accident, brushed against Lilias' thigh and she turned her head away sharply. She loathed this man with his full, sensuous mouth and small, lecherous eyes. There was something soft and white about him—like a slug, she thought—and she hated having him near her. Captain Clifton, on the other hand, plainly admired the lovely Mrs Colefax.

Lilias raised her voice and asked: "How is the war progressing, Colonel Fiennes? We had convinced ourselves that it would surely be over by Christmas."

"Yes, indeed," endorsed Regina. "Everything is getting so expensive. And some things are positively scarce."

Nathaniel Fiennes smiled uncomfortably. From the outset, he had found the Bristolians difficult to fathom, even the most ardent of Parliamentary supporters being worried about the effect of the war on trade.

"They want Heaven on Earth," he had written bitterly to a friend, "but only as long as the streets are paved with gold. They are like so many Shylocks, wringing their hands and crying 'Oh, my ducats!' and 'Oh, my daughter!' and not knowing which to choose."

He had, within the first few days of his arrival, abandoned his chilly quarters in the castle and rented a snug little house in Broad Street, next door to the White Lion. He had soon become popular amongst his neighbours, who found him mild-mannered and courteous. His soldiers, behind his back, referred to him in less complimentary terms.

"I am afraid we cannot hope for an early end of the war, Mrs Colefax," he said. "Not until His Majesty is soundly beaten."

Regina tried not to look shocked. She supposed that she was old-fashioned and that the world was changing. Values, she reflected sadly, were not what they were.

"And if the Parliament loses, Colonel Fiennes?" Lilias asked quietly.

Fiennes, who did not want to envisage any such thing, was saved from reflecting on how badly things were going by the entrance of Barnaby. Six pairs of eyes swivelled towards him as he staggered through the door. Hannah, Regina and Lilias exchanged involuntary glances of alarm; then Lilias rose and went to him, hands outstretched.

"Barnaby! We have been waiting supper for you. We have visitors, as you see."

"I know we have vishitors," he muttered. "Told me sho, thish morning."

He was making a visible effort to pull himself together. His eyes, liquid with drink, blinked owlishly in the light from the candles. Captain Clifton regarded him with overt contempt. He made it his business to know all the gossip of the town and was hand-in-glove with Clement Walker. He knew what was whispered about Barnaby Colefax, about his perverted tastes. He had seen him on more than one occasion, walking up High Street from the

57

Rummer, an arm flung around Phineas Leach's shoulders, the two heads close to one another, the lips smiling in mutual affection. And this half-man was married to the lovely creature whose every movement set the captain's over-inflamed imagination alight.

Mollie, who had been on the look-out for Barnaby's return, her cap set at an unintentionally rakish angle, announced that supper was ready, if they would be obliging enough to step into the dining-parlour.

"I hope you like stewed mutton with peppers and onions, Colonel," Regina remarked as she accepted the Governor's arm. "The mutton is our own salting. And to follow, there is a gooseberry cream, prepared as I know you like it. You see, I have been at some trouble to discover your tastes."

Major Langrish offered his arm to Hannah, and it was inevitable, therefore, that Captain Clifton should escort Lilias, with Barnaby bringing up the rear. Lilias found herself seated between the two of them at supper.

By tacit consent, the subjects of war and the Royalist preparations for an attack upon Bristol were eschewed, and the conversation turned on lighter matters. To go with the gooseberry cream, Lilias had made a Cornish apple tart, a pastry shell filled with stewed apples and spread with a rich, thick custard.

"Excellent! Excellent!" declared Colonel Fiennes, rubbing his hands as he sent up his plate for more. "You are a very lucky man, Mr Colefax."

Barnaby, so far, had contributed very little to the general conversation. In the aftermath of drink, he was passing from a state of euphoria to one of truculence and gloom. What had Phineas been doing in the Rose Tavern in the company of those men? For some obscure reason, the governor's innocent remark enraged him. "I'll thank you to keep your opinions to yourself," he snarled, glowering at the unfortunate Fiennes.

"Barnaby!" cried Regina, horrified, while Hannah

blushed for shame and Lilias sat as though turned to stone.

"'Barnaby! Barnaby!'" he mimicked. "Women! You're all the same. Hate you . . . hate you . . . "

"He's not been well," Regina flustered, hurrying to her nephew's side. "A touch of the ague . . . He's a little delirious."

"He's more than a little drunk," Captain Clifton sneered, not bothering to hide his disgust. His words dropped into the silence like a stone.

"B-Better than being a lecher," Barnaby hiccupped, leaning across his wife to advance his bloated face to within inches of the other man's. "I know all about your kind, Clifton, psalm-singing hypocrite that you are! Groping up the women's petticoats when you think that no one is looking. Canting swine!"

"For God's sake, Clifton!" Major Langrish got to his feet, forgetting the penalty imposed by his colonel for taking the Lord's name in vain. His one anxiety now was to avert a scene. "Let it go! You're right. The lad's blind drunk."

"I may be drunk," said Barnaby, "but I know what I've seen. I've seen him coming out of Bedminster Kate's, along the Backs. I know he's been feeling around my wife's thighs all through supper, and no doubt she's been egging him on."

There was a scandalised shriek from Hannah. Lilias closed her eyes, feeling sick. She had been as good a wife to Barnaby as she knew how, but she had realised from the beginning that there was something seriously wrong. She had thought, at first, that Barnaby's reluctance to make love sprang from a shyness and inexperience similar to her own. But as the months had dragged by and he had only inflicted his inexpert fumblings upon her when he was drunk, she had begun to suspect that matters were worse than she had feared.

Another shriek from Hannah and a bark of command

from Colonel Fiennes made her open her eyes. She saw the sprawled figure of Captain Clifton on the floor, and Barnaby, his fist clenched, staring down on his enemy in gleeful disbelief, still uncertain how the miracle had happened. When the burly captain had swung at him, he had ducked with all the drunkard's instinct for self-preservation, and then, again by instinct, aimed a blow at Clifton's chin. No one in the room had been more surprised than he when he had sent his assailant crashing to the ground.

Captain Clifton, the admonitions of his superior officers ringing in his ears, glared up at Barnaby as he fingered his swollen jaw. He had been made to look a fool in front of Lilias Colefax, and by her nasty little pervert of a husband.

"I'll get you for this, Colefax," he whispered, as Colonel Fiennes and Major Langrish began to make hurried excuses for their departure. "I'll get you for this if it's the last thing I do."

CHAPTER FOUR

"Chelwood! The very man I want to see." And Prince Rupert flung an arm about Priam's shoulders.

Oxford, whose venerable walls had, for centuries, echoed to nothing more exciting than theological argument and legal disputation, now rang with the sounds of a military encampment. Trenches had been dug across St Giles' meadows and along the back of Wadham. Grain was stored in Brasenose Tower, and Magdalen Tower was manned for observation. New Inn Hall had been converted into the Royal Mint, and all the college plate had been melted down to augment the Royal Treasury. New College had been fortified and its undergraduates formed into a regiment. The sombre black of academic gowns was enlivened by the rainbow flash of silks and satins. The exceptionally mild winter had meant early boating parties on the Cherwell, even if the delights of picnics were still some months away.

Prince Rupert, who had his headquarters at nearby Abingdon, had ridden over on this spring-like first of March expressly to find the Earl of Chelwood, and had been fortunate enough to come upon him directly, crossing Christchurch meadows.

"In what way can I serve Your Highness?" asked the Earl.

They redirected their feet towards the gently murmuring river, now whipped by a little breeze into sudden flurries of foam. The reeds stood sentinel, gleaming under the running light. Thin slats of sunlight paved the water with gold.

His recent failure to take the city of Gloucester had left Prince Rupert subdued, but today there was a burgeoning excitement in that handsome face.

"My lord," the faintest of German accents informed the Prince's speech, "you know Bristol, I think? Your estate, Lord Wilmot tells me, is not far from there?"

"Above Bath, Your Highness, between Cold Ashton and Lansdown. In answer to your question, yes, I know Bristol well."

"Good! Good!" The Prince nodded in satisfaction. "You could draw me a plan of the central streets? Particularly around—let me see—what is it, now?—ah, yes!—I have it! Particularly around the Frome Bridge?"

"I could, Your Highness." Priam hesitated. "May I ask what for?"

Rupert chuckled, his teeth gleaming whitely against his swarthy skin. "You may. But keep what I am about to tell you strictly to yourself. I know that I can trust you." He looked into the Earl's mystified face and laughed. "What would you say, my friend, if I told you that the second city in the kingdom, the city of the greatest military, strategic and monetary importance outside of London, might fall into our hands without a single blow having to be struck?"

*   *   *

"Why can't you come to the cock fight at the Bell?" Barnaby asked peevishly. "You like a good fight. And Robin Hedger is pitting his red pyle against Alderman Yates' Wednesbury grey. My money's on the grey."

"I can't come," Phineas repeated obstinately. He looked distressed. "Let the subject drop, Barney. You know I'd come if I could."

"You're up to something," Barnaby accused. "I know you, Phineas. You can't fool me."

The two friends were walking in the direction of the bridge, after a morning spent sampling the various delights of the Lamb, the Antelope, the Three Kings and the Bell, all hostelries in St Thomas' Street.

Phineas said: "I don't know what you mean."

"You're being damned secretive, that's what I mean. You keep going off at night on your own; and you've been very quiet for weeks." Barnaby caught hold of his friend's arm and demanded anxiously: "There isn't someone else, is there, Phineas?"

The narrow houses of the bridge towered on either side of them, and, as though conscious of scrutiny from a dozen unshuttered windows, Phineas withdrew his arm.

"No, of course there isn't. Don't be a fool."

The two young men huddled for a moment against a wall as a cart rumbled past on its way to the Redcliffe Gate, splashing them to the thighs with dirt and offal. When it had gone by, Phineas said, as though coming to a sudden decision: "Walk with me a little way along St Nicholas' Back, Barney. Your dinner won't be ready yet and there's something I want to say."

The Avon was crowded with shipping, bringing in food from Wales and Cornwall to victual the town in case of a siege by the Royalists. There was a long pause, then: "Well?" Barnaby demanded impatiently.

Phineas asked thoughtfully: "Barney, have you ever seen the King?"

"What's that to do with anything? No. Why should I want to see the King?" His eyes were fixed moodily on a ship down river, watching the sailors running up and down the rigging like ants, getting ready to sail to Ireland or America or some other far-off place beyond the reach of cousins and aunts and, above all, wives; beyond the reach of the whole race of women. Barnaby's eyes gleamed hungrily as he reflected on that small, enclosed, all-male world. "You don't talk about seeing the King in our house," he added. "Not with cousin Richard sitting in Parliament, directing the rebels' affairs."

"Rebels! You said rebels!" Phineas sounded eager, the dark eyes in the angelic face watching his friend intently.

"What's the matter with you, Phineas?" Barnaby's attention was now thoroughly caught by the other's unusual manner. "I only called 'em rebels because . . . well . . . it's just a figure of speech."

"Who do you hope will win this war, Barney? King or Parliament?"

Barnaby's eyes opened even wider. He had never known Phineas so serious. "Lord, I don't know," he answered carelessly. "It don't matter a jot to me either way, I can tell you that. I've problems enough of my own."

He was looking at the curve of Phineas' cheek, at the peach-like bloom of the skin, and fighting down the prickle of excitement which proximity to his friend always gave him. Not true . . . not true . . . The words beat like a captive bird inside his head, but, as always, made no sense through constant repetition.

"Years ago," Phineas was saying, "my father took me to London and I saw the King and Queen. Like little dolls, they were, fragile and exquisite. I've never forgotten them. They were walking along Cheapside in some procession or other to St Paul's. And everything was so gay: light and colour and movement. People were happy. There were maypoles in the street and plays at the Globe and bear-baiting and cock-fighting and a great market in the nave of St Paul's. On ordinary days, I mean, not on the day I saw the King and Queen."

Barnaby, who could not boast of ever having visited London, not wishing to be outdone, said: "Pooh! I can remember when Bristol was like that, with the midsummer bonfires on Brandon Hill, and the Easter and Michaelmas fairs down by the castle. Not like it is now, all psalm-singing and church every day o' the week—at least, 'tis amongst the Dissenters. And my cousin's one of them, so I should know. A proper Dismal Dora Hannah's become and no mistake."

"And they're doing away with Christmas and the Whitsunday games." Phineas shook his friend's arm in a fever of anger. "Life is becoming so drab, Barnaby! And it'll get far worse if Parliament has its way."

"Yes." Barnaby nodded gloomily. "The next thing you know they'll be saying that it's wrong for a man to have a drink, or making cock-fighting illegal. But there ain't much we can do about altering things."

"We could make sure the King wins the war."

"What? Go and fight for him, you mean?" Barnaby roared with laughter; then, seeing that Phineas was in earnest, toyed with the idea for a moment or two as a possible means of escape. But in the end he shook his head. "No, not for me, Phineas old son. I never take sides in an argument."

"I didn't mean actual fighting . . . But would you never consider making a stand?"

"What about? I didn't start this sodding war and I ain't going to be a hero in anyone's cause. *A plague o' both your houses*, that's what I say. And it's what you'll say, too, if you've any sense. Come on," he added, "it's time for my dinner. That's one thing I'll say for Lilias: she can cook."

Phineas shrugged and gave up. The two friends wended their way up High Street, unaware that Captain Clifton was watching them malevolently from the porch of St Nicholas' Church. Nor did they see his clenched hands, nor hear him muttering under his breath.

"A proper little David and Jonathan! Perverted filth! You'd better look out for yourself, Barnaby Colefax! I'm going to get even with you one day."

*   *   *

Robert Yeamans' house, number six Wine Street, was directly opposite the Guard House, not, perhaps, the most propitious place for conspirators to meet, except that it had a back door which opened into a narrow lane, convenient for assembly and dispersal.

On the night of March the second, seven or eight men were gathered in an upstairs room, their anxious faces nipped raw-red by the cold, for a blustering wind had suddenly sprung up. Numbed fingers closed gratefully around tankards of hot spiced ale with which their host's wife had thoughtfully provided them.

"None of you was followed?" Yeamans asked, when the more pressing of his guests' needs had been attended to.

"We took all the usual precautions," George Boucher answered gruffly, and the others nodded their heads in agreement.

Boucher thought that Yeamans looked pinched and ill with worry. It was a serious undertaking that they were engaged in, and the consequences could be disastrous if they were discovered. Boucher, like his friend, was a family man: between them, they had sixteen children. He was uncertain whether the plan to hand over the city to the King had originated with himself or with Yeamans. It was sufficient to say that, for months past, they had been doing a steady and judicious recruiting.

The men who had joined them were, for the most part, wealthy merchants like themselves, who considered that this war would be the ruin of their trade and hoped to see it ended as soon as possible. There was also a sprinkling of humbler folk and one or two surprises, like young Phineas Leach, whose motives were more obscure.

Four houses had been chosen as the focal points of activity: Yeamans', here in Wine Street; Boucher's, near the Frome Gate; Thomas Milward's, just outside the city walls; and Robert Luckett's, at the end of Duck Lane. Arms and ammunition had been secretly smuggled into all the houses. They were to be eked out with clubs, swords, staves and kitchen-knives.

The ringleaders of the conspiracy had always met at one or other of these dwellings, with an additional rendezvous at the Rose, in Temple Street. This latter was not often used, but often enough to have attracted some attention. It had been a mistake, Yeamans was the first to

66

admit it, for so many known Royalists to be seen in public together. Clement Walker, for one, had grown suspicious.

"March the seventh," Yeamans told his listeners, "has been fixed on by the Prince, when there will be something of a moon to light his way."

Henry Taylor of Broad Street grunted, showing the whites of his eyes like a shying horse. He glanced at George Boucher with raised eyebrows: surely they would do better without any moon at all? But Boucher was dreaming of a knighthood and no one else seemed disposed to cavil.

"George!" Yeamans roused Boucher from his reverie. "You know what you have to do?"

"Of course!" Boucher was indignant. "We've been over it so many times before."

But: "Go over it again," insisted Yeamans.

Boucher sighed. "The party which assembles at my house is to open the Frome Gate, having first secured St John's Gate with chains and padlock."

Yeamans turned to Robert Luckett. "And you, Rob?"

"We seize the Pithay Gate."

"And we," Thomas Milward put in, without waiting to be asked, "rush Steep Street and the Steps, coming to Boucher's aid should we be needed."

Yeamans nodded, his thin hands playing nervously with his empty ale mug, twisting it this way and that. "And my party," he concluded, "will seize the Guard House. Two guards have been bribed, and the rest we shall imprison in their own cells. Then we shall sweep the street with musketry fire from the High Cross to the castle."

Phineas Leach looked unhappy. "Is that necessary?" he asked.

Yeamans curled his lip. He had always regretted the addition of this young man to their party: it brought them no credit. But any recruit was useful and he had not dared to turn him away.

"It will serve as a warning to people to stay indoors. It will be after curfew and therefore no one should be hurt. If they are—" He broke off, shrugging. "Well, you can't make an omelette, Phineas lad, without breaking eggs."

"And the Prince? Where will he be?" asked Edward Dacre.

"On Durdham Down. His army will be disposed at strategic points above the city—Westbury, Horfield and at the gallows on St Michael's Hill. As soon as we've opened the gates, we ring the church bells. The watchword is 'Charles', and every man is to wear a white favour on his breast and in his hat. That way we shall be easily recognisable in the dark." Yeamans reached into a drawer and pulled out a rolled paper. "This is the proclamation which I shall read from the High Cross, offering protection to all who stand for the King and Protestant religion as practised by the Church of England."

"And those who do not? What of them?" Once more, Phineas Leach sounded a tentatively critical note, and once more Yeamans shrugged.

"They must take their chance," he answered shortly.

★　★　★

Regina glanced across the supper table and asked: "Must you go out again tonight, Barnaby?"

"Why, what is there to keep me here?" he demanded thickly. "What joys do you and my darling wife offer me if I stay at home tonight?"

"Barnaby!" Regina spoke sharply, sensing trouble, and glanced at Hannah for support. Getting none, she continued: "You have been out of the house every night this past week or more. You will give us all a bad name."

"He's out with that Phineas Leach," Hannah said viciously. "He's already given us all a bad name."

"Shut up!" Barnaby turned on his cousin, his lips thinning to a nearly invisible line. "Anyway, I haven't

68

seen Phineas for at least five days. I don't live in his pocket, you know." He glanced at his silent wife. "You're mighty quiet, Lilias, my love. What's the matter? Cat got your tongue?"

Lilias felt her temper rise and tried to control it. This unhappy marriage was as much her fault as Barnaby's. If she had felt any real affection for him, she might now be making some effort to understand him. As it was, she merely felt repelled. She no longer wanted him near her: she shrank, horrified, from his touch. Deep down, some still, small voice whispered that he needed her help; that his advances were a plea for her aid. But she did not wish to think about it. It filled her with dismay.

"No, the cat's not got my tongue," she answered coolly and turned towards Regina. "I meant to tell you, ma'am. I saw Colonel Fiennes today as I was passing the Tolzey, in conversation with Major Langrish. They both sent you their compliments, and the Governor hopes that you will do him the honour of dining one day with him, at the castle."

"Oh dear! That means he doesn't want to come here any more," said Regina, flustered. "That really was a most unfortunate affair. Not that I blame you, Barnaby," she added hurriedly. "You were provoked and had good reason to do what you did. At least, I think you did . . . I mean . . . Mollie!" Her voice rose on a shrill note of relief. "See who that is knocking at the door."

"Mistress 'Azard, mum," Mollie announced as Dorothy came briskly into the room.

"Ah!" she said, giving a brief nod which embraced them all. "I'm glad that everyone is here. Mayor Locke has just left our house—or may be still there, for all I know, gossiping to Hazard. Heaven alone knows what men find to talk about. But that's neither here nor there. The point is, he's had a message from Colonel Fiennes. Sir Ralph Hopton has won a victory for the King at Braddock Down, and it's Fiennes' opinion that the

Royalists will now abandon the siege of Plymouth and make a push towards Bristol."

"Mercy on us!" cried Regina. "Dorothy, whatever shall we do? I can't stand the thought of bloodshed. Fighting, perhaps, in our very own streets." And she burst into noisy sobs.

Lilias hastened to comfort her, while Hannah went for a glass of the cordial Regina always took on such occasions, and which Barnaby declared smelled suspiciously like brandy.

"But why should there be fighting in the streets, ma'am?" Lilias wanted to know "Plymouth and Gloucester have held out. Why shouldn't we?"

Regina brightened as she sipped her restorative, but Dorothy, seating herself in the best chair near the fire, pulled down the corners of her mouth.

"As to that, Lilias my dear, Hazard says that some of our defences are extremely poor, especially between Brandon and Windmill Hill Forts. Hazard says that Fiennes is too indifferent a soldier to see it. It's common gossip that when one of the men pointed out a weak spot in the fortifications, the Governor called him a saucy knave for his trouble. I tell you, Regina, I'm not the only one having second thoughts about Fiennes. Now, don't jump down my throat! I know he's a favourite of yours. But any man who is passably good-looking and gives you a civil time of day is a favourite with you. You've always been susceptible as long as I've known you. But why isn't Fiennes living up at the castle with his men, instead of burying himself down here in Broad Street? Answer me that if you can!"

"Well, that's as may be ... I'm sure I don't know." Regina, gaining a little courage from her cordial, added with more spirit: "Not that I mean any disrespect to the Reverend Hazard, Dorothy—I wish we had him at St Nicholas': he preaches a very good sermon—but I do think that Colonel Fiennes knows more about defence

70

and so forth than your Matthew. Or any common soldier. All the same, I do wish Richard were here, instead of wasting his time up in London."

"He's hardly wasting his time, mother," Hannah reproved her indignantly. "He's helping to govern the country."

"As to that, I've always said that that sort of thing is better left to the people who were born to do it."

Such heresy could not be allowed to pass unchallenged and both Hannah and Dorothy hurried into speech. Lilias, who had heard the argument before, slipped upstairs for a shawl, promising to look in on little Eliot as she did so.

The child, now ten months old, lay curled on his side, thumb in mouth, eyes fast closed. In the flickering light of her candle, Lilias thought how like his father he looked, and felt a sudden stir of affection for the absent Richard. She agreed with Regina in wishing that he were at home. His presence was so solid and comforting: nothing very dreadful could happen while he was near.

She tiptoed from the room and crossed the narrow landing to the one she shared with Barnaby, and found him waiting for her, sitting on the edge of the bed.

"What—what do you want?" she faltered.

He laughed unpleasantly. "Hardly the question, my dear, for a wife to ask her husband, considering the circumstances. I should have thought it was obvious."

She backed away from him, remembering the night he had tried to seduce her and her treacherous sense of excitement. Dear God! That he had ever excited her now seemed impossible, a far-off dream which reality had woven into the very stuff of nightmare.

"Don't touch me," she pleaded. "I don't want you near me. Go away, Barnaby, please, and leave me alone."

With an ugly noise, he was off the bed and crushing her in his arms. His hands, clammy and importunate, were fumbling at her skirts. She gave a little moan and

71

tried to push him away, sensing through her horror a repugnance which was as great as her own.

"You're like all the others," he said, and his face was so close that she could smell the wine on his breath. "You think I'm only half a man. So I'm going to prove to you that that's not true."

He forced her back on the bed, his body pinioning hers with its weight. She felt bruised, defenceless against his onslaught. Defiled. A wave of repulsion engulfed her, battering her against some distant shore where a dark tide ran. She thought, for one blessed moment, that she had fainted . . .

Barnaby rolled off her and sat, arms clasped around the bedpost, shivering and crying. Sweat beaded his forehead. His eyes were closed and he breathed hard, as though he had been running. Lilias lay where she was for what seemed an eternity, then got up and went to the basin and ewer which stood on a table in the corner of the room.

"Lilias!" Barnaby's voice was muffled, choked by tears. "I'm sorry! Sorry." She was vaguely aware that he was holding out his hand, but she ignored it and did not speak. "Help me! Help me, please! I'm begging you . . ." Still she said nothing, her back rigid with the implacability of youth. Silently she finished washing and went downstairs without a backward glance.

Dorothy Hazard had gone, Hannah was placidly sewing and Regina was reading a devotional book. Neither had time to notice her or suspect that anything was wrong. Gratefully, she sat down out of the range of the candles.

Presently she heard Barnaby come downstairs and the street door shut behind him.

★   ★   ★

It was late when Barnaby left Abyndon's—alias Jones', alias the New Inn, alias the Rummer—on the corner of

72

Venny Lane and High Street. It had one of the worst reputations of all Bristol's many inns, and by curfew, even Barnaby had had his fill of the reek of unwashed bodies and the smell of spilled, sour ale. He breathed deeply, filling his lungs with the cold, sharp tang of the river. The High Cross stood at the top of the street, veiled in shadow, backed by St Ewen's, with its delicate façade, and the looming bulk of Trinity. On either side of him, the houses rose, thin, blank-faced and eyeless.

At the crossroads, Barnaby hesitated. He did not want to go home just yet, to face again Lilias' rejection of him and the frayed emotions of the evening. He wanted to postpone harsh reality for as long as he could. He glanced blearily to his right, where the cobbles of Wine Street were tinged with silver under the rising slip of a moon. There were sounds of activity in the Guard House: a shout, someone laughing, then the sudden crash of a breast-plate dropped carelessly on the floor. A soldier stood silhouetted in the open doorway, peering out thoughtfully into the night.

A mangy cat, scrounging for food in the gutters, rubbed itself hopefully around Barnaby's legs, and he kicked it away with a curse. At the same moment, he was conscious of a movement in the mouth of an alleyway opposite. And as the soldier turned and disappeared inside the Guard House, someone slid furtively deeper into the shadows and was lost to Barnaby's view. He stood there, straining his eyes after the vanishing form, befuddled with wine and fresh air. Surely that had been Phineas! And yet . . . No, he must have been mistaken.

A rat shot like a bolt from a nearby house. The cat was on its tail in seconds, claws screeching for a grip on the slippery cobbles, spitting hate and fury after its escaping prey. Jolted out of his stupor, Barnaby swore, crossed over, leaving the High Cross behind him like some mourning ghost, and wended his way down Broad Street. As he neared the bottom, he saw the same stealthy figure,

73

now accompanied by another, slipping silently round the corner from Tower Lane, to be swallowed by the black maw of St John's Archway. It was, he was positive, Phineas Leach.

So there was someone else! Consumed by jealousy, Barnaby followed his quarry into the darkness of the archway and out on to the span of the sleeping Frome Bridge.

★   ★   ★

Prince Rupert and the Earl of Chelwood stamped their feet to keep them warm and clasped their arms across their chests. Overhead, a few defeated clouds lifted to unveil the stars. Around them, the grey twilight spaces of the Downs stretched remote and sinister, the humps and shoulders of thrusting rock recalling the grave-barrows of some long-dead, long-gone age. The tangle of trees known as Nightingale Valley foamed down the side of the Avon Gorge to the sluggish grey thread of the river. The city itself, sunk deep in its marsh, was a smudge of blackness below them.

★   ★   ★

George Boucher's house in Christmas Street adjoined the Frome Bridge. It was built four-square around a courtyard, supported on the bridge side by a colonnade of freestone pillars. The room in which Boucher and his friends were assembled overlooked and overhung the river.

Henry Taylor of Broad Street and Phineas Leach were the last to arrive, and the former had Barnaby Colefax by the collar.

"What the Devil—" spluttered Boucher, thunderstruck, as the unwelcome visitor was dragged inside. "Leach! If this is any of your doing—"

"The drunken sot must have followed us from Yeamans' house," Henry Taylor answered, before Phineas could reply. "He's far too drunk to know what's going on, but until all's over, he'll be safest under our care."

Boucher nodded grimly and, ignoring Phineas' half-hearted protestations, propelled Barnaby ahead of them, up the stairs. Twice Barnaby tripped and would have lain where he fell, but was hauled unceremoniously to his feet.

"There'sh no need t' be so bloody rough," he protested.

"Is everything ready in Wine Street?" George Boucher asked Taylor.

The other grunted assent. "But there's unusual activity in the Guard House tonight. Yeamans was very uneasy."

"He worries too much," said Boucher.

There was a barrage of questions from the other conspirators as Barnaby was pushed inside the room. He was thrust into a chair and Phineas knelt anxiously beside him. When explanations had been given: "We'll lock the idiot up," Boucher assured the others. "He must stay here for now, but when the time comes, he can join the rest of our prisoners in St John's crypt."

Barnaby's head was beginning to clear. A faint glimmer of understanding penetrated his wine-logged senses.

"Wha'sh goin' on?" he asked suspiciously. "I know shome o' you . . . Sheen you in the Rose in . . . in Temple Shtreet." He smiled, pleased at this feat of memory.

"Barney! For pity's sake, pull yourself together," pleaded Phineas. "Why did you follow me, you fool?"

Barnaby beamed at him seraphically and stroked his friend's hair. "Thought you was playin' me false . . . Don' think you are . . . Wha'sh goin' on?" he repeated.

"You'll find out soon enough," Edward Dacre promised him, not unkindly.

Barnaby felt sick and dizzy. He caught odd words, phrases, tantalising scraps of sentences of which he vainly tried to make sense. Boucher was handing out white favours, sashes for the breast and cockades for the hats. Phineas donned two of these and Barnaby watched in stupefaction.

"What you doin', Phin? Why you puttin' those white things on?"

"Oh, shut up, Barney!" Phineas cried in exasperation. "Why couldn't you have left me alone? Why do you have to come sticking your great nose in?"

For the second time that evening Barnaby felt rejected. Tears of self-pity rolled down his cheeks. Neither Lilias nor Phineas loved him . . .

There was a sudden loud knocking on the outer door, and a voice from below shouted: "Open, in the name of Parliament!"

The conspirators gaped at one another in stunned silence, horror and disbelief writ large on all their faces. Then the sound of hammer-blows, like thunder in the quiet, suggested that the soldiers had started to break down the door.

Boucher's face was grey with fear, while Henry Taylor, in bitter accents, unerringly named Clement Walker as their betrayer. Several others were in tears and most seemed too frightened to move. It was left to Edward Dacre to prove himself the man to be relied upon in an emergency.

"Douse the lights!" he ordered in his deep, clear voice and flung the shuttered windows open. Below him lay the banks of the Frome. It was low tide and the river oozed lazily between deposits of mud, like a snake which had sloughed its skin. Further down stream, ships rode like phantoms at their moorings. "Out of the window," Dacre commanded. "And pray that the mud will hold us."

There was a rending crash as the outer door gave way, followed, a moment later, by the clatter of feet on the stairs. Everyone in the room made a concerted rush for the window and the promise of freedom beyond. Barnaby rose from his seat, assisted by Phineas, his mind suddenly as clear as crystal. Fear made everything plain. This was a plot to let in the Royalist troops and Phineas was one of the conspirators. He remembered their talk on St Nicholas' Back and cursed himself for his blindness.

Panic seized him. Who would believe that his presence here was an accident? His friendship with Phineas was too well known: people would be bound to draw the wrong conclusion. He lurched towards the window, clawing and fighting his way on to the broad expanse of sill, then paused a second, clinging to a stanchion. Below, the mud lay smooth and almost phosphorescent. Over its slimy surface, strange scarecrow shapes heaved and floundered, slithering unsteadily to their feet. Two of them had found a board and were floating with it downstream.

Someone pushed Barnaby in the back. Even as he fell, hands clawing wildly at empty space, he was aware of firing from the house and the shadowy figures of soldiers racing along the banks. He hit the mud with a smack. It was in his eyes, his nose, his mouth, smothering him in its cloying embrace. His legs, weakened by too much wine, refused to obey him. Then someone had hold of his shoulders and was pulling him free. A hand smeared the mask of mud from his face.

"Barnaby Colefax!" hissed Captain Clifton. "Well, well, well! Not just a sodomite, but a treacherous one at that. A King's man! A bloody little Judas, who's not fit to live." Barnaby was spluttering, trying to get up, but two hands were pinioning him to the mud. "I'd let them hang you," Clifton went on, and Barnaby found himself mesmerised by the mad, furious glinting of his eyes. "But you might get off, mightn't you, my perverted little friend? Cousin Pride has influence in Parliament. So I think I'll do the hangman's work for him."

Barnaby was paralysed with fear. The next moment, he was face down again in the mud, a great weight holding him down. The blood was drumming in his ears and he tried to scream; the mud tasted salt on his tongue. He was being dragged down, and further down, into a gaping pit of darkness . . .

Captain Clifton grasped the limp wrists and hauled the body towards the bank, up over his ankles in slime. The mud yielded up its prey with a reluctant squelch, still sucking at the splayed legs and clawing fingers. Rolling the slack, pathetic figure over on its back, Clifton shouted: "This one's dead, Major Langrish!"

CHAPTER FIVE

"Lilias! Lilias! Wake up. Lilias!"

Lilias shook herself free from the cobweb of dreams to see Hannah bending over her. It was quite dark, except for a faint tissue of moonlight carpeting the floor, but she had the feeling that she had not long fallen asleep.

"Whatever is it, Hannah?" She sat up, pushing her hair from her eyes. "It can't be morning already." Even as she spoke, the absence of Barnaby's sprawled figure and his drunken snoring confirmed her impression.

"No, it's not morning." Hannah was impatient. "Mother and I have only just come up to bed. Listen! There it is again! Can't you hear it? It sounds like shots being fired."

The sound came once more, crisp and clear through the windless air; the undoubted crackle of musketry fire from the direction of Wine Street. Lilias got out of bed and ran to the window, opening the casement and peering as far as she could along Broad Street.

"Do you think we're under siege?" quavered Hannah.

"Ssh ... No, I shouldn't think so. The firing's too spasmodic. The start of a siege would be ... well ... noisier, I should think than this."

Regina came in, her night-cap askew, a cloak hastily thrown on over her night-rail.

"Girls! Girls! Whatever are we going to do? The Royalists are here, I'm sure of it. They say Prince Rupert lets his men do anything they like after he's sacked a town, especially with the women ... They say he's awfully handsome."

Lilias laughed, but Hannah exclaimed in horror: "Mother! You have a wicked, lewd mind. I shall kill myself rather than let one of the ungodly lay so much as a finger on me."

"So laudable," murmured her mother. "I wish I were one half as brave."

Lilias went to her and hugged her. "Dear ma'am, I'm sure there won't be any need for either your sacrifice or Hannah's heroism. I don't think for a moment that we're under siege. In fact, I rather think the firing has stopped."

There was silence while they all strained their ears. Someone was shouting in the distance, but otherwise all was quiet. Then came the sound of marching feet, just outside the window.

"A troop of soldiers," Lilias reported, "going in the direction of the Frome Bridge." And a few moments later, there came a further volley of firing.

Mollie Hanks, who had slept through the first disturbance, now erupted into Lilias' bedroom on the verge of hysterics.

"They're coming to get I! Those devils are coming to get I!" she gulped and plunged into the vacated bed, burying her head under the sheets.

"Mollie," said Regina awfully, "if you start screeching, I'll beat you black and blue. My nerves are in shreds already. Dear life! What's that?" She pressed a hand to her heart as there came a knocking on the outer door.

Lilias again peeped cautiously out of the window. "It's all right," she told the others with relief. "It's only Mistress Hazard."

"Well really!" gasped Regina. "I declare she's given me palpitations. Dorothy," she demanded sternly, a few moments later, as she admitted her friend, "must you bang on the door like that? It sounded like the crack of doom."

"Nonsense!" was the astringent reply as Dorothy led the way into the Prides' front parlour, where the remains of the evening's fire still lent a rosy glow to the room. "What's that hideous keening?"

"Mollie Hanks having hysterics. Never mind that.

Dorothy, do you know what's going on?"

"Not yet, but I've sent Hazard to find out. He'll be back, I hope, in a very few minutes. Of course, I had to rouse him. He sleeps like the dead. Now my first husband, Anthony Kelly—"

But the reminiscence was lost by the entrance of the Reverend Matthew Hazard, who, finding the street door on the latch, had made his own way in.

"I've seen Aldworth," he said in response to the ladies' eager questions. "It seems that Yeamans and Boucher and a number of others had made plans to let Prince Rupert and his army into the city tonight—"

"The fiends!" exclaimed Dorothy.

"—but Fiennes, it seems, knew all about it from the beginning. Clement Walker had already informed him that he thought something was afoot; then the two guards whom the conspirators thought that they had bribed went straight to the Governor and confirmed Walker's suspicions. So, all Fiennes had to do was to give them enough rope."

"They won't hang any of them surely!" cried Lilias, horrified.

Matthew Hazard shrugged. "I should think it extremely likely. Fiennes told the Mayor that he intends to make an example of the ringleaders, at least."

"And a good thing, too," snapped Hannah viciously. "That's the only way to deal with traitors."

Lilias felt confused. How could anyone be a traitor who was trying to assist the King?

"What was the firing about?" asked Dorothy.

"The party at Yeamans' house offered some resistance, but gave in when Fiennes threatened to bombard them with cannon."

"Well," Dorothy smiled approvingly, "it's a relief to discover that Fiennes has that much spunk. I've never liked the man," she added untruthfully. "All you can really say of him is that he's better than that debauched womaniser, Essex." She turned to Hannah. "But at least, now, we shan't be raped in our beds."

"No, indeed." And Hannah repeated what she had said earlier to her mother.

Lilias wondered idly why the minds of plain women ran so continuously upon rape. She also wondered, less idly, where Barnaby was, and why, since it was now long past curfew, he had apparently failed to come home. Or could it be that he was lying drunk in the kitchen?

The same thought seemed to strike Hannah, for she remarked bitterly: "Of course, the one man who ought to be here to protect us is out drinking somewhere, with his friends."

"But Richard's in London," Regina said vaguely. "And you, yourself, said that he—"

"I meant Barnaby, mother."

"Oh! But I don't think he'd be much good, dear. He was never one for using his fists. He hates violence of any kind ... Now, who on earth is that? It can't be more visitors, surely, at this time of night."

Hannah went to answer the knock on the door and returned with a pale-faced Major Langrish. He glanced uncertainly around the little gathering, then lowered his eyes, seemingly absorbed in the contemplation of his boots. He coughed awkwardly, shifted his feet, then said to Lilias, still not raising his eyes: "I am afraid that I have some very distressing news for you, Mrs Colefax."

*   *   *

She could not believe it! She would not believe it! Not that Barnaby was dead. She kept seeing him, sitting on the edge of the bed, and hearing his voice saying: "Help me! Help me, please! I'm begging you ..." And she had turned away. She had left him to fight his miserable little battle alone; and now he was dead. If she had responded to his appeal, he might still be alive. She had killed him as surely as the smothering river mud ... She shut

82

herself away in her room, refusing to see or speak to anyone for hours ...

At the end of the week, Richard came home, frantically summoned by Hannah, who was more concerned with her cousin's involvement in a Royalist plot than with the manner of his dying. But by then, Barnaby's innocence had been established, his reputation cleared by the testimony of young Pineas Leach.

"It was an accident," Richard said, patting Lilias' hand, "a most unhappy accident. He must have panicked and jumped with the others and suffocated to death in the mud."

Yes, she thought, it was fitting somehow that Barnaby should die in such a stupid and unnecessary fashion, choking out his aimless existence on the mudflats of the Frome, the victim of a double betrayal in which he had played no part. She clung to Richard's hand, unconscious of Hannah's basilisk stare, knowing only that his solid, comforting presence gave her the strength to bear the unbearable.

"Help me! Help me, please! I'm begging you ..."

Of all the conspirators, only Henry Taylor escaped, making his way to Prince Rupert at Clifton and riding with him to the safety of Oxford. The rest were chained by the neck and feet in the castle dungeons, under such appalling conditions that several died, including Phineas Leach. Governor Fiennes received the thanks of both Houses of Parliament and was ordered to proceed against the rebels with "all celerity and severity." He was particularly commended for his handling of the situation in Wine Street.

Feelings were running high. The hatred of Englishmen for Englishmen was increasing daily, and the division between Protestant and Catholic reached fever pitch. On April the fourteenth, the *Mermaid* and the *Sampson* sailed from Bristol carrying food for the Protestants of famine-stricken Ireland. No Catholic, on pain of death, was to touch it. But feelings between Dissenters and Episcopalians ran even higher. The Pope was hated hardly more than the King, who was execrated daily from every Nonconformist pulpit in the city. Grace Carey of St Augustine's Back dreamed of Charles Stuart's head crowned by a circlet of blood. The Church of England clergy were driven from their livings. And on May the eighth, Boucher and Yeamans were harangued all the way to their scaffold outside Yeamans' house in Wine Street by Dissenting clergy, and denied the ministrations of their friends. Their last prayers were interrupted by taunts from the crowd; and Captain Clifton hacked at the hands of Yeamans' brother-in-law, who tried to still the violent jerkings of the bodies.

"How can men do these things to each other?" asked Lilias, horrified. "Particularly in the name of religion."

"Blasphemy!" cried Hannah. "There is only one true way to worship God, and that is as it is shown to us in the Book of Revelations. *If any worship the Beast and receive the mark on his forehead, or in his hand, the same shall drink of the wine of the Wrath of God.*"

"But you can't all be right," shouted Lilias, losing her temper. "Not you and the Baptists and the Brownists and the Presbyterians and the Anabaptists and the Fifth Monarchists! And what about the King? He believes that he's right. And what about the Pope? He thinks—"

"Don't mention that henchman of Satan if you want to remain under my roof!" screamed Hannah. "There is one thing certain in all this world, Lilias Colefax, and that is that the Catholics are the work of the Devil."

The quarrel exploded like a clap of thunder, but there was more to it than a mere difference about religion. Underlying the theological arguments which were tossed, womanlike, heedless of either logic or relevance, at one another's heads, was the growing animosity of Hannah towards Lilias. Lilias, widowed, posed a threat which, married, she had never done. Richard had not returned

84

to London, declaring that Parliament could do without him for a while. And Hannah suspected that Lilias was the reason behind this resolve.

"Oh no, my love," Regina had said when Hannah voiced her suspicions. "He may find her easy to look at and pleasant to talk to—I'm sure we all do—but nothing more than that. Richard is devoted to you and your son."

"He doesn't love me any more," sobbed Hannah.

"Well, he won't if you continue like this," her mother had observed wisely. "There is nothing a man dislikes more than constant demands for reassurance and demonstrations of his affection. Unless it is a woman who cries."

But Hannah remained unconvinced; and Lilias' views on religion, striking as they did at the very roots of Hannah's belief, had proved the final straw. Words rapidly became inadequate; within minutes, both had resorted to blows.

It was Richard who separated them, pulling them apart with as little ceremony as he would have parted two squalling cats.

"I've a good mind," he told them furiously, "to horsewhip you both. Perhaps that would teach you a lesson."

Hannah dissolved into tears, but Lilias' eyes glinted dangerously. "Don't lay a finger on me, Richard Pride," she warned, "if for no other reason than I am pregnant."

She had suspected that she was pregnant about six weeks after Barnaby's death and was now sure of it. She did not want the child, conceived as it had been in such a fashion, in that last nightmarish encounter between her and her husband. It would be a constant reproach to her; a reminder that she had ignored Barnaby's plea for help; had turned from him at the moment when he had needed her most. She felt sure that she could not love this unborn child.

Fortunately, she had no time to brood. As spring slid

into summer, as June gave place to July, there was too much distraction, for Bristol was now seriously threatened by the King. The failure of the conspiracy to take it by stealth had in no way weakened the Royalists' determination that the second city in the kingdom should be theirs. Whoever held Bristol held the main shipping routes to Ireland and America. It was more important even than Plymouth, Gloucester or Hull, all of which were also in Parliament's hands. But they could wait. Ultimate success or failure in the war depended upon Bristol's capture, and Royalist hopes of taking it were running high.

The King's forces had had a string of victories, beginning on May the sixteenth with Sir Ralph Hopton's remarkable triumph at Stratton in Cornwall against impossible odds. On June the eighteenth, Prince Rupert fought a successful engagement at Chalgrove Field, near Oxford, resulting amongst other things, in the death of John Hampden. Meanwhile, Hopton had swept through Devon into Somerset, joining up with Prince Maurice and the Marquis of Hertford at Chard. There was a cavalry skirmish at Chewton Mendip: Bristol was slowly being ringed.

For the dithering Fiennes there was one last hope of averting the threatened siege. Between him and Hopton's army, advancing from the south, and Rupert and his army, advancing from the north, lay Sir William Waller's forces at Bath.

★ ★ ★

The early-morning distances were fretted with gold, the valleys flooded with shadow. Willow-herb, ragwort and the foaming heads of cow parsley starred the brooding woods and glittering meadows. The scent of wild thyme, thick like incense, rose from beneath the horses' crushing hooves. Patrick O'Mara could have fancied himself once more at home, riding out on a fine

July morning from his father's home near Waterford, in the company of that rash, fierce old man who had staked his life in a quarrel about religion.

Sir Connor O'Mara had never taken kindly to the Protestant creed, nor to the English neighbours who had bought the land next to his.

"Parvenus!" he would rage. "Jumped-up nobodies! Their ancestors made their money by trampling on the grave of the true religion! Servants of the Anti-Pope himself, that devil, Henry Tudor. May he rot in Hell! And now they come taking our good Irish land, watered by the blood of our heroes. Who are these Plunketts? Do they dare think that they are the equal of the O'Maras?"

Unhappily, the Plunketts did think so, unaware that family pride was the breath in the old man's nostrils.

"On my father's side are we not descended from the Mortimers? Mary bless their thieving souls! Isn't our family crest still the White Lion Rampant? But from my mother, God rest her, don't we go even further back to the mighty Brian Boru? And didn't I name this house Clontarf in honour of himself?"

His hatred of his neighbours had slowly smouldered until one day, after some real or fancied slight, he had roused his household on a punitive raid in the tradition of a more carefree and lawless age. He had been shot down by one of the Plunketts and carried back to Clontarf to die. An all-Protestant jury had acquitted his killer, and the big, rambling house with the leaking roof had passed to Patrick O'Mara.

Patrick had found himself destitute, with no means of paying even the most pressing of his father's debts.

"Sir Connor had no more idea of management than a baby," the lawyer O'Malley had told him repressively. "If you take my advice, you'll sell this place and use the money to pay what your father owes."

So Clontarf had been sold along with most of the horses, and Patrick had gone for a soldier of fortune. He was unmarried, his mother was dead, he was an only child; there was nothing to keep him in Ireland. The war in England had offered him employment and he had joined the troop of Sir Faithful Fortescue. He had not much cared, in his then state of mind, that he was recruited to fight for Parliament. But when he had discovered that he was to be employed in Ireland against his own countrymen, he had decided, there and then, to change sides. In the event, the decision had been made for him by his commander, who had switched his own allegiance before the battle of Edgehill.

And so here he was, on this warm July morning, riding with Sir Ralph Hopton's victorious Army of the West, out from Marshfield on its high, wide plateau, heading in the direction of Bath. With Hopton rode Prince Maurice, Sir Bevil Grenville and his Cornishmen, the Earl of Caernarvon and Sir Nicholas Slanning, with his company of heavy dragoons.

Sir Ralph Hopton was a Somerset man, whose conscience was deeply troubled by this war of father against son, brother against brother. It also disturbed the conscience of one of his dearest friends, the man whose army was drawn up on the neighbouring heights waiting to give him battle. There nestled in Sir Ralph's pocket a letter, received earlier that morning from Sir William Waller. One line would be for ever scorched on his memory.

"The Great God, who is the Searcher of my heart, knows with what a sad sense I go upon this service, and with what perfect hatred I detest this war without an enemy."

Sir Ralph's pendulous cheeks had quivered with emotion as he read those words, and the sad, bloodhound face had crumpled into tears. Now, however, with the scent of approaching battle in his nostrils, the professional soldier had replaced the private man. He had fought on the Continent in the religious wars and been

88

trained in the service of Count Mansfeld. His trained eye noted appreciatively Waller's dispositions on the crest of Tog Hill, his flanks protected by two thick copses, bristling with musketeers. A line of breastworks had been raised along the brow of the hill; and on the plain at Waller's back were reserves of horse and foot, guarding the steep downhill approaches to Bath.

Prince Maurice rode up.

"What do you think, Hopton? Can they be persuaded to come down? That position looks almost impregnable."

Sir Bevil Grenville called out: "My Cornishmen are willing to try an assault, Your Highness."

Maurice shook his head. "It would be suicide," he retorted.

Patrick O'Mara stretched his long legs and shifted his weight in the saddle. The fitful sunlight rippled and gleamed over his horse's hide, turning the glossy coat to spun gold. They were drawn up in a cornfield commanding a good view of Tog Hill. The trampled grain was studded with poppies, glinting among the crushed stalks like blood. The captain beckoned to one of his men, who, he knew, was a native of Gloucester.

"That house," he said, pointing to a soft, grey smudge and a spiral of smoke, away to his right, among the distant trees. "Whose is it? Do you know?"

"That's Westovers, sir. Belongs to the Earl of Chelwood. This is mostly his land, hereabouts."

"Ah!" Patrick nodded. "I thought it might be ... Hullo! What's up? Can you see what's happening?"

"Looks like we're retreating, sir. Back towards Marshfield." The trooper was disgusted.

"A feint," grunted Patrick. "I'll bet my last shilling. We're going to see if we can lure that wily old fox from his lair in the hills."

"About time, too, sir. I'm tired of all this hanging about, while the vanguard has all the fun."

Skirmishing had been taking place for the last two

hours, and the no-man's-land between the two armies was already littered with dead.

"Fun is it?" grinned Patrick, as he gave the order to withdraw. "We'll see if you still feel the same way by tonight."

★ ★ ★

The carnage was appalling. As darkness shrouded the Lansdown plain, Hopton knew that he had won a Pyrrhic victory. He, himself, had twice been injured: shot in the arm at the start of the battle and, later, thrown over a hundred yards when a gunpowder barrel had exploded.

Somewhat to Hopton's surprise, Waller had been taken in by the mock retreat and sent four hundred horse—Sir Arthur Hazelrigg's "lobsters"—to fall on the Royalist rear. It was then that the bloodiest fighting of the day had occurred, when Sir Bevil Grenville and his invincible Cornishmen carried Tog Hill in a running fight. Their ranks were torn to ribbons by volleys of musket-fire from the redoubts and breastworks at the top of the hill. Yet as one line of men fell beneath that murderous hail, another charged upwards to take its place. By the time the crest was carried, the victors were scrambling over mounds of their dead. Sir Bevil Grenville, whose courage and daring had inspired the Cornishmen throughout the day, was poleaxed in the moment of triumph. Immediately, his servant, Payne, a giant of a man, had put the thirteen-year-old John Grenville on his father's horse, and the weeping boy had led the final charge on the enemy position.

"Indecisive! Very indecisive!" Prince Maurice exclaimed, as Waller drew off his men to the safety of Bath, leaving Hopton and Maurice masters of the field. "With our advantages, we should have destroyed their entire army."

From the litter where he lay unable to move, Sir Ralph Hopton glared up balefully at the speaker.

"Had the cavalry, Your Highness, given more adequate support, your censure might be more appropriate." Privately he thought Maurice was growing very like Rupert, arrogant and self-opinionated.

"There will be trouble there," remarked Colonel Slingsby to Patrick O'Mara. "Their Royal High and Mightinesses make too many enemies."

"A pity," Patrick said, lying on his back and watching the rush of stars overhead. "They are the best cavalry leaders this war has seen. And as for today, Hopton is ungenerous. A charge uphill isn't easy. I was a part of it and I know."

Slingsby shrugged. "That's as maybe. Anyway, Waller's gone back to Bath with his tail between his legs. And I still say no thanks to His High Illustrious Arrogancy. No offence to you, O'Mara, who I'm sure fought bravely as always. It was just the leadership that was lacking." He gave a hearty, admiring laugh which echoed weirdly through the groans of the dying. "That old fox, Waller! Did you know that he left his light-matches burning on top of a wall, with rows of pikes propped up between them? If Hopton hadn't had the sense to send a man to investigate, we would never have known that he'd retreated. Now that's what I call a good soldier."

Patrick clasped his hands behind his neck and turned to look at Slingsby. "You know," he said, "the English must be the most xenophobic race in the history of the world."

"We're a plain-spoken race," the colonel retorted, nettled. "We don't go in for long, fancy words. You keep your heathen tongue to yourself, O'Mara, or for those who can understand it."

"The word 'xenophobia' is Greek and it means a hatred of foreigners. You dislike Sir William Waller and everything he stands for, yet you can speak of him with respect, even affection. Yet King Charles' nephews are almost universally reviled. And for no better reason that I can see than that they are both half-foreign. Even Hopton, who is a devoted admirer of their mother, has no place for her half-German sons."

Before Slingsby could refute what he secretly took as a compliment, Trooper Trenchard loomed up out of the darkness, and, leaning down, tapped Patrick on the shoulder.

"Excuse me, sir, but it's Westovers. You can see it from the ridge. It looks to me, sir, as though it's on fire."

*   *   *

Magdalen was half-asleep, worn out by the rigours of the day.

From the first sound of gunfire, early that morning, she had been coping single-handed with hysterical servants. The butler and housekeeper had retired to the pantry and drowned their fears in the Earl's best wines. The scullery- and kitchen-maids, raw country girls for the most part, had been scared out of their wits, screaming and crying. The upstairs servants had behaved little better; and even Miss Chillingworth, the children's governess, had taken to her bed and refused to get up. Several of the men had left to join Sir Ralph's advancing army, while the rest, less intrepid souls, had followed the example of the butler and Mrs Trowbridge.

But with the coming of dark and the subsequent silence, news of Hopton's victory had been sent by a neighbour who lived at Cold Ashton, and Magdalen had at last been able to relax, falling asleep in a chair by the library window. Her unquiet dreams were full of hysterical women and the pungent, bitter odour of smoke . . .

She jerked upright, her heart pounding in sickening alarm. For a moment or two she could not think what had wakened her; the same sense of unreality which had dogged her all day still clung to the edges of her mind. Then she saw it through the window: the jewel-bright lick of flame against the dairy and the barn, set on fire by some deserting soldiers. She saw that a shower of sparks had already set the bakery roof alight.

"John! Henry! Martin!" She had wrenched open the door which led into the courtyard, the cobbles a reflected lake of flame, before she remembered with horror that there would be no response to her summons. John, Henry and Martin, like the rest of the servants, were lying dead drunk in the butler's pantry.

Panic rose in a choking tide. Sparks, flying like will-o'-the-wisps, had settled on the thatched roof of the buttery. Tongues of fire, yellow, blue and gold, crept along the beams of the wash-house. Somehow those criminal, drunken fools must be roused from their stupor, or they would all be cremated where they lay.

Someone shouted and, in the glare of ruddy light, a party of horsemen galloped into the courtyard.

"Lady Chelwood?" called their leader, a tall, dark-haired man on a beautiful chestnut mare. He spoke with an Irish accent.

Magdalen gave a little moan and staggered towards him, hands outstretched. "Oh please! Help me! Please help me!"

The man leaned down, imprisoning the hands which fluttered so importunately against his knee. "For God's sake, ma'am, where are your servants?"

"The women are too frightened. The men are all drunk—those that haven't gone off and joined the army."

Patrick swore, then said briskly: "Don't worry, your ladyship. We'll soon have this little blaze under control." He smiled. "Just show me where the well is." Turning to Trooper Trenchard, who had dismounted and was hovering beside him, he added: "Take two or three men to the kitchen and get hold of every water-bearing vessel you can find. We could do with the milking pails, but it looks as though the dairy's alight. Now, ma'am, if you'll just show me that well—"

In less than two hours, the fire was under control, at the expense of a burned-out barn and dairy, and a wash-house that was badly charred. The buttery had sustained little damage and its contents were completely unharmed.

"For which, thank the Lord," Patrick O'Mara told Magdalen with a twinkle in his eye. "It would have broken my heart, so it would, to see all that precious liquor go up in smoke."

Magdalen smiled wanly. "Please help yourself, Captain. Also your men. I'm very certain you all deserve it."

"Thank you kindly, ma'am. But first, my troopers will get your servants on their feet."

He was as good as his word. Half an hour later, the shamefaced grooms, footmen and kitchen-boys, even the august Mr and Mrs Trowbridge, had been beaten and bullied to their senses and were setting about cleaning up the mess. Miss Chillingworth, regaining her usual calm, had also consented to give a hand.

In the shadowy library, Magdalen smiled at her rescuer. The solitude was blessed after the noise and terror of the past few hours.

"Captain O'Mara, I don't know how to thank you. You and your men have saved my home."

Patrick bowed gravely over the small, smoke-blackened hand, kissed the fingers lightly, glanced up—and fell in love.

CHAPTER SIX

Magdalen's hair was tangled, her dress filthy and a streak of black scarred one pale cheek. Yet nothing could disguise the remote, cool beauty, the gentleness, the innate sweetness of nature which had so moved the gallants and poets of King Charles' court to celebrate her virtues in verse and song. She was, thought Patrick with a sense of shock, exactly like the paintings of the Virgin: those lovely Raphael and Leonardo Madonnas, which must be as far from the truth as the fair-haired European-ised Christs were from the Jewish original.

Magdalen was looking at him now, her blue eyes wide, her sweet mouth trembling. She seemed vulnerable, yet he recognised a will of iron buried beneath the layers of timidity. It was a will which would keep her always on the straight and narrow path; which she would use relentlessly to drive her fragile body in the service of those she loved.

And she loved her husband, there was no doubt of that. Patrick saw her eyes flick constantly, as though drawn by some inner compulsion, to the portrait over the fireplace. Priam Lithgow, fifth Earl of Chelwood, stood there in all his painted glory, caught by Sir Anthony van Dyck in the pomp of satin and ermine. The improbably stiff pose against a back-drop of red velvet—one hand resting on the head of his dog, the other pointing to a muted autumnal scene beyond the fold of curtain—could not hide the essential virility of the man. Captain O'Mara was struck by something dark and brooding. He wondered suddenly, angrily, if the Earl made this gentle creature happy.

He ached to take her in his arms, to tell her that she was lovely, desirable, wanted. Instead, he bowed formally, cleared his throat like an awkward schoolboy and said: "I am happy to have been of some service to your ladyship."

"My husband wrote to me of you after, I think, the battle of Edgehill. You were with Sir Faithful Fortescue."

"And changed sides with him, too, my lady. The best day's work I ever did in my life." If for no other reason, he added to himself, that it brought me in contact with you.

"Your father, I believe, was a friend of my husband's father, the late fourth Earl?"

"They were at Oxford together, but then lost touch."

"It was fortunate, most fortunate, that you were in the vicinity today . . ."

The conversation petered out, killed by its own banality. He could not believe that two hours ago, in the cup of fire that had been the flame-lit courtyard, he had shouted and laughed and joked with her as though she had been one of his troopers.

Two little girls ran into the room and Magdalen bent to embrace them. "My daughters," she murmured, "Cassandra and Cressida."

And Patrick, who normally had an easy way with children, found that he had nothing to say. In that fragile web of candlelight and the Promethean glow of the dying fires, they appeared like their mother, ethereal, unreal, held within the magic circle of her arms . . .

He knew that he was being fanciful, he, Patrick O'Mara, who always kept his feet on the ground. But he felt stupid, tongue-tied, and it was Magdalen who broke the silence.

"Again, thank you, Captain." She held out her hands. "I cannot express how deeply I and mine are in your debt. Be very sure that my husband will hear of it."

Damn your husband, he thought, and realised with a sinking heart that her words were a polite dismissal. But

96

he could not take offence. She looked unutterably weary, almost as though she were about to faint. He made an inarticulate noise, kissed her hands and swung smartly on his heel. The library door shut with a smooth click of finality between them, closing her off from his view. Minutes later he was in the saddle, yelling for his troopers—"you pack of drunken, heathen, whoring knaves!" His mare bounded forward under the prick of a spur wantonly applied. Then he was riding back in the direction of Lansdown to get some sleep in preparation for the march next day.

*　　*　　*

The news of Lansdown was received in Bristol with horror.

"Mark my words," declared Alderman Cann, "we'll be under siege within twenty-four hours."

But the next information was that Hopton and Prince Maurice had withdrawn eastwards to Devizes, and Waller had marched out of Bath to engage them. Confident this time of victory, he penned the injured Hopton and his decimated troops inside the town's barricaded streets, ignorant of the fact that Prince Maurice and the Marquis of Hertford had already ridden to Oxford for reinforcements. What Waller did know was that much of the Royalist ammunition had· been destroyed in the explosion which had injured Hopton. He had reckoned, however, without the determination and ingenuity of his erstwhile friend.

Informed that no slow-match was left in the arsenal, Hopton commandeered all the bed-cord in Devizes. This, boiled, beaten and soaked in resin, proved an admirable substitute: the town still had not fallen to Waller on the morning of July the thirteenth. On that fateful day, the appearance of Prince Maurice with several thousand men ended Waller's hopes of·a successful siege. He withdrew his men hurriedly to the top of

Roundway Down to meet the attack on his flank; and there, with the larks wheeling and calling in the lambent air, the Parliamentary army suffered a catastrophic defeat.

The road to Bristol was now indisputably open.

* * *

On the morning of July the twenty-third, Lilias was roused by Regina shaking her arm. She sat up in bed, her heart slamming painfully against her ribs, poignantly reminded of the night of Barnaby's death.

"What is it? What's happening?" she asked. The sudden movement had made her feel dizzy, recalling that she was nearly five months pregnant.

Little Eliot Pride toddled in, making a bee-line for Lilias and calling her: "Pitty lady."

Lilias laughed, tickling him under the chin. His grandmother swept him up into her arms and kissed him.

"This is no moment for compliments, you rascal. Lilias, Dorothy has just been here—"

"At this time in the morning? Doesn't that woman ever sleep?"

"Will you be quiet and listen!"

"Mother!" Hannah hurried in, looking for her son. "I must finish dressing Eliot. And Richard wants his breakfast immediately. The Trained Bands are mustering at the Tolzey and he must be there in half an hour. Oh, and Mistress Hazard left you these instructions on how to make a fire-bag."

Regina looked dubiously at the piece of paper as Hannah bustled away, taking a protesting Eliot with her.

"Well, I don't know," she demurred. "Colonel Fiennes said to take all valuables to the castle for safe-keeping ... And I do have the silver-gilt candlesticks which were my father's, and that silver porringer which belonged to Great-aunt Susan, not to mention my mother's sapphire ring. But Dorothy says she wouldn't trust Fiennes with a crooked sixpence. Not that she means that he'd steal it or

98

anything like that, but just that she doubts his ability to hold the town against Prince Rupert. Of course, she wouldn't say so to anyone but me! You know how people love to talk. But Dorothy reckons we'd do better to make fire-bags, as they do in Massachusetts. She says they put all their valuables into a bag, and then in an emergency— fire or Indians or anything horrid like that—they simply grab it and run."

"Dear ma'am," Lilias cut in, stemming the torrent of words, "do please be calm and tell me what has happened."

Regina looked aggrieved. "But I've been trying to tell you, only people will keep·chattering . . . Are you feeling sick? Shall I get Mollie to bring you a draught?"

"Ma'am, the news!"

"Oh yes! As I said, Dorothy was here and Reverend Hazard had just that minute returned after being sent for by the Mayor. Prince Maurice and the Cornishmen have been sighted to the south of the city. Now, are you quite certain—"

"I shall be quite all right as soon as I am on my feet," Lilias assured her. "It was just that first moment of sitting up."

"Oh, my dear, I do so sympathise. I remember when I was expecting Hannah—"

"Mother!" Hannah's head reappeared around the door. "I've lost one of Eliot's shoes. Come and help me look for it. He's in to everything."

"Hannah!" Richard's voice was heard peremptorily from below. "Where's Mollie? And where's my break-fast? I particularly asked—"

"Oh dear!" wailed Hannah. "I don't know where the wretched girl has gone. Now Eliot's fallen off the chamber-pot. Mother!"

"Breakfast!" yelled Richard furiously.

"My, my!" exclaimed Regina, flustered as she always was at the hint of domestic discord.

"You help Hannah with Eliot," Lilias soothed her, "while I get dressed and attend to the food."

"Dear girl," breathed Regina, misty-eyed. "I didn't really want Barnaby to marry you, you know. But I'm very glad now that he did."

When Lilias entered the kitchen ten minutes later, Richard was closing the outer kitchen door.

"That was Jeremiah Godsey from Wine Street," he informed her. "Prince Rupert has been sighted on Durdham Downs by the look-out in the Brandon Hill Fort. They reckon he has about thirty thousand men."

"And how many have we?" asked Lilias, cutting a generous rasher of ham with hands that were not quite steady.

"About ten thousand—which should be enough as long as the defences hold." Richard sat down and watched irritably as Lilias fried the ham. "Why isn't Mollie doing that? You're not the hired help."

She smiled at him across her shoulder. Pregnancy had not diminished her looks; rather it had given her a glow, like the patina on an overripe plum. He noticed how full her breasts were, straining against the bodice of her gown. His hands began to tremble and his mouth felt dry. He addressed himself assiduously to his meal, and, after a moment, said thickly: "There's nothing to be afraid of, you know."

Lilias knew that he was lying for her sake and felt grateful. She was conscious, however, that her panic was laced with exhilaration, a quickening of the pulses at this break in the monotony of everyday existence. The prospect of fighting, of war itself, terrified her; but if everything could suddenly be made as it was yesterday, or the day before that, she knew that she would experience disappointment: a feeling of having in some way been cheated.

Richard laid down his knife and began probing his teeth with a small ivory pick. The warmth, the friendly smells of the ham and newly baked bread, made a little haven of intimacy, shared by the two of them alone. Soon, Hannah or Regina or Mollie would come in and the peace would be shattered. Richard sighed and put away his toothpick, spreading his hands across his stomach and feeling with satisfaction the hardness and flatness of his muscles. For all his weight and build, he had never allowed himself to run to fat. Surreptitiously he glanced at Lilias, and it came to him, unbidden, that he wished that the child she was carrying was his. The enormity of the idea made him choke over his beer, and when Lilias looked at him in concern, he blushed and began to stammer.

"You—you kn-know that this house is your home for as long as you wish to stay. Yours and your child's. Barnaby's child." As well to remind himself of the facts. "I—I hope you won't feel it necessary to return to Cornwall, or wherever it was you came from."

Lilias shook her head. "Not as long as you are willing to have me here. There is nothing for me in Cornwall now. During the last years of my father's life, we had become estranged from all our friends. Bristol is my home now, and I feel that I owe it to Barnaby to bring up his child here, as he undoubtedly would have wished."

"Yes. Poor Barnaby." He did not wish to think about her marriage to Hannah's cousin; to imagine her in another man's arms. Although he suspected, knowing Barnaby, that it could not have been a happy marriage: as well, then, that it had been so brief. "You will probably marry again," he forced himself to say, but his resistance to such an idea was overwhelming. It came to him that he was in love with Lilias and the knowledge disturbed him deeply.

"Perhaps. But not yet. Not for a while."

Relief flooded through him. "I must go," he announced abruptly, and got to his feet. "Lilias—"

"Yes?" She thought how impressive he looked in the

buff coat and red sash of the City Militia. She smiled at him with the affection and admiration of a friend.

"If anything were to happen to me, you'd look after Hannah and her mother? You're so much stronger than they are."

She felt frightened: suddenly the war seemed very near. She had not seriously considered until then the death of anyone she knew. She reached up and, to the surprise of them both, kissed him on the cheek.

"Yes, of course. I promise. But take care of yourself, dear Richard."

*　　*　　*

The following day, Captain Patrick O'Mara was involved in a skirmish around the Redcliffe and Temple Gates, at the same time as Prince Rupert, to the north of the city, was discussing his plans with his lieutenants. Fiennes had, naturally enough, refused the Prince's invitation to surrender, in spite of the fact that all the shipping in the Kingroad had been seized by the enemy. Prince Maurice, with the help of loyal sailors, had "persuaded" the masters to declare for the King.

"We must take the town by assault," Rupert said slowly; and the Earl of Chelwood and Colonel William Legge exchanged startled and troubled glances.

"Sir," ventured the latter, "surely we shall lose too many men?"

They were standing on the heights above the Brandon Hill Fort, looking down into the heart of the city. Far below them, the coils of Avon and Frome islanded the houses on a promontory of green. The Great Marsh lay, surrounded by trees and bushes, a dappled shadow outside the old medieval walls. Smoke curled from kitchen chimneys and, here and there, tiny figures moved across the open spaces of the quay. It looked peaceful, like some toy thrown down by a giant's careless hand.

102

"Sir," Priam said, adding his protest to Will Legge's, "there is so much water. The only approach without a river crossing is from the east through Lawford's Gate. One very narrow neck of land. From this side, the Frome Gate must be carried."

Rupert looked disdainfully down his nose. "You think us incapable of doing that, my lord? Then we must put our trust in Hopton to carry Bristol from the eastern side. But, for myself, I am not so pessimistic." He spoke over his shoulder. "What is your opinion, Colonel Washington?"

Henry Washington grinned. He was a cheerful man and his bland, somewhat eupeptic features belied a tenacity of purpose and a military ability which would find an echo in the following century in his cousin's grandson, George.

"Well, Your Highness," he drawled, "there will be plenty of resistance. The inhabitants, as far as I can gather, are mostly for Parliament and the Free Religion, and regard Your Highness as the Devil incarnate." Rupert laughed. "However, I think we can do it. A hard nut, but one which can be cracked."

The Prince nodded in approval. Henry Washington was a man after his own heart and one whose opinion he valued. He spread a rough map of the city on the ground.

"Two separate assaults, I think, gentlemen. Maurice and Hopton will concentrate on the Redcliffe, Temple and Lawford's Gates. On this side, we shall attack Windmill and Prior's Hill Forts, with a feint here at Brandon. Colonel Washington, that will be under your command. The password will be 'Oxford' and our colour green." He stood up again and turned to William Legge. "Will, get a message through to my brother. A council-of-war tonight, at Captain Hill's house at Redland. Hopton, I suppose, had better come, too." The Prince's dislike of Sir Ralph sounded plainly in his voice and Will Legge grimaced at his companions behind their commander's back. It was, his look implied, going to be an eventful evening.

*   *   *

July the twenty-fifth saw an attack on the Kingsdown line, but it was repulsed with heavy losses. All day long the guns boomed out over the city, and a pathetic trickle of refugees who had lost their homes began arriving from the heights around Cotham.

"Heaven help us!" exclaimed Regina as the guns roared out once more. "We're all of us going to be killed!"

Richard, who had come in for a brief rest after patrolling the streets all night, did not contradict her; and, on Hannah's clamouring for reassurance, he continued to look grave.

"A siege we could have withstood. Fiennes was expecting that and had made his plans accordingly. But Langrish says he is going to pieces in the face of this direct assault. He was advised this morning to occupy higher ground, but has obstinately refused to do so."

"But you say that the attack is being beaten back. Perhaps he is right to do so."

Richard shrugged impatiently. Women had a poor understanding of military matters. "Today, yes! But tomorrow? Fiennes' obstinacy could cost him the city."

"You think those devils will take the town?" cried Hannah in alarm, and he put his arm around her.

"It's possible. We must be prepared for the worst." Releasing her, he pulled on the buff coat and red sash which he had temporarily abandoned, and addressed himself to Lilias. "Go out as little as possible. The streets won't be safe with all the garrison and the ammunition-carts on the move from the castle." He stooped to embrace his son, and Lilias was again surprised that so big a man could be so tender and deft with children. "If the city should fall," he went on, straightening his back,

104

"and I'm not here, lock all the doors and bar the shutters. The Cornishmen are said to be in an ugly mood since the death of Sir Bevil Grenville."

Hannah made an inarticulate sound and clung to him. Lilias looked pale, and Regina was too frightened even to indulge in her sense of the dramatic. For once, she was absolutely silent.

"You'll try to let us know what's happening?" Lilias asked.

"If I can. It may not be easy." He gave her the glimmer of a smile. "If in doubt, go to Dorothy Hazard. There's nothing goes on in this city, but that woman's the first to know."

"You believe that there will be another assault tomorrow?"

"I'm sure of it. This was merely the preliminary skirmishing. Tomorrow, unless I'm very much mistaken, the Prince will launch an all-out attack."

* * *

A cannon ball, fired from the Brandon Hill Fort, hit the ground, showering Henry Washington with earth. Behind him stood the two houses he was there to defend, houses filled with stores and ammunition. In front of him, his men kept up a constant barrage of musket-fire against the outer earthworks of the fort.

The day was going badly, had been going badly ever since the over-eager Cornishmen had attacked half an hour too early, at two-thirty in the morning, and been repulsed with heavy losses. Lawford's Gate had been carried, but a sortie along the market to the gates of the castle had resulted in the deaths of three of their commanders.

Matters had not gone well, either, to the north of the city. Lord Grandison had been killed leading an attack on Prior's Hill Fort. Colonel Bellasis' attack on Jones' Fort had also been a failure; while Rupert, everywhere at

105

once urging on the laggards, had been unable as yet to breach the outer defences of the town. By mid-morning, some of the Royalist cavalry had withdrawn as far as Whitchurch, convinced that the day was lost.

It was at this juncture that Henry Washington turned to Colonel Harry Lunsford and said: "I could force the defences—just there!" Lunsford, wiping the blood and dust from his blackened face, followed the direction of his friend's pointing finger. "You see where I mean?" demanded Washington.

Lunsford nodded thoughtfully. Between Brandon Hill Fort and Windmill Fort was a hollow of rocky ground where the defences had been left unfinished. There was also a barn which would afford any attackers a certain amount of shelter.

"Furthermore," Washington continued, his practised eye assessing the range and scope of the forts' guns, "they can't bring their artillery to bear on the hollow. They don't have enough depression."

Lunsford grinned suddenly. "Fiennes is a fool," he said. "One piece of cannon there could have saved him the town. As it is . . . How will you do it?"

"Firepikes. Wildfire." Washington yelled for one of his men and gave him a message for Prince Rupert. "Ride like Hell and find His Royal Highness. Tell him I can breach the defence line near Brandon Hill Fort, and ask him for reinforcements."

*   *   *

"I want volunteers," Dorothy Hazard announced briskly, as she let herself into the Prides' small kitchen.

"Volunteers?" Regina twittered. "Whatever do you mean? You sound exactly like a recruiting sergeant."

"And that's what I am. Colonel Fiennes wants volunteers to help block up the Frome Gate with earth and wool-sacks. And as the men are all busy—making a great deal of noise and achieving very little, most of them—

I've promised to recruit the women for the task. Now come along, Regina! And you, Hannah. It will be better than sitting moping and wondering what is going to happen. Maria Holsworthy and Lady Rogers have already promised to help."

"Lady Rogers ..." The adamant refusal which had been trembling on Regina's lips faltered at this information. "Well, I suppose if Lady Rogers thinks fit ..."

"I'll help," said Lilias, wiping her floury hands on a cloth and stripping off her apron. "Mollie can finish making this pie."

"Good girl," approved Dorothy. "I didn't like to ask you in view of your condition—which, I may say, is beginning to show. You really should be wearing a looser gown than that. Fortunately, the men will be much too occupied to notice."

"You can't!" Hannah laid a restraining hand on Lilias' arm. "It wouldn't be decent to go parading about like that."

"Rubbish!" snapped Dorothy. "In normal times, of course, one wouldn't expect it; not in that dress, anyway. But these are not normal times, my dear Hannah. The forces of Beelzebub are hammering at our gates. It is up to us, the women of Bristol, to defend our native city against Satan's ravening hordes! We shall take our children in our arms, and as long as there is breath in our bodies—"

"Dorothy!" Regina, recognising what she called her friend's Sunday-go-to-meeting voice, remorselessly interrupted. "Dorothy, you cannot possibly think that Fiennes will surrender the city?"

"That man is capable of anything. A broken reed. But God will give us strength. Never forget that He is on our side. Now, come along all three of you. I don't want to hear any more 'ifs' and 'buts'. *Behold, I have refined thee, but not with silver. I have chosen thee in the furnace of affliction.* Isaiah, chapter forty-eight."

"That's all very well," Regina grumbled in a low voice to Lilias as they followed Dorothy outside. "But I would just as soon not be one of the chosen."

* * *

"Use the butt-end of your muskets," Washington yelled above the din. "You'll never take aim in this."

As his musketeers poured through the gap which was to be known to Bristolians for centuries after as Washington's Breach, they found themselves in a maze of narrow streets, a rabbit warren of lanes and alleys which burrowed in all directions down the hillside. The approaches to Bristol were steep, the city proper lying snug in its marshy bed, surrounded by hills and water. But since the Middle Ages, the town had spread beyond the medieval walls, climbing and clustering over the surrounding slopes in a rash of crowding houses and alleyways: a death-trap for an invading army.

The half-finished rampart had been levelled with halberds, and the ditch and hollow filled in with faggots so that the way was now clear for the horses. Washington had seized the redoubt and the few houses near, and was now awaiting the promised reinforcements. Lieutenant Rousewell, defending the breach, had just fallen, mortally wounded. Ammunition was running short.

"For God's sake," grunted Lunsford, "where's Rupert?"

Washington did not answer, his eyes on the overhanging houses. A moment later, his worst nightmare was realised when the inhabitants of Steep Street and Griffin Lane opened up a murderous cross-fire.

"Washington! Lunsford!" shouted a voice behind them.

"Bellasis," breathed Harry Lunsford thankfully. "Heaven be praised!" And with Bellasis and his men, he also recognised the Earl of Chelwood.

Half an hour later, Lunsford was dead, killed as he and

108

Bellasis charged Host Street and Christmas Steps, separated from the main attack by a sudden sortie from Windmill Fort led by the intrepid Captain Nevill.

Henry Washington and Priam, meanwhile, had led their men on a suicidal dash down Church Street, along Frog Lane and were, by midday, stabled in the comparative calm of Cathedral Close taking careful stock of their position. Their losses had been tremendous: the streets and lanes were piled with dead. Colonel Washington had miraculously escaped unscathed, but Priam had suffered a wound in his upper left arm and was weak from loss of blood. He resisted, however, all Washington's insistence that he withdraw to the safety of Redland and, knotting his sash tightly about his arm, managed to staunch the sluggish bleeding.

"The men are in an ugly mood," he said. "They've seen too many of their comrades slaughtered and there are bound to be reprisals. It will take every officer we can muster to keep them in order, once we've taken the town."

"We haven't taken it yet," Washington retorted grimly. But even as he spoke, above the medley of voices, the crash of musketry and the roar of cannon fire, came the sudden, imperative beating of a drum. "Listen," he breathed, shaking Priam's sound arm. "Listen! Fiennes is giving the signal for a parley."

*   *   *

The signal was also heard by Patrick O'Mara as Hopton's army entered on the southern side of the city, having finally forced a breach near the Redcliffe Gate.

It was heard by Richard Pride, in Prior's Hill Fort, where he had been sent with a message for Robert Blake, its commander.

And it was heard by Lilias, her dress torn, her face streaked with dirt, as she stood in Dorothy Hazard's battalion of women who had worked like slaves for the past few hours, diligently blocking the Frome Gate. "Listen!" shrieked Maria Holsworthy, as Lilias and Lady Rogers manhandled two more sacks of wool into place. "Surely ... that's the signal for a parley?"

The women stood still, every ear straining. The noise came again, the brisk rat-a-plan of a drum.

"You're right, Maria," Dorothy said slowly. "That lily-livered cur, Nathaniel Fiennes, is going to surrender our city. Ladies! Follow me! If the men won't continue this fight, then we shall!"

"Dorothy," Regina begged, as her friend set off at a trot across the bridge in the direction of Broad Street, "what are you going to do?"

"We are going to arm ourselves. With anything, ladies! Rolling-pins, scissors, kitchen knives, brooms. Anything you can lay your hands on to repel the forces of darkness and evil."

"Lilias," Hannah gasped, past enmity forgotten, "I'm frightened. We shan't stand a chance against armed men. And you know what they say about Prince Rupert: that he eats live babies for breakfast."

"That's nonsense," Lilias answered gently. "He can't be such an ogre as they make him out to be. But if it will make you feel happier, stay at home with Eliot. He needs his mother with him, whatever Dorothy may say. And keep your own mother with you, too. She's very tired. I'll go with Mistress Hazard and the rest."

"But you can't, not in your condition. You might harm the child."

"I shall be all right," Lilias replied, surprised yet again by the tingle of excitement which pulsed along her veins. Her eyes were already searching for a suitable weapon as they entered the over-crowded kitchen.

Governor Fiennes had advised, as long ago as last Easter, that every household should stock up with three months' supply of food. Consequently, four enormous smoke-cured hams hung like stalactites from the ceiling.

110

Barrels of salted fish, flour, corn-meal and butter stood ranged along the cooler, outside wall of the kitchen. The still-room was packed with preserves and pickles and the cellar was full of home-made wines and ale.

"Dorothy has taken leave of her senses," moaned Regina, sinking thankfully on to a stool. "I always knew it would happen one day. Why can't she mind her own business and leave the fighting to the men? I'm not going back with a broom or a rolling-pin . . . Lilias! What are you doing?"

Lilias, who had taken a knife from a kitchen drawer, sent Regina an impish grin.

"Dear ma'am"— she twirled the knife above her head as Regina and Hannah both screamed—"how do you fancy me as Queen Boadicea? No, no," she added hastily, "I was only joking. I don't think I could really kill anyone to save my life. I'll take the broom, instead."

"You're mad," moaned Regina, as Lilias moved towards the door. "You'll all of you get yourselves killed."

CHAPTER SEVEN

Just after noon, the Earl of Chelwood, forcing an entry through the Frome Gate, found himself confronting not the expected musketeers and pikemen of the Bristol garrison, but a bevy of determined, soberly dressed ladies, prepared to risk death and injury in defence of their homes. Priam's head ached and his arm throbbed. He was in no mood for what he considered to be mock heroics.

"Disperse that gaggle of geese!" he shouted to his lieutenant, and set an example by laying about him with the flat of his sword. For answer, he was dealt a stinging blow on the side of his head with a broom. With a curse, he leaned from the saddle and grabbed his assailant's wrists. "The city has surrendered, you wild-cat!" he shouted. "Now, go home where you belong, with your husband and children." He became aware of his captive's youth and also of the fact that she was pregnant. "For God's sake—" he began again furiously, but stopped, swaying from weakness, forced to release Lilias in order to hold himself upright in the saddle.

The broom clattered from her grasp and she put up her hands to steady him. "You're hurt, sir," she said in concern.

"It's nothing," he gasped, readjusting the sash around his arm.

A tall woman, who was plainly their leader and who had been calling on the Lord of Hosts to deliver them from the forces of evil, now stopped and stared at him.

"I know you, my lord," she shouted suddenly. "A lecher, a whore-monger, a frequenter of brothels! A follower of the Prince of Darkness!"

112

"Shut that old crone up," Priam said viciously to one of his men.

The rest of the women had now been disarmed of all the pathetic paraphernalia which was their only defence against armed and armoured men; brave women, Englishwomen, his own countrywomen, whose courage was being expended against their own kith and kin. The absurdity and horror of civil war struck the Earl more forcibly than ever.

"Go home," he repeated violently, giving Lilias a push. "For pity's sake, go home."

★   ★   ★

Lilias stood at an upper window staring down into Broad Street, which seemed on fire from end to end.

Ever since Fiennes and his garrison had marched out of Bristol early that morning, Royalist soldiers and sympathisers had been rampaging through the city, looting and raping as they went. Vainly, some of their officers had tried to control them, but the men had seen too many of their comrades butchered by the citizens to give any quarter now.

With the coming of dark, the marauders' torcnes flared and hissed against the soft summer sky. Strange goblin shapes cavorted and capered in the fiery dark, more terrifying now that their faces were hidden. Contorted shadows leapt and clung to the sides of the houses; voices were thickened by drink.

Behind Lilias, Hannah lay in bed, clutching Eliot. Regina sat in a chair by her side, a shawl draped over her night-shift, rocking herself and moaning.

"It's all right. It's all right," Lilias soothed, summoning up a courage she did not feel and wishing that Richard were with them. But he had not been seen since the previous morning. No one knew whether he was alive or dead.

Lilias moved back to the bed, putting her arms about

113

the distraught Hannah. As she did so, there came the sound of breaking glass as a stone crashed through the leaded panes of one of the downstairs windows.

"Oh, missus! Missus!" The door flew open and Mollie Hanks appeared on the threshold. "There's someone tryin' to get in. Aah!" She ended on a high pitched scream.

There was the splintering of wood as the street door was forced open. Mollie screamed again and dived beneath the bed. Hannah whimpered and held the peacefully sleeping Eliot tighter. Regina sat as though carved from stone.

More noises followed the first, spiralling up the well of the narrow stairs in a confusion of bangs and grunts. Someone was moving about in the room below, laughing and muttering drunkenly to himself.

"All my valuables," breathed Regina. "They're in that wretched fire-bag. Why, oh why, did I listen to Dorothy? Why didn't I take them to the castle?"

"Ssh," hissed Lilias. Slowly she reached for the heavy candlestick that stood by the bed, then she padded softly to the door. She paused, listening. Finally, she tiptoed out on to the small dark landing and peered over the head of the stair-rail. As far as she could make out, there was only one intruder, but the chances were that he was armed. Shaking with fright, her grip on the candlestick slippery with sweat, she edged her way silently down the stairs.

She had forgotten that the fifth stair creaked. As she froze against the wall, a man came cautiously from the little back parlour holding up a lantern. For what seemed an eternity, they stared at one another; then the man gave a long, low whistle.

"Now, here's a prize," he said at last, in a thick Cornish accent. "And what might your name be, my beauty?"

He laid down the trophies he was carrying—Regina's

114

fire-bag and a bottle of Richard's best wine—and started, purposefully, to mount the stairs.

"Keep back," Lilias warned him, producing the heavy candlestick from behind her skirt.

At the same moment, the man's eyes widened as he took in her condition. For a second or two, he hesitated, then shrugged and came on. He knew that to rape a pregnant woman was punishable by death but, in this case, the risk of being caught seemed worth it. He had rarely seen a more beautiful creature.

"I won't hurt you," he promised. "Not you, nor the child. Not if you do everything I ask."

Lilias felt sick. Her knees were trembling so that she could hardly stand, but she dared not call for help. The man was armed. She could see the haft of a plug-bayonet and, below it, the wide sheathed blade. Regina was elderly, Mollie Hanks hysterical and Hannah not yet recovered from the shock of Richard's disappearance. To bring any one of them to her defence with a shout for assistance might result in two injuries instead of one.

"I won't hurt you, my handsome," the man said again; and at the sound of that typically Cornish endearment, Lilias had an idea. The man probably spoke the old Cornish tongue, and to hear it now, under these circumstances, might be enough to unnerve him. As he put out a hand and grabbed her sleeve, Lilias began to say the Lord's Prayer out loud.

"*Agan Tasn'y, us yn nef, Benygys re bo dha Hanow, Re dheffo dha wlascor, Dha voth re bo gures y'n nor kepar hag y'n nef . . .*"

The ruse worked. The man's step faltered, his outstretched hand wavered just long enough to give Lilias her chance. With all the force she could muster, she brought the candlestick crashing down across his wrist, and he let out an ear-splitting yell. Regina's voice called tremulously: "Lilias, is anything wrong?" but was half-lost beneath the man's flurry of oaths.

115

In the light of the lantern his eyes glared redly, while with his injured right hand he clawed desperately for his knife. Somehow he managed to grip it, and Lilias saw him advancing towards her, the broad blade raised. She stood transfixed, like a rabbit threatened by a snake. Some part of her brain told her that he meant to kill her and urged her to run. But her legs refused to obey and she stayed where she was, unable to move . . .

The flash and deafening report of an explosion broke the deadly spell. In total disbelief, she watched the man keel over, blood gushing from his mouth, his staring eyes glazed first by astonishment, then by death. She heard Regina scream from the head of the stairs and then the sharp staccato rattle of Hannah's terrified questions.

Standing by the outer door, the pistol still smoking in his hand, was the officer who had handled her so roughly the previous afternoon. As she watched, he tore off his coat to smother the flames of her assailant's broken lantern, then pitched headlong, unconscious, at her feet.

*   *   *

Priam opened his eyes at the touch of a cool hand on his brow. A calm voice said: "Keep still, or you will set your wound bleeding again."

He was lying between clean sheets in a strange room which, judging by the unguents and salves ranged along a shelf near the bed, undoubtedly belonged to a woman: presumably the woman who was bending over him feeling for his pulse.

She was extremely beautiful, that was his first thought. His second was that he had seen her before. As memory sharpened, he murmured, half to himself: "Of course! The wild-cat of the Frome Bridge." He added as an afterthought: "Your husband should take more care of you. What sort of cowards are Bristol men to allow their womenfolk to do their fighting for them? And then run away and leave them unprotected?"

116

"I have told you," Lilias admonished him severely, "to lie still and not excite yourself, or you will have a recurrence of your fever and have to be bled again. And if it makes you feel any better, sir, my husband is dead." She saw his quick glance at her thickening waistline and flushed. "He died five months ago. It was an accident. The house you are in belongs to his cousin's husband, Mr Richard Pride. Now, do you think that you are strong enough, if I support your shoulders, to sit up and drink this broth?"

Priam stared up at her, still a little bemused. "Richard Pride? Richard Pride? I know him. One of those damned rebels who's a friend of Pym and Fairfax. Where is he now? Sat safely at Westminster, I'll be bound. Are you all alone here, Mistress . . ."

"Colefax. And I am not alone. Mrs Pride and her mother, Mistress Regina Stillgo, also live here. Nor have you any cause, sir, whoever you are, to cast such a slur on Mr Pride's reputation. He is not at Westminster, he is here in Bristol." The icy rage in Lilias' voice melted into concern as she added anxiously: "Though God knows where. He has been missing since the surrender."

The Earl closed his eyes, then said: "I remember now. One of Hopton's Cornishmen was trying to rape you . . . How long have I been here?"

"A night and almost a day. Now, sir, this broth is rapidly getting cold. If you could manage to sit up . . ."

"What is happening in the city?" Priam painfully eased himself away from the pillows. An arm came round his shoulders and his head was cushioned against the girl's soft breast.

"It's quiet now . . . No, don't try to hold the spoon. Just open your mouth . . . there . . . like so. We shall manage very well, I think. Prince Rupert has brought most of your men under control, and one or two of the ringleaders have been shot."

She did not think it necessary to add that there were

117

still reports of unpleasant incidents; still the thirst for revenge by the families of Boucher and Yeamans. For the most part, tempers had cooled; and the natural urge of all Bristolians, whatever their political creed, to get on with the daily business of buying and selling, had brought peace to the streets far sooner than could otherwise have been expected.

After a few mouthfuls of Regina's rabbit broth, it was obvious that the patient was tiring. Lilias put aside the spoon and bowl and carefully lowered him to the pillows.

"This is your room," Priam accused her faintly. "I've turned you out. Where are you sleeping?"

"In the attic, with the maid, Mollie Hanks. I've slept there before and I am perfectly comfortable. So don't let us have any argument about that."

He smiled weakly. "Has anyone ever told you that you are a managing woman, Mistress Colefax?"

Lilias regarded him seriously. "My father always used to say that I'd grow into one when I was older."

"And how old are you?"

"Seventeen, if the date of my birth is correct. And incidentally, sir, although you know my name, I don't know yours."

"Chelwood," he answered simply.

"The Earl of Chelwood? Of Westovers?"

"The same. You sound surprised." But she didn't: she sounded suddenly wary. "What have you heard about me?" he added.

He expected evasions, half-truths, embarrassment, and was momentarily nonplussed by the directness of her reply.

"My cousin-by-marriage, Mr Pride, says that you are an atheist and a lecher ... I can see nothing in that, my lord, which can possibly amuse you."

"It's just that no one has ever said those things to my face before. Oh, I'm not a fool: I know they're said behind my back. But very few people will risk offending

118

the great Earl of Chelwood by telling him what they really think."

"Greatness, my lord," Lilias replied, adopting Hannah's best sententious manner, "is in the mind, not in a title." And without waiting to see what mortifying effect this would produce upon the Earl, she picked up the bowl and spoon and went downstairs. But she had an uncomfortable feeling that her patient was laughing.

As she opened the kitchen door, a familiar and most welcome figure met her gaze.

"Richard!" She started forward, both arms outstretched, heedless of bowl and spoon. "Where have you been? We were all beginning to think you must be dead."

Regina was sitting in the corner, quietly sobbing with relief. Mollie Hanks was noisily weeping and Hannah was clinging to her husband.

"He was in Prior's Hill Fort," Hannah said, "and news of the surrender failed to reach them until twenty-four hours after everyone else."

"And even then," Richard went on, "Robert Blake refused to believe it, until the Prince sent a message threatening to hang us all unless the fort was evacuated immediately." He took the bowl and spoon from Lilias' precarious grasp. "Who do these belong to?"

And so the story came tumbling out: of the scene on the Frome Bridge; of the Cornishman's attempted rape and Lilias' rescue; a riot of half-sentences, contradictions and amendments poured out by four excited female voices, from which Richard was forced to deduce more than he was actually told.

"Chelwood!" he muttered, displeased, when quiet was at last restored.

But however much he disliked the Earl, Richard realised that he could hardly turn from his door the man to whom Lilias owed her life, and one, moreover, who was wounded. He shrugged, accepting that he would have to make the best of things.

"I'll go up and see his lordship later," he said. "Now, for pity's sake, get me some food."

★   ★   ★

"A visitor to see you, my lord."

Priam, now almost recovered, glanced up from his seat by the window and looked at Lilias. Against his will, this girl intrigued him. From Regina, who could be twisted around his little finger, he had learned the story of Lilias' birth, upbringing and marriage, and the circumstances of Barnaby's death. He had also, from the things which Regina had not said, learned a great deal about Barnaby himself.

The Earl had met many beautiful women in his time. He had married one of the loveliest, and been smiled upon by the flower of the English court. Yet not one of these women had ever affected him as did Lilias Colefax. From the first, she exerted over him a most powerful fascination. He told himself severely that it was nothing more than animal lust, sparing a wry smile for his present impotent condition. There was no man living who would not be attracted by that face, by that incipient womanhood, with its promise of ripeness to come. And he fought desperately the conviction that there was more to his feelings for Lilias than that. He had always thought himself immune from what other men called love, from that humiliating dependence upon another's every whim. He detested the thought of self-surrender. And Lilias gave him no encouragement. She seemed unaware of his existence, except as a conqueror of war.

"A visitor?" He tried to keep his pleasure at seeing her out of his voice, and succeeded in sounding distant and frigid.

"A Captain Patrick O'Mara from the garrison."

This time, the Earl could appear genuinely pleased and rose unsteadily to his feet.

"Sit down, my lord! Sit down!" The tall, lanky

120

Irishman was forced to stoop as he came through the doorway. "The Prince has sent me to enquire how you are."

"Mending fast. I shall be with him at the castle in a day or two. Come and sit down, and tell me the news."

"I will. But first, I must tell your lordship something which concerns you more closely. An incident, my lord, touching your wife."

Twenty minutes later, Priam was staring at Patrick O'Mara with horrified eyes.

"You mean that not one of those damned rascals would go to my wife's aid? My God, O'Mara, they'll pay for this when I get my hands round their cowardly throats!"

"It won't happen again," Patrick reassured him. "By the time my troopers had finished with them, every man jack of them was thoroughly ashamed."

"They'll be more than ashamed." The Earl's face was dark with suppressed passion. "I shall close up Westovers and get Magdalen to France or Holland until this bloody war is over."

"It might be for the best," Patrick agreed sombrely. "Lady Chelwood is too gentle a person to exert much authority over her servants."

"Yes." Priam was struck by the contrast between Magdalen and Lilias Colefax. With that managing female in charge at Westovers, no one would have dared to disobey. In charge at Westovers . . . In God's name, what was he thinking of? "I owe you a debt of gratitude, Captain, which I can never hope to repay. If there is anything I can do for you at any time, you have only to command me."

"That's all right, my lord," Patrick answered in his easy way. "I was glad to have been of service." Magdalen's face swam for a moment before his eyes and was hurriedly dismissed. "The Prince sent me to warn you that His Majesty and the Prince of Wales are expected in Bristol. They are to lodge in Small Street, so His

Highness thinks that you may hold yourself in readiness for a visit."

"This visit to Bristol is one of congratulation, I take it, to Prince Rupert?"

The Irishman laughed, pulling down the corners of his well-shaped mouth. "Hardly that, I'm afraid; the Prince and Hopton have fallen out over the governorship of the city. Rupert wants it for Maurice and the worthy Sir Ralph wants it for himself."

Priam groaned. "Why do people dislike Rupert so much? He's the best general we have, for all his foreign ways." The Earl did not notice the ironic quirk of his companion's eyebrows. "God help us if the rebels ever find a general one half as good."

"Amen to that! And talking of rebels, my lord, you seem to have fallen into a nest of them here. The owner of this house, I understand, is a member of this infamous Parliament. And the young gypsy who showed me upstairs was decidedly unfriendly."

"Gypsy? Oh! You mean Mistress Colefax. Yes ... I suppose she does have the look of a gypsy."

"It's that very black hair. Not exactly the colouring of a typical Sassenach, begging your lordship's pardon."

"She's Cornish. A Celt, like yourself." Priam was abrupt. He did not want to discuss Lilias with Patrick O'Mara.

But when the Irishman had gone back to Bristol Castle and his garrison duties, the Earl found that he could not get rid of Lilias from his mind. What, he wondered, did she feel about him? Did she, indeed, feel anything at all?

*   *   *

Lilias was not as indifferent to the Earl's presence as she would have liked him to think. She listened to everything that Richard had to say about him and about the things he stood for—repression, tyranny, the suppression of religious liberty and thought—but for the

122

first time in her life was nagged by doubts. She had never, until now, considered politics: the rights and wrongs of the present struggle. She had imbibed from an early age the opinions of her father, which had been the same as those of her husband's family and friends. She had accepted the words of Dorothy Hazard and Parson Pennill without question. Seen through their eyes, the world was a simple place: good and evil, black and white, these were the standards by which they judged.

Now, suddenly, the world had turned grey; there were shadows and nuances of colour she had not perceived before. It was possible for a man to be her enemy and yet to save her life at the risk of his own. It was possible for Regina to deplore his morals, yet to describe him as a charming and chivalrous man. It was possible to discover that Prince Rupert was not the Devil incarnate, and that many of his soldiers were ordinary, decent, kindly men. She was confused and took refuge in silence.

On the Earl's part, it was increasingly in vain that he told himself Lilias was taciturn, ill-natured and ill-mannered, a peasant with nothing more to recommend her than those extraordinary looks. She had only to be in the same room for more than a minute for instinct to scream at him that this was totally untrue. By the time of King Charles' visit to Bristol at the beginning of August, Priam was forced to acknowledge that he was at last in love.

King Charles had arrived ostensibly to settle the dispute between his nephews and Hopton; but, in fact, the matter had been satisfactorily concluded before his arrival in the city. In reality, the visit was to receive a "gift" of twenty thousand pounds from the "repentant" citizens. A medal was struck with the King's head on one side, and a view of the city and the legend CIVITAS BRISTOLIA REDUCTA, 1643, on the other. Altogether, the Bristolians, with the exception of a diehard few like Dorothy Hazard and Denzil Hollister, thought it a cheap enough price to pay for the immediate resumption of trade.

"Although, mind you," declared Mayor Aldworth to ex-Mayor Locke, "I'm not saying I'm glad it's happened, because I ain't. Throwing good money after bad is something I can't abide. Nevertheless—"

"Things could be a good deal worse," nodded John Locke. "A bit of lickspittling does no one any harm, provided it's done in a good cause."

This being the general consensus of opinion, King Charles and the Prince of Wales found a warmer welcome from the citizens than they had been led to expect. His Majesty lodged in Small Street at the house of Mr Colston, and Prince Charles, Prince James and Sir Edward Hyde next door. It was, therefore, but a brief step from one street to the other for the King to visit the Earl of Chelwood, who, he was informed, was lying wounded at the home of a Mr Richard Pride.

"P-Pride?" stammered the King, his round, glossy eyes suddenly as blank as two pebbles. "I seem to recall this M-Mr P-Pride. A M-Member of P-Parliament, unless I'm much m-mistaken. He made himself a n-nuisance over the soap m-monopoly."

"Your Majesty is not mistaken," bowed Sir Edward Hyde, his round head bobbing like a Hallowe'en apple, thought the young Prince of Wales irreverently. "But he will be loyal enough now, sire, if he knows what is good for him."

Richard, however, made certain that he was not at home when the King and Prince of Wales called in Broad Street. Taking Hannah and Eliot with him, he went on a visit to Regina's sister at Abbot's Leigh.

"But what will His Majesty think," Regina wailed, "if you are not here to receive him?"

"His Majesty will know very well what to think," her son-in-law retorted grimly. "But if he's wise, which I doubt, he'll do nothing about it. In any case, I rely on the good sense of Prince Rupert to restrain him."

"But how are Lilias and I to manage on our own? I do think you might think about us!"

"You'll be all right, mother," Hannah told her angrily. "You're really a monarchist at heart. You think that because a man is born to a crown he merits some special consideration."

"Oh, hush do!" Regina begged in agitation. "Someone might hear you. Things are different now. It's not Nathaniel Fiennes up at the castle."

"No. He's facing a court-martial for surrendering Bristol. *Let the saints be joyful in glory: let them sing aloud upon their beds. Let the high praises of God be in their mouth and a two-edged sword in their hand to execute vengeance . . .* Psalm one hundred and forty-nine."

"I sometimes feel," Regina whispered guiltily to Lilias, when she had sped her daughter on her way, "that religion has become a disease with Hannah."

The following day, she and Lilias stood in the newly swept and polished front parlour to make their curtseys to the King and Prince. Because of the smallness of the house, all but two of their gentlemen-in-waiting had remained outside lounging about in the sunny street, laughing, ogling any pretty woman who passed and exchanging jokes. "Generally behaving," Denzil Hollister later reported to Dorothy Hazard, "like the godless creatures that they are."

While Regina, all a-flutter, conducted King Charles upstairs to greet the Earl, Lilias was left below to entertain the Prince of Wales; and this first meeting with her future King took her by surprise. She knew that the Prince was four years younger than herself, and had been expecting a child. But this tall youth of thirteen, already over-topping his diminutive father by several inches, was very much of a man, as his sparkling eyes informed her when he gave her his hand to kiss.

"Mistress Colefax, an honour. More: a pleasure."

125

Lilias sank into her second curtsey of the afternoon, and was raised to find herself looking into a swarthy face framed by hair nearly as dark as her own. But this was no gauche boy. The glance the young Charles Stuart sent her was as knowing and as old as Adam: swift, appraising, from under half-closed lids, making her feel completely naked. She, who was rarely discomposed, blushed hotly and stammered as she offered him a chair.

Their conversation from then on, seemed to be conducted on two levels; what the Prince said with his lips and what he said with his eyes.

"I understand that we have to thank your ministrations, Mistress Colefax, for nursing Lord Chelwood back to health."

What hair, what lips, what breasts! I should like, Mistress Colefax, to take you to bed.

"Your Highness is very kind. But I owe the preservation of my honour, if not my life, to the Earl of Chelwood."

"Ah, yes! One of Hopton's marauding Cornishmen. A savage race."

You would not preserve your honour long with me.

"I, too, am Cornish, Your Highness. Not all Cornishmen are savages, I do assure you."

"If you say not, Mistress Colefax, then I take your word. I should never dream of contradicting a lady."

I should like to undress you very slowly and take you here and now, in this room.

Lilias found that she was losing the thread of his spoken conversation, so potent were his thoughts and desires. It was positively immoral in a boy of his years . . .

Thankfully, she heard the King's high, light voice and the Earl's deeper, answering one. A door closed and there was the sound of footsteps on the stairs. Another moment, and His Majesty re-entered the parlour with Regina, still flustered, hard on his heels. The two gentlemen-in-waiting drew themselves up smartly and bowed. The Prince and Lilias rose, the former going to stand beside his father.

The King graciously extended his hand to Lilias, then turned to take farewell of Regina.

"I am sorry to have m-missed M-Mr P-Pride." The doll-like features were set in lines of disdain, the little body rigid with affront and disapproval. "Nevertheless, to yourself, M-Mistress Stillgo, m-my thanks."

What the King said and did after that, Lilias could scarcely remember later. Odd words and phrases occasionally floated back to her, but when they did, they served merely to remind her of the lazy, lecherous gaze of the young Prince of Wales.

And for his part, the Prince locked away in his memory the vision of cloudy dark hair, brilliant blue eyes and a pair of excitingly full red lips.

CHAPTER EIGHT

On an early spring day in the year 1645, Bristol Castle was still cold and gloomy. Ghosts of its past haunted the draughty corridors; the evil deeds done within its walls seemed to hang over it, like a pall. The Earl of Chelwood shivered and turned from the narrow window, going back to the warmth of his spluttering fire. Outside, the sky was blue, rinsed here and there to a delicate green. Little clouds, fragile as blown glass, danced to the tune of a following wind. Carriages clattered by over the city's dusty cobbles, their drivers magnificently careless of life and limb. People argued, shouted, cajoled, reviled, all in the name of the great god Commerce. But inside the castle there was an air of gloom, much of it emanating from the mood of the inmates.

Priam had been a member of the Royalist garrison for almost two years: two years which had seen the high hopes of the King's army crumble into dust. *Bristol taking, Gloucester shaking, Exeter quaking,* so had run the popular rhyme in the August after Prince Rupert's successful assault on Bristol. But Gloucester had not fallen. The Prince's plea to take the city by storm, as he had Bristol, had been rejected by the King as too costly of life. Later in the same year, there had been heavy losses during the indecisive fight at Newbury; and in the November, Waller had gained his revenge by beating Sir Ralph Hopton at Farnham. Arundel Castle had surrendered, also to Waller, the following January of 1644.

To make bad worse, it was learned that the King was planning to bring over Irish Catholic troops to fight on his behalf. The outcry, even among Royalists, was prolonged and deafening, and had led Parliament to enter into a Solemn League and Covenant with the Presbyterian Scots ... Priam stared into the heart of the dying fire with its caverns and waterfalls of burning gold, while the tally of defeats, of mistakes, of crass stupidities totted themselves up in his reeling brain.

But no previous disaster—not Waller's second defeat of Hopton at Cheriton, not the fall of Exeter, not the Queen's flight to France—had prepared men's minds for the tragedy of last summer; for the utter defeat of Prince Rupert at Marston Moor.

The news of Marston Moor had been received in Bristol with a feeling of incredulity. No one, neither friend nor foe, could believe that Rupert—Rupert the Invincible, Rupert the Devil—could ever be so soundly beaten. The name of the man who had commanded the victorious Parliamentary forces had hitherto been known only to a few. Lieutenant-General Oliver Cromwell's rise to prominence in the rebel army had been steady but unspectacular. Yet those who knew him well had recognised his genius for war. But since last July, his name had become a household word, to be spoken of in the same breath as Fairfax and Essex, and soon to be mentioned before them . . .

Someone knocked at the door, and Priam called: "Come in!"

The door opened and Trooper Trenchard appeared, bringing himself smartly to attention.

"Sir! Mr Pride is here. He says you're expecting him. It's about his application for a pass to go to London."

"Ah, yes. Show him in."

Trenchard wheeled about and disappeared again. His footfalls echoed hollowly in the bare outer room.

Priam rubbed his left arm, which was throbbing painfully. It was partly due to the trouble which his wound still gave him that he had been left here as a member of the Bristol garrison. It was also partly at his own request, so that he could be near to Westovers in case of further trouble, Magdalen having flatly refused to leave England without him.

129

But he knew his reason was a lie, a carefully fostered illusion to hoodwink himself and others. He walked back to the window, staring down on the dense cluster of roofs: arsenal, store-house and barracks. The river was bustling with the morning's traffic, an artery carrying the life-blood of the city. The houses of Countess Slip, on the further bank, were huddled together like a village of toys . . . But Priam saw none of these things, only the face of Lilias Colefax.

His love for her grew more intense. He hardly ever rode over to Westovers these days; he could not face Magdalen's trusting eyes. Yet he had nothing to be ashamed of; he made no conscious move, ever, to come in contact with Lilias. It was inevitable, however, that they should meet. Richard Pride was one of Bristol's leading citizens, and as Hannah despised all social functions, Lilias frequently accompanied him instead. Consequently, she and the Earl often found themselves guests at the same table. Moreover, when her child was born in the December of 1643, a daughter, christened Judith, she had asked Priam to stand as godfather. He had saved her life and she could do no less; but it forged one more link between them.

The Earl felt trapped, the victim of a passion more lasting, more binding and more hopeless than anything he had ever dreamed of. He went back once more to the fire and waited for his visitor.

Richard Pride was shown in by Trooper Trenchard and stood just inside the door, staring heavily at the Earl. The old animosity was still there, sparking between them. Priam seated himself behind the littered table which served him as a desk, and indicated another chair.

"Sit down, Mr Pride, if you please."

"I prefer to stand, thank you, my lord."

"Very well." Priam shrugged and picked up a paper. "I have here yet another application from you for a pass to visit London. I thought I had made it clear after each of your previous requests that you will not be allowed to travel beyond the city limits."

Anger flared behind Richard's eyes, but the heavy-jowled face remained impassive.

"And I have told you, my lord, that I have business associates there. I have obligations to men who loaned me money when times were bad, because of the soap monopoly."

"The Jews!" Priam's voice was scornful. "Trust your sort to run to the Jews!"

Richard answered steadily: "I have good friends around Smithfield and Cheapside, it's true, but it was not from them that I borrowed. The Spaniards' interest rates are too high for me. My money came from fellow Bristolians, such as William Penn."

"Penn? A loyal King's man? You ask me to believe that he lent you money in direct defiance of the known wishes of the King?"

"He didn't enquire why I wanted it, my lord. He lent it to me as a fellow citizen in distress."

"My God!" the Earl burst out. "It's true that Bristolians hang together. It's true what people say, that you're no better than the Jews."

"No better than Our Lord, then."

"Don't you spout religion at me!" Priam was on his feet and shouting. His dislike of Richard Pride had grown out of all proportion during the past two years, but he refused to admit the reason: the suspicion that Richard, too, was in love with Lilias Colefax. He caught at the fraying edges of his temper and continued more calmly: "You are a Member of Parliament, Mr Pride. Your reason for wanting to go to London is to resume your seat in that iniquitous assembly. No doubt you wish that you had had a hand in January's bloody doings, as you probably had a hand in the death of Strafford."

"If you are referring to the execution of Archbishop Laud, my lord, I was not in favour of that proceeding,

131

and had I been permitted to take my rightful seat in Parliament, I should most certainly have opposed it. As you well know, I am a practising member of the Anglican Church."

Yes, he was, damn him, thought the Earl. Why wasn't he a canting Puritan like his wife? A Dissenter, like so many of his Parliamentary colleagues? Not that religion, or its denominations, meant anything to Priam, who had long ago dubbed it all a bag of moonshine. But Richard Pride's solidly orthodox beliefs made him less easy to despise and offered less reason for denying him a pass to visit London.

Nevertheless, dislike made Priam obstinate. He had good cause to regard Richard Pride as an active enemy of the King and to keep him where he could see him, under his eye.

"No, Mr Pride, your request is refused. You must continue to be confined within the city boundaries."

*   *   *

"But Richard," protested a tearful Hannah, "you can't get out of the city without a pass."

Her husband glanced up from packing a saddle-bag, and patted the crumpled, tear-stained cheeks.

"If Lilias plays her part, then I can do it."

"Lilias! Always Lilias! Why not me?"

Richard sighed wearily. "Because you'd be too frightened, sweetheart. You'd too easily give me away."

"But if you get out," said Regina, adding her objections to her daughter's, "you won't be able to come back."

"No. Not as long as the Royalists hold the city. But that may not be for long. The King's forces are losing ground every day. Fairfax is bound to make a push towards Bristol soon."

"Then wait," begged Hannah reasonably. "Wait until then. Then you'll be able to go to London any time you choose."

132

"No," Richard answered, fastening the last buckle. "I owe Penn and the others money, and I must repay it while I can. Now that Penn is married and has a son, I wouldn't want him to find himself embarrassed because of me."

"Nonsense!" declared Regina stoutly. "A rich Dutch woman will have her pockets well lined, you may be sure of that."

"Margaret Penn is Irish," Richard answered patiently. "It was her first husband who was Dutch."

"Then he was rich. Dutchmen always are. He'll have left his widow well provided for, and William Penn will reap the benefit."

"A debt is a debt," Richard retorted stolidly. He did not add that he felt atrophied from lack of action, suffocated by his household of women.

Lilias came in pulling on her gloves, a warm cloak thrown around her shoulders. "I'm ready," she said quietly, but her voice trembled a little.

"Hiding in a cart among crates of soap!" Hannah exclaimed scornfully. "It's so undignified."

"These are undignified times, my love." Richard kissed her perfunctorily on the cheek. Then, conscience smiting him, he seized her and kissed her on the mouth, smiling down at her. "I'll write to you as soon as I get to London."

"And if you don't get through the gates?"

"You'll know within the hour, and may come to visit me in the castle dungeons."

Hannah gave a little moan and clung to him. He stroked her back awkwardly.

"There, there. It won't happen if Lilias can persuade the soldiers not to look too closely at the cart. So long as she gives them her nicest smile."

Hannah drew away abruptly, her eyes dwelling jealously on Lilias.

"So that's it! That's why Lilias must go and not me.

She's prettier, is that it? I couldn't fascinate the soldiers, but Lilias can."

"Hannah." Lilias came forward, laying her hand placatingly on the other girl's arm. "It's not like that, Hannah."

"Yes it is! Why do you lie? Richard has always thought that you are prettier than I am."

"She is prettier than you are," Richard said, his patience snapping. God! How glad he would be to get away from this hissing, purring, clawing world of women!

"Beauty, after all, is only skin deep," said Regina, adding her hopeful mite.

But her daughter was not to be soothed. She backed away from Richard, refusing to wish him "God speed!" Then, at the last moment, she ran out, calling his name, attracting the attention of two Royalist officers on the opposite side of the street and almost giving everything away.

Richard and Lilias walked to the stables in Tower Lane, where one of the boys from the soap works was waiting beside a cart. At the sight of Richard, he pulled his scrubby forelock, as the foreman had warned him to do.

Richard took Lilias by the shoulders and looked earnestly into her face. "If you feel you can't go through with this, my dear, you know you have only to say."

"Is it so vital that you go to London? We shall miss you very much."

His heart missed a beat, and it was a second or two before he could trust himself to speak calmly.

"It's not just the money, Lilias: that's an excuse for Hannah and her mother. And if I'm caught, they certainly wouldn't believe that that's my only reason."

"What then?" Lilias looked frightened and he gripped her shoulders harder.

"I know the dispositions of all the defences of this city.

There have been a lot of changes during the past two years. And if Fairfax does attack, it will be of the greatest value to him to have such information."

"Richard!" Lilias' hands fluttered agitatedly against his breast. "You know they'll say it's treason, and they'll hang you."

He covered her hands with his own capable big ones. "Only if I'm caught. But you must draw back now, if you want to. I have no right to ask you to do this thing."

She smiled bravely. "You know I'll do it," she said. "I owe you more than I can ever repay."

"You don't owe me anything: certainly not your life! So, if we are caught, you must say as I do, that you were totally ignorant of my presence in the cart. They might not believe it, but I shall swear to it on oath. So mind you back me up. We don't want young Judith without a mother. But I trust it won't be necessary. Just smile at the soldiers at Lawford's Gate and you'll have them eating out of your hand." She nodded. "Now, you and the boy help me into the cart and see that the packing cases are well distributed around me. And let us hope that you're not stopped by any well-meaning friends who want to know what you're doing."

They reached Lawford's Gate without incident, however, the cold spring weather keeping most people indoors. There they were halted by the soldier on duty, who came out to inspect the cart.

"Trooper Trenchard!" Lilias exclaimed, smiling valiantly although her lips felt stiff and her voice sounded unnatural in her ears.

"Mistress Colefax." Trenchard returned her smile delightedly. He was one of her most ardent admirers. "Where are you going with this . . . with this . . .?"

"Cartload of soap. I am taking it to Mr Pride's agent at Kingswood for delivery in Bath. Mr Pride, as you know, is unable to leave the city."

Trenchard frowned. "Surely one of the men at the

works . . ." he began, but Lilias interrupted him, prepared for this question.

"I asked to be allowed to go. I felt so cooped up. A drive into the country will do me good. And as they are short-handed at the works, Mr Pride agreed."

"Unaccompanied?"

Lilias indicated the tail-board of the cart, where the young factory lad sat swinging his legs and whistling. "Not quite alone, as you can see. And the roads around Bristol are quite safe now, thanks to your very active patrols."

Trenchard grinned, pleased at the compliment. Such praise was worth having from so anti-royalist a family as the Prides were known to be.

"Very well, Mrs Colefax. But I'll have to examine the cart."

Lilias' heart beat quicker and she made a great effort to stop her hands from trembling. There must be no tell-tale signs to give Richard away. His life depended on her. She summoned up all her courage.

"Is that absolutely necessary, sir? I'm very late now. I promised Mr Pride that I would be at Kingswood by midday—his agent is waiting, you understand—but, unfortunately, I allowed myself to be delayed by the shops in the market. You know how it is, Mr Trenchard—" she leaned towards him confidentially, so that he could smell her perfume "—when Mother Casey has a new consignment of ribbons."

"Well, no," he answered, laughing, looking into the lovely face only an inch or two from his. "But I understand how it is for ladies." He felt intoxicated by her nearness. "Very well, Mrs Colefax, if you assure me that it is indeed soap that you carrying, you may pass."

Lilias, feeling both relieved and guilty, and praying that this conflict of emotions was not showing on her face, bestowed on Trooper Trenchard her most bewitching smile. As the cart moved forward, she saw out of the

136

tail of her eye the tall, rangy Irishman, Captain O'Mara, coming leisurely out of the gate-house, and: "Is everything all right, Trooper Trenchard?" she heard him ask.

The soldier's reply was lost in the clatter of the wheels as the cart rumbled underneath the echoing archway.

* * *

"You were in charge, Captain O'Mara," Priam said coldly. "It was up to you to see that your men did their work properly."

"Sir." The Irishman, very straight and stiff, stared doggedly at a point on the opposite wall.

"Well? What have you to say for yourself? Richard Pride, in defiance of my orders has left the city and is now, presumably, in London. His wife is saying openly that he escaped in a cart full of soap. I have been made to look a fool and all through your negligence."

"Trooper Trenchard has been severely punished, sir. And . . ."

"And?"

"I think Mrs Colefax should be arrested, my lord, for aiding and abetting Richard Pride to break the law."

"Mrs Colefax says that she knew nothing about her passenger until she reached Kingswood. I am willing to accept her word."

"My lord!"

Priam saw disbelief writ large on Patrick O'Mara's face and recognised it as an echo of his own. Did he in truth believe in Lilias' story, as he told himself he did? But he would rather not go into that. It was easier to vent his spleen on the Irishman who, in his heart of hearts, he did not really like. For all his sophistication, the Earl was English enough to give way now and then to the unreasoning, arrogant prejudices of his race.

He unbent a little, but too late to salvage Patrick O'Mara's pride. "We will say no more about it, Captain. Trooper Trenchard has been punished and will be more

137

alert in future. Just keep a sharper eye on the rest of your men."

He nodded dismissal and Patrick went out, his face pale with anger. He was still shaking with temper as he descended to the great hall of the castle.

"You look annoyed, Captain," observed a voice. "May I be permitted to know the reason?"

Patrick looked round with a start, then bowed. "Y-Your Highness," he stammered. "I didn't see you there."

The Prince of Wales, standing with his back to the fire, laughed. "You are most freely forgiven, captain."

Young Charles Stuart had been sent by his father to be Captain General in the West, and had made his head-quarters in Bristol. Patrick O'Mara found him a convivial youth, already a hard drinker and with a roving eye for the women; as unlike the King, his father, as he could possibly be.

The Prince repeated, but on a deepening note of enquiry: "May I be permitted to know the cause of your anger, captain?"

"I-I would rather not say, Your Highness. I beg your pardon. No offence is intended."

"From you, Captain, none is taken. You like me. I can see it in your face. And that is always a recommendation." He laughed, genuinely amused. "I don't find so much favour, I fancy, in the eyes of others. The Earl of Chelwood, for example." And Charles grinned shrewdly, his teeth gleaming whitely against his olive-coloured skin. "He doesn't care very much for my morals. Oh, not my immorality as such, but he deplores my habit of bedding with the wives of respectable men. He says it makes trouble, and he's probably right. But it's odd when you consider how much he would like to lay the lovely Mrs Colefax."

"Lilias Colefax?" Patrick glanced up sharply.

The Prince lounged across the hall, hooking one leg

138

over a corner of the table and sitting precariously on its edge.

"Oh come, Captain, you disappoint me." The fifteen-year-old youth smiled, as one man of the world to another. "Haven't you noticed how often the Earl finds excuses to be at the same city functions as the lovely Lilias? The flimsiest of pretexts will do."

"But ... he's married," Patrick protested feebly.

The Prince gave a roar of laughter. "My dear man, if that were a barrier to copulation we should all be living like monks. Don't tell me that you've never slept with a married woman? Or maybe two?"

"But the Earl is ... different."

"Different? Well, yes, if you mean that he goes whoring rather than wenching." Charles rubbed his chin thoughtfully. "But I can't blame any man lusting after Mrs Colefax."

"He's a sensual man. At least, I've always thought so. But his wife is ... beautiful." Patrick found it hard to convey what he really meant.

"But cold?" suggested the knowing young man seated before him, giving a broad wink.

"A Madonna," breathed Patrick involuntarily.

The Prince of Wales' eyes opened very wide. "So-ho!" he said. "Sits the wind in that quarter? Here's a pretty kettle of fish. You'd like to seduce the Countess of Chelwood, and the Earl would like to do the same by Mrs Colefax."

Patrick flushed to the roots of his hair and began to revise his opinion of the Prince. "I have had the honour," he answered stiffly, "of meeting the Countess only once. I thought her—"

"A Madonna. Yes, you told me." The Prince slid off the table and went back to the fire, from where he regarded the Irishman thoughtfully.

"Your Highness knows that I am a Catholic," Patrick said defensively, misinterpreting the Prince's stare.

139

"So is my mother," Charles returned indifferently. "It is not your religion, Captain, that bothers me."

"What then, Your Highness?"

"This deification of an almost unknown lady. It smacks of a romantic soul."

"And that is to be deplored?"

The Prince looked at his companion with an old man's eyes set in a young man's face, eyes heavy with foreboding of the future.

"Perhaps not," he answered quietly. "But it is an anachronism in this day and age when there is no longer room for chivalry." He gestured desolately with his beautiful hands. "The world has grown sober and men have lost their taste for gallantry, their love of laughter. Their God is now the terrible Jehovah of wrath and retribution. Too many men can read, and the written word is replacing the loveliness of stained-glass windows and the old medieval plays. Old values are dying. No, keep your romantic notions while you can, Captain O'Mara. You will need them in this grey and dismal age."

And long after the Captain General in the West had withdrawn to Oxford to rejoin his father, Patrick O'Mara recalled that cynical, dark face and heard those half-mocking words. He began keeping a watch on Priam's movements and soon realised that the Prince had not spoken idly. On several occasions, when he found himself in the company of the Earl and Lilias at the dinner-table of mutual friends, he sensed the undercurrent of emotion between them. He acquitted them of either contriving to meet or of making any overt display of their feelings. There was no gossip about them, so Patrick supposed that others had noticed nothing. Perhaps he would have noticed nothing except for the Prince's words.

Anger licked through him. He had disliked Lilias ever since she had helped to smuggle Richard Pride out of the

140

city, and Trooper Trenchard had been beguiled by those lovely eyes. Trenchard had been flogged for his negligence, but his disgrace had also implicated his commanding officer. Lilias Colefax had made a fool of Patrick O'Mara, as well; but he doubted that she had made a fool of the Earl. It was obvious to him now why Priam had insisted on believing her story: it was a natural desire in him to protect the woman he loved.

And that thought would send Patrick grumbling and bawling at his men, who complained that he had altered and was not the easy-going officer they had originally known. How dare the Earl betray, even in thought, that lovely and virtuous creature whose heart he would give anything on earth to call his own? It would serve his lordship right if, after all, Lilias did not return his love; if he, Patrick O'Mara, was mistaken.

But he was not mistaken. Lilias had been in love with the Earl from the first moment of seeing him; that moment on the Frome Bridge when he had leaned from his saddle and pinioned her against his plunging horse. But why, she wondered, lying sleepless at night, the eighteen-month-old Judith curled against her side, why had her heart suddenly betrayed her for this one man above all others? What was there in that angry, harsh-featured face that had made her fall in love once and for ever?

If affection had come later, after he had saved her life and lain a helpless invalid in her arms, then she might have been less sure of her feelings: gratitude and circumstance might both have played their part. But she had loved Priam from the first, when he had merely been her enemy. And a bad-tempered enemy at that, she recalled with a rueful smile, seeing once again the blazing blue eyes, feeling the merciless grip on her wrists and hearing the contemptuous command: "Disperse that gaggle of geese!"

She had an idea that Priam returned her love, yet at no

141

time during the two years since the capture of Bristol by the Royalists had he hinted, either by word or look, that he regarded her as anyone but a woman who had a claim on his gratitude. He was loyal to his wife. He would never speak.

*　　*　　*

On a hot June morning, Lilias was helping Mollie in the kitchen, preserving fruit and making pickle. The big earthenware jars stood ready to receive the strawberries, cocooned in their sugar-syrup and freshly picked from the garden. A riot of vegetables and spices sprawled in colourful confusion across the scrubbed tabletop, ready to be chopped and pickled.

"Coo, I'm glad them bells 'ave stopped," said Mollie with feeling, as she searched for the knife which she had, as usual, mislaid. "Fair give me 'eadache, they did."

The bells had been pealing on and off for the past few days to celebrate Royalist victories in Scotland.

"Although," Dorothy Hazard had confided to Regina only that morning, "there are rumours of a very serious Royalist defeat somewhere near Naseby. But they—" she jerked a thumb, indicating the direction of the castle "—aren't saying anything about it."

Understandably, Lilias thought. "Mollie," she said severely, inspecting the contents of the big copper pan hooked over the fire, "have you been eating these strawberries?"

"Who? Me, missus? Never! You can't 'ave counted them proper."

"I don't need to count them," Lilias complained. "Each time I look into this pan, the amount has dwindled. You really are the greediest girl I know."

Mollie studied her face carefully, then, seeing the lurking twinkle, grinned in return. "Well, I'm 'ungry, missus. Food's scarce these days. I know it's the same fer all of us, but I'm a growing girl." She was seized by sudden alarm. "You won't tell Missus Stillgo?"

142

"No, nor Mistress Pride. But don't take any more, or there won't be enough to fill one jar, let alone two. And then you'll be sent to bed without any supper ... There, there! You don't have to hug me like that. I've quite lost my breath, and look! I have sugar all over my skirt ... What were you saying about old Mr Curtis?"

"'Im that lives in Small Street? Powerful bad 'e was last night. Or so Mrs Curtis told my ma. An' my ma told me when she come with my clean clothes this morning."

"What's wrong with him?" Lilias asked idly, beginning to ladle syrup into one of the jars.

"Dunno. 'Orrible sick 'e was, by all accounts." Mollie wiped her hands on her apron, her face lit up by ghoulish glee. "All black 'e was. An' a terrible great swelling in 'is groin."

The spoon fell with a clatter from Lilias' suddenly nerveless hand. When she spoke, her voice was little more than a croak and fear squeezed at the pit of her stomach.

"Did ... did your mother say anything about a rash?"

"Like smallpox, you mean?"

"No. Just on the chest. Like a ... like a ring of roses."

> Ring o' ring o' roses
> A pocketful of posies,
> Atishoo! Atishoo!
> We all fall down.

The ancient and sinister rhyme jingled menacingly through Lilias' head, that childish game played in imitation of the plague and first heard in England three centuries earlier, in the year of the catastrophic Black Death.

"Dunno." Mollie sniffed and wiped her nose on her sleeve. "Ma didn't say nothing so far's I can remember."

"Are you sure? Think, Mollie! It's important."

Mollie thought, but shook her head. Her memory was never of the best. "I could slip round to Ma Curtis and ask," she volunteered.

143

"No!" Lilias was emphatic. "And don't take the children for their walk this afternoon. Not until we know something more about it."

But by nightfall her worst fears were confirmed. Three cases of plague in addition to John Curtis had been reported. Such outbreaks were common in the long hot days of summer, when the rivers ran putrid with excrement and refuse rotted in the streets. But the visitations varied in extent and intensity, and this one promised to be severe. Food and medical supplies were as short in Bristol as they were in every Royalist-held town. Nothing more clearly underlined Parliament's growing tally of victories than the conditions of increasing distress in those cities which were garrisoned for the King.

"We must apply to the castle for passes to take the children to safety," said Regina. "To my sister's at Abbot's Leigh."

"And quickly," agreed Lilias. "In a day or two, perhaps less, the city boundaries will be sealed and no one allowed to pass beyond the limit. I'll see the Earl of Chelwood in the morning."

"It's only a small house," Regina said slowly. "I doubt if Lucinda can accommodate us all. Two adults at most, and the children."

"In that case, I shall stay," Lilias said firmly. "I have had the plague and was lucky enough to recover. They say that you can't catch it twice."

"But you can't stay here on your own," Hannah objected. "One of us must stay here with you."

"I shall have Mollie."

"No, Mollie must go with the children. Mother will never cope with them alone."

"All the more reason for you to go!" cried Lilias; but Hannah leaned back in her chair, dispiritedly shaking her head.

"No. I've felt so tired lately and Eliot is more than I

can manage. He likes being with mother. She spoils him. Don't try dissuading me, Lilias, my mind's made up. I am going to stay here, with you."

CHAPTER NINE

Lilias and Regina both knew that it was useless to argue with Hannah once she had made up her mind. The streak of obstinacy in her—attributable, according to Regina, to the late Miles Stillgo—was very strong. Moreover, Hannah had not been well of late, and Lilias suspected that she was pining for Richard.

The following morning, Lilias went to the castle, to find herself only one of a throng of people all applying for passes to leave the city. For more than an hour she sat in the great hall, easing her way along the wooden benches lining the ancient walls; watching the bustle of soldiers passing in and out; listening to the order barked along a chain of command; commiserating with the man on her left, who complained of the shortage of food; smiling at the little boy on her right who sat wanly, lifelessly almost, on his mother's knees. And then, at last, she was shown into a small dank room.

"Name?" the Earl of Chelwood snapped, without looking up from his papers.

"Colefax. Lilias Colefax."

Priam's head jerked up as though pulled by a string. His heart began to beat suffocatingly, as it always did at the sight of her.

"Mistress Colefax." He managed to keep his voice steady. "And what can I do for you?"

"I want passes to leave the city, my lord, for Mistress Stillgo and Mollie Hanks, so that they can take the two children to safety."

"Passes?" he answered coolly. "Why don't you just smuggle them out, Mistress Colefax, preferably in a cartload of soap?"

The bitterness in his voice took her by surprise and she

146

flushed. "I told your officers, my lord—" she began woodenly.

"Oh, I know what you told them, Mistress Colefax. But you can't really think that I'm that much of a fool."

Her blush deepened. "Then why didn't you have me arrested?" she demanded bluntly.

The Earl put the tips of his fingers together and regarded her across them. His heart was pounding as if it would burst. "I've often asked myself the same question," he murmured. The thin lips grew thinner until they almost disappeared. The grey eyes were as hard as slate. "But what good would it have done, except add, perhaps, one more casualty to the sum total of this loathsome war? What pleasure would it be to me to see you suffer, even though you enjoyed making a fool of me?"

He knew the accusation to be unjust; that, as she was now protesting, her action had been unprompted by any consideration of him. Somehow that only made it worse. Yet he had no right to feel this agonising sense of betrayal because of her loyalty to another man. He could never mean anything to her, as she could never mean anything to him.

"My lord!" Her voice rose on a note of anger. "These passes that I ask for are not for myself or Mistress Pride. They are for Mistress Stillgo, who is elderly, and our children, so that they may go to safety during this outbreak of the plague."

"You are not afraid to stay here?"

"Mrs Pride refuses to leave Bristol. For myself, I have had the plague and so don't fear it."

Damn her, he thought. Why did she look at him just so, with that mixture of childish defiance and odd, womanly dignity? Why did he want to take her in his arms and kiss her, protect her, cherish her; all those emotions which he ought to feel, and never had done, for Magdalen? No other woman had ever made him feel this way.

Lilias swayed a little on her feet. During the past few weeks, as food had become scarcer, the contents of the Pride larders had been shared amongst neighbours and friends. Each day saw the ration grow smaller: soon there would be very little left.

"You're unwell!" The Earl's voice was harsh with concern. He got up and forced her into his chair.

"No, no! It's just that I haven't had too much to eat these last three days."

Priam knelt beside her, noticing for the first time how pale she was. He took one of her hands in his, gently chafing it. "I'll send for some wine," he said.

"My lord, please don't. The hall is full of people far worse off than I am. Things have only just started to get difficult for us, thanks to my cousin's foresight. But most of the people out there have been short of food for months."

He knew that, of course, without her telling him. Parliamentary attacks on Royalist supply-waggons had become increasingly effective, and their ships were successfully blockading the Bristol Channel. And now the plague had come to add to their miseries.

"I'll give you the passes for Mistress Stillgo and the girl," he promised. "But you and Mrs Pride should also get out of Bristol."

Lilias shook her head. "We have nowhere to go, my lord. Mistress Stillgo's sister has a house at Abbot's Leigh, but it is too small to accommodate us all."

It was selfish to feel glad that she could not escape from danger, but at her words he knew a sudden lifting of the heart. She was so close to him; he had only to take her in his arms, lay his head on her breast and tell her that he loved her . . . There would be no going back. His boats would be irrevocably burned . . .

There was a knock on the door and Captain O'Mara entered. "Sir—" he began, then broke off abruptly as he took in the scene: Lilias Colefax seated in Priam's chair

148

and the Earl kneeling by her side.

The Earl sprang up, flushing. "Please to wait in future, Captain," he snapped, "until I tell you to come in." Then, despising himself for feeling forced to explain, he went on: "Mistress Colefax is not very well."

"Indeed. I'm sorry." Patrick's tone was cold. Yet again, this girl was the cause of his being reprimanded, this gypsy, this upstart daughter of an impoverished renegade parson, who had made herself somebody by marrying money, and who should, even now, be languishing in gaol. "I should not have troubled your lordship, but the Mayor and Sheriff are here to see you. Seven more cases of plague have been reported within the past hour. They are very anxious to know what you wish to be done."

"Very well, I'll see them." Priam had recovered his poise. "Give me a moment or two to write these passes, and then you may show His Worship in."

*　　*　　*

It was two days after Regina had left, accompanied by little Judith and Eliot and the terrified Mollie, that Hannah complained of feeling unwell.

"Just an ague," she said. "I shall be over it in a couple of hours."

She spoke with such confidence that Lilias felt reassured and sat on, after Hannah had gone to bed, stitching a new dress for Judith. Through the leaded panes, she watched the daylight drain away like sea-water before the advancing dusk. The street cries and bustle of the city were stilled, after all the clatter of the day.

Conditions in Bristol were now very bad. New cases of plague were reported every day and the total deaths had already exceeded one thousand. Food was becoming impossible to obtain. The villagers of Shirehampton and Sea Mills would advance no further than the outskirts of the city. Many people were afraid to leave the shelter of their homes, and were discovered, days later, dead in their beds. And every night after dark, the rumble of the carts over the cobbles would begin, accompanied by the mournful cry of "Bring out your dead!"

Lilias shivered, picturing the waxen corpses piled on the bare boards of the tumbrils. She felt suddenly lonely and afraid. She thought of Priam, of the way he had knelt beside her that morning, of the urgency of her body in response to his, of her overwhelming desire that he should make love to her . . . She shook herself mentally. He was madly in love with his wife, everyone said so; and she felt a furious surge of jealousy for this woman whom she had never seen. It was arrant stupidity to want so badly something she could never have. Magdalen Chelwood was good, virtuous and beautiful; Regina had told her so, and others all agreed. The Earl was a very lucky man and knew it. What would he want with her? In his world, she was a nobody; a person of small account. Yet surely—surely!—she had not been mistaken in thinking that he felt something for her?

"The man is dissolute! A lecher! A reprobate!" Dorothy Hazard's oft-repeated words came back to Lilias. "A disgrace to the name of gentleman!"

Was that how he wanted her? As just another woman to put into his bed? Just another conquest? Somebody to laugh about afterwards with his friends? She would not think of him any more. Resolutely Lilias put away her sewing, picked up her candle, made sure the windows and doors were fastened and went slowly up to bed.

As she reached the head of the first flight of stairs, she heard a delirious cry, like an animal in pain. It was a cry she recognised, a cry which took her back three years and more to that hideous moment when she had first realised that her father had the plague. It was a cry which turned the blood to water in her veins.

Hannah! She recalled with a growing sense of chill that Hannah had sneezed with peculiar violence several times

150

that evening.

Atishoo! Atishoo!
We all fall down!

Even as she stumbled towards Hannah's room, the cry came again. Lilias pushed open the door, knowing full well what she would find.

Hannah lay naked on the bed, a black swelling festering in her groin. On her thin breasts was the tell-tale rash like a circlet of roses, and she was throwing herself feverishly from side to side. The pillow was covered with vomit, a dark and sickly greyish-green.

Lilias ran from the room on legs that trembled, knowing that she did not have much time. Bubonic plague struck so swiftly that it was possible to be perfectly well in the morning yet dead by nine o' clock at night. The next few hours were like a nightmare, during which she boiled water, tore up linen and frantically bathed, lanced and poulticed Hannah's stricken body. There was no time to feel tired or sickened by the disgusting stench; there were only fleeting minutes as she fought desperately for Hannah's life.

But it was a vain struggle, as she had feared from the first. The disease was too virulent and Hannah's resistance too low. Towards dawn, the fever slackened and Hannah lay quiet, drenched in sweat as her failing senses gradually cleared. She was dying; Lilias recognised the signs: the pinched nostrils, the stertorous breathing, the flesh falling away from the bones . . .

"Lilias!" The name was hardly more than a whisper, a sigh from between Hannah's cracked lips.

"I'm here. What is it?"

"Promise me—" Hannah stopped, struggling for breath.

"Lie still. Don't try to talk."

"Not much time . . . Promise me . . ."

Hannah was trying to sit up, and Lilias lifted her, cradling her against her breast.

"Promise me—" the voice was a little stronger now "—that you'll look after Richard and Eliot."

Lilias remembered Richard asking her much the same thing on the morning of the first Royalist attack. She felt suddenly trapped. She did not want these demands on her loyalty, these claims on her time and affections. But the Prides had been good to her, they had a right to expect something in return.

"Promise me!" Again the two words were repeated.

"Richard will do what is best, you may be sure, both for himself and the child," Lilias whispered gently. She doubted if the meaning of her words got through, but the reassurance in her voice was all that was needed.

Hannah nodded, smiled and closed her eyes. Then her head slipped forward and sideways.

*   *   *

"I have come," Priam said, "to offer my condolences on the death of Mrs Pride." His eyes wandered round the quiet, darkened room, and he seemed for the first time to sense the emptiness of the house. "Are you staying here all alone?"

"Yes . . . I suppose I've had no time yet to feel lonely. If I do, there is always a bed for me at Mistress Hazard's." She tried to speak levelly, to keep things impersonal, in order to subdue the rapid beating of her heart.

"If there is anything I can do," Priam offered, "you have only to command . . . What has happened to . . .? What arrangements . . .?" He broke off, knowing the fate of most victims of the plague and afraid that it must have happened to Hannah.

"Mistress Hazard attended to the burial. She obtained permission from your Captain O'Mara for the body to be interred in the sect's own burial ground. Hannah was a Separatist, you know." He nodded, and she continued with an effort: "We could not allow the body to be

152

thrown into the common pit, if only for the sake of her husband."

"Does Mr Pride know?" Priam stumbled a little over Richard's name. The escape was still a festering sore.

"No. I have been unable as yet to send word to him. I am told that no one is any longer allowed out of the city."

"No." The Earl hesitated. "Rebel scouts have been sighted near Clifton. We are expecting an assault almost any day. You should not stay here on your own."

"I am among friends in Broad Street. And I am able to look after myself."

"Yes, so I recall." He smiled faintly. Was not that air of self-sufficiency a potent part of her charm? "Nevertheless, I should be happier to know that someone was here with you."

The concern in his voice surprised her. She tried to smile, but, to her horror, the tears welled up and ran down her cheeks. All that she had borne during the past few days, the unhappiness, the horror, seized her by the throat, racking her with unexpected sobs.

Priam moved closer. They were much of a height—he had never before realised how tall she was—and they stood there in the dark of the shuttered room almost touching, breast to breast. Her spurt of emotion died, leaving her with a drained and helpless feeling. Her body felt light, as though at any moment it might float away. Tears pricked once more behind her lids.

"I-I'm sorry," she stammered. "I'm tired. Forgive me."

"No, I am the one who should ask forgiveness, bothering you with my presence at a time like this."

Something in his tone made Lilias glance searchingly at him. Priam could not properly see her face, shadowed as it was by her hair. The room lay grey and still all about them, a thin rim of sunlight edging the shutters . . . Then she was in his arms, pressed so close that she could hardly breathe. She could hear the ragged beating of his heart. His lips were on hers, crushing, bruising, until her senses swam under his touch.

They were both intoxicated. Nothing in the experience of either had prepared them for a passion such as this. It was a madness: a beautiful, blessed madness, and her body trembled uncontrollably against his. He was murmuring her name over and over, into her hair . . . Lilias . . . Lilias . . . She had never known that it could sound so sweet. She felt the pressure of his thighs as he began to bear her, unresisting, to the floor . . .

She wrenched herself free. "No, my lord! No!" The words were torn from her in a sort of gasping cry. "We must not! It would be wrong."

"For God's sake," he said hoarsely. "You can't refuse me now! Lilias—"

"No, my lord!" she repeated. Her voice had risen on a note of panic and she eluded his supplicating hands. If she let him touch her again, she was lost. "I beg you!"

Priam's arms dropped slowly to his sides and he gave an ugly little laugh.

"My dear girl, you flatter yourself. I have never forced myself on a woman in my life—" he thought fleetingly of Magdalen "—and have no intention of doing so now." His tone was contemptuous. Disappointment had created in him the desire to wound.

But it was more than disappointment, more than lacerated ego or thwarted male pride. He needed Lilias as he had never needed any other woman; certainly not Magdalen, who indulged him in what she considered to be the less desirable aspect of marriage, because it was her duty and she must bear him a son. She did not enjoy making love, and she made the fact plain. Until today, he had accepted the fallacy that marriage and passion were separate bedfellows, that only women of a certain type could give pleasure in bed.

But those few moments when he had held Lilias in his arms had taught him that love and passion could go

154

hand-in-hand. He had no doubt now that Lilias loved him as he loved her. She had opened the Gates of Heaven—and now, for some prudish reason, was about to slam them shut. He seized her by the shoulders, forcing her round to face him.

"I love you," he said thickly. "I shall love you all my life, I think." He pulled her close against him and felt her body begin to yield.

Neither heard the street door open and shut, but a moment later, Dorothy Hazard's voice called peremptorily: "Lilias! Lilias, are you there?"

Priam cursed. "Tonight," he whispered. "Promise me that I may come back tonight."

Promise me . . . Promise me . . . A disturbing echo of Hannah and Richard sounded in his words. Lilias put the memories they conjured up from her mind. She drew a little away from the Earl without breaking the circle of his arms. She cupped his face in her long, thin hands and kissed him swiftly on the mouth.

"Tonight," she said. "Come through the garden from Tower Lane."

A few moments later, Priam had taken his leave and Dorothy Hazard was staring after him in open disapproval.

"And what did he want, eh? It doesn't look good, Lilias my dear, to entertain men—particularly," she added viciously, "that sort of man—when you are alone in the house. I wish you would reconsider and come to stay with Matthew and me."

"Thank you, Mistress Hazard, but I am perfectly all right. And his lordship," Lilias continued tranquilly, "came merely to offer his condolences. He probably will never come again."

*　　*　　*

"Gentlemen." Prince Rupert glanced at the faces round the table. "I think we can hold Bristol for at least

155

four months. Anyone talking of surrender will be hanged."

Priam, listening to the uncompromising words and noting the expression that went with them, decided that Rupert had changed since he last saw him. Gone was the devil-may-care young cavalry leader who had inspired so many glorious charges. In his place was a man embittered by defeat, and defeat not only at the hands of the enemy. Rupert's disagreements with his uncle had been too numerous and too vociferous to be kept secret. If, thought Priam, King Charles had listened to his nephew as much as to his wife, there was every possibility that his cause would have prospered. As it was, the Royalist forces were everywhere in retreat. Their one hope lay in the fact that they still held Bristol.

But for how long? Rumour said that Cromwell himself would lead the besieging forces, and his name alone struck terror into Royalist hearts. How many of the raw lads who made up the Bristol garrison would stand and fight against the men who were being called Ironsides, even by foe as well as friend? It was Cromwell's initiative which had formed and trained the New Model Army, creating a fighting machine second to none out of labourers, apprentices and tradesmen.

Everything that could be done, had been done to make the city safe and withstand a protracted siege. Cattle from the surrounding countryside had been driven into the Great Marsh. Two thousand measures of corn had been brought from Wales. Supplies of ale had been stored in St Nicholas' crypt. Parts of Bedminster and Clifton had been razed to the ground to make the city approaches more difficult to traverse. The old Windmill Fort, re-named Royal Fort, had been enlarged and protected by walls. Additional guns masked the Frome and Lawford's Gates. The castle defences had been repaired and strengthened. With Prince Rupert had arrived a formidable string of Royalist generals.

156

But it was neither of the forthcoming siege nor of hardships to be endured that Priam was thinking as he listened to the Prince's words. He was remembering the beauty of Lilias' face and dreaming of the night to come. And when they were at last dismissed from the council-of-war, he summoned Patrick O'Mara to his room.

"I want you to cover for me tonight, Captain," he said with one of his rare intimate smiles. "I have an assignation with a lady."

The Irishman set his shoulders to the door and looked at the Earl across the small bare room. "No," he answered quietly.

Priam stared, unsure that he had heard aright. But there was a grim defiance in the other's face which told him plainly that he had. He moved to the table which stood beside the window, and sat behind it. He felt slightly reassured by this change of position; the emphasis was no longer on friend and friend, but on commanding officer and subordinate.

"Is this mutiny, Captain?" he asked gently.

But Patrick O'Mara had steady nerves. He said: "If you wish to report the matter to the Prince, my lord, I am willing to accompany you straight away."

The Earl's thin mouth twitched in vexation. The man had him in a cleft stick and knew it. Once more he tried the assertion of authority. "That is an order, Captain."

"And one, sir, which I cannot obey."

Priam bit his lip. O'Mara had right on his side. He was ordering him to connive at breaking the rules. He said angrily: "Why do you refuse me tonight? You've done it willingly enough before, as I have for you. As we all have, at one time and another, for each other."

"And as I would now for you, if this were a case of plain and simple whoring."

The Earl's eyes blazed furiously as he got to his feet. "And what, precisely, does that mean, Captain?"

"That the woman in question is not a prostitute of the

157

town but a respectable Puritan lady. I know where you went this afternoon, my lord." He knew, without being told, by the look of exultant happiness that transformed Priam's face.

"And what does a respectable Puritan lady mean to you, you Irish Papist?"

Patrick flushed angrily. "Not very much, sir, in the normal way of things, except that, sooner or later, it would be bound to cause trouble—as you yourself pointed out to the Prince of Wales. In this instance, however, that is not my concern. My concern is that you are in love with Mistress Colefax."

As he spoke, Lilias' face flashed before him, a black pearl to Magdalen's white diamond; a painting by Breughel, compared with the delicacy of a Raphael Madonna . . .

"And what business is that of yours?" The question was flung at him, almost drowned by anger.

"None, my lord, until you involve me in that business. And I thank God and His Holy Mother that you have, for now you have given me the right to speak my mind."

"I have given you no such right," Priam began furiously, but the Irishman interrupted him.

"We won't argue that point, my lord. But I intend to speak, all the same. You are married to a beautiful and gracious lady who quite obviously adores you. If she did not, perhaps I would have held my tongue. But your wife loves you, my lord. You have no cause, that I can see, to look elsewhere for consolation."

Priam's anger froze, turning to self-justification as Patrick O'Mara touched an over-sensitive nerve. "Cause!" he exclaimed with a bitter laugh, turning and walking to the window. "What do you know about my marriage?"

It was Patrick's turn to be on the defensive. "Not much, maybe. But enough to recognise a truly good woman when I see one."

158

"And that prevents me from falling in love with somebody else?"

"No, perhaps not. But it should prevent you from doing anything about it."

Priam pressed his hands to his eyes, bright suns, orange, red and crimson, rolling up inside his lids. Why was he listening to this presumptuous fool? Was it because he spoke with the voice of Priam's own conscience? It was true that he loved Lilias, loved her with his whole being. If he did not, it would not matter. He could make her his mistress and then discard her, as he had done with so many others. His marriage would not be threatened . . .

God! God! God! Without realising what he was doing, be banged his fist against the wall. It was only when he saw the streak of blood across his knuckles that he was conscious of what he had done. He made himself think of Magdalen, conjuring up that pale and quiet face, looking deep into the ghostly, accusing eyes, and knew how great was his betrayal. For if he could not love her as she deserved to be loved, then at least she need never know it.

"You told me once," said Patrick O'Mara from behind him "that you were in my debt, that I had only to ask a favour and you would grant it. I am imploring you now, my lord, for your sake as well as my own, not to visit Mrs Colefax tonight."

Priam turned and looked wearily at the Irishman, understanding for the first time what lay behind the other's request. The irony of the situation was appalling. What tricks life played on its victims, and love was its most potent weapon. He said, not meeting Patrick O'Mara's eyes: "At least, I must see Mrs Colefax and explain."

"If you do," Patrick replied, "you are lost."

"Oh, God damn you!" Priam shouted, his hands clenched suddenly at his sides. He rocked menacingly on the balls of his feet, and the Irishman tensed himself, waiting for the Earl to spring. But nothing happened. Priam controlled his anger and said in a restricted voice: "Yes, you are right. And it is not the sort of reason anyone can explain."

He must send no letter, either. Lilias must believe him indifferent. Soon, in any case, their ways would part: the Earl had no faith in Rupert's ability to hold the city when confronted by the combined talents of Cromwell and Fairfax. Better that she should live her life with no regrets for the might-have-been. For Magdalen's and his daughters' sakes, he and Lilias must tread their separate paths.

Patrick, watching Priam closely, saw him come to a decision. The man looked haggard, but Patrick could not pity him. The Earl had Magdalen and that should be enough. It would have been enough for Patrick O'Mara, had Fate otherwise decreed. At least, he had performed for his lady the only service that he could. She would never hear of it, but the secret knowledge warmed his heart.

He glanced once more at the Earl and recognised that Priam would not, now, go back on his word. He sketched a salute and slipped quietly from the room.

*   *   *

Lilias shivered as she stepped out of the wooden tub, placed before the kitchen fire, the water dripping from her body.

The hot July day had drawn to a flamboyant close, trailing ribbons of crimson glory across a darkening sky. She had ventured to open a window at the back of the house, but had been forced to close it again in a hurry. The stench of the plague-ridden streets and the fetid rivers had been worse than the former closeness. So she had done everything she could to make the house smell sweet. She had brought in flowers from the neglected

160

garden, where they were growing in rank profusion, and she had burned some of Regina's scented lozenges, their perfume rising like incense in the gathering dusk. Then she had bathed, heating buckets of water over the kitchen fire, and emptying them into the wooden tub.

She thought unwillingly of Regina and Richard, having no doubt at all what their reactions would be if, somehow, they could be apprised of her intentions. They would be the same as those of almost everyone she knew, the same as her own first reaction.

But her own protest had been lost as soon as it was uttered, swamped by the intensity of her feelings. She had hardly been aware of Priam's cruel words, only of the white look of agony in his face. And suddenly she had felt that nothing else mattered: not the loss of reputation nor the horror and ostracism of friends; not the injury to Magdalen Chelwood; not the laws of God nor Man. Nothing mattered except the love she and Priam felt for one another.

Now, hours later she still had not changed her mind. She ran her hands slowly over her naked body, caressing it as Priam would caress it that night. It was smooth and taut, the belly muscles firm, even though she had had a child. But Judith had been such a little baby. She was still thin and weak, with no hidden promise of Lilias' beauty, and looking more like her father every day.

But Lilias did not want to think of Barnaby. She stood on tiptoe and looked at her reflection in the polished brass warming-pan that hung on the wall. Even its distorted image told her that she was beautiful: something she had never depised, in spite of all Dorothy Hazard's warnings about vanity. And tonight she was more grateful than ever for the dramatic dark looks bequeathed her by her Cornish forebears.

CHAPTER TEN

Priam could not sleep. He paced up and down his room, listening to the cries of the sentries as they changed the watch, staring out across the blackness of the castle's inner ward. Tonight, more than any other, the evil of the place seemed to rise up and haunt him, the gibbering ghosts squeaking and fleeing before the waxing moon. He thought of Lilias, waiting for him in the quiet house; waiting and waiting for the lover who never came ...

He was at the door of his room, his hand on the latch, before he realised what he was doing. The temptation to go to her even now, to get someone else—Slingsby or Murray or jolly John Russell—to cover for his absence, was overwhelming. Why had he listened to Patrick O'Mara? Why had he given the impertinent Irishman his word? What right had any man to interfere in his affairs?

No man had: it was his own conscience which had stopped him. He pressed his hands against his burning lids, trying to blot out the picture of Lilias' face and to prevent the fierce, aching longing to hold her in his arms. He lay on the bed and closed his eyes, but sleep refused to come. All he could think of was that tall, slender body and the cloudy mass of dark hair ...

He rolled off the bed with an oath and yelled for his orderly. After a moment or two, the man appeared from an adjoining room, his face still blotched with sleep.

"You called, sir?"

"I did. Get dressed." Priam, ignoring the man's look of astonishment, pressed some coins into his still limp hand. "Go to one of the brothels along the Backs—Kate's in Welsh Back, or Molly's on the Quay—and tell either of those Lady Abbesses that tonight I want only the best. The very best. A girl who can entertain and keep a man's mind from his troubles. For God's sake, go on, man! Don't stand there gaping!"

⋆　　⋆　　⋆

"You're looking worn out, child."

Dorothy Hazard seated herself in Regina's carved armchair, her back poker-stiff as always, and regarded Lilias with concern.

"I haven't been sleeping too well lately, that's all."

"Obviously not. You're exceptionally pale and you've lost weight. But then, you've been through a very great deal. It's a pity that you haven't more faith to sustain you. Matthew says that you've given up going to St Nicholas' altogether. Well, the Lord knows that I hold no brief for the established Church, but you would be welcome, you know, at any of our meetings."

Lilias sat down opposite her visitor and leaned back thankfully in her chair. "I know that," she answered gently. "Thank you."

"Richard, I presume, is still in London. You haven't been able to get word to him yet?"

"No letters are allowed out of the city."

"Ha! The Devil Prince is getting jumpy. But that means that you've no news of Regina's return, either?"

"No. She, also, is in ignorance of Hannah's death. It won't be a happy homecoming for either of them."

"Richard," Dorothy barked, "should never have gone away. He should have stayed here, where he could do most good. There are plenty of other fools in Parliament to carry on the work without him. Men! They die as selfish as they were born, and we poor women bear the brunt . . . You know, my dear, you really don't look well. You look extremely out of sorts to me."

Lilias gave her a smile which was lop-sided with the effort. "I feel well enough, but the heat is tiring and our food supply has run so very low."

Dorothy snorted. "Don't I know it! The Reverend is

the smallest eater, but I have a job feeding even him. The authorities have opened a kitchen in Wine Street and people are pooling what they have left, but the bulk of the city's supplies is finding its way into the castle; feeding those sons of Beelzebub and their doxies." Her face thinned in righteous disapproval. "There are goings-on there which no Christian women should tolerate in their midst. Lady Rogers and I intend presenting a petition to the Prince."

"Goings-on?" queried Lilias vaguely, only half-concentrating on what Dorothy was saying.

"Goings-on." Mistress Hazard nodded an outraged head. "Women—if, in Christian charity, one can call them women—are admitted to the castle every night from those dens of vice along the Backs and Quay. They say the Earl of Chelwood is the worst, but that's only what I should have expected."

Lilias' attention was caught and her heart lurched unpleasantly. "Are you sure of that?" she asked.

Dorothy's blue eyes snapped with anger. "Of course I'm sure. That man has had an evil reputation from the time he was old enough to call himself a man. Besides, I have it on the authority of Denzil Hollister, whose cousin is custodian of the castle library."

There was no doubting the word of the eminent Mr Hollister, the purity of whose morals was a byword in the city. Lilias got up and walked to the window, looking out on a wrack of feathered cloud imprinted against the blue. Pictures crowded through her mind: of herself wandering aimlessly about the house, certainty, then hope, gradually dwindling to despair; of herself in her lonely bed, staring with hot eyes into the unfriendly dark; of herself waiting for a message, for some word of explanation, which was never sent, and which, it appeared, now never would be.

She had been nothing to the Earl of Chelwood but a momentary infatuation, an assignation which he had

164

intended to keep as long as nothing more amusing offered. She had been mistaken in thinking that he felt for her what she felt for him. She had almost betrayed her friends, their kindness and their trust, for something which had proved to be worthless. Lilias took a deep breath. She must be strong-minded. She must put the memory behind her and not let herself be wounded by a man who was unworthy even to unlace Richard Pride's shoes ... Odd, how many times she had thought of Richard during these past few days, of his strength and warmth and honesty.

She turned back from the window and smiled at Dorothy. She refused to cry. Priam Chelwood was not worth a single moment's distress. She would think of him no longer.

★   ★   ★

By mid-August, Henry Ireton was stabling his horses in Bedminster churchyard, Fairfax had reconnoitred the city and established a battery above Totterdown, and four regiments were stationed along the Somerset loop of the river as far as the Malago stream. Waller barred the road to Kingswood and Easton, and Cromwell had made Wickham Court at Stapleton his headquarters. With him, he had brought Richard Pride, with his inside knowledge of the Bristol fortifications.

On a thundery late August day, Richard found himself in the long room at Wickham Court, where Cromwell and the other Parliamentary leaders had met to discuss Rupert's refusal to surrender the city.

"They say that the plague is still rife," Fairfax observed, and Richard shuddered inwardly, wondering how his family had fared. "If we attack now, we shall endanger the lives of our men."

Cromwell stared lugubriously at the speaker. "I have prayed," was his answer, "and it is the Lord's will that we make this attack."

Fairfax stifled an exclamation of impatience, but his little shift of irritation did not escape Richard's eyes, nor those of a man seated on the opposite side of the table. Thomas Rainsborough smiled sardonically.

"If the commander-in-chief is afraid—!"

"I am afraid of some things," Fairfax retorted sourly, "as all right-minded men should be. I am afraid of risking my soldiers' lives by exposing them to unnecessary danger. I am also afraid, colonel, of the way in which you and your men behave. Try to remember, sir, that we are fighting our own countrymen, Christians, like ourselves, not a bunch of red-skinned savages."

Thomas Rainsborough curled his lip. His sisters had married into the Winthrop family of Massachusetts, and his regiment was officered entirely by volunteers and recruits from New England.

"It will not be easy," Fairfax went on, "to take the city by storm. Prince Rupert is not another Nathaniel Fiennes."

It was Cromwell's turn to make an impatient gesture. "We shall be like the Israelites before the walls of Jericho!" he thundered. "We shall sweep all before us, trusting in the Lord!"

"I should prefer to trust in our own good sense," Fairfax replied tartly, and turned to hear what Henry Ireton was saying.

"What will be the watchword?" Ireton wanted to know.

Cromwell answered decisively with the one word "David!" and Fairfax's pointed beard quivered imperceptibly. Surely Oliver did not really see Rupert in the role of Goliath? "But after the outer defences are carried, the cry will be changed to 'The Lord of Hosts!'"

★   ★   ★

It was on September the tenth that the outer line of Bristol's defences was carried, and the cry of "David"

166

gave place to "The Lord of Hosts", ringing out trium-
phantly over St Philip's Marsh. Hugh Peters, who had
accompanied the New Model Army as one of its chap-
lains, rendered to the Almighty perfunctory thanks, but
intimated that it was no more than he had really
expected. God should know by now on which side his
bread was buttered.

The assaults had continued for more than two weeks in
the most inclement weather. Rain and autumnal mists
had turned the ground into a quagmire. Tents and
clothing were saturated, and constant forays and sallies
from the town kept the besiegers for ever on the alert. It
was, moreover, a race against time. Spies reported that
the King was getting ready to move from Oxford, and
that Lord George Goring was marching north from
Chard.

One one occasion, the mists were so thick that Colonel
Okey charged straight into the Royalist ranks and was
promptly taken prisoner. This was during a skirmish
around Washington's Breach, when Sir Horatio Carey
and six hundred foot tried to force a passage from the re-
named Royal Fort and were driven back with considerable losses. The day before, Prince Rupert had made a
similar sally through Lawford's Gate and been repulsed
by Colonel Montague.

On September the fourth, however, the weather had
begun to clear, and the guns of the Montpelier lunette
had kept up a continuous barrage against Prior's Hill
Fort. The fort was later captured by Thomas Rainsborough and his troops, and every man in it put to the
sword. Two days later, Fairfax wrote to Rupert, reminding him that two of Fairfax's uncles had died in the
service of the Prince's mother, and begging him again to
surrender.

"Does he think that I shall betray my uncle as the price
for his?" Rupert demanded furiously of his captains, and
countered with a courteous proposal that he be allowed to
send a message to the King.

167

"A bid to gain time," laughed Cromwell, happy, as always, in the heat of battle. "Tell him his request is refused."

Fairfax wrote once more, politely; and the two commanders were still haggling in this gentlemanly fashion when "The Lord of Hosts!" echoed from St Philip's Marsh, was taken up and re-echoed by Waller and Jackson, as they approached with their men along the road from Stapleton, and shouted by the cavalry of Desborough and Graves as they trotted up the old Roman causeway. Ninetree Hill reverberated to the cry, and it was heard as far away as Cotham and Redland. Colonel Welden's men yelled it as they launched an attack against the Redcliffe wall, having successfully crossed the Avon on rafts. Lawford's Gate rang with it, as the pioneers levelled the ramps and bridged the ditch and the gate fell with its twenty-two guns. From Back Avon to Wade Street and up to the castle walls, the city was in Parliament's hands.

Rupert, his face grey with fatigue and haunted yet again by the spectre of failure, called for a meeting of his captains. Without exception, they voted in favour of surrender.

★   ★   ★

On September the eleventh, 1645, the Royalist garrison marched out of Bristol and the city was once more held by Parliament. Even the Royalist sympathisers were too weary and too demoralised to care. Plague and starvation had taken too heavy a toll.

Lilias did not go to see the defeated garrison ride out, banners bravely flying, drums defiantly beating, vanishing in the direction of Oxford across the sunlit spaces of the Downs. She did not see the Earl of Chelwood; but then, she never wanted to set eyes on him again. She felt bruised in spirit and desperately tired. She attended Dorothy's Separatist meetings, but still found no comfort

168

for the soul. She was being punished, and rightfully so, for the evil she had contemplated doing. She had meant no more to the Earl of Chelwood than one of the city's many whores.

Somewhere at the back of Lilias' mind was a nagging doubt, the germ of a suspicion that if she made enquiries, probed a little deeper, she might possibly discover that she did not know the truth. But she did not enquire; refused to probe. She told herself that the passion which had gripped her had been a midsummer madness, setting all her values and teachings at naught. She would not acknowledge the hurt or the wounded pride, and saw only that she had been made a fool of. She put all thoughts of the Earl from her mind and went steadfastly about her daily tasks. And now, on this windy September morning, Priam had gone: she could not contact him again, even if she wished.

The house seemed so empty. All the noise and bustle—the shouting, the tramping, the cheering—was outside, in the streets. She would call on Dorothy and together they would watch Fairfax and his men march in. Lilias seized a cloak and stepped outside the door. She glanced towards the High Cross, where crowds were gathering, and saw a stocky figure, sitting squarely astride his horse, jogging down the street in her direction. There was something familiar about the figure, something she knew. She hesitated, then suddenly began to run . . .

Richard was already dismounting. He looked so dependable, so solid, so trustworthy and so sane that Lilias was shaken by an upsurge of affection.

"Richard!" she cried, holding out both her hands, tears coursing down her cheeks. "Oh God! Dear, dear Richard!" And before she knew it, she was folded in his arms.

*　　*　　*

"Lilias!"

She awoke from her first deep sleep to see Richard standing in the bedroom doorway. His white night-shirt glimmered palely against the darkness of the landing. She sat up in bed, hair tumbling untidily about her shoulders.

"Richard? What is it? Can't you sleep?"

He shook his head, enquiring hesitantly: "May I come in?"

Lilias bit her lip, uncertain what to say.

Dorothy Hazard, who had visited them that evening to offer Richard her condolences, had had no doubt whatsoever.

"You must come and stay with us, Lilias, until Regina and the children return from Abbot's Leigh. You cannot possibly remain under the same roof with a man who is not your husband."

Lilias had thought fleetingly of Priam.

"Dorothy, I know that it's improper and that people might talk. But how can I leave Richard alone tonight, when he is still overcome by the news of Hannah's death? It would be a cruel, a callous, thing to do."

"You had to do it. Why can't he? Men," Dorothy had added, from her experience of two husbands, "remain children for just as long as we foolish women let them."

"It wasn't so bad for me. Hannah didn't mean so much. Dorothy, I'm sorry, but I have no choice but to stay."

"We-ell—" Dorothy considered the matter doubtfully, but finally gave in. "As long as it is only for tonight, and as long as it's kept a secret . . . But if anyone asks me, I shall tell a lie and say that you were staying with me. I daresay you'll come to no harm."

Lilias, appreciating the enormity of the sacrifice that Dorothy was prepared to make, had kissed her cheek affectionately.

"Oh, go along with you!" Dorothy had exclaimed,

pleased all the same, and had eventually taken her leave.

Supper had been a silent meal, both Lilias and Richard busy with their own reflections. Later, Lilias had wished Richard a subdued good-night, picked up her candle and gone to her room, not expecting to see him again until morning. Now here he was, coming forward to sit on the edge of her bed, as Barnaby had once done years ago.

"I keep thinking of Hannah," he said miserably, like a little boy. "I know I shouldn't have gone away."

Lilias held out a hand and his fingers closed over it, pleading for reassurance.

"Richard, your being here wouldn't have prevented Hannah contracting the plague. I found out afterwards that she had been visiting a family whose son died the very same day."

"Did she suffer much?"

"Not for long. You know how swiftly it strikes. It was over in a few hours for Hannah."

He nodded sombrely, then said: "I was never in love with her, you know."

Lilias felt a little shocked by this stark admission, but answered gently: "No, I know. Or, at least, I guessed. But I think you were fond of her, all the same."

Richard shifted his position on the bed and cleared his throat, awkward because he knew he should not be there. "I wasn't really fond of her," he muttered at last. "She irritated me more than anything."

"Why are you telling me these things? Why now? They're nothing to do with me."

"Yes, they are." He released her hand and bunched his own together in his lap, staring down at them as though he had never seen them before. "I'm telling you now because I suppose I feel guilty—guilty that I don't feel more grief. Do you find that hard to understand?"

"No ... I felt the same way when Barnaby died. I cried for days, but I was really crying for my own lack of pity. Why did you marry Hannah?"

171

He shrugged. Everything was very quiet, just the Watchman now and then crying the hour. The frenetic bustle of the day was over; the marching and counter-marching of troops; the arrivals and departures; Richard returning, Priam gone. Cromwell and Fairfax were now ensconced in the castle apartments where only last night Rupert and his captains had taken their last fitful and uneasy sleep . . .

Lilias had to smother a cry, so sharp and intense was the pain inside her. After two years, Priam was no longer near. She wrapped her arms around herself as though to staunch the bleeding of some internal wound. He hadn't loved her; he had made a fool of her. She must hang on to that.

Richard was speaking. She tried to remember what it was that she had asked him.

"I married her for convenience, I suppose. I was thirty. I wanted to settle down. And when my mother died five years ago, it seemed natural to think of a wife. I'd known Hannah most of my life. She came of a good Bristol family and had money of her own . . . And that reminds me, I must see Lawyer Fothergill as soon as possible."

Lilias grimaced to herself under cover of the darkness. It was true: money and the acquisition of yet more money was the driving force of most Bristolians. "Weren't you happy with Hannah?" she asked gently.

"I wasn't unhappy—not until you came along." He saw her swift, defensive movement and possessed himself of her hands once again. "Lilias, don't be angry with me. I know it's not the time nor place to say anything yet, but I can't help myself. I've loved you from the first. You're so beautiful, but it isn't just that. You're so kind, so calm, so . . . so strong!"

Strange, she thought, that they held this mutual appeal for one another; that each needed the other's gentleness and strength. And yet . . .

172

The Earl seemed to be standing beside her in the dark; the little room was suddenly full of his presence. Was he thinking of her? Longing for her, even as she was longing for him? She knew that she was being stupid and fanciful. He was the man who had been willing to take advantage of her for no better reason than his own arrogant pleasure. He would have seduced her and left her. She had been saved from her own folly because he had found somebody better; some whore from the Bristol brothels, who had promised him a more exciting time . . .

"Lilias!" Richard's voice cut insistently across her wandering thoughts. "Lilias, I'm asking you to marry me."

"But . . ." Her head ached, her mind felt bludgeoned.

"Oh, not now. Not at once. Not for a year, perhaps two. Not until a respectable period of mourning has passed and Regina has had time to get used to the idea. But you'll have to marry again some day, and Eliot needs a mother . . . Judith needs a father . . . I'm being clumsy. I can't make pretty speeches. That's not what I meant to say."

"No . . . Dear Richard, I understand."

She ought to refuse. Another marriage, like her first, for all the wrong reasons, was asking for trouble. But Richard was not Barnaby. He offered the kind of affection poor Barnaby had never been able to give. Richard loved her, would give her security and peace of mind. Lilias felt as if she were drifting: a complete suspension of time and will. She was so tired of wondering what the future might hold, so tired of not belonging. And there was Judith to consider: this house had become their home. To marry Richard was the obvious solution.

And so she said to him, as she had once said to Barnaby: "Yes, I'll marry you, dear Richard. When the time is right."

173

He heaved a great sigh, as though a weight had been lifted from his shoulders. Then he moved, crushing her againt his chest. She thought in a moment of panic: "No! No, I can't marry him!" She remembered her feeling of complete surrender when the Earl had taken her in his arms. There was nothing of that here: just a suffocating sense of masculinity and the weight of Richard's body against hers.

He released her, looking shamefaced. "Not now," he said thickly. "Not until we're married." She thanked God wryly for the Puritan conscience. "I'll ride over to Abbot's Leigh tomorrow and bring Regina and Mollie and the children back. I don't think that I could trust myself alone with you in this house for one more night."

★   ★   ★

"How long can you stay?"

Priam looked down into his wife's anxiously smiling face and answered: "Only an hour or two. The Prince gave me leave to visit you before we march on to Oxford. We have broken our march at Marshfield."

"So short a time!" Magdalen's eyes were filled with tears, but she made a brave attempt to smile. "You're looking thin; I expect you're hungry. I'll go and order food at once."

"Wait. I've brought a visitor with me. Someone, my dear, to whom we both owe a very great debt." Priam's tone was bitter, but she noticed nothing, as he indicated Patrick O'Mara, standing just inside the door. Magdalen went forward with a glad little cry.

"Captain! How happy I am to see you again! I have always felt ashamed that I did not thank you properly that night."

Patrick raised one of her outstretched hands to his lips. His fingers were not quite steady. "Lady Chelwood. Your very devoted servant." He was acutely conscious of the Earl's mocking eyes upon them. Was this Priam's way of getting his own back? He had been a fool to agree to come. But when the offer had been made—"My wife will never forgive me, O'Mara, if she knows that you were so near and I did not invite you"—he could not resist the temptation. To see Magdalen's face, to hear her voice again, had suddenly become a craving.

"Say that you have forgiven me," she was saying, and he blinked.

"Forgiven you?"

"For my treatment of you that night. I behaved with shocking rudeness."

"You were kindness, itself."

"I dismissed you most abruptly."

"You were tired and frightened. I hope that your servants were severely punished."

"By me, yes," struck in the Earl. "Most of them were dismissed. Magdalen would have let them off more lightly. But then, she could never say boo to a goose."

The Countess flushed and looked abashed. Patrick unclenched the fist at his side and purposefully kept smiling.

"But then, it was not you, my lord," he pointed out, "who had to engage new servants. A difficult task, I suspect, in these extremely troubled times."

Magdalen threw him a glance full of gratitude, and the Earl laughed.

"You have found yourself a champion, sweetheart. Now, where is that food you mentioned?"

"Yes, of course." She hurried away in the direction of the kitchens.

Half an hour later, they sat down to a laden table. Priam laughed shortly. "So near and yet so far," he murmured. "We could have done with some of this food in Bristol." He remembered all that Lilias had endured, and anger licked through him.

Patrick, recognising the shuttered look on his face and knowing what the Earl was thinking, hated him for his

175

betrayal of Magdalen. He ought to feel sympathy, he supposed, their situations were so much the same. And yet not the same, for Patrick's love hurt no one.

The talk was desultory, all three suddenly afraid to look into the future. No one knew what the King would do, now that his armies were defeated.

"Will you return to Ireland, captain?" Magdalen wanted to know, and Patrick paused, in the act of slicing an apple. He had not, until that moment, considered it.

"Yes, I suppose so," he answered slowly. "His Majesty will need soldiers there. Ireland, at least, remains loyal to the King."

"Catholic Ireland!" Magdalen exclaimed unhappily, then stopped, blushing. "I—I'm sorry . . . I expect . . . Are you—? I didn't think . . ."

"You never do, my love," Priam said caustically. "And to save Captain O'Mara the misery of your embarrassment, shall we change the subject? May I see the girls?"

What had got into him? he wondered. Was he trying to show himself, or Magdalen, or O'Mara just how unpleasant and ill-mannered he could be? Some devil drove him. He guessed that the Irishman was in love with his wife, and wanted to hurt Patrick through her.

Lady Cressida and Lady Cassandra Lithgow had both grown and were more articulate than either their father or Patrick remembered them. Cassandra, the elder, was more like her mother, inclined to be shy, and with the same, soft, vulnerable mouth. But Cressida, at four years old, was fully aware of her charms, flirting outrageously, as did most small girls, with her father. Priam sat her on his knee.

"The age of innocence," he remarked mockingly. "The only period in a child's life when her father appears in the guise of hero."

"Oh, no!" protested Magdalen quickly. "My father . . . I mean, I always felt . . ."

176

"That your father was always a hero? But then, my love, your age of innocence, fortunately for us all, is still with you."

Magdalen was silenced. Patrick longed to smash his fist into the Earl's hard, cynically smiling face. He had hoped, by this visit, to cure himself of an infatuation for a woman he had only seen once: to prove to himself that it was a false emotion, born of the circumstances and his romantic recollections. But now, he knew it was not. Love at first sight was not just a poet's fantasy: it had happened to him.

And as he and the Earl rode away from Westovers to rejoin Prince Rupert at Marshfield, Patrick O'Mara had to accept the fact that he was as much in love with Magdalen as ever.

PART TWO
1649–1651

The glories of our blood and state
Are shadows, not substantial things,
There is no armour against fate,
Death lays his icy hand on Kings.
Sceptre and Crown
Must tumble down
And in the dust be equal made
With the poor crooked scythe and spade.

James Shirley, 1596–1666

CHAPTER ELEVEN

The room at the Bear Tavern near Cheapside where the Prides always lodged when they came to London was warm and comfortable. The windows had been newly glazed to keep out the draughts and the all-pervading smell of the Fleet. It was far enough for safety from the tumble of streets known as Alsatia, where crime flourished in every noisome tenement and alley, and where a man dared not walk alone after dark if he valued his purse and his life.

The street-cries—"What do you lack?" "Fine laces and ribbons!" "White vinegar, only the best!" "Cabbages and turnips, cheap at the price!"—the rumble and rattle of the traffic and the cries of the water-men were muted, like the distant booming of the sea. But with the coming of dusk, the noise had not slackened, as revellers and disturbers of the peace disputed their arrest with the constable and his Watch. The drivers of hackney coaches, waiting in clusters at every street corner, fought each other for the custom of fares, travelling for a shilling a mile to Kensington or Islington or one of the other outlying villages.

Lilias had washed and changed into the dress of dark red wool which Richard had given her for Christmas. She tried to think of her three children, Judith, Oliver and little Geoffrey, left with seven-year-old Eliot in Regina's charge, and picture what they would be doing. But she could not. The scenes of that January day in Westminster Hall, the clash of argument, the angry words, pursued one another relentlessly through her brain.

"Sir! The charge has called you Tyrant, Traitor, Murderer and Enemy of the Commonwealth of England. It would have been well if any one of these terms might have been spared you."

"This man, Charles Stuart, is guilty of the blood of his subjects, even as David was guilty of the blood of Uriah!"

"Sir, you have indulged in the crimes of a veritable Caligula!"

"The said Charles Stuart shall be put to death by the severing of his head from his body."

Lilias, from her seat in the public gallery, had been one of the few who could see the King's face clearly throughout the days of his trial. The wooden barriers, the pikes and heads of the surrounding soldiers had hidden the prisoner completely from the spectators in the body of the Hall. She had looked at the man she had last seen in the parlour of the Broad Street house, and been unable to detect in him any fear of his approaching death. Charles Stuart had denied the legality of the court, refused to plead and reduced the entire proceedings to a shambles.

Lilias knelt before the fire, holding out her hands to the blaze, for the evening was exceptionally cold. The King on trial; the King condemned to death; it was as though the world as people had always known it was coming to an end. Safety seemed suddenly an illusion. Lilias wished that Richard would come. She wondered what was detaining him at Westminster, and was afraid she knew. He was signing the death-warrant of the King.

Since their marriage in the March of 1646, Richard Pride had grown in importance. He had become a friend of Cromwell, now a very powerful man. Lilias could understand the attraction. They were very much alike: both outwardly strong but inwardly vulnerable and dependent for stability upon their women. Lilias had discovered Richard's dependency in the first few months of her marriage. He liked to have her near him, to reach out occasionally and touch her. And when he had been selected as one of the commissioners to try the King, he had insisted that she accompany him to London.

"The boys are old enough," he had said, "to do without you for a while. And they are fond of Regina. They'll stay with her and Mollie without any fuss. Besides, Judith is a big girl now, and can give her aunt a hand."

The six-year-old Judith had flushed at this praise. She was fond of her stepfather and of Regina, but the great passion of her life was Eliot.

"Eliot says—" prefaced most of her remarks, until Lilias felt that she could slap her. She loved Eliot almost as much as her own two sons, but she resented Judith's uncritical adoration.

"Eliot is not God, Judith," she had once admonished her.

"But sometimes he thinks he is," Regina had put in tartly. She was surprisingly free from prejudice where her only grandson was concerned. Indeed, Lilias occasionally fancied that Oliver was her favourite.

Oliver had been born to Lilias and Richard in December, 1646, and, just over a year later, Geoffrey had arrived. His birth had been difficult, and the doctor had warned Lilias that she would probably have no more children.

"We have four between us," Richard had consoled her gruffly. "If it is God's will that we have no more, we have still been sufficiently blessed."

Lilias had smiled tremulously, holding on to his hand, knowing what it cost him to say that, for he longed for a daughter of his own. She was not in love with him, but her affection went deep. What had happened to the Earl of Chelwood she had never enquired, but Westovers was empty, the Countess and her children, by all accounts, fled to Holland.

Lilias got up from the fire and paced restlessly about the room. Beyond the window, the dusk was cold and bleak, a fleece of dirty snow lying across the roof-tops. She picked up and put down the presents—a jointed doll for Judith, a ball-and-cup for Eliot, ninepins for Oliver and a brightly coloured bell for little Geoffrey—bought in the great market held daily in the nave of St Paul's. She wished that she were at home and Richard with her, instead of getting himself embroiled in state affairs.

She heard a step on the stair and ran to the door. "Richard!" she cried thankfully and kissed his cold lips. "Come in by the fire. I'll send for something to eat. Your hands are like ice."

It was only as her husband followed her into the room that she realised he was not alone. Lilias looked in surprise at the fussy, voluble little man who entered with them.

"My friend, Hugh Peters," Richard said. "He used to be minister at Salem and knows your father's friend, Governor Winthrop."

The little preacher turned at once towards her. "A great and glorious day, Mrs Pride! Praise be to the Lord for all His marvellous works! Your husband and I have just come from Westminster where he has set his hand to the document which will sever the arch-traitor's head from his body. Glory be to God!"

Lilias gripped her hands together until the knuckles shone white. "Richard, is this true?" But she knew without asking that it was.

Richard sat down heavily on a stool near the fire and waved Hugh Peters to a chair. "There was no other signatory from Bristol, and Oliver wished for all the major cities to be represented."

"Then Sir Henry Vane, as Lord High Steward, should have signed."

"That man." Richard spat. "He refused even to sit as a commissioner."

"No. He's not such a fool. He refuses to put his life in jeopardy."

Hugh Peters, in spite of being taken aback by her vehemence and the solemnity of the moment, neverthe-

184

less felt a stirring of some emotion he had long thought dormant. Really, Lilias Pride was a remarkably handsome woman. He judged her to be some twenty-three years old.

"What do you mean, 'refuses to put his life in jeopardy'?" Richard asked, bewildered.

The landlord bustled in with a laden tray. "I saw your honour come in and have taken the liberty of bringing food. Baked carp, roast chicken, bacon pie and some minced collops on the side. Then, to follow, a syllabub and an apple tart. Just a light repast, but I trust it will meet with satisfaction." He smiled ingratiatingly, wiped his hands on his apron, placed a jug of ale to warm on the hearth and bowed himself out. He had always prided himself on knowing which guests to flatter.

"You'll eat with me, Mr Peters?" Richard enquired, pulling up his stool to the table.

"No, I thank you. I have already eaten with General Fairfax. Mrs Pride, you were saying?"

"I was saying that my husband is putting his life in danger by signing the King's death-warrant. Suppose that one day the monarchy is restored?"

But neither man would suppose anything so foolish.

"My dear Mrs Pride, have no fears on that score," implored Hugh Peters. "The rule of God's Saints on Earth will last for ever. It is prophesied in the Bible, and we—" his globular dark eyes shone with excitement "—are destined to see the beginning of this glorious reign." The little preacher's voice took on the stentorian ring which had so often overawed his congregations at Salem. "Thanks be to God, we have freed ourselves from the shackles of Anti-Christ. Never again will the Scarlet Whore of Rome flaunt herself naked in this Christian country. The rule of bishops will never again return to plague us."

"But the rule of the Stuarts might."

"Lilias, hold your tongue," Richard said quietly. He

rarely raised his voice, but there was a certain tone that Lilias recognised, a warning note that she had tried his patience too far. "You are talking arrant nonsense. And how often must I tell you that political matters are not for women to meddle in? Mr Peters, let me press you, at least, to a piece of this pie. I can highly recommend it. The landlord's wife is an excellent cook."

For answer, Hugh Peters patted his thickening paunch and laughed. "I am getting too fat already. Over-indulgence in food, as in everything else, is a mortal sin."

Lilias, who had gone to sit on the window-seat, returned to the attack. "Who else has signed?" she asked.

"What?" Richard was impatient.

"Who else has signed?"

"Oh, Bradshaw, Cromwell, Ireton, Valentine Walton ..." Richard cited more names, some of which were familiar to Lilias, some not. But most were names of repute, and she felt no surprise that Richard had added his own to the list. It was not the names of religious fanatics like Thomas Harrison which had impressed him, but those others—John Hutchinson, Lord Grey, Thomas Scot, John Carew—whose owners he so greatly admired: men who thought as he did, that the monarchy had grown oppressive and unjust. Richard added: "As long as the King lives, everything that Parliament has fought for will be put at risk."

"But if you kill him," Lilias persisted, braving his displeasure, "you give the title to his son, who is young and free, and has all the charm his father lacks to win men to him." And women, too, she thought, remembering the appraising glances of those bold black eyes and the gentle, lascivious curl of the lips.

"No, no! You don't understand, Mrs Pride," cried Hugh Peters. "We shall abolish the monarchy by Act of Parliament as soon as the King is dead.

Lilias sighed. Men were such fools. They had such

186

touching faith in bits of paper and the power of a few lines of writing in some musty statute book.

Feet clattered on the stairs. There was a loud rap on the door and Richard called: "Come in!" Both he and Hugh Peters stared in astonishment at Colonel Okey.

"John!" Richard rose, holding out his hand. "You're just in time to take a cup of ale. Better still, stay and eat with me. I hate eating by myself, and my wife—you know my wife?—has already supped, and Hugh, here, says that he's getting too fat."

"A cup of ale, if I may, but that's all. This cold has dried my throat. Richard! I've come to fetch you back to Westminster. Cromwell is in a rare taking. They've just got wind of a plot to rescue the King ... Thank you." Okey took the ale and gulped, wiping his mouth with the back of his hand. Cutting across Hugh Peters' exclamations of dismay, he continued: "One of Fairfax's agents came in half an hour ago with the news. Oh, there's no danger, not now. We know who and where the conspirators are. The chief one is holed up in some br—" Okey glanced quickly at Lilias, then amended hurriedly "—in some house of ill-repute in Southwark. Cromwell's sending troops to arrest him tonight, but he wants you to come, too, so that there will be no mistake. Someone—Desborough, I think—said that you know him."

Richard dabbed grease from his chin. "I know him? Who is he, then?"

"The Earl of Chelwood," Okey snorted.

Lilias' heart gave a great thud and she felt as though she were going to be sick.

"Chelwood? I thought the man was in Holland. The fool!" Richard was contemptuous. "I should have credited him with more sense. Such plots can never be kept a secret. What about the rest of the conspirators?"

"They're already being rounded up. But Cromwell wants sure identification of the ringleader."

Richard crammed the last of the apple tart into his

187

mouth, at the same time getting to his feet and dragging on his coat, which he had thrown over the back of the chair.

Hugh Peters was clucking like an outraged hen. "Where is this . . . this place?" he asked.

"Southwark. Gibbet Lane, near the old Globe Theatre."

Lilias noticed that Okey did not hesitate to speak in front of her. Like Caesar's wife, she was above suspicion.

Richard kissed her abstractedly. "Don't wait up," he said. "I shall probably be late."

She smiled mechanically and made some reply which, even to her own ears, sounded like nonsense. But neither Richard nor the other two men seemed to notice, and, a moment later, the door closed behind them, leaving her alone in the room.

She stood perfectly still, recovering from the sound of the Earl's name which had been almost like a physical blow. Then, as the numbness left her and feeling crept back, she wondered what she ought to do. But why should she do anything? What was the Earl of Chelwood to her? And at once the answer came: the man who had saved her life. Could she stand idly by now and do nothing to repay her debt? Whatever else she did or did not feel for him, she owed him that at least. But there was the question of loyalty: Richard was her husband and Priam her enemy. Moreover, it was dark, and an unaccompanied woman in the streets at night was fair game for any thief or cut-throat who happened to be abroad . . .

Yet even while she argued with herself, she was pulling a cloak from the travelling chest at the foot of the bed and tying the hood tightly beneath her chin, to conceal as much of her face as possible. From her reticule, flung carelessly on the window-seat, she dragged a strip of black velvet, thanking Heaven for the prevailing London fashion. No lady with any pretension to style went out of

188

doors without a mask. Finally, she changed her thin satin slippers for leather shoes and chopines to keep her out of the melting snow. Then she crept cautiously down the stairs, past the crowded tap-room and slipped, unnoticed, into the dark.

*   *   *

Fortunately, there was no moon, and the icy sleet kept most people indoors. Lilias began to run, but the cobbles were too slippery with mud and refuse, and after a moment or two she was forced to slow down. How much advantage did she have? As long as it took Richard and Okey to get to Westminster, to see Cromwell, to receive orders and to set out with a detachment of soldiers to arrest the Earl. Where would they cross the river? From Westminster Stairs to Lambeth, probably, and thence skirting Lambeth Marsh to Southwark. If she took a boat from the Three Cranes, she could be rowed directly across to the tangle of streets and alleyways near the Globe. After that, she would have to ask someone the way.

The boatman eyed her curiously, but took her two-pence and motioned her to sit in the stern under the canopy. She was glad of the shadow it afforded, and relieved that the other passengers, who had only paid a penny, remained in the bow, exposed to the elements. For the first time since Colonel Okey had uttered the name of the Earl of Chelwood, Lilias had time to think seriously about what she was doing. She was risking her own safety and Richard's reputation for a man for whom she could have sworn she felt nothing. She had not consciously thought of Priam for a long time now, and was astonished at the violence of her reactions to the knowledge that he was in danger. He was an enemy of everything that her husband and, therefore, that she, as an obedient wife, held dear. He was plotting to rescue the King on the very eve of his execution, and for that his own life would undoubtedly be forfeit. Lilias found that her nails were biting into the palms of her hands, tucked inside her muff. And by the time that the boat went aground on the opposite shore, she was terrified that even now she might be too late to save the Earl.

As the boatman helped her out, she asked: "Do you know where Gibbet Lane is?" And realised as she spoke that she did not know which house she wanted.

"Gibbet Lane?" The boatman hesitated, plainly at a loss whether to tell her or not. "What does a woman like you want with Gibbet Lane?"

"There's someone there I must find," she answered desperately.

The boatman could not see her face or figure under the mask and all-enveloping cloak. She sounded young, but she might be older. "Daughter run away from 'ome, 'as she?" he asked sympathetically. "Got 'erself into bad company?"

"What? Oh . . . yes . . . yes, that's it." Lilias snatched thankfully at the story which the man had offered her so opportunely. "I think it's near the Globe."

"Well, the theatre, itself, is a bit further back, in the fields. But Gibbet Lane's near 'ere." The man pointed across the narrow strip of shingle to the gaping mouth of a street immediately ahead. "Up there and turn right . . . Look, missus, why don't you stay 'ere an' I'll call out the Watch? The constable'd go in and find your girl."

"No! No . . . please. I don't want any fuss. My husband doesn't know . . . I shall be all right. And thank you."

The shingle crunched under her feet and the chopines rang hollowly on the wooden steps which led up to the entrance of Fishmonger Alley. A man lurched out of an unlighted doorway and lunged for her, muttering drunkenly. With a little of sob of fear, Lilias dodged his outstretched hands and plunged forward into the darkness. A shutter was flung open above her head and

190

someone leaned out, emptying a slop-pail into the street. Mud and filth spattered her cloak. An opening loomed on her right. A lantern, hung high on the wall, illuminated the sign "Gibbet Lane."

It was a narrow cul-de-sac of five or six houses at the most, and beyond them stretched the dimly seen fields and the ghostly circle of the Globe. The theatre was shut now, like the Bear Garden and the Beer House further down river. But which house was it? She couldn't knock on the doors of them all . . .

A door opened and a man slouched out. There was the clink of money changing hands as the brothel-keeper wished her customer good-night. Before she could shut the door again, Lilias darted forward and slid inside.

" 'Ere! What the 'ell—? Blimey! 'Oo are you?"

Behind the lady abbess, two girls, partially clothed, were lolling on the dirty stairs. The place stank of stale food, sweat and human ordure. Lilias pressed a hand to her mouth as she began to retch.

" 'Ere's a dainty madam," sneered the proprietress over her shoulder, and both girls sniggered. "And what might you want, yer ladyship?"

"I'm looking for the Earl of Chelwood," Lilias said.

In spite of the feeling of nausea which threatened to overpower her, she was watching the woman closely. A sudden wariness leapt into the other's eyes and was gone on the instant. But it told Lilias all that she wanted to know.

"The Earl of 'oo, dear? Blimey, 'ear that girls? 'Er ladyship thinks we got earls amongst our clients."

The taller of the two whores got up and descended the stairs, swinging her hips in a practised manner, her heavily rouged cheeks in startling contrast to the pallor of the rest of her face. The faded blue eyes, sunk deep in their sockets, looked at Lilias with undisguised hostility.

"We don' 'ave earls 'ere, my duck," she said, smiling and showing a hideous fringe of broken teeth. "We don'

191

'ave interfering busybodies, neither. We've got a way of dealin' with little peeping posies like you." She turned to the madam. "Shall I fetch 'Ob, then?"

"Yes. I think you'd better . . . Wait a minute, 'ere 'e is."

A big, evil-looking man in a stained leather jerkin came through from the back of the house, and Lilias felt her skin begin to crawl with fear.

"No, wait, please." She stretched out a hand, thankful that she was wearing nothing but her plain gold wedding-band, although even that might prove too much of a temptation for her companions. "The Earl's in danger. I've come to warn him. Soldiers are on their way from Westminster to arrest him."

The madam sucked in her breath and her eyes narrowed. "No, keep off," she said to the single-minded Hob as he advanced purposefully on Lilias. "'Oo are you?" she demanded, suddenly fretful.

"That doesn't matter now. For Heaven's sake, take me to the Earl if you know where he is. I must warn him before it's too late."

"She could be a bleedin' spy," suggested the girl still on the stairs.

"True. Well, we'll know what to do with 'er if she is. We don' like our clients being pestered. Take off that mask and let's 'ave a look at your face."

"Let me see the Earl," Lilias pleaded desperately, as she removed her mask. "He will be able to vouch for me."

The brothel-keeper prised a strand of meat from between her teeth and spat it on the floor, considering this proposition.

"All right," she agreed at last, and Lilias heaved a sigh of relief. "But if you're lying, my girl—" She did not finish the sentence, but drew her finger suggestively across her throat. "'Ob!" She jerked her head towards the door. "Look outside and make sure this ain't a trap."

192

Hob disappeared to prowl the length of the little cul-de-sac, then returned, shaking his head. "No one that I can see."

"Right. Across the street. Number three. Old Mother Tankerville's, may she rot in 'ell! Been undercuttin' my prices lately."

Lilias followed the madam across the cobbles, where the dark shapes of rats foraged for food amongst the garbage, and into a house as evil-smelling and as dirty as the other.

The madam rapped on an inner door. "Tankerville! Got a visitor for you."

A woman, as fat as the first madam was thin, erupted suspiciously from her room, and was brought up short by the sight of Lilias.

"Gawd!" she exclaimed. "What a looker. Don' tell me you turned 'er down."

"It ain't like that. Come inside yer den an' I'll tell you. 'Ob. You stay there and watch 'er ladyship like a 'awk."

Dear God, thought Lilias. At this pace, she and Priam would still be here when the soldiers came. Her ears were already on the alert for any tell-tale sounds. A few moments later, however, she was being conducted up the rickety stairs by a reluctant Mrs Tankerville to a room at the back of the house. A door creaked protestingly open.

"Someone t' see you," Mrs Tankerville said. "You'd better take a look at 'er an' see if she's as friendly as she says. If not, we'll know 'ow t' deal with 'er. Yer lordship needn't worry."

The door swung wider and the Earl stood on the threshold, frowning.

"What the—? Mrs Colefax!" He sounded stupefied. "What on earth are you doing here?"

"You do know 'er, then," Mrs Tankerville conceded grudgingly, a tigress balked of her prey.

"What? Oh ... Yes, I know this lady. Come inside, Mrs Colefax, please."

The door shut on the curious face of the brothel-keeper, and Lilias found herself alone with Priam for the first time since that afternoon in Broad Street four long years ago. Before the Earl could speak again, she hurried into speech.

She had to repeat her story twice before his brain, recovering from the shock of seeing her, had grasped all the salient facts. He asked slowly, his mind reeling from this second shock of the blow to all his hopes: "You say that all my friends have been arrested?"

"Yes, according to Colonel Okey. And I see no reason to doubt his word. Their hiding-places, and yours, are all known to him."

"Someone must have betrayed us," the Earl said bitterly. He drove a fist into his open palm. "But who, in God's name? Which of them was it?"

"Does it matter now?" Lilias cried frantically. "You must get away from here at once." She looked with sudden compassion at the dark circles under his eyes, and at the face which had grown even thinner with the privations of the past few years. "Quickly," she went on, as he did not move. "There is nothing you can do on your own to save the King. His Majesty is too well guarded."

The Earl passed a hand across his eyes, trying to unclog his mind.

"Wait," he said. "There's something I don't understand. Why are you in London with Richard Pride?"

"He is my husband," Lilias answered. There was a pause. "We have two sons," she added.

Priam stared at her. She was Richard Pride's wife. She was married to a man who, the Earl knew, was one of the commissioners who had tried the King. Well, it was inevitable, he told himself wryly, that believing herself spurned by him, she should have turned to someone as much in love with her as Richard Pride had so obviously been. Was she happy with him? She did not look unhappy, and for that, Priam supposed, he should be thankful. But he was not. What, then, did his arrogant male pride want? That her life should be blighted? That she should waste it in mourning for a man who had been at pains to make it clear that she meant nothing to him? The Devil take Patrick O'Mara and his medieval notions of chivalry! He should have been born five hundred years earlier, when men made ballads to their lady's eyebrow and risked life and limb for nothing more than a smile. He should have been a troubadour at one of the Angevin courts of love in a less cynical and prosaic age than the present . . .

"For Heaven's sake, my lord," Lilias was saying, her fingers gripping his arm. "We must go. The soldiers will be here at any moment."

He turned to a table and began sweeping the papers from it, piling them on the hearth, where he set them alight. The leaping flames lent an eery glow to his face, like blood.

"You came here alone to find me and warn me?" His voice sounded odd. "You came through the London streets by yourself? Weren't you . . . weren't you afraid?"

"Yes, of course I was afraid," she cried in exasperation.

"Then why did you do it?" He stood up, staring into her eyes, as though trying to fathom some secret. Her own eyes fell before his insistent stare.

"I don't know," she said violently, "except that I can't bear to see anything trapped . . . For pity's sake, my lord, let's go! My life will be as much at stake as your own if I am found here."

"Forgive me. I wasn't thinking. Seeing you again like this has made me stupid." He found his cloak and wrapped it round him, unsheathing his dagger from his belt. He moved towards the door.

"Why here?" The words were jerked from Lilias before she knew what she was saying. She licked her lips, hesitated, then said steadily: "Why a brothel?"

He smiled mockingly. "Does it shock your good Puritan soul? You see, I trust these people."

"Why?"

"Because they are my friends and because their livelihood is in danger. They will be hounded into extinction once your Puritan friends are in control."

"The oldest profession?" Her smile glimmered, and he caught his breath. Motherhood suited her: her figure had filled out. It made her more beautiful than ever. "Can even the Dissenters put an end to that?"

"They'll try."

"Where will you go now?"

"Back to my wife and children in Holland. If I can get clear away. But here and now, I am escorting you back to your lodgings. Where are you staying, Mrs Pride?"

"The Bear, in Cheapside. But you mustn't come. I cannot let you. My lord, you must realise the danger that you're in."

"What greater safety could I ask," he demanded ironically, "than being in the company of one of the commissioners' wives?"

He opened the door for her and they descended the stairs. There was so much left unsaid between them, but this was neither the time nor the place to say it. The silence was alive with unasked questions, with answers that would never, now, be given. As they gained the foot of the stairs, Mrs Tankerville emerged into the ill-lighted passage, and, at the same moment, there was a thunderous knocking on the door.

"Open in the name of the law and Parliament!" shouted a voice which Lilias recognised as Colonel Okey's.

CHAPTER TWELVE

They all three stood rooted to the spot. Lilias felt as though her feet had turned to lead. Through lips stiff with fright, she whispered: "Is there another way out?"

The Earl shook his head. "Only to a path through the fields. If they have any sense, Okey will have that covered."

As he spoke, a slatternly maidservant came in from a door at the end of the passage, snivelling that there were soldiers in the kitchen. Lilias looked in horrified despair at Priam.

"Only one thing for it," hissed Mrs Tankerville, pushing them towards one of the doors that lined the passage. "That room's empty. Get in there and get undressed."

Lilias gasped. She saw the Earl glance, like a hunted animal, from side to side. Then he said quietly: "There's no help for it."

There was more knocking. "If you do not open this door," Colonel Okey was shouting, "I shall order one of my men to shoot off the bolt."

"I'm comin'. I'm comin'. No need fer vi'lence," grumbled Mrs Tankerville, and she turned to the Earl. "Fer Gawd's sake, get in there an' do as I say. An' pray 'ard that I can persuade 'em you've already left."

The door shut on Priam and Lilias, leaving them in the dark. As her eyes grew accustomed to the gloom, Lilias could see that the room contained only a bed.

"Take your cloak and gown off," the Earl ordered her in a restricted voice. "Loosen your hair around your shoulders and then lie down."

Lilias' frantic hands tore at laces and ribbons, and she heard the ripping of cloth as she pulled at the bodice of her dress. Priam had discarded both cloak and jerkin. His tall figure, in breeches and shirt, was pressed to the crack of the door. As silently as possible, he eased it half an inch wider.

"Oh, 'e's bin 'ere, all right," Mrs Tankerville was whining. "An' don' I know it! Gone off in a 'urry, like, an' not paid me a bleedin' penny. Food 'e's 'ad, not to mention other 'ome comforts, an' now 'e's gone, like what I said. An' not so much as a farthing."

There was the low-pitched growl of a man's voice, angry and frustrated. Lilias could not catch what he said.

"Lor' bless yer honour, you can see 'is room if you want to." Mrs Tankerville sniffed. "Smells like 'e's bin burnin' something." There was the sound of feet on the stairs, as someone clattered up and then down.

"Clean as a whistle, Colonel Okey, sir," reported a voice. "And the woman's right. He's been burning papers in the hearth. Not long ago, I should imagine . . . No, sir, only ashes."

The voice which Lilias took as belonging to Colonel Okey spoke again, followed by Mrs Tankerville's cackle of laughter.

"You can look if you like, an' welcome. Everyone to 'is own pleasure, that's what I say. I've never bin one fer lookin', meself. I 'ope your lads won't be too embarrassed, the God-fearing boys that they are. Jus' open the doors an' peep in, my dears. There's nowhere anyone can 'ide."

Priam closed the door and was across the room in two swift strides, lying down beside Lilias on the bed. He loosened his shirt, tugging it free of his breeches and gently drew her against his naked chest. He threw one of his legs over both of hers. She could hear the slamming of his heart as it knocked against his ribs, and lay, petrified, her face concealed beneath the sheltering hunch of his shoulders.

Doors were being opened and shut; there were indig-

198

nant cries and low, embarrassed mutterings. Then the door to their room was set ajar and the Earl clamped his mouth on hers.

"It's all right, Mr Oliphant, sir," Mrs Tankerville called out. "Jus' some peepin' Toms of soldiers come to see what the likes of you an' me gets up to."

The Earl grunted. Lilias was conscious of his weight, her mind a riot of emotions, of which fear was now only a part. Desire, shame, a hideous feeling of betrayal all jostled for position in her teeming brain. Richard was somewhere outside: innocent, trusting Richard who thought her asleep in bed in the inn at Cheapside.

There was a stifled apology and the door shut again. The pale gold wedge of lamplight from the passageway disappeared, and the darkness closed about them, thick and blinding. Priam eased off her and tiptoed to the door, once more edging it open. After what seemed an eternity, he said quietly: "I think they're going." Then, after another minute: "It's all right. They've gone."

Lilias sat up and began to dress, glad that the Earl could not see her face. She was aware of him watching her from the door.

Should he tell her the truth? he wondered. Tell her what had really happened on that night four years ago? He had sensed again tonight, while he had held her body close to his, her longing to surrender, had known again the passion which seemed to flare between them at a touch. He wanted her! Dear Lord, how he wanted her! His desire had not diminished with the years.

But what could he offer her except a life of poverty and exile, of estrangement from her children, of the precarious pleasure and dubious honour of being his mistress but never his wife? And what of Magdalen and his promise to Patrick O'Mara? And what of Richard Pride? Pride was a good man. That was the trouble with this war: there were always too many men worthy of respect on the opposite side.

"We must go," he said harshly, "as soon as I am dressed." And he began savagely pulling on his clothes.

As they emerged into the passage, Mrs Tankerville came in from the street.

"They've gone," she announced, smiling, and Lilias could see the remnants of beauty in the battered old face. "They've searched opposite an' they'm satisfied at last that you ain't in Gibbet Lane. They've moved off St Mary Overis way. They'm probably goin' back across the Bridge."

"Then we'll take a boat," said Priam. He leaned forward and kissed the woman's lined and dirty cheek. "You're still the best-looking whore in Southwark."

She screamed delightedly. "You go an' tell that to the yeomen of the Tower! Not but what I wasn't once. All the actors from the Globe used to ask fer me. Will Shakespeare, Dick Burbage, Ben Jonson. But that was forty year ago, before I started losin' me hair an' teeth." She sobered. "Take care of yerself, me lord. Don' fall into the 'ands o' them dismal Desmonds. As fer you, young lady, if you ever wan' a job, I'll give you one. With a face like yours, you'd make this place a fortune." And she shuffled off along the passage to placate two dissatisfied clients, angry at the recent interruption of their pleasure.

The Earl glanced fleetingly at Lilias and opened the street door. "Time we were going," he said.

*   *   *

"You didn't catch him, then?"

"No." Richard spoke almost with relief. He had not relished the role of Judas, however much he might dislike the Earl.

Lilias, curled against his side, felt the same sense of surprise that she had experienced on their wedding night at the strength of that stocky body. Dressed, Richard gave the impression of a man who might in old age run to

200

fat. But it was an illusion created by his ill-fitting clothes. At thirty-eight, he was, stripped, an extremely fine figure of a man, firmly fleshed and sinewed. She could feel now the ripple of muscle over chest and thigh.

"And the plot is scotched? There is no chance now that the King will be rescued?" She had to ask the question for the sake of her uneasy conscience.

"There never was. Chelwood and his friends were fools even to think that they could try."

"And was it one of their own people who betrayed them?" Had the landlord, or the landlord's hawk-eyed wife, seen her come in, creeping up the back stairs, like a thief in the night? And if they had, did they think that she had taken advantage of her husband's absence to keep some secret assignation? Would they say anything to Richard?

Her mind was in turmoil. She could have sworn, lying on that bed in Priam's arms, that he did after all feel something for her, that there must be an explanation of his former conduct. But the cold, silent journey back to Cheapside and the formal, stilted thanks had only repeated the pattern of their previous relationship. She was nothing to him now, as she had been nothing to him in the past and would, most certainly, be nothing to him in the future.

Richard had not bothered to answer her question. His mouth, hot and urgent, was seeking hers. She thought again of Priam, of the touch of his lips, his half-naked body; then gave herself up to her husband's needs.

*   *   *

On Sunday, January the twenty-eighth, Hugh Peters preached to the soldiers quartered in St James's Palace on a text from the prophet Isaiah.

All the Kings of the nations, even all of them, lie in glory, everyone in his own house. But thou art cast out of thy grave like an abominable branch ... Thou shalt not be joined to them in

201

burial because thou hast destroyed thy land and slain thy people . . .

It was a vicious attack upon the condemned King, and one which would be remembered in later years. Immediately afterwards, the little preacher took to his bed with a mysterious illness which, declared the King's friends, was a sure sign of God's displeasure. In fact, it was a recurrence of the fever which had plagued him from his Salem days. He explained as much in a note to Richard Pride, excusing himself from their engagement to attend the execution together. Richard therefore went alone.

The Earl of Chelwood was also present, his hat pulled well down over his eyes and a two-day growth of stubble on his chin. He was amongst those who watched the King and his escort of troops cross the frost-bitten park between St James's and Whitehall, and mount the little wooden staircase near the tilt-yard. The cluster of roofs which marked the rooms and galleries of the Cockpit were covered with a scattering of snow, and the bare branches of the trees were etched like skeletons againt the sparse, dead, winter landscape. Later, the Earl found himself in the square in front of Whitehall Palace, wedged between a farmer and his son, who told him that they had come all the way from Guildford.

"A bad business," the elder man muttered uneasily. "A very bad business, indeed."

There was a strange atmosphere amongst the crowds, which stretched as far as the eye could see. Although the usual assortment of piemen, balladmongers and pedlars moved between the people, doing their customary brisk trade, there was none of the air of carnival which commonly attended public executions. There seemed, rather, as hour after hour dragged by and still the King did not appear, to be a suspension of life, a frozen, dream-like quality which made the whole scene unreal.

The King had entered the palace at ten o' clock. At midday, the rumours began.

"This gentleman here," whispered a fat woman, standing next to the farmer, "says that young Gregory has refused to carry out the execution, on account of the King's divinity, and him being feared for his mortal soul."

The gentleman referred to turned round and nodded in the farmer's direction. "I've jutht been told," he lisped, "that volunteerth are being brought from Colonel Newthome's wegiment."

"Bloody rubbish, if you ask me," said a thin dark woman who, by the smell of her, was a Billingsgate fishwife. "I reckon they never meant to execute 'im at all. The trial an' that was just to put the fear o' God into 'im and make 'im better be'aved in the future."

"Well, I heard," declared a masked lady in a silken hood, drawing back fastidiously as the fishwife looked in her direction, "that the Dutch ambassadors have demanded the King's release. Otherwise, their government are threatening war."

Priam, who might have said so much, contributed nothing. The tension and lack of food were making him dizzy.

It was after two in the afternoon when the executioner and his assistant, both masked and wearing heavy frieze coats, stepped through a window of the banqueting hall on to the scaffold. Seconds later, they were followed by the King and Bishop Juxon, spiritual adviser and confessor during the long weeks of His Majesty's ordeal. The block had been set low and staples driven into the boards, so that the King could be tied down, should he struggle. It was a needless precaution: no one was calmer than Charles Stuart himself as he prepared to die. He spoke briefly to his people, warning them of the tyranny under which they now laboured.

"I die a Christian," he attested, "according to the profession of the Church of England, as left me by my father."

Then he put off his cloak and doublet, his insignia of the Garter and the George, and prayed a while with Bishop Juxon. At last, he lay down with his head on the block, the straggling grey hair gathered into a small white cap.

"Stay for the sign," he commanded.

The executioner cleared his throat. "I will, an' it please Your Majesty."

The unwitting irony of the reply was lost on young Gregory's listeners. Bishop Juxon's lips were moving in prayer.

A fearful silence had fallen on the crowds, and Priam felt as if he were going to faint. The King stretched out his arms. The axe rose and fell. And as the grizzled, bleeding head was held aloft, a terrible groan burst from the spectators.

As soon as the King was dead, two troops of horse dispersed the crowds. Within thirty minutes, the space in front of the banqueting hall was empty. The people who jostled past Priam as he made his way to Westminster Stairs seemed bewildered, and everywhere there was an unnatural calm. What would happen now that there were no heralds to cry: "The King is dead! Long live the King!"?

Priam pulled his shabby cloak about him, a poor protection against the icy wind. The Stairs were slippery with frost and he almost lost his footing as he clambered aboard an uncovered boat.

"Where to?" grunted the boatman, but did not look up. An air of gloom hung over everything. On the busy river, no one whistled or sang.

"Billingsgate," Priam said tersely. And God send that the Frenchman had waited for him as he had promised.

"I can wait until the thirtieth, monsieur, but I must sail then on the evening tide. But it would be safer if we sailed at once."

"I can't leave yet," Priam had replied. "Not until I

find out what has happened to my friends. I might be able to do something for them."

But the other conspirators were in the Marshalsea prison, heavily chained and guarded ...

"You saw 'im, then?" the boatman was asking. "The King, I mean."

"Yes, I saw him."

"Made a good end, I daresay. 'E always 'ad dignity, I'll give 'im that."

Priam made no reply. His head throbbed and he was weak from hunger. He itched from flea-bites acquired during the past two nights holed up in some thieves' den in Alsatia. He had not dared to return to Southwark. Gibbet Lane would most certainly be watched. With luck and a following wind, he would soon be back in France, and from there he would join Magdalen and the children at The Hague. What would happen to them all? Would he ever see Lilias again? He felt desperately tired, drained of all desires but that one.

"Dear God," he prayed, he who never prayed, who did not believe in God, "let me see her again. Just once before I die."

He could not know that at that very minute Lilias, too, was praying for the self-same thing, staring from the window of the Bear in Cheapside. The door opened, and she turned. Richard was standing in the doorway.

"Is it done?" she asked.

"Yes, it's done." Richard Pride kissed his wife. "The body will be buried at Windsor."

"Can we go home now?" Lilias whispered, and he smiled and drew her to him.

"Yes," he said gently, stroking her hair. "Now we can go home."

★   ★   ★

Patrick O'Mara read the paper aloud.

"When Satan showed Our Lord all the kingdoms of

205

the earth, he did not show Him Ireland, reserving that place for himself. And Satan hath kept it ever since for his own peculiar use ..." He broke off, roaring with laughter, and enquired: "Where in God's name did you get this thing?"

The girl in bed beside him grinned. "Is that what it says? Honest to God?" She giggled. "No wonder Father Hennessy had such a black face. He brought it back with him from Dublin. He says Cromwell's soldiers are nailing them up everywhere."

"They would be."

"Why?"

"Because they're frightened to death that King Charles the second—the Black Boy, God bless him!—will try to invade England from here."

Bridie O'Flynn rolled on to her back. "Now there's a boyo I'd like to meet. They say he's powerful good with women, lad that he is, and all. They say his mistress has just had a baby."

"Lucy Walters? Who told you that? Father Hennessy, I'll be bound. He's the biggest gossip between Antrim and Cork."

Almost absent-mindedly, Patrick began to fondle his companion's breasts, and Bridie looked at him in resentment. Her red lips pouted. "Don't you feel anything at all," she demanded, "for the women you go to bed with?"

"Not much. Why should I? I pay you well."

"Jesus, mercy! That's all you men ever think of, money!" She added curiously: "Haven't you ever been in love with anyone?"

A tide of colour crept up Patrick's neck and then receded. "That's none of your business," he answered violently. "Besides," he continued on a softer note, "you'll go blabbing it out to Father Hennessy, and before I know it, half Ireland'll be privy to my affairs. You're as bad as he is when it comes to holding your tongue."

"You have been in love, then! I thought so! A woman has ways of knowing these things." Bridie laughed delightedly, entwining her thin legs with his. "Who was she? Come on, tell! You can trust me, honest! I promise I won't say a word. Sure, an' I believe she was married." She considered him thoughtfully, head on one side, eyes as bright and enquiring as a bird's. "Holy Mother of God! I do believe ... She was, wasn't she? I do believe you're in love with one o' them black Protestants."

"It's none of your damned business," Patrick repeated again. He pulled himself free of her embrace, got out of bed and walked to the window, where he opened the wooden shutters.

The September sun slanted across his naked body, warm and heavy like fur. People were already astir in Drogheda's busy streets, driving their cattle to market, emptying the night's excrement into the central drain, and everywhere talking nineteen to the dozen. The noise and stench made Patrick swear and turn away from the window.

"You'll catch your death, stood there in all your glory!" Bridie was regarding him coquettishly from the bed, her young body inviting him to come and take her.

He smiled, good humour reasserting itself, and looked down on her from his considerable height. She wondered who he was seeing with that calm, faraway gaze. Not Bridie O'Flynn, that was certain. She stuck her tongue out, rolled off the bed and began pulling on her coarse woollen stockings.

"If you don't want me any more, then, I might as well go. I've plenty more clients among Sir Arthur's garrison. And when Old Noll and his soldiers get here, who knows? I might even corrupt a good Protestant or two."

Patrick's gaze focused on her sharply. "Don't wish that on us, even in jest. I tell you, those soldiers of Cromwell's mean business. We're Catholics, my girl, and they hate our guts."

Bridie glanced up at him, at first startled, then frightened. "I didn't mean it. Holy Mary, you don't really think—? Oh, go on with you, you old Job's comforter! Our defences are the best in Ireland. Young Tom Mortimer told me so, himself."

Patrick snorted. "Tom Mortimer! A boy still wet behind the ears, who doesn't know his cock from his elbow!" There was an urgent rapping at the door and Patrick grabbed a blanket, throwing it round him. "All right! All right! I'm coming."

His body-servant stood outside. "Sir Arthur wants to see you, Captain. You're to come at once. The rebels have been sighted, sir. They're within ten miles of the town."

Patrick nodded and slammed the door with a curse. So much for their commanding officer's vigilance! And even with this information to hand, Sir Arthur Aston seemed to be making no move to bar the city's gates. Some of those seemingly innocent country folk down there could well be Cromwell's troopers in disguise. It was a ruse which Old Noll had been known to use.

Patrick grabbed his clothes. "Off you go, and quick!" he said to Bridie, giving her a slap across the buttocks. "There's going to be trouble. Go to Father Hennessy at the church. He might want assistance with the wounded."

The rebels had been sighted, his servant had said. But who, today, were the rebels? King Charles the first of sacred memory had been executed on January the thirtieth, and it was now the beginning of September. In the intervening months, the English Republic had been accepted by most of the major powers of Europe. Horror had been expressed, and condolences showered on the dead King's family; but only the Irish, the Scots and the English Royalists had made any move on behalf of King Charles the second. The Dutch, the Spanish and even the French were all treating with Lord-General Fairfax.

Sir Arthur Aston was waiting impatiently in his quarters at the Mill Mount for the arrival of his captains. He was seated with his peg-leg stuck out uncomfortably before him: his real one he had lost fighting the Turks. All sorts of stories were current concerning this artificial limb, the favourite being that it was made of solid gold, and Sir Arthur was inclined to encourage such tales, adding as they did to his consequence. He was a man over-confident in his own capabilities; or, at least, so thought Patrick O'Mara. Others agreed with him.

"The man's an ass," Lieutenant John Mortimer, elder brother of young Tom, confided to Patrick, half an hour later as, together, they mounted the stairs to Aston's rooms. "Did you know that the stupid old sod wrote to Ormond only last week, telling his lordship not to come to our assistance?"

"Go on with you, Jack! You're pulling my leg."

"I'm not, as God's my witness! I only wish I were."

"But in Heaven's name why?"

"Said it would be an unnecessary waste of Ormond's ammunition and a criminal risking of the lives of his men. The silly bugger thinks that our defences are impregnable. But enough of that. How was the gorgeous Bridie last night? Knows a thing or two does that one. Surprised even me, and I've been around, as I don't really need to tell you."

Patrick returned some joking answer; but it was not of Bridie O'Flynn that he was thinking as he listened with half an ear to the monotonous tones of Sir Arthur Aston. He was picturing Magdalen: the set of her delicate head; the endearing trick she had of smiling with her eyes, even when her mouth was serious. She was constantly in his thoughts. No other woman had ever compared with her or captured his imagination so completely. He had heard that she was in Holland and her husband with her. He hoped savagely that the Earl was caring for her as she deserved. He had never regretted his interference in

Priam's affairs. A woman like Magdalen ought never to be betrayed for a gypsy such as Lilias Colefax . . .

Lieutenant John Mortimer kicked him on the ankle. With a reluctant sigh, Patrick redirected his wandering thoughts and tried to concentrate on Sir Arthur Aston's mouthings.

★   ★   ★

Magdalen, Countess of Chelwood, crouched nearer to the fire. The little room was cold. Bitter winds, blowing from the east, rattled and tore at the shutters. Draughts like knives cut under the doors. The Hague was in the grip of winter.

The house which Magdalen and her family had lived in for the past few years was between the Binnenhof Palace and the old Spanish prison, a neat Dutch house with pointed gables. They lived, as countless other English exiles lived, on the charity of the good Dutch citizens. It was fortunate that the Princess Mary, eldest of the murdered King Charles' daughters, was married to the Staatdholder, William. The Dutch had been horrified by the King's execution, but had still come to terms with the new English government.

"Vat are ve do to?" Mevrouw Bogardus had demanded of her tenants, the broad face above the spotlessly clean white collar indicative of dismay. "Ve need to trade vith your country."

The wind took hold of the shutters and shook them violently, and Magdalen went over to make sure that they were fastened. She stared out briefly at the dull, flat landscape before blotting it out, tears in her eyes. Homesickness overcame her, homesickness for wooded hills, soft blue distances and sunlight playing on water. She longed to see again the crumpled fronds of pale new bracken and trees purple with rain; to smell the scent of honeysuckle and hear the early-morning birdsong in the woods. She pined for Westovers and the rolling, rain-

210

smudged hills of Bath . . .

The door opened and Priam came in. She went to him with a glad little cry, her one sure rock in a world which suddenly seemed to be built on sand.

"You're cold. Come and sit by the fire. I've warmed some ale for you."

"Ale?" The Earl could barely smile, he felt so tired and dispirited. "How did we manage to afford such luxury?" A thought struck him. "You and the girls haven't been going without proper food?"

"No such thing. Cressida earned it for you. She has been running errands for Mevrouw Bogardus."

"Which the Mevrouw has lain awake at nights thinking up, I've no doubt. 'Oh, I have forgot ze bread. How careless I am! Perhaps ze leetle von vill go and I vill pay her half a guelder.'"

Magdalen laughed, pouring the ale into a cup from a cracked blue jug on the hearth. "Half a guelder! Nothing so extravagant, I can assure you. The Mevrouw, like all good Dutch women, is thrifty." She handed him the cup and noted with satisfaction a little colour creeping back into his thin pale face. He had never been really well since his return from England last February after that abortive plot to rescue the King. He had shut himself away for days on hearing of his fellow conspirators' executions. How he himself had escaped, he would never say. Magdalen sensed some mystery there. She pulled off one of his wet shoes, noting with a despairing sigh that there was a hole in the sole of the left one. They had no money to buy a new pair. "What did Sir Edward Hyde want?" she asked, after a moment's silence.

"To tell me that all hope of an invasion from Ireland is at an end. Cromwell and Ireton have been everywhere victorious. Resistance has been ruthlessly crushed. Drogheda was sacked under circumstances of the most gruesome barbarity."

"Drogheda?" Magdalen caught her breath. "Surely

211

... that Irishman, Patrick O'Mara, was there? With Aston's garrison? At least, he was when he wrote to us last. Priam, do you think—?"

"I daren't think," he answered shuddering. "If he was there at the time of the siege, it will be a miracle if he's still alive."

The Earl could not repeat to her the terrible tales told to him by Edward Hyde.

"I love my country," the Chancellor had said to Priam, tears furrowing his flabby cheeks, "but this has made me ashamed to be an Englishman. It was one of the most bestial crimes in the annals of our nation. A blot on England's fair name."

Aston, it appeared, had run short of ammunition, and the "impregnable" defences had been breached within hours by Cromwell, at the head of his men. Most of the garrison had been slaughtered, including Aston, whose peg-leg had been torn from his mangled body and hotly disputed over by two of Cromwell's troopers—but had turned out to be made of wood after all. After that, neither man, woman nor child had been spared.

From Drogheda, Cromwell had marched south to Kilkenny and Wexford, whose inhabitants now had little stomach for a fight. And every Catholic priest found by the triumphant English had been battered to death in the name of religion.

"How can anyone talk about a God of love," Priam burst out, "when He allows such atrocities to be perpetrated in His name?"

"Hush! Hush!" Magdalen cried, startled and distressed by his outburst. His lack of faith had always troubled her, but she had not realised till now that it had gone so deep. To her, who believed implicitly in eternal damnation, who prayed every night of her life to some bearded patriarch who resembled her long-dead grandfather, her husband's denial of the Christian faith was frightening. Yet the need to protect him was paramount. She would

212

gladly go in his place if she could to whatever smoking Hell awaited unbelievers after death.

She sat on the floor, one cheek pressed against his leg, her hands clasped protectingly about his knee. The Earl looked down at her, his anger evaporating. He put out his hand and touched the fair, shining head ... A dark-haired ghost brushed momentarily between them, but Lilias Pride was not for him: his happiness must lie here, with Magdalen. After a while, he put his arm about her shoulders. And so, listening to the rising wind, they stayed.

CHAPTER THIRTEEN

Little Oliver Pride was three years old and his face was set in the same mulish lines that his father's assumed when he made up his mind to something. But there all points of resemblance ended. Oliver was a thin child with a white slip of a face beneath a thatch of dark hair. His eyes, a bright blue, were never still, darting from one point of interest to another. His sharp little nose quivered constantly in anticipation of every new event. He was impervious, declared his mother, to any concept of right or wrong.

"He's young, the precious lamb. He'll change," Regina protested each time the child received a whipping.

But Oliver showed no signs of repentance, nor of changing, either. To Lilias' oft repeated cry of: "Oliver! Why did you do it?" the inevitable reply was: "Because I wanted to."

Geoffrey, a year younger and his brother's persistent shadow, was of a very much sweeter disposition. "My little angel," Regina called him; and although Lilias scoffed, she had to admit that there was something very vulnerable about this youngest of her children.

But of Richard Pride's three sons, the one most like him was Eliot, a stolid, unexciting boy who, in this May of 1650, would shortly be celebrating his eighth birthday. He had his father's thickset body and the dogged look of Hannah in his eyes. Judith Colefax still adored him. They stood together now, much of an age and height, their air of solid rectitude inflaming young Oliver still further.

"I want to go," he declared mutinously. "I want to go. Oliver wants to go out to supper."

214

"Oliver wants a thrashing," Lilias retorted, dangerously calm. "Little boys of your age, Oliver, do not go out to supper. Now, be good. Geoffrey's not making all this fuss."

Geoffrey blinked at this mention of his name, as though suddenly recalled from some secret world of his own, and embraced his mother effusively about her knees. His brother regarded him with undisguised contempt, then opened his mouth and screamed.

Richard came in, buttoning his coat. It was of dark green cloth with silver buttons, and Lilias thought that he looked particularly fine. He took in the situation at a glance, set his recalcitrant son across his knee, pulled up the night-shirt and gave Oliver a vigorous spanking. Then he set him down, howling, on his feet.

"And if you don't do as your aunt Regina says and go to bed this minute, you will get the biggest whipping of your life," his father told him.

But Richard's bark, as his family well knew, was very much worse than his bite. In an age of autocratic parents, he was a very indulgent father. Too indulgent, Lilias sometimes thought: Oliver needed a much firmer hand.

"Eliot, be a good boy and help your grandmother put the little ones to bed," she said, bending to kiss her stepson. "And Judith, don't forget to say your prayers."

"No, mother." Judith obediently put up her face to be kissed in her turn. It did not bother her that Lilias was going out. She had Eliot, and that was all that mattered.

"They're tired, bless them," Regina said. "Going to see the ships come in has worn them out. It was a very exciting morning."

"I saw the ships! I saw the ships!" Oliver chanted, recovering mercurially from his spanking and beginning to jig up and down.

"I saw Captain-General Cromwell," Eliot reproved him, "and that was much more exciting."

On that hot May day, the Captain-General of Ireland

had landed in Bristol, his triumphant Irish campaign behind him. The threat of a Royalist invasion from that troublesome island had been eliminated once and for all.

"Will you really see Cromwell tonight?" Eliot wanted to know. His father's friend had become a hero in his eyes, to be spoken of with bated breath.

"I shall be as close to him tonight as I am to you now," Lilias promised her step-son. "Well, almost as close. Mrs Jackson will be in the place of honour because she's the hostess and also the Mayor's wife."

"Not if Myles Jackson can help it," Regina chuckled drily. "He'll quite likely tuck her and those plain daughters of his away in some dusty corner. I've always thought that he had a penchant for you, Lilias my dear. You're certainly a great deal more decorative."

"Mother-in-law!" Richard spoke sharply, frowning Regina down, and she grimaced in comic dismay at Lilias.

Lilias laughed and kissed her husband's cheek. "Don't be such a prude, Richard my love. You should be proud that other men still admire me."

"Still?" He looked at her with love as he returned her embrace. "You talk as though you're as old as Methuselah. Now, we really must be going, or we shall be late. And you know how Oliver hates unpunctuality."

Mayor Jackson lived in the corner house between the Shambles and High Street, within the shelter of St Nicholas' Gate. The house and prosperous greengrocer's next door, belonged to Denzil Hollister.

Mrs Jackson and her daughters had slaved all day to make the house worthy of the most important of their visitors. Candles blazed everywhere like votive lights and dripped their scented wax on the polished floors. The furniture had been rubbed until it shone and the curtains taken down and shaken. Bowls of flowers had been placed at strategic intervals to drown the smell of the kitchens.

216

Mrs Jackson presided nervously over the laden table, her pale eyes darting between guests and servants, plainly apprehensive that something might go wrong, and eager to impress the guest-of-honour.

The Captain-General of Ireland was seated on her right, and on his other side sat Lilias Pride. This had been at the Mayor's insistence, and not without a great deal of opposition from his ladies.

"She will shock him," Carrie Jackson had roundly declared, with all the bitterness of the plain woman for her more beautiful sister.

"Pooh!" Myles Jackson had waved this objection to one side. "General Cromwell's not such a Puritan as you think him."

"Obviously not," Mrs Jackson had sniffed, finding herself most unexpectedly in agreement with her husband. "Not if that daughter of his, Elizabeth, is anything to go by."

All the same, she was glad to note that Lilias had abandoned her usual ringlets in favour of a more sober hair-style. Her gown, too, although clearly London made, was a plain dark blue, its only decoration bands of cream linen edging the wrists and throat. Yet, in spite of it all, Lilias still managed to look like some exotic bird which had strayed into a nest of starlings. It really was, Mrs Jackson thought, most provoking. She hoped that the Captain-General would not notice.

Oliver Cromwell, however, was enjoying himself. Good food, good wine and the company of a beautiful woman, he was averse to none of these things. He talked to Lilias of her children, and being himself a family man, found her quick-witted, intelligent and charming. His great boisterous laugh frequently rang out, belying his terrible reputation.

Yet the other side of his character was also true: the midnight wrestlings for the salvation of his soul and his fear of eternal damnation. Before the outbreak of war, he had sometimes feared for his reason, but action had proved to be the antidote for many of his ills: it was the drug which his restless soul craved.

This evening, however, he was in expansive mood, more than ready to listen to the request put to him by some of Bristol's leading merchants once the ladies had withdrawn upstairs.

Robert Cann leaned forward, hands clasped in front of him on the table, glancing at his friends for support. Robert Yate and Thomas Speed nodded encouragement.

"You have something you wish to say, gentlemen?" asked the Captain-General, noting these preliminaries with a certain grim amusement.

"General Cromwell," Robert Cann began, "my friends and I have a proposition which we would like to put to the Government, and we are hoping for your support. We want to buy the concession for your remaining Irish prisoners."

"With what object, gentlemen?" The heavy eyebrows were raised and the wart seemed to quiver on Cromwell's chin.

"The colonies, particularly the West Indies and Virginia, are extremely short of labour. Men are urgently needed to work on the plantations. Every owner who returns has the same sorry tale to tell: crops rotting in the fields for the want of a few hundred men."

"So?" Cromwell leaned back in his chair, hands folded across his stomach. "But surely, gentlemen, we have not emptied our gaols?"

Thomas Speed decided that it was time to lay their cards on the table. "General Cromwell," he said, "this war has cost us dear. It has taken a sad toll of our businesses and trade will take time to recover."

Mayor Jackson put in, in support of his friends: "We had to pay very heavy compensation to the King for giving our backing to Parliament."

Cromwell smiled. "I see. You mean that there is no

218

money to be made in the deportation of criminals?"

"Yes ... No! That is ... No!" Robert Cann avoided the General's eyes. It was possible to make a profit out of the sale of common felons, but the less said about that illegal practice the better. "But if we were allowed the concession for your Irish prisoners, then we could ... well ... we could ..."

"Make a nice little profit and do the whole thing legally!" Cromwell laughed and turned to Richard. "Are you in this consortium, my friend?"

"No. I am against trafficking in human flesh, as these gentlemen well know," Richard answered with acerbity.

"Phaw!" Robert Yate had flushed uncomfortably. "That's a great deal too nice. Slavery has been accepted practice since the days of ancient Rome."

Richard shrugged. "That's true," he agreed. "Nevertheless, I feel in my bones that it is wrong."

Cromwell held up his hand to silence the others' outraged protest. "In certain circumstances," he said, "I would agree with you, my friend, but we are talking now of the Catholic Irish. Those who listen to the teachings of the Catholic Church are *deceitful above all things and desperately wicked.* These people have, in the past, tried to lead us into the bondage of Rome, and will do so again if they are not stamped out. They have flouted the teachings of the Lord of Hosts. They bring His wrath upon themselves." For a moment, Cromwell's face was transformed by zeal, lit like a lamp from within. The heavy folds of flesh seemed to lift and melt as he felt the power of the Word surge through him. This was his true destiny: the destruction of evil in the form of the Catholic Church. "Very well," he went on, "you shall have your concession, gentlemen. And so shall the wicked perish."

While his two friends expressed their heartfelt thanks, Alderman Cann said nothing. Cromwell, eyeing him narrowly, enquired: "Is there something further, Mr Cann, that you wish to ask me?"

"It's just this, General. I don't know what conditions are like in the Irish prisons, but I can make a good guess. Oh, please don't misunderstand me. The heathen should not be housed in comfort. I'm not the man to advocate that. But some of the colonists are just a shade pernickety about getting value for their money. Our Virginian friends in particular aren't going to buy any rubbish."

Cromwell nodded. "I understand their point of view. So what, Mr Cann, are you proposing?"

"Well ... I don't know about Yates and Speed here, but I'd like to see a sample of what I'm buying. Now, I can't waste valuable time on the trot to Ireland and back. There's things I have to see to here. So, if it could be arranged, I'd like a batch of prisoners sent over to look at, say, from Waterford gaol."

Robert Yates and Thomas Speed murmured their approval, while Cromwell thoughtfully chewed his lip. Finally, he said: "I don't see why not, gentlemen. If Parliament agrees to give you the concession—and I can't see any reason why they won't—then I'll write an order personally to the Governor of Waterford gaol and have a batch of prisoners sent to Bristol expressly for your approval."

The three men were immediately wreathed in smiles, grunting their pleasure and gratitude. Mayor Jackson raised his glass.

"To the Captain-General of Ireland, gentlemen! To his victories at Drogheda, Wexford and Kilkenny."

They all drank enthusiastically and Cromwell raised his glass in return.

"To commerce, gentlemen, the lifeblood of this country! To Bristol and its continuing prosperity."

★   ★   ★

"Are you sure that you won't come with us?" pleaded Regina.

Lilias shook her head. "You know how I hate fairs,

220

Regina dear. And the Bridgwater Michaelmas Fair is always so extremely noisy. And my head hasn't recovered yet from the ringing of those bells. I'm sure they've been ringing for ever."

"But, my dear, Dunbar was such a very great victory for General Cromwell . . . Are you really certain that you won't come with us?"

"Don't press her, mother-in-law," Richard said, coming into the room, dressed ready for travelling. "All the same, my love, I wish you'd let Mollie remain here with you."

"What a fuss," laughed Lilias, "for a two-night absence. I've stayed alone in this house for a lot longer than that. And I'm surrounded by friends. You'll need Mollie to help look after the children."

"There are two of us without her."

"And there are four of them. It will be a full-time job for just one of you, keeping an eye on Oliver."

At the mention of his son, Richard's face darkened, but Lilias noted that there was a glint of pride in his eyes nonetheless. "That boy ought to be whipped every day of his life. It's the only way we'll ever control him."

"Yes, I can just see you doing it." Lilias kissed her husband's cheek affectionately. "You really should be starting, if you hope to reach Axbridge before dusk."

There was a scuffle in the passageway, and Mollie Hanks shrieked: "Oh, drat the little varmint!"

Oliver careered into the parlour, making straight for the sleeping cat. He tweaked its tail, screamed delightedly as it awoke spitting, tugged its ears and leapt out of the way of its slashing claws.

"Oliver!" shouted his father sternly, while Lilias and Regina looked helplessly at one another.

"What are we going to do with him?" his mother asked.

"Perhaps the journey will tire him out," suggested Regina hopefully, tying the strings of her hood firmly

221

beneath her chin. She began shepherding the other children towards the door.

"Oliver," said Richard, "you'll ride pillion with me. Then I shall know where you are and what you are doing."

They all proceeded into the street. As Lilias shut the door of the travelling-waggon on Regina, Mollie Hanks and the other three children, the alarm bell sounded from the castle.

"What on earth—?" began Richard, a worried frown creasing his brows. He hailed Matthew Hazard, who was coming towards them down the street. "Reverend! Do you know what's happened?"

The Reverend Hazard pulled off his hat and came to stand beside the carriage.

"One of the Irish prisoners that they brought in this morning has escaped, that's all. He won't get far. All the gates are being watched. The soldiers will soon have him back under lock and key."

"Oh Heavens!" exclaimed Regina, and Richard looked thoughtfully towards his wife.

"No," said Lilias firmly, reading his thoughts. "You can't possibly disappoint the children now. They've been looking forward to this for months. They've talked of practically nothing else all summer. Don't worry! I shall bar and lock all the windows and doors. And as the Reverend Hazard says, the man won't be at liberty for long."

"Oh, missus!" Mollie wriggled forward anxiously in her seat. "The kitchen door to the garden's open. I forgot to lock it."

"I'll do it at once, the very moment I go in," Lilias promised. "Now, really, you must set forward. You don't want to be travelling in the dark and your rooms are bespoken at the inn. Have a good time at the fair, and bring me home something nice."

As Richard still hesitated, Matthew Hazard smiled

222

reassuringly. "Rest easy, Mr Pride. We shall see that no harm befalls her."

Richard nodded, still vaguely uneasy, but forced against his will to be satisfied. Lilias was right: the children were too excited to bear disappointment calmly. So he kissed his wife once again and gave his horse the office to start. The travelling-waggon rumbled ponderously up Broad Street in his wake, the children leaning out and waving furiously through the window.

"Do you wish me to come in with you, Mistress Pride?" Matthew Hazard asked, as the little cavalcade disappeared in the direction of the Redcliffe Gate.

"No, thank you, reverend. I shall be quite all right. It's broad daylight, and it is possible that the prisoner has been retaken by now. At least, I hope so, if only for the sake of Alderman Cann's probable apoplexy."

"Indeed! He won't take kindly to the loss of thirty guineas' worth of Irishman!"

They both laughed, and Matthew Hazard went off up the street again, letting himself in at his own front door. Lilias went through to the kitchen.

It surprised her a little to find that Mollie had not only left the door unlocked, but wide open as well. The scent of late roses drifted in from the garden and the warm September sunlight paved the kitchen floor. Lilias stood for a moment, staring out at the grass and the bronzing trees and the rosy-red roofs of the houses in Tower Lane glowing above the old grey wall. Then she stepped back inside and closed the door . . .

The first thing she was aware of was the point of a wicked-looking knife—her own carving knife—levelled at her breast; the second was the black-bearded scarecrow who was holding it. They both stood, frozen into immobility like the courtiers of Polydectes looking upon the Medusa's head. Then the black beard split, revealing some excellent teeth, as the scarecrow gave a mirthless grin.

"Well, well, well! Lilias Colefax, by all that's holy!"
The man moved swiftly, gripping her mercilessly by one wrist. "One shout, one false move out o' you, me darlin', and you're as good as dead."

The suffocating beat of her heart subsided a little as Lilias managed to gasp: "Captain O'Mara? What—what are you doing here, like this?"

The grip on her wrist tightened and the grin became more wolfish. "Oh, I'm one of Cromwell's prisoners of war. One being sold into slavery on the American plantations by your fat Bristol merchants. Or hadn't you heard? But I'm sure you had. And probably approve. What does it matter, after all, what happens to one or two Catholics?"

"You won't get away with it," Lilias said, breathing more easily as familiarity began to make her feel safe. "You'd far better let me call the soldiers and give yourself up now. Then they might take a more lenient view." She tried an experimental step towards the door.

An arm came around her, clamping her body against Patrick's with such force that she cried out in pain. The point of the blade was pricking at her throat.

"Don't make any mistake, Mrs Colefax," Patrick O'Mara hissed in her ear. "I'll kill you as soon as look at you if you don't do what I say. I'm not the man I used to be. I've been a prisoner in an English gaol. I was at the sack of Drogheda. I've seen sights and heard sounds that I'll never forget until my dying day. I've seen women with their breasts cut off, babies spitted like chickens, human heads used as footballs." She whimpered and he laughed. "That, me darlin', is nothing! Just a few of the lesser horrors I could tell you. And all done to shouts of 'Alleluia!' and 'Hosanna!' and 'Praise the Lord!' So, you see, I'm in no mood to treat an Englishwoman very gently." He released her and she fell against the table, rubbing her bruised and smarting wrist. "Right. Now we understand each other. Who else is in the house?"

224

"No one," Lilias said, betrayed by panic into telling the truth. "I'm alone, I swear it. Mrs Stillgo and my husband and children have gone to Bridgwater Fair."

"Your husband?"

"Richard Pride."

"So he married you, did he?" The Irishman laughed softly. "I'm not surprised. I used to watch him stripping you with his eyes. The canting, hypocritical Puritan!"

"He is none of those things," Lilias retorted, stung into sudden anger. "Richard Pride is a very good man."

"I'll take your word for it. As far as I'm concerned, he's an inhabitant of this accursed city, and that's enough for me. Well, well! It seems my luck is in. An empty house—or almost empty. Except for one woman, who is going to do just as I say." Lilias glanced at him sharply, and again he laughed. "First things first, my dear. I'm starving. You'll get me something to eat."

There was a thunderous knocking on the street door, and a voice shouted: "Mrs Pride! It's Colonel Scroop. Will you open up, please? There's something urgent I have to tell you."

Lilias jumped, and Patrick was immediately by her side. "Answer the door," he said, "and remember, I shall be right behind you. At the first wrong word, this knife goes straight between your ribs."

Lilias had no doubt by now that he meant it. Taking a firm grip on her bolting senses, she preceded him along the passage to the door and opened it just wide enough to see Colonel Scroop. Beyond him, in the sun-dappled street, was a *posse* of his soldiers.

"Mrs Pride, there's a prisoner escaped from the castle. One of the Irish prisoners who were brought ashore from Waterford this morning. One of my men thinks he might have come this way, because there was a sighting in Tower Lane. You haven't seen anything of him?"

"No, but I'll lock all the doors. My husband and Mistress Stillgo are away. They've taken Mollie and the children with them."

"Alone, are you? Will you be all right? Would you like one of my men to stay with you until the prisoner is found?"

"No! No, thank you, colonel," Lilias stammered hastily. "I—I'm not feeling too well. I shall probably go to bed early."

Colonel Scroop nodded abruptly and turned to issue further orders to his men. Lilias closed the door and was engulfed once more by the gloom and creeping shadows of the passage. Patrick O'Mara motioned her with his knife back in the direction of the kitchen.

*　　*　　*

He wiped the bread around his plate to mop up the last of the gravy, then sat back with a sigh of repletion.

"You can cook, Mrs Pride, I'll give you that. And now, me darlin', I'll tell you what I want you to do." Lilias noticed that Patrick O'Mara's Irish brogue was thicker than she remembered it, as though by discarding the English accent which education and upbringing had imposed upon him he could identify more closely with his oppressed and persecuted race. "I want you to bring that bath in front of the fire and fill it up with water. Thanks to the hospitality of the English Republic's prisons, I'm a walking mass of corruption, as no doubt your pretty nose has noticed."

Lilias licked her lips. "I'll have to go to the well in the garden for water."

"No you won't, me darlin'. There's a water-barrel there in the corner. I can see it with me own eyes, so don't play off any of those tricks on me. Heat some of that and fill the tub ankle-deep. I shan't be sitting down. I'm sure a twice married lady such as yourself won't find it too embarrassing. You've seen a naked man before."

By the time Lilias had done as he bid, it was growing dusk. She closed the shutters and lit the candles. Then

226

Patrick laid his knife on the table.

"Sit there," he commanded, "where I can see you. Between the bath and the kitchen fire. That's right. And don't try anything foolish, or I'll have this knife into you before you can reach the door."

He undressed by the simple expedient of ripping apart the rotten and filthy rags that he was wearing and dropping them where he stood. As he stepped into the tub and Lilias handed him the soap, she saw that his emaciated body was covered with flea-bites and sores.

"Not a pretty sight for a lady's eyes," he remarked grimly, "but I'm one of the better preserved ones, or else I shouldn't be here. You ought to see some of the sights I've left behind in Waterford gaol." He stooped and began splashing himself with water.

Lilias sat down, her fear again beginning to recede. "How do you intend getting clear of the city?" she enquired.

"We'll talk about that in the morning." He saw her startled glance and smiled. "Did you think I was going tonight? Oh no, my dear. I haven't slept in a bed for over a year. That's a pleasure I'm not denying meself. As to how I get out, you might help me there. You made a fool of me once. You smuggled your husband out of Bristol right under my nose, and earned poor Trooper Trenchard a flogging."

"The fortunes of war, Captain," she said, in a voice which somehow did not seem to be her own. She was not really conscious of what she was saying.

"As far as I'm concerned, Mrs Pride, I'm still at war. I'd cut any Englishman's throat for twopence."

"That's foolish." She eased her weight forward from the back of the chair and advanced one foot before the other. "There are good and bad in every nation. You can't condemn a whole race."

"Can I not?" He stooped to retrieve the soap, and Lilias propelled herself forward and up, making a dash for the door.

There was a flurry of water, a rainbow spray of drops, sparkling like diamonds in the light, and she was violently forced back against the wall. The Irishman's body was slippery with soap, but his strength was still too much for her. With one wet hand, he roughly jerked up her chin.

Lilias screamed and the sound enraged him. It brought back a memory of Bridie O'Flynn as he had last seen her, lying in her own blood, her throat cut from ear to ear, and one of Cromwell's soldiers still raping her. He recalled the mutilated body of young Tom Mortimer, both legs lopped off at the knees. And, just before someone had hit him that swingeing blow to the back of his head, he had heard the hair-raising screams of old Father Hennessy as he was battered to death by the troopers. And here before him was this woman whom he hated, a woman who had twice made him look a fool and whose very existence posed a threat to Magdalen, whom he loved.

Lilias divined his intention before he was aware of it himself: Patrick recognised only the urge to hurt and wound, and the blood-red desire for revenge. She had a brief, vivid recollection of that night with Barnaby; after that, there was nothing but the violent onslaught against her shrinking flesh. She lay on the ground, conscious only of his breathing and the savagely thrusting movements of his body . . .

Lilias moved, easing her bruised and aching bones. She must, she thought, have lost consciousness for a moment or two, for Patrick O'Mara was standing by the table, his head averted, the light slithering across his still-wet skin. Slowly she dragged herself on to her elbows and experienced again that sense of degradation which any sort of violence brought in its train.

Patrick turned his head and looked at her for a moment or two without speaking. Then he said in the

228

voice she remembered, the Irish brogue nothing more now than a faint echo: "If you want me to say that I'm ashamed of myself, I am. I'd also say I'm sorry, but it wouldn't do any good." He took a cup and crossed to the water-barrel in the corner. After a moment, he returned and knelt beside her, lifting her with one arm, his other hand holding the water to her lips. She gulped it greedily and felt a little better. Still with his support, she got up and sat down in her abandoned chair. He went on: "I've no excuse, except that war—bestiality—brutalises others in its turn."

Lilias raised her head at that, and, for the first time, looked him full in the eyes. "Yes," she said at last, "I do, in part, understand." And the odd thing was that she did. In that moment, her terror and self-pity seemed to drain away, and she realised something of what he had suffered during the past terrible year. "Where will you go?" she asked.

"If I escape, do you mean? Back to Ireland if I can. I've cousins in County West Meath who'll shelter me . . . The Saints know why I'm telling you this. You have every cause to betray me."

She did not trouble to deny it. She knew, and he knew, that she would not do so now. Some subtle change had taken place during the last few minutes. The victim-victor relationship, interchangeable between them, had vanished. In its place was a grudging comprehension that everyone was, in some part, a casualty of war. Evil begot evil, feeding from within.

After a while, Lilias stirred, and Patrick said abruptly: "I must be going." He glanced down at his naked body and grimaced wryly. "But hardly like this. Do you have anything of your husband's that I can . . . borrow?"

"There might be something." Strange, she thought, how they both tacitly accepted now that she would help him. "No, wait! There's an old suit of Barnaby's—waistcoat, jacket, breeches—that no one will ever miss.

229

And he was more your height and weight. I'll fetch it."

She went upstairs, washed and changed her dress, then did her hair. In the distance, she could hear the plaintive voice of the night watchman. Her mind still felt numb. When she returned to the kitchen, Patrick O'Mara was sitting by the fire, the linen towel thrown round him like a Roman toga. Silently she held out Barnaby's old clothes.

As he began to dress, she said: "I thought you were staying here the night? You can do so, if you wish."

He glanced at her oddly. "You wouldn't be afraid?"

She smiled, and he was suddenly aware that she had a sense of humour, something he had not credited her with before.

"What of?" she asked. "I have already lost my honour. There's only death."

Perhaps there was something to be said for the Earl's infatuation, after all. She certainly was a remarkable woman.

"I never intended staying," he said in reply to her question. "I only said that to frighten you. Darkness is my best—my only—friend."

"You can't escape, you know. Every known exit from the city will be guarded. Scroop will have his patrols along every inch of the walls. His pride is at stake. He won't be worsted by a Catholic Irishman."

"Perhaps you're right," Patrick answered grimly. "But at least I must try, having got this far." He smiled at her ironically. "Aren't you going to wish me luck?"

Lilias said vehemently: "I wish you God-speed—if only to worst Alderman Cann and his friends and this infamous trade."

"Well, well." He walked over to her and again lifted her chin, but this time gently. "I never thought to hear such a thing from the lips of an Englishwoman."

"I'm Cornish," she said fiercely. "A Celt, like yourself. But there are many English people, many Bristolians even, who hate this infamous trade and would prevent it if they could. As I told you, you can't condemn a whole race because of the evil of a few."

"No." On a sudden impulse, he bent his head and kissed her mouth. The next moment he was gone, the click of the door-latch sounding loudly in the stillness.

The following day, Lilias heard from the Reverend Hazard that the prisoner had been recaptured.

CHAPTER FOURTEEN

"For God's sake, sire, you must fly!"

The Duke of Buckingham, Lord Wilmot and half-a-dozen others crowded round the King, catching at the big grey's bridle. All around them the town of Worcester was acrid with smoke as Cromwell continued his bombardment. The Earl of Derby appeared, his left cheek bleeding from a sabre cut. From head to foot, he was covered in dust.

"Dalyell's brigade has surrendered," he gasped. "And Fleetwood has forced the Teme at Powick Bridge."

The young King's voice was husky with despair as he stared into the faces of his friends.

"The Scots! For Heaven's sake, gentlemen! There must be some way of making them fight."

"Sire, they won't budge. General Leslie himself cannot make them move."

"Traitors! The damn traitors!" Buckingham exclaimed, tears of frustration and rage coursing down his cheeks.

They were joined at that moment by the Earl of Lauderdale, his horse's hooves slithering dangerously on the blood-soaked cobbles. "Your Majesty," he panted, "the rebels are in the town. For Sweet Christ's sake," he added, addressing the other men, "get His Majesty out of this."

"I'll not go back to Scotland," the King said mutinously, snatching his bridle from their importunate hands.

"Sire, we can decide that later," his friends urged despairingly. "For the moment, we must get you clear of the town."

"The St Martin's Gate," insisted Major Carliss. "Hamilton's holding the rebels around Castle Hill, and Rothes and his men have blocked Friar's Street."

Half an hour later, the King and his party were clear of the screaming hell of Worcester and galloping along the Wolverhampton road. Dusk had fallen, bringing to a close that terrible September day, turning the trees to a rusty black, a small breeze tossing them against the skyline. September the third, 1651; a year to the day since Cromwell's previous great victory at Dunbar. The twenty-one-year-old Charles Stuart thought that it would be for ever etched on his memory.

"When I die," he said, with a shaky laugh to his friend, the Duke of Buckingham, "they'll find 'Worcester' engraved on my heart, as 'Calais' was said to be engraved on Queen Mary's."

"We should have stood a chance," cried Buckingham, "if only the Scots had supported us. In God's name, why wouldn't they fight?"

"Too late to ask that now," grunted Derby, as the little cavalcade came to a halt in the shelter of a copse.

"I'll not go back to Scotland," the King repeated with a finality which told his listeners that he meant it. "I'll not go back to be humiliated and preached at twenty-four hours a day by those damned Covenanters, as I have been for the past year and a half." Again he gave a laugh that cracked in the middle. "Do you know that Argyll even made me do penance for my mother's and father's sins?"

"But if you don't go back to Scotland, sire," asked Derby, "where will you go? Without the Scots, you won't stand another chance of invading England."

"I haven't stood a chance with them," the young King snapped. Then his sweet smile flashed out. "I'm sorry, my lord. I'm tired and very hungry."

"Good God, what are we thinking of?" expostulated Lord Wilmot. "His Majesty must be got to shelter, and soon."

"But where, sire, do you intend making for?" persisted the Earl of Derby.

"France," said Charles firmly. "Somewhere I must be

233

able to find a ship whose master is willing to carry me to France."

"But, sire, think!" Buckingham was horrified. "That means disguise. It means entrusting your sacred person to all sorts and conditions of common men."

A chuckle escaped the King. "I'll be safer with common men, George, than I'll be with any of you. No, no, my lords! I'm serious! We must all disperse. We must all find our own way home. Home!" he repeated brokenly, and turned his head away.

"But where tonight, sire?" Wilmot asked. "First things must be thought of first."

Derby jostled his mount a little nearer. "There is a house I know of, near Tong in Shropshire, belonging to a very loyal family, the Giffards. If we ride all night, we can cover the forty-odd miles before daybreak. Once there, we can decide what to do."

There was silence, each man sunk in his own dark thoughts. Then the King roused himself and nodded briskly. "Lead us to this house of yours, my lord. The rest of us will follow."

*   *   *

"I'm going to see the ships come in! I'm going to see the ships come in!" Oliver danced around the room in excitement, feet twinkling across the stone-flagged floor. His half-sister, Judith, caught him by the arm.

"This is a solemn occasion, Oliver. A funeral procession." She turned to her stepfather, who sat by the fire, his feet in a steaming mustard-bath, his shoulders draped by a blanket. Richard was in the final stages of a very bad cold. "Papa! Please speak to Oliver or he'll disgrace me and mama and the boys."

Richard grabbed his errant son in mid-flight, drawing the child to his knee. Oliver sobered immediately. He was a little in awe of his father, the one person in the world for whom he had any respect.

234

"Oliver, you will behave yourself this morning. Any adverse reports from your mother and you know what you can expect."

"Yes, papa," Oliver answered demurely. "But why do I have to be quiet?"

"Because, as Judith told you, this is a solemn occasion. General Ireton is dead. He died in Ireland—"

"Fighting the wicked Papists?" Oliver's eyes lit with anticipation. He loved stories of violence and sudden death.

Richard hesitated. Henry Ireton had, in fact, died of pneumonia, but his death had indirectly been brought about by zeal in the course of his duties. Cromwell's favourite son-in-law had neglected his health, and his illness had been the fatal result.

"Yes, fighting the wicked Papists, as it is the Christian duty of everyone of us to do. His body is to be buried in Westminster Abbey ... Do you know where that is?"

"London, papa."

"And who founded it?"

"Edward the Confessor, papa," Oliver murmured, playing with one of the buttons on his father's coat as his attention began to wander. It was one of the ironies of life, Richard reflected with a sigh, that learning came so easily to Oliver—he soaked up facts like a sponge mopping up water—but meant less than nothing to him. Oliver would never love knowledge for its own sake, only if he could shape it to his ends.

"Yes, very well. And today, General Ireton's body is being brought ashore, here, at Bristol, after being carried across the sea from Ireland. And from here, it will begin its journey to London. Now do you understand why it is such a solemn occasion? Why we can't have little boys dancing and singing and shouting? Do you?"

"Yes, father."

"And you will be good, and not cause your mother any trouble?"

"Aren't you coming?"

"No. I'm not feeling well enough yet."

Lilias came in, drawing on her gloves, Mollie Hanks, with Eliot and little Geoffrey, behind her.

"Regina will be staying with you to see that you take your medicine," she said, dropping a kiss on the top of her husband's head. She eyed her elder son with misgivings. "I only hope that Oliver is going to behave."

"Yes, I promise," said Oliver, and Lilias breathed a little easier. "My sacred promise—if you'll take me shopping in the market afterwards."

Richard raised eyes and fists to Heaven.

"Oliver," said his mother resignedly, "you'll never drown."

"Why not?"

"Because you were surely born to be hanged. All right. I'll take you to the market afterwards. Do you have any money to spend?"

He nodded. "Aunt Regina gave me twopence for finding her keys—" no one knew that he himself had hidden them "—and I have a whole shilling that I've saved."

"You're mercenary," said Judith in that virtuous tone which always annoyed him. Oliver lowered his head and ran at her, butting like a goat.

Quickly, before anyone realised what was happening, Eliot stepped between them, swinging his half-brother up into the air, high above his head. It was a form of attention which delighted Oliver. He was still shrieking with excitement when Regina entered, cradling the latest addition to the family in her arms. At once, and without ceremony, Eliot put him down and hurried over to look at little Morwenna.

"I've never seen a boy so devoted to a baby," Judith remarked scornfully, her body rigid with jealousy and bitter hurt. She did not like this little half-sister of hers, who had been born three months earlier and who absorbed everyone's attention, even Eliot's. Oliver, who would normally have protested loudly at being thus abandoned, made no demur, and went over to look at the bundle gurgling milkily against Regina's shoulder. Richard's eyes lit up, and he held out his arms for this child who was the centre and delight of his life.

Lilias felt, as always, the panic which stemmed from concealment. She had not been prepared for the depths of Richard's devotion to the longed-for daughter, but did not see how, in any case, she could have told him the truth: that Morwenna, whom she had named after the Cornish saint, was really the child of Patrick O'Mara. To have revealed this fact, would have raised unanswerable questions. Why had she not raised the alarm after the Irishman had left her on that fateful night? Why had she never mentioned the episode to anyone? Why ... why ... why?

In the first panic of finding herself pregnant, the only solution had been to let it pass as Richard's child; and his happiness at the prospect had seemed to justify the deception. Now she was not so sure, but the damage was done, and it was far too late for the truth. It was fortuitous that Patrick O'Mara's colouring was almost identical with her own, and everyone assumed that the baby was taking after her mother.

"Come along," Lilias urged the others briskly, and put her arm around Judith's taut little shoulders. How thin she was, fine-stretched like a vibrating wire. Lilias wished, with a sigh, that the child would get over this unreasoning passion for Eliot.

At last they were ready to leave, and proceeded in the direction of the castle. The funeral cortege was met by the Mayor and civic dignitaries at the Water-Gate to a salute of twenty-one guns, while the citizens lined the banks in solemn homage. Oliver stood with exemplary stillness while the black-draped coffin was borne ashore, and uttered not a sound until he was at last free to escape to the stalls of the market.

They walked along by the weir and around by the castle ditch. Oliver danced ahead of them all the way, proudly cracking his little whip with its gold-mounted handle, a birthday present last December from his father. Judith walked sedately as always, catching hold of her mother's hand.

The stalls were set out in the wide-open space in front of the castle. Oliver gave a little crow of delight and ran forward, jingling the coins in his pocket. But he was not quick to spend them, his mother noticed; in that he was a true Bristolian. He made certain that he got value for his money. Judith bought swiftly and methodically, already knowing what she wanted. She moved purposefully from stall to stall, Eliot following her like a faithful shadow. Geoffrey was tired and moping, and had to be carried in Mollie Hanks' strong young arms.

The guns were still booming out from the castle walls, the puffs of smoke hanging like clouds in the upper air. Lilias called to the children that they must be getting home for their dinner.

"No!" said Oliver defiantly, and pranced away, flicking his whip.

"I'll 'ave the 'ide off 'im," shrilled Mollie. "A right varmint, 'e is, and that's the truth."

Lilias, conscious of people staring, made a grab for her son, but Oliver evaded her clutching hands and nearly fell under a horse's hooves. Only the dexterity of the rider prevented an unfortunate accident. Lilias dealt the shaken Oliver a resounding slap and turned to thank his preserver.

There were two horses: a gentleman on one and, on the other, a lady seated pillion behind a groom. It was the groom who had so nimbly avoided disaster. The gentleman and lady both seemed in an impolite hurry to be gone, and Lilias' thanks and apologies were received with

238

perfunctory smiles. The groom, however, touched his hat and advised her not to worry: boys, he added, would always be boys.

"Will!" the lady said urgently. "We must be going."

The gentleman put in: "We cannot stand here all day, Jackson, talking to strangers."

The servant hurriedly begged pardon and asked for directions to the Redcliffe Gate. "For there are so many alterations since I was last here," he added, "that I find myself quite at a loss."

"You know Bristol, then, sir?" enquired Lilias, and saw the lady nip the groom's arm.

"A little, ma'am," he responded briefly, and it was plain that he would say no more.

"We did ought to be getting back, missus," urged Mollie, when Lilias had given the necessary directions and the little cavalcade had moved on. "It do look as though it's coming on to rain."

"Yes, very well, I'm coming." But Lilias spoke absent-mindedly, staring after the retreating figures, a puzzled frown on her face. Something about the groom had struck her as familiar, something to do with his eyes. He was, she judged, a very tall young man, with skin weathered to a most unlikely shade of walnut-brown, an ugly man from what she had seen of his face, although that admittedly was not very much, shaded as it had been by the slouched brim of his hat. She racked her brain for the solution . . .

"Lilias! Lilias!" She became aware of an imperious voice, and realised that a travelling-chariot had drawn up beside them. A face very like Regina's, but with more force of character, was peering at her from over the door.

"Aunt Codrington!" Lilias stepped forward to greet Regina's sister. "What are you doing in town?"

"I've come to see my plaguey lawyer, that's what. Pettigrew! The man's an idiot. All men are idiots, if it comes to that. Codrington was a little better than most, I

suppose. Shouldn't have married him if he hadn't been."
She glared at Oliver. "That child will come to a sticky
end."

Lilias laughed. "You saw what happened, then?"

"Indeed I did. That child has the luck of the Devil."

"Won't you come home and have dinner with us, now
that you're here?" begged Lilias. "Regina will be so glad
to see you."

"I was going to call on you, in any case. Hate dining at
inns. Get in, all of you. Only keep that boy under
control."

A few moments later, as the rain began to fall in large,
pendulous drops, spattering and jumping on the cobbles,
Lilias, Mollie and the children were safely ensconced in
Aunt Codrington's coach and being rattled in the direction of Broad Street.

"What's all the fuss?" demanded the old lady. "I
heard the noise of guns." Lilias told her, and Aunt
Codrington pulled down the corners of her mouth.
"Ireton, indeed! Jumped-up Jack-o'-nobody! This war'll
do us no good, mark my words. The English are snobs:
they like an aristocracy. If we get rid of one lot, we'll
make ourselves another. But it won't be the same.
Cromwell! Who's he? The great-great-grandson of a
Putney brewer!"

"Hush, aunt, I beg you. Don't talk like that in front of
Richard."

"Oh, I know what that precious husband of yours
thinks of Oliver Cromwell ... Be careful, man!" she
yelled at her coachman, as they lurched perilously into
Wine Street. "You nearly had us over! Servants! He's no
more fit to drive a coach than I am, but what can you do
in these days? Where is Richard, by the way? Skulking
off, I daresay, leaving you to look after the children."

But no one was more sympathetic when she saw
Richard's plight, and almost before she had greeted
Regina she was recommending half a dozen remedies.

240

"It's no good, Lucinda," her sister protested. "Lilias and I have the works of the world to make him swallow even the most innocuous herbal draught. What he needs, of course, is a change of air. Bristol is so damp in the autumn."

"It's always damp. That's why I live at Abbot's Leigh ... Now! There's an idea! Why don't Lilias and Richard come to stay with me? Oh, only for a day or to, until you're better, Richard dear. Regina won't mind looking after the children."

"We're always imposing on mother-in-law," Richard began doubtfully, but it was obvious that the proposition pleased him.

"Regina likes being imposed upon," Aunt Codrington declared bracingly. "She's that sort of woman. She was that sort of a girl." Regina blinked at this unexpected view of herself. "Well, that's settled," her sister went on. "You can both come back with me this afternoon. Tell that Mollie what's-her-name to pack your things."

And settled it was. Lucinda Codrington had never been known to take no for an answer.

As they sat down to dinner, Richard enquired of Lilias: "Did you hear any news?"

"News?" she repeated blankly, her mind on what dresses she ought to tell Mollie to pack.

"About the traitor, Charles Stuart," her husband said impatiently. "Is there any news yet of his capture?"

"Oh, that! No. None. At least, I heard nothing. He seems to have vanished into thin air. Either that, or he went back to Scotland, after all."

"The Scots deny all knowledge of him," Regina said. "Goodman Lewis' son has just returned from the north, where he's been on business. He declares there's no knowledge of him there."

"A very good thing if he does escape, if you ask me," pronounced Aunt Codrington, ignoring Lilias' warning frown. "One king executed is enough for any generation.

241

We don't want this boy going the same way as his father. And it's no good looking at me like that, Richard Pride, because that's my opinion and I'm changing it for no one. Not for you, nor Fairfax, nor your precious Noll Cromwell, himself. Now, eat up your dinner and let's be going. I want to get home before dark."

*   *   *

"An invitation to supper from my neighbour, Mrs George Norton," said Aunt Codrington, bustling into her little parlour, the just-delivered note clutched importantly in her hand. "Very worthy people and highly respected. She's expecting almost any day now."

Lilias withdrew her gaze reluctantly from the view beyond the window. The Abbot's Leigh woods were beautiful in autumn, a golden torrent, shot through with eddies of scarlet and copper, burnished slopes reaching down to the old grey river.

"Then does this Mrs Norton really want us upsetting her rest, aunt, even for part of an evening?"

"Lord bless you, Eleanor Norton doesn't mollycoddle herself, my dear, like some of your fine town ladies. And she wants me to meet two very close friends who have recently come to stay, a Mrs Jane Lane and her cousin, Henry Lassels."

Richard, however, when the invitation was put to him, begged to be excused. His cold, though mending, was still inclined to be heavy.

The Nortons' house, as Lilias first saw it in the soft evening light, was a low, rambling building with tall chimneys and an imposing flight of steps leading to a central door. Trees flanked the out-buildings, and there was a bowling-green as well as some pleasant formal gardens. The late sun glinted on its many windows.

Mrs Norton, who looked, indeed, very near her time, welcomed Aunt Codrington and Lilias effusively, graciously accepting their apologies for Richard's absence.

242

She begged leave to introduce her friend, Mrs Jane Lane.

Jane was a small, delicate girl of rather fragile beauty, and Lilias recognised both her and Henry Lassels at once.

"We met!" she exclaimed. "Two days since, in the market at Bristol. My little boy nearly ran under your horse's hooves. He was only saved by the skill of your groom."

Jane Lane smiled nervously, looking very much as though she regretted this second encounter. Reluctantly she extended her hand.

"You mean William Jackson," she murmured with constraint. "He is not, strictly speaking, my groom, although he is travelling with us. He is a poor tenant-farmer of my brother's."

"And has been extremely unwell, poor lad," George Norton put in. "Ever since he arrived here, he has been suffering from a tertian ague."

Before Aunt Codrington could make herself free of an unfailing remedy for this particular complaint, a large, pompous man, who had been introduced as Dr Gorges, former chaplain to His Majesty King Charles the first, said frowningly: "I have some knowledge of physic and could have assisted the unhappy, afflicted fellow. But both Mrs Lane and the patient himself have refused my ministrations."

The worthy doctor had plainly been wounded in that most vulnerable spot, his pride, and Jane and Henry Lassels hastened to reassure him.

"It is just that William Jackson is so accustomed to the illness, that he is capable of ministering to himself."

"It certainly hasn't affected his appetite," Eleanor Norton contributed drily. "Pope tells me that when Mr Jackson is able to rise from his sick-bed, he positively haunts the kitchens."

At that moment Pope, the tall, stately butler, announced that supper was ready, and Lilias was

escorted into the dining-room by young Mr Henry
Lassels. He made the usual polite enquiries about her
visit to Aunt Codrington and the state of her husband's
health, and touched lightly upon their encounter in
Bristol Market; but it was obvious to Lilias that he was
extremely ill at ease. Some of her questions he answered
almost at random.

A preposterous conviction was growing in Lilias'
mind, fostered by the memory of Mr Jackson's eyes. And
the information, dropped during some teasing banter on
the part of their host, that William Jackson had a truckle-
bed set up in Henry Lassels' own room, gave her further
food for thought.

"Yes," cried Mr Norton, carving a pair of broiled
fowls dressed in parsley sauce, "Henry is so nice that he
must have someone sleep in the same room as he does. I
pity that poor William Jackson, Henry, upon my word I
do, being constantly at your beck and call."

"I consider it a most unhealthy practice, allowing a
sick man to sleep in the same chamber as oneself,"
declared Mrs Norton roundly.

Lilias glanced at her curiously. It was apparent from
the tone of their conversation that neither she nor her
husband entertained any suspicions of Mrs Lane's servant, and Lilias scolded herself for her wild imaginings.
Yet the suspicion persisted all through supper, so that
she, like Mr Lassels, was hardly able to keep her mind on
what she was saying. Twice she saw Aunt Codrington
frown at her, and was thankful when the meal was
concluded.

Mrs Norton suggested a turn in the gardens. "There
are still many flowers worth seeing, Mistress Codrington,
even for the time of year."

It was beginning to grow dusk, but there was still
sufficient light to see the view and admire the distant
vista of the Avon Gorge. Lilias was reminded poignantly
of that very first night when she had walked into Bristol

244

with her father. Mrs Norton and Aunt Codrington were busy exchanging recipes for salves and herbal ointments, and the two men had disappeared about business of their own. Lilias therefore found herself in the company of Mrs Jane Lane.

"You are making a lengthy visit to Mrs Norton?" she enquired.

"Yes ... no ... that is, I really cannot say," was the faltering and somewhat ambiguous reply. "But—" Jane Lane recovered her composure a little "—I hope to stay at least until Mrs Norton is delivered."

Lilias returned some noncommital answer and the conversation flagged, each woman busy with her own secret thoughts. Was it the King? Lilias wondered for the hundredth time; while Jane Lane silently bemoaned the incident which had thrown this old acquaintance of His Majesty in their path. Moreover, an acquaintance, according to Mrs Norton, who was now married to a friend of Noll Cromwell's. She shivered suddenly. "Let us go in," she said. "It's beginning to get very cold."

As they mounted the steps and entered the lighted hall, they were rejoined by their hostess and Aunt Codrington. Almost at the same moment, a door at the back of the hall opened and a tall young man came through. In one hand he held a tankard of ale and in the other an enormous hunk of bread and cheese. He stopped, patently disconcerted at the unexpected meeting.

Jane Lane cried in a small, breathless voice: "Why! William—!"

"Ah, Mr Jackson!" exclaimed Mrs Norton, amused. "I am relieved to see that you are feeling so much better."

The man scraped his feet in an awkward fashion and bobbed his head. "The fever comes and goes, ma'am, thank you."

Lilias stared at him, fascinated. His hair had been

245

roughly cut and hung untidily about his none-too-clean collar. His face—she judged him to be twenty or thereabouts—was, as she had previously thought, an unnaturally dark shade of brown. The backs of his hands were the same peculiar hue, and in places, Lilias noticed, it was blotched and streaky. And William Jackson was well over six feet in height, for all that he tried to appear shorter by stooping.

He glanced up and his eyes met hers. There was no hat now to shield them, nor to disguise their deep velvety brown. The look was as bold and appreciative as it had been that day in the Broad Street parlour, although it was tinged at present with a certain apprehension. Lilias felt rather than saw Jane Lane's furtive glance in her direction, but she was riveted by the grimace of comic dismay masking the young King's face. Charles Stuart was evidently a man who could laugh, even when threatened by danger.

With difficulty, Lilias prevented herself from bobbing a curtsey and turned away, engaging her hostess's attention. "William Jackson" crossed the hall and unhurriedly mounted the stairs.

"I think, my dear," Aunt Codrington decreed, "that it is time for us to be going. It is only a short walk, but I had rather accomplish even so brief a journey while there is still some light. These are such dangerous and unsettled times."

The services of one of the Nortons' servants was pressed upon them, but both Lilias and Aunt Codrington declined.

A voice spoke from halfway up the stairs.

"I should be pleased to offer my services to the two ladies, ma'am, and escort them home," offered "William Jackson".

Jane Lane started forward, wide-eyed and frightened. "No, William! Your fever—you cannot!"

"Nonsense!" exclaimed Mrs Norton stoutly. "He has

been upstairs in that room far too much in the past two days. It will do him good to make himself useful and get some fresh air. As for his fever—" Mrs Norton nodded significantly towards the empty tankard now swinging from the King's slack finger "—it seems, if only temporarily, to have left him."

Jane Lane was overruled, both by her friend and by "William Jackson" himself. Clasping a thick cudgel thoughtfully provided by Mrs Norton, he escorted Lilias and the unsuspecting Aunt Codrington the few yards down the road to the latter's door.

As they bade him good-night and turned to go in, Lilias said quickly: "There! I almost forgot! Mrs Norton asked me especially for my recipe for starching lace, and I came away without telling her ... Mr Jackson! A moment please! I have a message for Mrs Norton. Go on in, aunt, and I'll follow."

She ran down the path and overtook the King, who was standing in the shadow of some trees. Forgetful of the proprieties, Lilias anxiously took hold of his arm.

"Sire," she said in a low voice, "there are no ships sailing from Bristol to France for at least a month. I know, because troopers were in the city last week making enquiries."

The King grimaced, his face suddenly white beneath its coating of walnut-juice, the youthful lines sagging into a caricature of cynical old age.

"So ... Ah, well, Lord Wilmot will have had a fruitless journey today, I fear." He sighed. "It seems I must move on again ... Poor Jane. She was hoping to stay awhile with her friend, but that will now be impossible."

"Will it, sire?"

"Of course," he answered, genuinely astonished. "My claims on her must naturally come first." It was said without arrogance, a simple statement of fact. Lilias reflected that Charles Stuart would have to be very

247

careful. Even in disguise, his air of authority and consequence shone through.

"Sire," she urged, "I should advise you not to tarry in this part of the world too long. Bristol is and always has been staunchly for Parliament, and now for the Republican cause."

The King smiled and her heart seemed to twist within her breast. What charm, what fatal charm, these Stuarts had.

"But not you, Mrs Pride?" he asked gently.

"You have nothing to fear from me, sire."

"Have I not?" He stood looking down at her for a moment or two. A little breeze sifted through the branches overhead, rippling the dying leaves from red to bronze. The long shadows crept silently towards them over the grass and a late bird sang. "You're beautiful," he said at last, "and I always have something to fear from a beautiful woman."

Before she could divine his intention, his arms were around her, his lips on hers, his whole body aflame with passion. Then he released her with an unsteady laugh. "Good-bye, Mrs Pride. I hope we shall meet again one day, in happier times." He pushed past her almost roughly, and vanished along the dusty road.

Lilias stood looking after him, until he was swallowed by the dusk.

*   *   *

Late the following evening, Lilias was sitting quietly in Aunt Codrington's parlour sewing and listening to Richard, who was reading aloud, when Aunt Codrington herself came in, bursting with news.

"Mrs Norton, poor soul, miscarried during the night, only a few hours after we left her. I warned her against eating those oysters. There's an 'r' in the month, I said."

"Miscarried! Poor woman!" Lilias said quickly. "Is there anything that we can do?"

248

"We-ell ... " Aunt Codrington was doubtful. "Very poorly indeed, the report from Mr Norton said. No visitors advised at present."

"But at least she has this Mrs Lane staying with her," Richard put in. "That must certainly be a comfort."

"But she has not! At least, not after today. It appears that at supper-time tonight, Mrs Lane received a letter telling her that her father has been taken ill. She and Mr Henry Lassels must leave first thing tomorrow morning."

Aunt Codrington prattled happily on giving them further details, but Lilias had ceased to listen. So the most wanted man in the whole of England was leaving Abbot's Leigh. She stared out of the window at the shadowy garden, remembering the King's burning kiss. She had only to lift her voice to send him to certain death. Why then did she not do it? She was married to a devout Republican, a friend of Cromwell's, a man who would never forgive her if he ever discovered that she had let the arch-traitor escape. But Lilias had no time for these male ideologies. Womanlike, she found instinct and intuition more reliable guides and always acted accordingly.

She blew Richard a kiss with no feeling of guilt. Men were too prone to be guided by their heads; women listened to the promptings of their hearts.

PART THREE
1660–1663

O, my America! my new-found-land.

John Donne, 1571–1631

CHAPTER FIFTEEN

The April day was cold. Thin streamers of light laced the threatening clouds, and Lilias quickened her steps, calling to Judith and Morwenna to do the same. "It looks like rain," she said.

Judith, now a thin, angular girl of sixteen, admonished her half-sister sharply: "Don't dawdle. You hear what mother says!"

Lilias wondered for the hundredth time why Judith disliked Morwenna so much, but knew the answer without stopping to think. Eighteen-year-old Eliot, now the head of Pride's soap works since Richard's decline in health, made no secret of the fact that Morwenna was very much his darling.

"What's there to sulk about in that?" Oliver would demand when Judith moped. "He can't marry her. She is related to him by blood as much as she is to you. Not that he'll marry you anyway, if you go about looking like a slab of sour cheese."

But her half-brother's argument was disregarded by Judith, even while she acknowledged its apparent truth. She resented Morwenna's increasing influence over Eliot, was jealous of an affection which she had never inspired and, above all, was deeply envious of the fact that Morwenna had inherited Lilias' good looks.

"It's not fair!" she would burst out every now and then to Regina. "We both have the same mother. Why should Morwenna be as she is, while I . . . I only look like me?"

Morwenna came running after them now, her cheeks whipped to a delicate rose by the wind, her blue eyes sparkling, tendrils of black hair escaping from under her hood. Lilias recognised one of those fleeting resemblances to Patrick O'Mara which made it so certain that Morwenna was his child. Thank God, she reflected, that no one else even remembered the Irishman's existence, let alone what he had looked like. Richard adored Morwenna; she was the apple of his eye and the truth would undoubtedly kill him.

Richard's health had been failing for some years. He had never really recovered from the trouble which had plagued him on that long-ago visit to Abbot's Leigh. It had meant his gradual withdrawal from public life at a time when his friend Oliver Cromwell was going from strength to strength, becoming Lord Protector of England and very nearly King. The paths of the two men had inevitably parted, the intimacy between them sinking into mutual goodwill. And now, Oliver was dead—had been dead for well over eighteen months—and his son, Richard Cromwell, ruled as Lord Protector in his stead.

The first drops of rain splattered on the dusty cobbles as Lilias and the two girls quitted the open space of the market and entered the maze of brash young streets sprouting over the site of the vanished castle. Five years earlier, on Cromwell's orders, Bristol Castle had been demolished; six hundred years of history had vanished in as many days. As she hurried between the crowding houses, some of them still smelling of raw timber and fresh paint, Lilias thought: "This was the keep." Here, Priam had lived for the two years of the Royalist occupation; here his feet had trod, his voice had sounded ... Lilias gave herself a mental shake. She was thirty-four, too old for that sort of romantic nonsense. It was doubtful if the Earl even remembered her name.

She had been aware for the past few minutes of a crescendo of noise, but had been too absorbed in her own thoughts to pay it much attention. Now, however, as she and her daughters turned right towards New Gate and left into Wine Street, it became too persistent to be ignored. She heard shrieking, shouting and the smashing of windows. Morwenna and Judith cowered against her in alarm.

A man scuttled past them, his high-crowned hat pulled down over his eyes, his cloak liberally besmirched with mud.

"Excuse me, sir!" Lilias caught his arm. "Can you tell me what the disturbance is about?" The man seemed disinclined to wait, but Lilias tightened her grip. "What is happening, sir?" she persisted, planting herself firmly in front of him and blocking his line of retreat.

"It's the apprentices, ma'am," he said hurriedly. "Now, please let me pass. Honest, God-fearing citizens such as ourselves are not safe."

Lilias made no effort to move. "What about the apprentices?" she asked. "Why are they making all this din?"

The man's gaze sharpened in sudden recognition. "You're Richard Pride's wife. Get home, ma'am, I do implore you. The apprentices are in an ugly mood and half of them are drunk."

The distant ebb and flow of sound was growing to a deep-throated roar, and the man tried to push past Lilias. She let him go just as the Watch clattered under the arch of New Gate, and a flutter of scarlet near the High Cross announced the arrival of the Mayor to read the Riot Act. At the same moment, a rabble of apprentices erupted into Wine Street from St Mary-le-port and Dolphin Lane. There was a brief struggle with the militia before the ringleaders were marched off under guard. Without these firebrands, the rest of the apprentices were quickly subdued—although not before one or two heads had been soundly knocked together—and the Mayor did his duty and read the Riot Act. Lilias tapped young Joseph Leach, nephew of the long-dead Phineas, on the shoulder. The boy turned, then pulled off his scruffy hat, twisting it awkwardly between his hands.

"What's going on, Joseph? What's this all about?"

"Oh . . . just high spirits I reckon, Mrs Pride. High spirits that got a bit out of hand."

"It sounded like it. Whose windows were you breaking?"

Young Leach blushed and looked embarrassed. "Just windows," he muttered.

"Puritan windows," hissed the pimply-faced youth beside him. "Denzil Hollister's, for one."

"But why?" Lilias was both puzzled and uneasy. During the last ten years or so, apprentices' riots had become a thing of the past.

"Haven't you heard, missus?" enquired another boy, as the Mayor's peroration came to an end and the crowd began to disperse. "They say General Monck's bringing back the King."

"The—the King?" Lilias faltered. Yet even as her mind rejected such an incredible idea, the small cold hand of fear began squeezing at the pit of her stomach.

"That's right, missus. They're sayin' 'e sent Sir John Grenville out to Spain last month, and that the Black Boy and 'is court've moved to Breda. That's in Holland," Lilias' informant added helpfully, and she nodded.

"Who told you all this?"

"News was brought in to the Mayor this mornin'. General Monck is marching south from Scotland and is going to call a Parleyment. My dad says it'll be the first for years."

"He's lying!" Judith exclaimed angrily. "Mother! Tell him it must be a mistake. England is a Republic now."

Was it a mistake? Lilias doubted it and bit her lip. Richard Cromwell was a weak, ineffectual man who had never wanted to inherit his father's great position. And ever since Oliver Cromwell's death, a strong tide of Royalist sympathy had been running. Denzil Hollister had told Richard only the other day that men were

256

openly drinking the King's health in more than one of Bristol's taverns.

"They want to bring back the rule of Anti-Christ," he had spat. "But the rule of God's Saints on Earth will last for ever."

But Lilias guessed that this yearning for the return of the monarchy had nothing to do with religion or politics. People were starved of entertainment, longed for the theatres, cockpits and beer-houses to be re-opened, wanted to dance once more around the maypole every spring and make love to girls by the light of the midsummer bonfires. She reflected briefly that if the news was really true, then Priam would be returning; would be living again at Westovers; would be near to her. But almost as the thought entered her head, she realised that Richard would be in danger; that he could never stay in England under the Stuarts. Whoever else the King might forgive—and she had no doubt that that easy-going monarch would be as lenient as he could—Charles Stuart would be urged, and probably would wish, to take vengeance on his father's executioners. Mercy would be in short supply for those men who had signed the late King's death-warrant.

*　　*　　*

"I tell you, Pride, that if you don't leave this country, you are as good as dead. Your name was very near the top of the list."

William Goffe's gaunt figure towered over his listeners, reducing the front parlour of the Broad Street house to doll-like proportions. He had ridden through the night from London and looked exhausted.

Six days had gone by, days which had steadily confirmed, hour by hour, the fact of the restoration of the monarchy. Morwenna began to shake with sobs, and Eliot, watched by Judith's jealous eyes, put his arm around her.

"Shush, love, don't cry. It's not certain that father will have to go away."

"If he doesn't," William Goffe reiterated, "he's a dead man. As I should be." He snorted contemptuously. "Oh, some will buy their freedom. Some will cringe and crawl. But not me. And not you either, Richard Pride. You're not that sort of man."

Richard said nothing, looking at the faces of his family gathered anxiously about him. Regina was crippled with rheumatism, a shadow of her former self. But Eliot was a good boy, strong and level-headed, the image of what Richard himself had been at eighteen years of age. The business could safely be left in his eldest son's capable hands. Judith was a sensible girl, with all of Lilias' domestic skills; she and the faithful Mollie could easily run the house between them. Twelve-year-old Geoffrey was a dreamer, but oddly practical also, and apprenticed to old Fothergill the lawyer. Then there was Oliver, reluctantly learning the soap-making business and far too astute for a boy of thirteen. He was the only one of his children whom Richard found it hard to understand. Oliver was extremely handsome in a sharp-featured, predatory fashion, reminding Richard of a hawk waiting to swoop on its unsuspecting prey. And, finally, there was Morwenna.

Richard's heart contracted, as always, at the sight of this dearly beloved child. Like her mother in colouring and beauty, she had enchanted him from the minute she was born. He had always longed for a daughter, and Judith—plain, hard-working, estimable Judith—had never been a substitute for the one he had not had. After Geoffrey's birth, Richard had resigned himself to the inevitable, convinced by the doctor that Lilias was unlikely ever to conceive again. And then, incredibly, she had announced herself once more pregnant. Richard's first joy had been muted by considerations for Lilias' health, but when she had been safely delivered

258

of a daughter, his happiness had known no bounds. And as the child grew up, she had entwined herself still further about his heart. Next to Lilias, he loved her better than anyone else in the whole world, and the thought of having to leave her brought him close to tears.

He would not let himself think that this parting might be final, that he might never see any of his children again. It was true that he could not stay in England. Indeed, he had no wish to remain, to see his life's work crumble into dust, to see everything that he had struggled for handed back to the hated Stuarts. He believed devoutly in the Republic.

He looked up at Goffe. "You say that Dixwell and Whalley are also going to New England?"

"Yes. For myself, I have friends at Hadley in Massachusetts and I shall go there."

"What of the other signatories?"

"Cawley, Ludlow, Phelps and, I believe, Broughton and Lisle have already left for Switzerland. Some will go to Germany. Okey, Barkstead and Miles Corbet are seeking refuge in Holland."

Lilias' hands suddenly tightened on the back of Regina's chair. The mention of John Okey had brought back the memory of that night, eleven years earlier, the last time she had set eyes on the Earl of Chelwood. She could smell again the sour stench of the brothel, feel again the pressure of Priam's mouth on hers as they lay together on the creaking bed, expecting every moment to be discovered. . .

"Massachusetts!" Richard's voice cut across her thoughts. "Lilias' father was a friend of Governor Winthrop's."

"John Winthrop died," Lilias reminded him gently, "a few months after the King's execution."

"It doesn't signify." A little colour had crept back into Richard's cheeks and he leaned forward almost eagerly in his chair. "New England, Lilias, A new life. A new beginning." The words echoed queerly from the half-forgotten past. "We could make a fresh start, and eventually send for the family to join us."

"Not me," Regina interrupted him, sadly but firmly. "I'm too old. When I die, I want my bones to rest in Bristol soil. But the children must join you as soon as they are able. Lucinda and I will manage very well."

Lilias glanced at William Goffe and recognised that he was as doubtful of this happy outcome as she was herself. She foresaw years of living in hiding, even in New England. There was still a minority of colonists who were hardened monarchists. But it would be wanton cruelty to burst Richard's bubble of illusion, to snatch from him the one hope which would make this uprooting bearable. Her heart went out to him, loving him in that instant with all the savage protection of a tigress for her young. For a moment or two, she hated Charles Stuart and everything he stood for with an intensity equal to that of the most hardened Republican. She knelt by Richard's side, thinking how ill he looked.

"We'll begin our preparations to leave at once," she said. "William Goffe is right. We have very little time. They say that Monck has already despatched the ship which will carry the King back to England."

*   *   *

Magdalen stood among her half-packed belongings and stared around the sunny room.

"It will seem strange not to be living here any more," she murmured. "After all these years."

Cassandra nodded, misty-eyed. "Poor Mevrouw Bogardus! She was crying so much that I couldn't bear it. I had to leave her and come upstairs."

"What nonsense!" Lady Cressida Lithgow slammed shut the lid of a travelling-chest and looked at her mother

260

and sister in disgust. "Here we are, going home—the one thing we've all been praying for, and talking of, for years—and you are both practically in tears. We've lived through a miracle! Four months ago, the King was a hopeless exile, banned from France, banned from Holland and living in threadbare poverty in Spain. The English Republic appeared as safe as houses and likely to remain so for the next five hundred years. And yet, here we are! Packing! Going home to mother's beloved Westovers. We ought to be the happiest women on earth."

"We are, we are!" laughed Magdalen through her tears. "It's just—oh, I don't know! Of course, we're happy. And why *my* Westovers? Don't you remember it at all?"

"Not much." Cressida sat down on the window seat beside her mother. "The only thing I recall vividly about it, is its being on fire. There was a very tall man there, but I don't think that it was father."

"No. He was an Irishman called Patrick O'Mara. It was after the battle of Lansdown. He helped us put out the fire."

"Did you ever see him again?" asked the romantically-minded Cassandra.

"Once . . . He wrote to us for a while, but he was at Drogheda just before the sack. We never heard from him after, so we presumed that he must have been killed."

"How sad." The ever-ready tears sprang to Cassandra's eyes, while Cressida looked at her mother, suddenly alert. There had been a tender note in Magdalen's voice which, usually, she reserved only for Priam. Cressida was so accustomed to the fact that her mother loved their father to the exclusion of everyone else, herself and her sister included, that her curiosity was immediately aroused. Was it possible that Magdalen had been fonder of this Irishman than she realised?

261

There was the clatter of hooves in the courtyard, followed by the indignant flapping of wings, as the Mevrouw's doves rose in a white cloud to make way for the solitary horseman.

"Father," said Cressida, and pushed the shutters wide, watching Priam as he slid to the ground and tossed his reins to the waiting groom.

Her father interested Cressida far more than either her mother or her sister, whom she loved, but thought rather dull. It was partly the Earl's reputation which intrigued her—knowledge culled over the years by her sharp little ears from scraps of overheard, adult conversation—but, also, a growing conviction that none of them really knew him. There was a part of his life which was his alone. Cressida had first become aware of it one day years ago, when her father had taken her and Cassandra skating on one of The Hague's frozen canals. She remembered the day perfectly, the roads still muffled with snow and everything sprayed silver with frost. A girl had gone past on a sledge, her cheeks flushed with the cold, her eyes sparkling, her head thrown back on a shout of laughter and her hair floating behind her in a jet-black cloud. The Earl had stared after her as though he had seen a ghost. His hands had gone out in a small jerky movement which had made him appear half-lost. There had been a look on his face which Cressida could recall even now: a yearning, a longing, an agony of spirit which seemed to stem from his very soul . . . A moment later, seeing Cressida's eyes upon him, his face had been wiped clean of all emotion as, with the bland, attentive smile she knew so well, he bent to hear something that Cassandra had to say.

The Earl glanced up now and waved to Cressida. A few moments later, he was in the room, brushing aside their eager questions in his haste.

"Just give me a change of linen and a fresh pair of boots. I must leave for Scheveningen within the hour."

262

"But why?" Three tongues clacked the question simultaneously, and Magdalen cried reproachfully: "Priam! You promised that we should all go together."

"I know and I'm sorry. But I have very pressing business with the King. I've made arrangements for you to travel with the Dennisons, but I must be on my way at once."

"But what can possibly be so pressing that it can't wait a few more hours?" Magdalen spoke almost angrily for her.

But Priam did not even hear her, so intent was he on bundling his shaving gear into a saddle-bag. He yelled out of the window to his groom to have fresh horses saddled, perfunctorily kissed his wife and daughters and swung on his heel.

"I'll see you later, in Scheveningen," he said.

"Well!" exclaimed Cressida, sitting down once more on the window seat. "Whatever has got into father?"

*   *   *

Lilias lay curled, as so often in the past, against the warmth and comfort of Richard's side. It was very late. After going to bed they had talked long into the night, holding hands like two frightened children suddenly face to face with the unknown.

If she pinched herself, Lilias wondered, would she wake up? But this nightmare was real. In a few days' time, she and Richard would be sailing thousands of miles away to a country as strange to them as the back of the moon. She rolled on to her back, staring with eyes now grown accustomed to the dark at the well-known room. Every crack in the ceiling was a well-charted map, every contour of the furniture a familiar landmark. She wondered if she would ever see any of them again.

And yet, did she and Richard really need to run away? She had saved the Earl of Chelwood's life and later, by her silence, the King's. Surely both these facts must count for something. If they stayed, if she pleaded for clemency for Richard, would Charles refuse to intervene, even though her husband was a regicide? She remembered the way the King had kissed her, that night at Abbot's Leigh.

But such a course of action was impossible. Not only would the truth shatter her marriage, but Richard would never consent to stay on those terms. She had the power to save her husband but dared not use it. She would have to go with him to America, to finish that journey on which she had set out from Cornwall over eighteen years ago.

Lilias cuddled once more into Richard's side, noting as she did so how thin he had grown. The flesh now sagged on his once firm body and when she touched his ribs, she could almost count the bones. Sometimes at night, he would break into a sweat, and every winter he was plagued by persistent bouts of coughing. How long could he endure the rigours of life in the colonies, a hunted fugitive from the King's officers and spies? She had never been in love with him, but this quiet, honourable, steadfast man had inspired in her a loyalty and affection which would lead her if necessary to offer up her life in exchange for his. She wrapped her arms about him, fiercely protective. No one should harm him if she could prevent it.

★   ★   ★

Scheveningen was aswarm with Royalists, all at a fever-pitch of excitement.

"Not elbow room for a mouse," declared the cheerful young man who introduced himself to the Earl of Chelwood as "your lordship's obedient servant, Samuel Pepys," and who directed Priam to the house where the King was lodged.

It took the Earl two hours to obtain an audience, so thick was the press of courtiers in the outer rooms; but as

264

soon as Charles saw him, Priam's welcome was assured. Thrusting his arm through the Earl's, the King dismissed the rest of his importunate followers, including the opulent lady who was clinging to his arm, and led the way to his bedchamber.

"The only place where I can get any peace these days," he said, grinning like a schoolboy who had escaped from the classroom. He added with a laugh: "I never knew I had so many friends."

"You'll have plenty of those now, sire. May I ask who was the lady, or would that be indiscreet?"

The King smiled cynically. "There's nothing discreet about Barbara Palmer, my friend. That was her husband Roger you observed hanging on her sleeve."

"A complaisant looking gentleman," the Earl remarked drily.

"Oh, very. Until recently, the lovely Barbara was Lord Chesterfield's mistress."

"But not any more, I imagine."

Charles gave his slow, lazy smile that suddenly aged him from mischievous schoolboy to world-weary man.

"Not any more, as you say. The lady and, of course, Lord Chesterfield have both been extremely accommodating."

"And, one imagines, the lady's husband."

"He, too. But then, he is hoping to become a viscount at the very least. However, you didn't seek an audience with me to discuss the Palmers."

"No. Your Majesty, there is a favour I want to beg of you."

"You too," murmured the King, motioning the Earl to sit with him on the bed.

As he did so, Priam was startled by the sight of gold coins scattered over the coverlet. He picked one up and handed it to the King.

"The money!" cried Charles, clapping a guilty hand to his head. "Part of the fifty thousand pounds that

Parliament sent me to cover the expenses of the voyage. I'd never seen so much money in all my life, and I emptied it on to the bed to show to my brother James and my sister Mary. We must have missed some of it when we gathered it up." He grinned, once again the schoolboy. "And now, what was this favour you wished to beg of me, my lord?"

"Does Your Majesty recollect Mistress Lilias Pride of Bristol? Ah! Mistress Colefax she would have been when you knew her."

"I recollect her well. Better, my lord, than you could imagine."

The Earl glanced sharply at the King, but let the cryptic utterance pass without comment. He licked his dry lips and asked hesitantly: "Did you know, sire, that her present husband is one of the Regicides?"

A hard look came into Charles' lean face. "So this request concerns the wife of one of my father's murderers, my lord?"

"Sire, Mrs Pride saved my life when I was in London on the eve of his late Majesty's execution. Forgive me for raising such a melancholy subject at a time of such general rejoicing, but I owe my existence to Lilias Pride, and therefore dare to beg clemency for her husband."

The King got up and walked to the window, looking out on all the bustle of the quayside below. He was silent for a moment, then turned and smiled. "You had no need to plead for my intervention, my lord. You see, I too owe Lilias Pride my life." And in response to the Earl's look of amazement, he briefly recounted the events at Abbot's Leigh. "So I am also in the lady's debt," he concluded. "You have my permission to send word to her that she has nothing to fear from me."

Priam bowed and withdrew. But as he made his way towards the harbour, where the *Naseby*, now tactfully renamed *The Royal Charles*, lay at anchor, waiting to

266

carry the King and all his entourage home to England, the Earl was afraid that even now he might be too late. It was possible that his bird had already flown.

CHAPTER SIXTEEN

A chill wind blew off the sea as Lilias rounded the point by the South Battery and made her way along the wharf of Boston harbour. To her left rose the hill crowned by a fort raised in the late Governor Winthrop's time; ahead of her lay the narrow muddy streets leading off to Trimount and Boston Common. She turned her feet in the direction of King Street, where she and Richard lodged with some friends of the present Governor.

It was two years since she had first seen the wooden pier of Boston's Long Wharf, the famous three-mounded hill and the cluster of houses which made up the chief city and port of Massachusetts. Built on a peninsula jutting out into the Charles River, Boston had struck her as a bleak and unexpectedly foreign place, reminding her painfully that she was thousands of miles from home and everything she held most dear.

But her homesickness and fear had been partly assuaged by the kindness and warmth of their reception. To the colonists, particularly to the Puritans and devout Republicans of the Bay Colony, the restoration of the monarchy could only be deplored, and the Regicides were regarded as martyrs and heroes. It was a view endorsed by the hanging, drawing and quartering of poor Hugh Peters who, although he had not signed the late King's death-warrant, had been marked out for Royalist vengeance ever since the sermon he had preached before King Charles' execution. All the Harvard undergraduates, defying royal displeasure, had plunged into mourning for the barbarous death of their co-founder.

Horror had mounted in the colony at the news of further executions, climaxing at the beginning of 1661 when it was learned that the bodies of Cromwell and

Henry Ireton had been exhumed, and the grisly remains exhibited on the gibbets at Tyburn. And a year later, in the January of this year of 1662, a former Governor of the colony, Sir Henry Vane, had also died on the scaffold.

It had been Lilias' intention that she and Richard should travel on to Pequot and seek help from the son of her father's old friend, John Winthrop the younger. But Richard's health, already undermined by the parting from his family, had seriously deteriorated during the voyage and, within a few days of landing, he had been laid low by a raging fever. He had been almost bed-ridden ever since, and what had been intended as a brief stay in the home of Elizabeth and Makepeace Farleigh had become a permanent lodging.

"Eh, but I'm glad to have thee, lass," Elizabeth Farleigh would say each time that Lilias made tentative plans for her own and Richard's future. "No children, and Makepeace busy all day in the shop! There's always a demand for shoes, thank God, what with the disgusting state of our roads."

But behind the genuine pleasure in their company, Lilias sensed that both Elizabeth and Makepeace Farleigh thought that their stay would not be of long duration. She saw the way in which Elizabeth would glance at Richard and then at her husband, as though to say: "There's one that's not long for this world."

Lilias herself refused to believe it. She could not visualise life without Richard after all these years. With every ounce of her magnificent strength she willed him to live. But fear nagged at her every night when she felt the skeletal thinness of his body and listened to his painful breathing.

Other worries beset her. The money they had brought with them was running low, and it was impossible to send to England for more. An early letter from Regina had reported soldiers in the city making enquiries for

Richard Pride, and although neither she nor the children had been troubled since, it was obvious, she wrote, that Richard would be arrested if his whereabouts ever became known. She begged Lilias not to write, for letters could so easily be intercepted and the King's agents were everywhere. The militia daily patrolled the quay, and Regina herself would only write when she could find an absolutely reliable friend to carry her letters. So much, thought Lilias, for the gratitude of a King and an Earl. She felt deeply angry and bitter.

She entered the Farleighs' kitchen, where Elizabeth was baking bread. Her hostess looked up and smiled, wiping her hands on a cloth. Elizabeth Farleigh was fifty; a plain, homely woman who still spoke with the intonation of her native Yorkshire dales.

"Eh, thou looks bonny. Reet healthy. I was saying t' Makepeace only t' other day, I don't know a prettier woman than our Mrs Pride."

Lilias laughed. "The walk did me good. I went as far as the Common, then came the long way back by Windmill Point." Her eyes went to the table and a half-full bowl of gruel. "Couldn't he eat anything again?"

"Nothing t' worrit about, love," Elizabeth Farleigh answered as comfortably as she could. "He doesn't like porridge as we make it here. Thou knows that. He's no stomach for Indian corn. Besides, he has a visitor."

"A visitor?" Lilias was immediately alarmed.

"No need t' tak on, now," her hostess soothed. "It's nobbut Mr Winthrop, who's in Boston on business. Now, don't start fussing with dishes. Just go on up. A visitor'll do you both good."

Lilias smiled gratefully. But when she had tidied her hair, smoothed down her dress and mounted the stairs to the long narrow room on the first floor which she shared with Richard, she found her husband looking extremely ill. John Winthrop, who was standing miserably at the foot of the bed, came forward at once as soon as he saw

270

Lilias, his hand held out in greeting. A pleasant man of fifty-six, he was now Governor of Connecticut, and in that capacity had recently obtained a charter from the King making Connecticut and New Haven one colony. Lilias knew how busy he was, and was grateful to him for sparing the time.

"I wish it could have been for a happier reason, Mistress Pride," he said, with the faintest of Suffolk accents, a legacy from his boyhood and early manhood years at Groton. He saw the anxiety leap into her eyes and pressed the hand he was still holding. "Don't be alarmed, ma'am. It's nothing to do with your husband. But John Okey has been arrested and executed."

Again Lilias was back in the Southwark brothel, holding on to Priam's arm, hearing Okey's voice as he shouted: "Open in the name of the law and Parliament!" Priam, to whom she meant so little that he had not even intervened with the King for Richard's life!

"Okey! Executed!" Her eyes went to Richard, and as John Winthrop released her hand she moved quickly towards the bed. She could see that her husband had taken the news badly. "I thought he had escaped to Holland."

"Indeed he had. He was a good man, as you know. A good Republican and a devout Anabaptist." The Governor drew a deep breath. "That is what makes it all the more difficult for me, Mrs Pride, to be the bearer of these tidings. For you must know that it was my own cousin, George Downing, who betrayed him."

"But I don't understand!" cried Lilias. "George Downing was the Lord Protector's Scoutmaster-General."

"And is now buying himself back into royal favour. He probably has a knighthood in view." Winthrop's tone was bitter. "In the circumstances, and knowing Mr Pride to be a friend of John Okey's, I felt that I must bring you the news myself."

"Thank you. That was kind of you. I think, if you don't mind, that we should leave my husband now to rest."

At the foot of the stairs, John Winthrop detained her. "Mistress Pride, I had no idea that your husband was so ill. I would not, had I known, have added to his burden for the world."

Lilias was at once defensive. "Your news was certainly a shock to him, Mr Winthrop, but that, I am convinced, is the only reason that he looks so pale. There is nothing wrong with my husband that time and rest will not cure."

She saw the fleeting look of disbelief in the other's face as he uttered some polite response. But all John Winthrop said was: "Mistress Pride, I have dabbled a great deal in medicine. I know something of the curative properties of minerals and plants. When I return home, I shall, if you permit, send you some of my Rubila. It is a concoction of my own; a compound of antimony, nitre and tin. I have found it efficacious in helping to cure most known diseases."

"That would be very kind of you, Mr Winthrop," Lilias replied.

"I would do anything," he assured her earnestly, "for those whom I admire. For those who fought for the Cause at home. The shame which my cousin Downing has brought upon the family will be hard for us all to bear. We feel that, in the eyes of the world, we are all sullied."

"Mr Winthrop," Lilias answered quietly, "if there is one thing which life has taught me, it is that every man has the right to be judged on his own merits, and not on those of his family or friends."

John Winthrop smiled and again pressed her hands. "Thank you for that," he whispered. "God keep and preserve both you and your husband."

*   *   *

272

The Earl of Chelwood stared around the little parlour of the Broad Street house like a man in a dream. So many memories came crowding back: Lilias in his arms, the feel of her body yielding to his, the brush of her hair against his cheek, her soft lips pressed to his ... It seemed like yesterday, not seventeen years ago. He felt that if he shut his eyes for a moment and opened them again, he would see her walk through the door ... But it was a hopeless dream: Lilias was gone. A whole waste of ocean flowed between them, and all because his messenger from Scheveningen had not reached her in time. Well, perhaps it was better so. Her staying could have changed nothing between them...

Nevertheless, when the door did at last open, he jumped, his heart giving a stupid, half-expectant leap. But it was only Regina Stillgo, much older than he remembered her, one of her gnarled hands gripping a cane on which she leaned. The Earl went forward to offer her his help, but was waved unceremoniously aside.

"I can manage without your assistance, thank you, my lord." The eyes, which Priam remembered as gentle and mildly flirtatious, now snapped at him fiercely. Nor was there any smile to mitigate their wrath. "And what is it you want? If you have come to spy for your royal master, rest assured that you will get nothing from me. I have no idea where my son-in-law is." Regina lowered herself slowly into a chair. "And why aren't you in London," she demanded, "dancing attendance on our new Portuguese Queen?"

"The wedding was in May, ma'am," Priam answered gently. "The junketings are long since over."

"Hmph..." Regina mellowed a little at his conciliatory tone. "What I said just now was not strictly true, but I have no intention of telling you Richard Pride's whereabouts. You're not dragging him back here, as Okey was dragged from Holland, to turn him into gallows' meat."

273

"I have no desire to know Richard Pride's whereabouts, ma'am.. That is not why I am here. I am established at Westovers for the summer with my wife and daughters, and as Judith Colefax is my god-daughter, I came to enquire after her health, and to know if there is anything I can do."

"Your god-daughter?" Regina's eyes narrowed into a fretwork of wrinkles as she searched her memory. "So she is! I had forgotten. Well, I suppose you've had precious little chance to acknowledge the connection for the past seventeen years." The rigid back relaxed slightly and the ghost of a smile entered the tired old eyes. But Regina still looked less pliable than of old. Since her sister's death the preceding year, something of Lucinda's mantle had settled about her shoulders. "And what sort of help do you propose to offer her, my lord?"

"I know that things cannot be easy for you, with so many under one roof. I wondered if Judith would consider coming as companion to the younger of my two daughters."

There was an indignant snort from the doorway. "No thank you, my lord, she would not!"

Judith herself stood there, glaring balefully at the Earl, her brusque rejection of his offer hanging heavily in the air.

Priam's first reaction was that this plain, awkward girl could not possibly be Lilias' child; it was as though a swan had given birth to a duck. But a second glance showed him that there was a similarity between mother and daughter, a similarity not of looks—Judith was all Barnaby's child in that respect—but of character. Lilias' determination not to be worsted by life was also apparent in Judith's face as, indeed, it was in the face of the young man who had come in behind her. Regina made the necessary introductions.

"My great-niece, Judith, as you have probably guessed. And this is her half-brother, Oliver."

"Oliver Pride," the young man said with a trace of defiance and, coming forward, he bowed ironically to Priam. There was no self-consciousness about him. He was, thought the Earl, an extraordinarily self-possessed young man, for one who could not be much more than sixteen. He went on: "And you, sir, are the Earl of Chelwood. I saw you last autumn, one day when I was riding to Bath, and my half-brother told me who you were."

"Indeed?" said Priam politely, for once at a loss for words.

"Yes. My lord, I overheard your offer just now concerning my half-sister, and your reason for making it. But as Judith has so ungraciously refused you, may I propose myself in her place? I should make an excellent secretary."

Judith and Regina began a chorus of protest and apology, but the Earl was merely amused.

"How old are you, Mr Pride?"

"Fifteen and a half, my lord. Sixteen in December. The very last day of December," Oliver added, as one wishing to make everything clear.

"A little young for my secretary, Mr Pride, don't you think?"

"No, sir, if you'll forgive me, I don't. I can read and write fluently in both English and French. I have a smattering of Latin and a head for mathematics. Ask my aunt, here. Ask my half-brother. I am assisting Eliot for the moment in the soap-making business, but I feel that it is a waste of my talents. I could be extremely useful to you, my lord."

"You certainly have a high opinion of yourself," the Earl murmured thoughtfully. But he did not seek confirmation of Oliver's claims from Regina; the boy was so patently telling the truth. Priam found him conceited, but amusing . . . and he was Lilias' son. The Earl rose abruptly from his chair.

"If you are sure, Mistress Colefax," he said, turning to Judith, "that you do not wish to accept my offer—?"

"And live on your charity? No, my lord, I thank you! I want nothing to do with the murderers of Thomas Harrison, John Okey and the rest."

"Judith!" Regina exclaimed warningly, but the Earl silenced her with a lift of his hand.

"In that case, I see that I am wasting my time. Yours, also." He looked at the expectant Oliver, and was reminded of a dog waiting for a bone. "You, on the other hand, Mr Pride, seem flatteringly eager for my company. Discuss the matter with your family. Then, if they all agree and you still feel the same way, come and see me again at Westovers and we'll discuss the matter further. Mistress Stillgo, your very obedient servant. Now I must take my leave."

*　　*　　*

"Must you go out?" asked Richard.

He was fretful today, and his enforced bed-ridden situation seemed to irk him more than usual. Lilias could not disguise from herself that his condition had worsened in the months since he had heard of Okey's arrest and execution. She stooped and kissed him, saying gently: "Elizabeth will be disappointed if I don't accompany her. And she and Makepeace have been so kind. . ."

"Yes, I know. I know." Richard gave a shamefaced smile. "What is this convention—or synod—all about?"

"It's to decide the question of Church membership. You remember, Richard, I told you. It's to decide if people who are not Separatists—or of the Elect, as they call it here—can have a voice in the running of the Bay Colony. Elizabeth is anxious to back Richard Mather, who thinks that they should. Makepeace is doubtful. He inclines to young Increase Mather's point of view that they should not. And they want me to go along to act as a sort of buffer between them."

276

"Increase Mather? Is he the sharp-faced young man who came to supper the other night? The one who treated me as though I were some kind of plaster saint?"

Lilias chuckled. "Hush, dear! You don't mention the idols of the heathen in Massachusetts. Yes, that's the one. He has just returned home, after taking his Master's degree at Trinity College in Dublin. Although the mind boggles at the thought of him in that Catholic country. No doubt he saw himself as a missionary amongst the pagan. But he certainly seems to be a well-regarded young man, especially since his engagement to Maria Cotton. Now, where's that new book that Pastor Mather so kindly lent you?"

Richard produced the Reverend Michael Wigglesworth's long and gloomy poem, entitled *The Day of Doom*, which was enjoying considerable success throughout most of the American colonies, and opened it reluctantly. He could not really believe in the avenging Jehovah portrayed by Mr Wigglesworth, nor in the doctrine that only the Elect of God would enter Heaven, everyone else being consigned to the fires of Hell. All the same, he made a pretence of reading, in order to set Lilias' mind at rest. It did not matter that he would throw the book aside as soon as she had left the room, as long as she thought him contented.

Lilias went downstairs to join Elizabeth, feeling guilty. In her pocket nestled a letter from Eliot, delivered to her that morning by the master of the *Falkland*, which had just docked in Boston harbour. Lilias knew how much a letter from home meant to Richard, but until she had prepared his mind for a part of its contents, she dared not let him see it. On the bend of the stairs, and in the light from the big high window, she took out the crumpled paper and read the offending passage yet again.

". . . And so, after much discussion with Oliver, and after much cogitation on my own part, and feeling that in your absence I stand to the others *in loco parentis*, I

277

agreed to let Oliver go. I hope you will forgive me, my dear father, but there was no possibility of consulting you, and Oliver will never take kindly to trade. He has neither the temperament nor the aptitude for it. He will be much happier in Lord Chelwood's employ. Moreover, I feel that in these uncertain times, for us to have a friend, literally, at court can do nothing but good. I know that you will find this sentiment reprehensible; and knowing, also, your feelings regarding the Earl of Chelwood, I must crave your forgiveness. But it means one less mouth to feed, and there are few such opportunities open to the son of a Regicide. I believe that I have made the right decision. . .."

Lilias' heart was slamming against her ribs in the same thunder of agitation that she had felt on first reading Eliot's letter. The Earl had not forgotten her then, nor that he was Judith's godfather. She grimaced wryly to herself. Small shrift he must have received from Judith in any plans he had made concerning her! But Oliver! Priam's secretary! She could just manage him proposing it. That boy had always had enough self-confidence for two.

"Lilias! Art thou there, lass? It's time we were going." Elizabeth's voice floated up to her from the bottom of the stairs. Lilias hastily folded up the letter and returned it to her pocket.

"I'm just coming," she said.

*　　*　　*

The North Road Church was full to overflowing to hear both Richard and Increase Mather put their points of view. In the end, it was a victory for the liberals, the vote going in favour of an extended franchise, and young Increase bowing gracefully to the will of the majority. He was less amenable, however, as they left the church in the waning light of the rain-washed evening. He took Makepeace Farleigh by the arm.

"We may have been forced to concede a point today,

my friend," he whispered, "but I shall make no such concession in the case of this new-fangled sect calling themselves the Society of Friends." Increase gave his thin-lipped smile. "Do you know what they are calling them in Dublin? Quakers! Because they quake and sob whenever they pray. Devil's spawn would be more accurate! Ah . . . excuse me, Makepeace, Elizabeth. Your servant Mistress Pride. I see my intended father-in-law. I must go and pay my respects." And Increase turned abruptly in the direction of a group gathered about the Reverend John Cotton.

"There is nothing wrong in valentines *per se*, my dear sir," the Reverend Cotton was instructing a friend in carrying tones. "But for young girls to write the names of young men upon them and then to draw them out of a hat, that can only be regarded as a game of chance and therefore an abomination in the sight of the Lord. Frivolity in any guise is greatly to be deplored. These colonies are not, I repeat *not*, to be founded upon such frivolous pastimes. Nor upon lascivious dancing nor the singing of wanton ditties!"

Lilias felt suddenly depressed. She had lived through so many years of gloom and repression that she longed, just for once, to wear bright colours, to go to a theatre, to watch the May-Day games or do any one of those silly and, yes, frivolous things which she remembered from her youth. She dimly recalled the itinerant groups of actors, jugglers and mummers who travelled the hot, dusty roads of Cornwall every summer, surrounded by eager, laughing crowds of people. But all that had vanished after the end of the war, and particularly after Cromwell had become Lord Protector. And now when, to judge by Judith's disapproving letters, the restoration of the monarchy was bringing back the gaiety and laughter to Old England, she was banished to the New, and to a sobriety of which even Dorothy Hazard would have approved.

279

"Thou art day-dreaming again, lass," Elizabeth Farleigh said, taking her hand. "Come on! Goody Machin wants us to meet a family who arrived this morning by the *Falkland*. Nice people, she says. Father, mother and two young sons. And they come from thy part of the world. That must be them, standing by the porch. Goody! Introduce us to thy friends. Mistress Pride is from Bristol, which is Gloucestershire way. Perhaps they might know one another."

Something about the man's back seemed vaguely familiar to Lilias, and for some reason there sprang into her mind a picture of herself seated on the cart at Lawford's Gate that cold spring day, while Richard crouched concealed amongst the crates of soap. Then at Elizabeth's words, the heads of the little group turned— and Lilias found herself staring into the at first astonished, then malevolent eyes of Trooper Trenchard.

★   ★   ★

"But why art thou so certain that this man—what's his name?—Trenchard—will go t' Governor?" Elizabeth asked for perhaps the tenth time, pausing in the task of helping Lilias and Richard to pack their few belongings into their battered travelling-chest.

Makepeace Farleigh, a dour Lowland Scot, who was assisting Richard to dress, looked up impatiently.

"Will ye no stop askin' foolish questions, woman! The lass has told us why. This man's nae friend tae either o' them. An' with guid reason. Eh, Richard, man, ye're as weak as a cat."

"But if he goes to the Governor," Elizabeth persisted, "this Trenchard will have to admit that he fought for the King."

"There's nae law against it, woman. Particularly," Makepeace added drily, "since the King has been restored to his throne."

"But the Governor knows about Richard."

280

"Aye, but not officially. Once Richard's presence here is brought to his notice and a charge laid, the Governor'll no be able to ignore him. He'll be bound to inform London and arrest Richard as one o' the men who signed the late tyrant's death-warrant. Can you stand up, Richard, lad, while I help you intae your breeches?"

Lilias pushed her hair back from her forehead and cast a hunted glance around the familiar room. "There . . . I think that's all . . . Elizabeth, are you sure that this cousin of yours in Jamestown won't turn us from her door? We shall be complete strangers to her, after all."

"Of course she won't! See, I've written her this letter explaining who ye are. Put it away safely in thy reticule." Tears sprang to Elizabeth's eyes. "It's all so sudden . . . Art thou sure, Makepeace, that *The Pride of the Bay* is sailing tonight, and not on the morning tide?"

"Of course I'm sure, woman! Do you take me for a fool?"

His wife, however, continued to clutch at straws. "But why are we so certain," she demanded, "that the Governor will inform the King?"

"Because it is his duty."

"But he's defied the King often enough before."

"Exactly," snorted her husband, wrapping a heavy travelling cloak about Richard's emaciated frame. "He's defied the King over the secession of New Hampshire and over the royal decree that the Church of England should become the official Church of Massachusetts. He can't go on defying His Majesty or *we* shall be fighting a civil war. Mrs Pride understands that right enough."

Lilias smiled wearily, her mind still reeling from the shock of seeing Trooper Trenchard again. She said: "Elizabeth, it's no use pretending, my dear. The Governor will have to throw Richard as a sop to the King while he fights him on other, far more important issues. It's time we moved on, in any case. We've trespassed on your hospitality for far too long."

281

"What nonsense!" Elizabeth drew Lilias towards the window out of earshot of the men. "Richard's in a bad way, hinny. Just listen to him cough . . . He'll not stand the journey well."

"I know, but there's nothing else we can do. It's the greatest luck in the world that *The Pride of the Bay* is sailing on the evening tide."

"I realise that, but . . . just be prepared, Lilias, that's all I'm saying."

Lilias glanced at Richard. "I think I've been prepared for a long time now, though I wouldn't admit it, even to myself." She went across the room and put her arm around her husband's shoulders. "If Makepeace and I support you, my dear, do you think that you can make the stairs?"

"I'm not an invalid," Richard snapped pettishly. But by the time he had negotiated the stairs and lower room, he was thankful to clamber into the back of the Farleighs' waggon. "No soap-crates this time," he said, grinning feebly at Lilias.

And when he was at last aboard *The Pride of the Bay*, he was completely exhausted and could only sink on to the bed in the tiny cabin put at their disposal by the Master. Elizabeth and Makepeace sat with him for a while, but the ship was almost ready to sail.

"I'll come on deck with you," Lilias said when they were finally forced to leave. "Richard—" She broke off, realising that he was already asleep.

"Let him be, lass." Makepeace stood looking down on his erstwhile guest, then stooped and pressed Richard's shoulder. It was a gesture of farewell and somehow to Lilias seemed significantly final.

Once on deck, she watched while the Farleighs clambered into the little boat which would carry them ashore. A cold wind was blowing from the north, and the lights of the Boston houses were strung like diamonds along the water's edge. Overhead, a sail tautened and flapped and the ship trembled with sudden life. The sailors were shouting, running, their bare feet slapping along the deck, to obey the Master's orders. And Lilias, her eyes blurred with tears, realised that she and Richard were fugitives once again: people without a home, setting out yet more into the terrifying unknown.

CHAPTER SEVENTEEN

Lady Cassandra Lithgow pirouetted in front of her bedroom mirror, watching the light ripple across the heavy folds of pale blue satin. Then she added a deep collar of Honiton lace and stood back to consider the effect.

"What do you think, Cressie? Will it do? Cressie! Do stop looking out of that window and attend to me. Will it do?"

Cressida reluctantly turned her head. "Will what do? Oh, the collar. Well, if it's for my lord Hartford's delectation, he'd probably prefer the dress without it."

"Don't be so indelicate, Cressie. This gown is cut far too low."

Her sister smiled. "For country bumpkins here in Somerset, perhaps. But Hartford is used to London fashions, and they say that Mrs Palmer—I beg her pardon! My Lady Castlemaine—has set a standard in dress that is positively indecent."

"That settles it then," Cassandra said firmly. "The collar stays. I will not be thought to be aping that horrid creature. And Hartford positively loathes her. He says she's fast."

"That man is either a prig or a liar," Cressida stated calmly, once more turning to look out of the window. "I can't think what you see in him."

"He's handsome, he's rich and he adores me," her sister answered frankly. "And I'm very fond of him," she added swiftly, forestalling Cressida's acid retort. "And Papa and Mama are pleased with my choice. I don't turn down suitor after suitor."

Cressida sighed. "No . . . Poor Mama! I really am a trial to her. But she's gradually becoming resigned to my

284

being an old maid." She stretched her arms above her head in her boyish fashion, scandalising her more decorous sister. "Oh, Westovers is so lovely this time of year. I wish Papa would let us live here all the year round."

"Pooh! I don't believe that. You're far more restless than I . . . Why do you keep looking out of the window? You've been staring at something for the last half-hour."

"Not something. Someone," Cressida corrected her softly.

Cassandra hurried to her sister's side, pushing the casement wider and peering down into the courtyard below. The Earl was there, talking to one of the gardeners and, a respectful pace or so behind, stood his secretary, young Oliver Pride.

"Now, there's what I call an interesting man," Cressida murmured thoughtfully.

"Oliver Pride!" Cassandra was scathing. "Oh, he's handsome enough, I grant you. Conceited, too, for who and what he is. But interesting? Besides, he's years younger than you are."

"Only five," Cressida answered a little too promptly. She saw her sister's quick, suddenly searching look, and coloured. "Sixteen—seventeen in December. Although, as you say, love, a mere baby compared with my sere and yellow twenty-one years." She rose gracefully, slipping an arm about Cassandra's waist. "You look beautiful. Hartford will be enchanted and probably insist on bringing forward the date of the wedding. And now I must go and help Mama choose the flowers to decorate the dinner-table. It's not every day that my only sister gets herself betrothed."

But in spite of her words, when Cressida emerged a few moments later into the courtyard, she made no attempt to turn in the direction of the hothouses, but went instead towards the formal gardens. Her father had now drawn some way ahead and was consulting with the workmen who were digging a new ornamental lake between two avenues of trees. Oliver turned his head at her approach.

"Lady Cressida." He bowed, his good-looking young face impassive above the plum-coloured coat.

He really was extraordinarily handsome, Cressida thought, with that very dark hair and those startlingly blue eyes. But that was not why he intrigued her: during the past few years she had displayed her indifference to even handsomer men than Oliver Pride. No, her interest had first been aroused because she sensed that Oliver was a part of that mystery which surrounded her father. Why should the Earl take such an interest in a Regicide's family? How did he come to be godfather to Oliver's half-sister Judith? And why was Oliver's colouring so exactly that of the young girl she had noticed that long-ago day at The Hague, when her father looked as if he had seen a ghost?

Because he was five years younger than herself, Cressida had at first approached Oliver as she would any young man so much her junior and her father's servant: with a touch of amused condescension. It amazed her now to remember it, so rapidly had she come to accept him in all ways as an equal. In mind, she had discovered him far more adult than many of the older men she knew who had been paraded by her parents as prospective suitors. Cressida suspected that Oliver Pride had been born old, that he was ambitious, cunning and as cold as ice. Why then did this not very attractive combination of attributes so appeal to her? She herself was impulsive, warm-hearted and needed a great deal of love. It was, therefore, patently ridiculous to lose her heart to a man such as Oliver Pride; but love was never reasonable and, in her experience, always had about it a touch of the absurd. What made Cassie love a stick like Hartford? What made her mother adore her father as she did, when her adoration was so obviously not returned?

286

"Mr Pride! I wanted a word with my father." What a lie! "But I see he is busy. A very pleasant morning, is it not?"

"Very pleasant, Lady Cressida. Cold, but that is only to be expected at this time of the year. The trees look beautiful. Autumn has always been one of my favourite seasons."

"Mine, too." Another lie. She hated the autumn and its melancholy that was akin to tears. "If my father does not need you for a while, Mr Pride, will you walk with me to the hot houses? I have promised my mother some help with the flowers. We will ask my father's permission as we pass."

Oliver bowed again, his outward calm belied by his racing thoughts. This strange girl, who reminded him of his mother in her strong independence of mind, liked him. He could not be mistaken: she made it too plain, for all that she thought that she did not. He was neither flattered, nor amused nor embarrassed as many another young man of sixteen would have been. He was too busy calculating how the fact could be turned to his advantage.

"I should be honoured, Lady Cressida."

"And delighted, Mr Pride?" Her laughing eyes challenged him, and moved him to an unexpectedly spontaneous grin.

"And delighted, naturally, Lady Cressida."

She cocked her head thoughtfully on one side, like an interested sparrow. "I'm not sure that delight is an emotion that comes naturally to you, Mr Pride . . . Oh, bother! Now what does Williams want?"

The stately footman had picked his careful way across the damp lawns and was speaking to the Earl. And from the manner in which their heads turned in Oliver's direction, it was not difficult to deduce that he was the subject of their conversation. Then Priam nodded and Williams trod purposefully towards Oliver.

"Mr Pride. Your brother, Mr Eliot Pride, has called to

see you and begs a word. You will find him awaiting you in the housekeeper's room."

Oliver looked startled, as well he might. It must be something very serious indeed to bring Eliot within a mile of Westovers. His dislike of the Earl was as intense as their father's.

"Very well," Oliver said. "With his lordship's permission, I shall come at once." He smiled regretfully at his crestfallen companion and followed the footman into the house.

Eliot was standing awkwardly in the middle of the housekeeper's sunny little parlour, patently ill at ease. Every rigid line of his thin body proclaimed his urgent desire to be gone.

"Eliot!" Oliver went forward, holding out his hand. "What brings you to Westovers this day? All's well at home, I trust? Aunt Regina? The girls? Geoffrey?"

"Yes, yes," Eliot said hastily. "It's not that." He raised his eyes to his half-brother's face and Oliver saw that he had been crying. It shocked him in the same way that a child was shocked by a parent's grief. Eliot had always been the strong one of the family on whom the others leant. "It's father," he went on. "We had a letter this morning from your mother, delivered by the master of *The Virgin Queen*, out of Virginia."

"*Virginia?* But—"

"Apparently father was recognised in Massachusetts and they had to leave in a hurry. They went, or, rather, sailed for Virginia, but father died during the voyage." Eliot's voice broke and he paused a moment, mastering his emotion. Then he finished: "His body was buried at sea."

*   *   *

Richard died in Lilias' arms during the first night out from Boston. The effort and excitement had proved too much for his already over-burdened heart.

288

Lilias awoke from an uneasy, wave-tossed sleep to hear him calling her. His voice was so faint that at first she thought it merely an echo from her own disturbed dreams, and by the time that she realised her mistake, he was sinking fast. She raised him in her arms and he smiled faintly, just brushing her cheek with his lips.

"Love..." The word was like the flutter of a moth's wing as the creature beat its way towards warmth and light. Then death rattled its grim warning in his throat. Lilias was barely conscious of the hot tears raining down her face as she sought to remember the Anglican Office for the Dead. But her mind was numb, paralysed with grief; and all that came into her head was Simeon's Song, the *Nunc Dimittis*. "Lord, lettest now Thy servant depart in peace, according to Thy Holy Word..."

The ship rolled as a wave took it, lifting it, then dropping it again into the heaving depths. Once again, Richard breathed the word: "Love..." And then he was gone, only the empty shell, the husk, lying there, held against her breast.

How long she had stayed like that Lilias did not afterwards remember. She was overwhelmed by her terrible sense of loss, of affection, for this man whom she had grown to love as she had loved her father, a love rooted in respect for his honesty and integrity and because he was persecuted for doing what he thought was right.

Richard was buried at sea the following day as the ship ran past Long Island. And two weeks later, Lilias found herself alone in Jamestown, the guest of Elizabeth Farleigh's cousin, Caroline Meake. The lady had accepted Lilias into her home in the same unquestioning way that all colonists seemed to do: glad of a fresh face, of company and of news from the land of their birth. But Caroline Meake was not as affluent as the Farleighs, and Lilias knew that her presence could soon prove an embarrassment to her hostess. It would be many months before her letter to Eliot was delivered and he could send her the money for her passage home. In the meantime, she had only a few guineas left and must set about earning her own living.

So one evening, as Caroline sat spinning by the light from the whale-oil lamp, the friendly clacking of the wheel an accompaniment to the ghostly whistling of the wind in the chimney, Lilias asked: "Do you know of anyone hereabouts, ma'am, who might be willing to employ me?"

Caroline Meake paused in her work, eyeing her visitor doubtfully. "We-ell," she said at last, "I did hear that a housekeeper was needed at Clontarf . . . No, no, my dear! Forget that I spoke. That wouldn't be suitable at all."

"Clontarf, ma'am? What, or where, is that? The only Clontarf I've ever heard of, was a battle in Ireland."

Caroline looked bewildered. "As to that, my dear, I couldn't say. But this is a tobacco plantation about five or six miles from here, and not at all the place for a decent Christian woman such as yourself."

"Why not, ma'am? What's amiss with this tobacco plantation?"

"For one thing, the owner's not married. A bachelor," Caroline added unnecessarily, then, with a glance over her shoulder, lowered her voice. "There are rumours of—well—Goings-On! Women . . . You know what I mean. And furthermore, the owner's an Irishman. There's no proof, you understand, that he's a Papist. No Masses. No priests. And, of course, there *are* Protestant Irish. Although, no doubt, a thieving, drunken bunch of rogues like the rest of them. At all events, he has a great deal of trouble getting decent bodies to work there. Which is probably why he pays so well."

At Caroline's last words, Lilias pricked up her ears and began to take a serious interest in the dissolute Irish owner of Clontarf. "Pray, ma'am," she asked, "what is this gentleman's name?"

290

Her hostess was immediately flustered. "Oh dear! I've no head for names. Whatever is it, now? I know it's one of those fairly common Irish names . . . O'Brien? No . . . O'Malley? I don't think so . . . Wait! I have it! O'Hara! Yes, that's it, I'm sure."

"And you think that this Mr O'Hara needs a house-keeper? Do you think that he would accept me if I applied to him for the position?"

"Oh, my dear, there's no doubt that he'd accept you. Elsie Brownlow told me herself that she had met him a fortnight back, and that he was at his wits' end. . ." Caroline's voice tailed off and she looked distressed. "But I really shouldn't have mentioned it. Please forget that I said anything, and I will start enquiries tomorrow for any employment there might be in Jamestown."

Lilias smiled at her reassuringly. "Please don't put yourself to the trouble, ma'am. My mind is quite made up to offer myself for the post of Mr O'Hara's house-keeper. On your own admission he pays well; and that must necessarily be my prime consideration." She leaned forward and squeezed her hostess's hand. "Please don't worry about me. There is no need, you know. I am perfectly capable of taking care of myself."

*　　*　　*

Geoffrey Pride, now fourteen years of age, leaned against the door of the musty lawyer's office and waited for his master, "Old" Fothergill, as he was known to all Bristolians, to transact his business.

When Old Fothergill had announced that Geoffrey was to accompany him on this visit to London, Geoffrey had been both pleased and excited. But once the capital was reached, his emotions, he found, were mixed. His father's stories of London, remembered from his youth, pictured a very different city: one of sober, honest, God-fearing men slowly clearing the streets of vice and corruption. But it was not like that at all. Ladies of the court flaunted themselves abroad next-door to naked, dresses cut revealingly low across their breasts. There were theatres, bear-baiting and cock-fighting; and places where women, naked from the waist up, leant out of windows, calling shamelessly to the men below. Piles of rubbish polluted the gutters.

Here at Smithfield, it was not quite so bad; at least it was spacious and clean. Channels had been dug to drain away the water and refuse into a small brick enclosure known as Smithfield Pond. The old horse-pool had been sanded over and the springs which had fed it dammed up. A railing guarded the central market-place, which had been raised and paved. The elm trees had been felled and the stumps made into seats. Earlier in the century, a crop of new buildings had mushroomed nearby, and Hosier Lane and Chick Lane had grown into thriving centres of commerce. Brokerage-houses had become common with the gradual return of the Jews.

Yet even here, Geoffrey did not feel comfortable. He supposed that Aunt Regina was right when she called him a prude. But he could not help what he was. It was not his fault if he did not like the same sort of things liked by other boys, if he shrank from all forms of excess, drunkenness and swearing and the soft, preying hands of women. . .

A voice said: "It's Geoffrey Pride, surely?" A young man, some three or four years older than himself, had stopped beside him, hand extended in greeting. A pair of large, dark, liquid eyes smiled down into his. "William Penn," the young man went on. "We met a few years ago, during one of my father's periodic visits to Bristol. Your father and mine are friends." He added on a lower note: "I was sorry to hear that Mr Pride had been forced to go abroad."

"He—he's dead," Geoffrey stammered. He had been fond of Richard in his quiet, undemonstrative way, and the wound of his bereavement was still too raw to bear any probing. He went on in a rush, to prevent any expression of sympathy: "I remember you well. But I think you haven't been in Bristol for some years?"

"No. We've been in Ireland, on the family estates. You may recall that my father was in disgrace after he failed to capture Hispaniola for the Lord Protector."

"Oh . . . I'd forgotten . . . But he did capture Jamaica instead."

"A poor substitute, Old Noll thought it. However, we're back in favour now. Back with the King. Back in this rag-bag of a city."

"You don't like it either." Geoffrey sounded relieved.

"Not much. But I'm off to Paris next week. Two years at the college at Saumur. It's a Huguenot college," he added quickly, seeing Geoffrey's eyes widen in horror.

"Ah . . . you'll like that, I daresay."

The other smiled his gentle smile. "Yes, if only to get away from my father. He and I don't get on."

"I didn't know. I'm sorry."

A thought struck young William. "You don't live in London now, do you?" he asked.

"No. I'm here with my master, Lawyer Fothergill, on business."

"The law, eh? I'm going to be apprenticed in Lincoln's Inn when I return from Saumur. Perhaps our paths will cross again, Mr Pride."

"I hope so. I'd like that," Geoffrey added naively. It was a long time since he had felt drawn to anyone as he did to William Penn.

The other, as though he felt something of the same emotion, again took Geoffrey's hand and shook it vigorously. Then he walked off quickly, turning into Hosier Lane.

"Well, that's something satisfactorily settled," said Lawyer Fothergill's voice behind Geoffrey, as he descended the creaking stairs. "Now, my lad, I want you to come with me as a witness when I call on that rogue, Rodriguez."

★   ★   ★

Clontarf was a low, two-storeyed, white building, set near the edge of the plantation. It was surrounded by the living-quarters of the slaves and indentured servants, by the workshops and curing-sheds and by the mill and garden, where enough food was grown to make the estate independent of the outside world. It had, too, its own wharf on the river, where the great hogs-heads of tobacco were loaded on to barges and ships.

A somewhat slatternly girl opened the door to Lilias and showed her into a long, narrow, sparsely furnished room. Little had been spent on luxuries, although tobacco planters were notoriously rich. And Mr O'Hara, according to Caroline Meake, was no exception.

Lilias wandered round the room, drawing her fingers across a table-top and regarding their dusty tips in disgust. Disorder and slovenliness still irritated her as much as when she was young, and she yearned to set this untidy house to rights. If for no other reason, she hoped that Clontarf's owner would give her the job.

She wandered over to the window and stared out at the quiet plantation, for autumn and winter were the fallow seasons, the time of rest and relaxation. Lilias had only been in Virginia for a matter of months but even so, she could not fail to realise how tobacco—its planting, growing, curing and, above all, its selling—dominated the life of the colony. Spring and summer were the busy months, when plantation owners watched over the sprouting plants with loving care; when slaves—deported criminals for the most part—hoed and weeded and discouraged the armies of caterpillars and worms; when every cloud in the sky caused acute anxiety, for a storm could ruin a crop in minutes. And when the leaves were just turning yellow, they had to be picked and dried and tied into "hands", then dried again on the sticks in the barns. Then, and only then, could the planters begin to take their ease. . .

The slatternly girl put her head around the door again. "'E's jus' come back," she informed Lilias dully. "I'll go an' tell 'im you're 'ere. It's Muster Day," she added by way of explanation.

"Muster Day?"

"Tha's right," the girl grunted, and withdrew.

Lilias shrugged and let her go. She heard the clatter of horses' hooves outside and men's voices raised, some regretfully on a note of farewell, others laughing, accepting the owner's invitation to step inside and take some refreshment. The shrill note of the little servant girl cut across their deeper tones, then the sounds became muted as host and guests entered the house. Evidently, the other plantation owners had no fear of corruption from a possible Irish Catholic, although Lilias suspected that Mr O'Hara was not introduced to their wives and daughters. Perhaps he did not care. He had no wife or daughter of his own to be slighted.

She cast another glance around the room, trying to catch some echo of its owner's personality, some tiny hint of taste or preference which would warn her what sort of a man she might expect. But there was nothing. The room was as impersonal, as devoid of character, as an empty barn.

There was a quick, firm tread in the hallway beyond. A voice said: "In here?" and then the door-handle turned. A moment later, Lilias found herself face to face with Patrick O'Mara.

* * *

Lilias was the first to recover her composure, outwardly at least. She dropped her prospective employer a polite curtsey and took covert stock of him beneath her lowered lids.

He was taller than she remembered, still as lean as

ever, his face and hands tanned by the wind and sun. His clothes were old-fashioned, even by the Bristol standards of two years earlier, but he sported one of the long, elaborately curled wigs which King Charles was making all the rage in London. The old litheness and grace of his movements was marred by a very slight limp.

For his part, the astounded Irishman saw the woman of whom he had such ambivalent memories now grown to full maturity, that extraordinary beauty mellowed and ripened so that it was at its zenith. Even the shabby black dress could not diminish it. And in the silence, the recollection of their last meeting loomed and grew until it hung between them like a monstrous shadow.

Lilias found her voice at last. "I—I'm sorry to be so stupid, but they told me . . . that is . . . I mean, I was expecting a Mr O'Hara."

"It's a common error," he answered, clearing his throat and mechanically motioning her to a chair. "Won't you please be seated, Mrs . . . I assume that it is still Mrs Pride?"

"Yes." She sat down on a dusty chair and stated baldly: "I am a widow. My husband died some months ago. Since then, I have been the guest of Mrs Caroline Meake in Jamestown."

"A widow. I see." Patrick moved like a somnambulist and seated himself astride the room's only other chair. "Or rather, I don't see. Mrs Pride, how do you come to be in the Americas?"

Lilias lifted her chin, partly in defiance, partly to observe him better. Morwenna's likeness to him was really quite remarkable.

"My husband was a Regicide," she told him bluntly, feeling that nothing but the truth would serve.

Patrick O'Mara's eyes widened in understanding. "So! Richard Pride signed the King's death-warrant, did he?"

"He did what he thought to be right," Lilias said fiercely.

296

Patrick made no answer for a moment: she could not begin to guess what was passing through his mind. Then he said slowly: "I was not aware that we were sheltering any of the Regicides in Virginia. Massachusetts now . . . I believe there are three or four of them there."

"We came from Massachusetts," Lilias answered levelly. "My husband had been ill for some time. The voyage was too much for him. He died on board *The Pride of the Bay*."

"May I ask why you left Massachusetts?"

"I was recognised." Lilias looked him in the eyes and half-smiled. "By Trooper Trenchard, who had just arrived in New England with his family. That should appeal to your sense of poetic justice, Captain O'Mara."

"*Mr* O'Mara," he corrected her, then threw back his head and laughed. "Trenchard, eh? Well, well! Life has a nasty habit of coming full circle, hasn't it, Mrs Pride? So, you want a job. May I ask to what end?"

"To the end of earning my living, sir." Her tone was waspish. "I have neither friends nor relatives here. And I need money if ever I am to return to England." Her own curiosity concerning him, she reflected, was likely to go unsatisfied. She could hardly question the man she hoped would be her employer.

Patrick, reading her thoughts in her eyes, took pity on her. "It is possible, in this country, Mrs Pride," he informed her gently, "for a slave who behaves himself to earn his manumission. Just as in the days of ancient Rome. But unlike ancient Rome, a freed slave here can, if he is industrious and prepared to work all the hours God gave him, become in time one of the masters. After your Bristol aldermen shipped me to Virginia—where, incidentally, I fetched the unprecedented sum of fifty guineas: Alderman Cann was, I trust, well pleased—I served as a slave for five years." His shoulders eased themselves almost imperceptibly under his coat. "I still have the stripes to show for it. Then, after I was freed, I

297

worked like a—" he grinned ironically "—like a slave for another four years until I had money enough to buy myself this plantation. It had been run down by a worthless owner, who sold it for a nominal sum to pay his gambling debts. Fortune, however, fickle jade that she is, decided that it was time to smile on me at last. I had three exceptional crops, and now ... well, now I'm a wealthy man." He saw Lilias' disparaging glance around the room and again he laughed. "As you have no doubt been informed, my dear, I can't keep servants; not, at least, those who are any good. The worthy local ladies suspect that I'm in league with the Pope—or the Devil." He shrugged. "In their book, it comes to the same thing."

"And are you? A Catholic, I mean?"

"And if I am, does it make any difference to you?"

"None whatsoever." Lilias regarded him straitly. "I'm not very religious, I think. Are you willing, Captain O'Mara, to give me the job?"

He returned her gaze somewhat enigmatically. At last he asked: "Are you willing to take it? Considering what ... what happened between us the last time we met?"

"Perfectly willing. You were not yourself then. Besides, I have told you, I need the money."

"You're a strange woman. I wonder if I ought to agree? For your sake, not for mine. Looking as you do, and with my reputation as a loose-living Irish Papist, you will have little reputation left to you. You will no longer be accepted in Jamestown."

"So I have already been warned by Mrs Meake. It doesn't matter as I don't intend to stay. When I have earned enough to pay my passage home to England, I shall go."

Patrick grimaced. "At least you're honest." It was his turn to let his eyes wander round the threadbare room. "You will have your work cut out to make anything habitable out of this place."

298

"Oh, I shall do it, never fear." She added, with a touch of bitterness: "I was never intended to be a fine lady."

At this moment, a voice from the other side of the closed door was heard calling: "O'Mara! Where the devil have you got to? Come on, man! You're missing the fun."

A thick-set, red-faced man appeared in the doorway, a full tankard of cider in his hand. At the sight of Lilias, however, he faltered. And as his gaze sharpened to take in her face and figure, his lascivious little mouth curled into a grin. "I beg your pardon. I didn't know you had company, my friend."

Patrick rose and answered coolly: "Not company exactly, Thompson. This is my new housekeeper, Mrs Lilias Pride."

The other's already prominent eyes boggled in speculation. Then he chuckled deep in his throat. "Housekeeper, eh? My God, if you don't get all the luck, O'Mara! How did you get wind of her? Hey, wait until I tell the others! You'll be the most envied man for miles."

"You see what you must expect," Patrick said when the man called Thompson had gone, guffawing loudly, to join the rest of his drinking companions.

"I have told you, it won't trouble me," Lilias answered tranquilly. "For the first time in my life, I have no one's reputation to think about but my own. It gives me a wonderful sense of freedom."

He nodded as though he understood. "I'm sorry," he said, "to inflict this bunch of Hell-rakes on you, but it's Muster Day." Then, seeing her look of enquiry, and remembering that she had been in Virginia for only a few months, he explained: "During this quiet time, between harvest and planting, every able-bodied man has to turn out to practise with the militia. But, needless to say, drilling is not the only occupation of the day . . . Very well, Mrs Pride, it is settled. The job of housekeeper is yours. When can you start?"

"At once, if you will be so good as to send one of your men to Jamestown to pick up my things. I will give him Mrs Meake's direction."

"It shall be done. And now, if you'll excuse me, I'll tell the girl to prepare your room." He paused, his hand on the door-knob, as though he wished to say something more but did not know how to begin. At length, he asked: "I suppose . . . I suppose you and your husband left England before the King . . . or any of the exiled Royalists returned?"

"Naturally."

"Naturally," he repeated, then went out quietly, closing the door behind him.

CHAPTER EIGHTEEN

"I wouldn't mind," Judith said angrily, "if she were some help about the house, but she isn't."

"But, my dear," Regina reasoned wearily, "she's only a child."

"Child! She's twelve years old. When I was that age, I was a great help to you and Mama."

"You were always such a good girl," Regina offered placatingly.

Judith slapped some dough on to a marble slab and began to knead it furiously. "And much thanks I ever got for it."

"Now, my dear, you know that's not true."

"Yes it is. And you know it's true, aunt!" Judith overrode Regina's feeble protest. "But that's not the point. With Mollie married and gone, and you not having been well, I have to run this house single-handed. I have to look after you and Eliot and Geoffrey. And Morwenna! She does absolutely nothing and no one takes her to task. No one complains. Not you, not Geoffrey—not Eliot."

Regina raised her shrewd old eyes and studied Judith's set face. Eliot! There was the nub of the grievance. If Eliot were not so fond of Morwenna, Judith would be perfectly content, for she had inherited all of her mother's domestic virtues. But it was Morwenna who had inherited Lilias' beauty. She enchanted everyone she met. Poor Judith, Regina thought. She hadn't only her father's looks to contend with, but also Barnaby's peevish nature. Like him, she alienated those very people she most wished to attach.

Regina moved her chair a little closer to the kitchen fire. In spite of the warmth of the spring day, she still felt cold. It had seemed such a never-ending winter. The news of Richard's death had hit her hard. Somewhere, deep down, she had always cherished the hope of seeing him again. She had always liked him, even though she had stood a little in awe of him. She had not altogether liked it when he had married Lilias, but it had proved a good marriage and Lilias had stuck loyally by him. . .

The heat of the fire was making her sleepy. Her thoughts fused into an irregular pattern. A riot of pictures tumbled through her mind, without sequence or order: the birth of Eliot, her only grandchild; Lilias, as she had first seen her, an already beautiful girl of sixteen; Dorothy, leading the way to the Frome Gate to defy Prince Rupert and his men; the King, standing in her own front parlour . . . The pictures whirled and kaleidoscoped together. After a while, she began to snore.

Judith's thin mouth set like a trap and she pummelled the dough even harder. Then she began to roll it. She was making rabbit pie because Eliot liked it: it was infuriating because it was also a favourite of Morwenna's.

The latch of the kitchen door clicked and her half-sister came in, eyes sparkling, her dark hair tossed by the wind.

"I'm home," she announced buoyantly, "and I've brought Eliot with me. I called in at his dull old soap-works and persuaded him that he needed a rest."

Eliot followed her into the kitchen. "Minx!" he said, tweaking one of the curls which framed her laughing face. "You're forcing me to set a bad example to the hands."

Morwenna pouted and kissed his cheek. She was already very tall for her age. "You know that's not true," she scolded him. "You're always working. You're out of here at the crack of dawn and not back again until nearly midnight."

"An exaggeration, miss," Eliot smiled, slumping into

302

the chair opposite Regina's. "Grandmother is well away, I hear."

"Let her be," advised Judith. "She has been extremely unwell all day. But Morwenna's right," she added grudgingly. "You work too hard. Look at you! You're far too thin and there are circles beneath your eyes."

"It's not easy," he retorted, "when there are five of us to feed. Particularly when you are the son of a Regicide." His tone was bitter. "There are a lot of people nowadays who have forgotten their own part in the war and how they cheered at the death of the King. They are all loyalists now and don't want to buy from me."

"Then why won't you take my money, that I inherited from my father?" Judith demanded angrily. "Is Mr Pride too proud?"

It was an old, childish joke between them, but this time Eliot did not smile.

"Judith, we have had this out before. That money is your dowry. It belongs to you and your future husband."

His cousin's mouth opened, then shut again, thin and almost bloodless. Morwenna wondered what had annoyed her half-sister this time, but Judith's sour moods were too frequent to give her much pause for thought. Besides, she had other matters weighing on her mind.

"Eliot," she said, going to kneel beside his chair, "when is Mama coming home?"

"Soon. I am only waiting for a ship whose master I can trust absolutely, to send her the money for her passage." He glanced sideways at Judith as he spoke. It struck him as odd that she had never offered to help her mother. Once when he had broached the subject to her, she had snapped at him, bad-temperedly.

"The soap-works belong to her now that father is dead. I see no good reason why I should provide the money."

Morwenna got up and began to flutter aimlessly about

303

the kitchen, finally coming to rest beside the table where Judith was working. She picked up some trimmings of the dough and began to fashion them into a flower. Judith's precarious hold on her temper snapped.

"If you have nothing better to do than that," she shouted furiously, "you can help by setting the table for supper."

Morwenna looked at her, aghast. "Of course. I'm sorry." She hurried guiltily from the kitchen.

"Must you speak to her quite so harshly?" Eliot asked. "I know she's thoughtless, but. . ."

"That's right," Judith interrupted him, "you take her part! You always do, you and Aunt Regina!" And, bursting into noisy tears, she too ran out of the kitchen. The door slammed behind her and a moment later Eliot heard her overhead in her room.

He stood up, irresolute, wondering if he ought to follow; but he was sick to death of her petty tantrums and could hardly force his way into her bedchamber. He leant over his grandmother and gently shook her by the shoulder.

"Grandmother! Grandmother, wake up, please. I want to talk to you about Judith."

But there was no response, and it suddenly occurred to Eliot that Regina had not been snoring for the past few minutes. A cold fear gripped him as with trembling fingers he felt for her pulse. But the wrist lay slack and lifeless in his hand.

*　　*　　*

Lilias opened her eyes and lay for a few moments, wondering what had awakened her. It was very dark and, for the moment at least, very still. The only sound was the sighing of the wind through the trees; and even after several months, she found it difficult to adjust to the quiet. No city, certainly neither Bristol nor Boston, was as silent as this strange wild country at night.

They had been odd months, with an armed neutrality carefully preserved between herself and Patrick O'Mara. No reference to the past had been made since that first, uneasy interview: always they were employer and employed. Lilias had wrought wonders in the creature comforts and general standard of living at Clontarf. The house-servants, at first disinclined to take her seriously because of the way she looked, dismissing her as just another of the master's women, soon discovered their mistake. The girls were set to clean and scour and mend, while Lilias herself took charge of the kitchen. With full stomachs, she reasoned, they would be a great deal easier to manage; and her reputation as a cook began to grow. In the surrounding countryside, amongst the men at least, an invitation to dine at Clontarf soon became highly prized and a matter for eager acceptance. Yet however much young bucks like Giles Thompson tried on these occasions to catch a glimpse of the lovely Mrs Pride, they were always disappointed.

"Keeping her for yourself, you sly devil, eh?" Thompson would roar, nudging Patrick in the ribs and remaining unconvinced by his host's cold rebuttal of the accusation.

Lilias was well aware that her reputation was damaged beyond repair. On her rare visits to Caroline Meake, she was icily received by the other ladies of Jamestown. She was unconcerned, however, by the gossip. Soon she would have earned enough money to return to England, and that was all that mattered. And she had no need to go into Jamestown if she did not wish it: the plantation was almost entirely self-supporting. And what few commodities could not be grown or made, were brought up river to the private wharf and unloaded by the slaves.

These deported criminals and ex-prisoners-of-war—for the Bristol merchants had done a thriving business with the Scots as well as the Irish during the years of the Protectorate—were kept in subjection by foremen with evil-looking whips. They were as well treated at Clontarf as anywhere, as far as Lilias could judge, although the fact that Patrick, too, had suffered as a slave in no way softened his attitude towards them.

Once, and only once, in the very first week, had Lilias ventured to protest against a flogging. "You, of all men," she had reproached her employer, "should know what it is to suffer as a slave."

"Oh, I do," Patrick had informed her silkily. "I also know every trick and ruse of which the criminal mind is capable, and the dangerous volatility of desperate men. You content yourself with running the house, Mrs Pride, and leave me to run my plantation."

"Perhaps if you had been flogged—" Lilias had foolishly persisted, but had had no time to get further.

With an oath that had blistered the air, he had ripped off his coat and shirt and turned his back towards her. She had seen at once the deep criss-cross scarring of healed stripes.

"And no doubt," he had whispered viciously, "Trooper Trenchard could show you the same."

After that, the relationship between them had deteriorated to one of chill politeness and wary respect, each taking care to keep as much as possible out of the other's way. If he wished her to stay beyond the span of time she had allotted to herself, he gave no hint of it; nor did he once offer her a word of praise for the changes she had wrought at Clontarf. For her part, Lilias wanted none, preferring to forget that he was Morwenna's father. She had very little time to feel lonely or to miss Richard, so busy was she kept reorganising the house. It was a challenge in which she revelled, inducing a housewifely order out of chaos; and every night throughout the whole of that winter, she fell asleep as soon as her head touched the pillow.

With the coming of spring, there was still plenty to occupy her time. She saw less and less of Patrick as, with

306

the end of the fallow season, with last year's crop safely converted into cash, he was out and about, superintending the planting of new seed. And now, with the young plants needing constant attention, he rode out every day overseeing the slaves. The hospitality and jollification of the winter months ceased, each planter similarly occupied. There were one or two dinner parties, but not, Lilias noted, of a very convivial nature. There had been one such meeting this very evening at Clontarf, but no one had got drunk and it had broken up early. Lilias, glimpsing the huddle of heads around the dinner table and hearing the earnest murmur of voices as she crossed the hall, had concluded that it was a business meal. She had retired to bed after supervising the clearing away of the dishes, and had fallen asleep at once.

Now, however, she was inexplicably awake, her ears straining into the eerie silence. Then she heard it: the dull thud of hooves galloping fast along the dirt road that led to the house from the landward side of the plantation. The faint drum-beat increased in intensity as she slid out of bed and made her way across the room to her window. This gave on to the yard at the back of the house, and as she peered out, she saw the dark shadow of a horse plunge to a standstill below her. The young lad who looked after the stables ran forward from the darkness of a doorway where, presumably, he had been on the watch and waiting. He gentled the spent animal as its rider slid awkwardly to the ground; and even in that dim light, Lilias could see that the man was clutching his shoulder. The boy exclaimed, and the deep, quick tones of Patrick O'Mara bade him be silent. There was some further brief altercation between them, then the boy led away the horse, and Lilias, whose eyes were now accustomed to the darkness, saw that the animal's hooves were muffled with rags. Patrick lurched unsteadily into the house.

Pausing only to throw a wrap around her night-shift and to light her bedside candle, Lilias descended to the deserted kitchen. She was surprised, as she passed the staircase window, to note that first lightening of the sky which heralds dawn.

Patrick was leaning against the well-scrubbed table, easing himself out of his coat, and Lilias' upheld candle showed the spreading stain of blood across his sleeve. He glanced up sharply as she entered, then hissed: "What in God's name do you think you're doing? Douse that light for Mary's sake!"

She did as she was bid, hurrying forward and pushing him on to a stool. The growing pallor of the sky beyond the uncurtained window was sufficient for her to see by.

"You're hurt," she breathed, seizing a pan and going to the water-barrel in the corner of the kitchen.

"One of the militia men's bullets winged me, nothing more." But his voice was faint.

Lilias put the pan of water on the table and began tearing a clean pudding cloth into strips. After one look at Patrick's face, however, she abandoned this task and ran into the living-room, where a decanter of brandy stood on the sideboard. She splashed some into a glass with a hand which was not quite steady, and returned to the kitchen to find Patrick slumped down almost to the floor. She raised him with difficulty, forcing the spirit between his bloodless lips.

He spluttered and, to her relief, revived a little, enough at any rate to drag himself back on the stool and to sit passively while she ripped open the left breast of his shirt. The wound was, indeed, only a flesh one, the bullet having passed cleanly through his shoulder. The copious bleeding made it look worse than it actually was; and as soon as Lilias had staunched this with a wad of linen bound tightly into place, a little colour began to creep back into Patrick's face. He took another swig of brandy and revived yet more.

"You're the first woman I've ever met," he said with his mocking smile, "who doesn't faint at the sight of blood."

"I've lived through two sieges," she reminded him tartly, binding another strip of linen around his shoulder.

He raised his good arm and put it about her neck, hoisting himself uncertainly to his feet. "Get me up to bed, and fast," he commanded. "I gave them the slip about three miles back when we all dispersed. But they won't be long picking up my trail."

"They? We?" she queried, supporting him as best she could as they moved towards the door and into the hall. But before he could reply, she added: "If someone's after you, as I gather they are, I'd better go back as soon as possible and clear up the kitchen. And what about your horse?"

He grinned weakly. "What a practical woman you are, Lilias Pride. The boy will have seen to the horse and hidden it. But you're quite right. Let me hang on to the stair-rail, here, while you attend to matters in the kitchen."

By the time that Lilias had thrown away the blood-tainted water, tidied away the torn cloth and made certain there were no bloodstains on table or floor, Patrick had managed to haul himself halfway upstairs. As, with Lilias' assistance, he reached the landing and long corridor at the top, he paused, his head jerked upright, listening.

"I thought I heard hoof-beats," he murmured. "Wait! I was right. There they are again. Listen! A fair way off still, but coming fast. Get me undressed and into bed. When they knock on the door, delay as long as possible. And remember, you haven't heard or seen a thing."

"And how will that serve you?" Lilias demanded impatiently. "It won't prove that you haven't been out or done whatever it is you've been doing. I don't know what you've been up to, Mr O'Mara, but there's only one way to save you now. You'll have to get into my bed."

* * *

Lilias drew the bolts of the big front door with shaking hands, but the face which she presented to the captain of militia was one of sleepy indignation.

Captain Marston, who was just preparing to hammer the oak and shout "Open in the name of the King!" was startled by the appearance of Mrs Pride. He had been expecting one of the house-servants, whom he could bully.

"M-Madam!" The Captain stammered a little. "I should be glad of—I mean, I demand a word with Mr O'Mara."

"At this hour of the morning, captain?"

"That, madam," said Marston, recovering his poise, "is not your concern. Just take me to him." And without waiting to be invited, the Captain pushed past her into the hall. Two of his men followed. The others, plainly acting on instructions, remained outside.

"I'm afraid that I cannot take you to him," Lilias began. "Mr O'Mara is naturally asleep. However—"

"Upstairs, lads," ordered Marston. "Grab him before he has time to escape down the back flight. Not that it will avail him much. Hawley and Rogers are waiting to nab him if he does."

"Captain, I must protest—" Lilias began again, but was thrust back by a powerful arm as Marston and his men made for the stairs. She ran after them.

"Wait! Please, Captain! You don't understand..." She prayed to Heaven that she could play her part convincingly.

On the landing, Captain Marston paused to refresh his memory. He had been a guest of Patrick's often enough and knew the location of his bedchamber.

"The first door on the right, lads. And don't stand any nonsense. You probably won't have to. We winged one of them, and I've a fancy that it was O'Mara."

"Wait! Please!" Lilias tried again, but was again ignored. Captain Marston strode after his men.

310

"Now then, O'Mara—" he began, only to break off short as he surveyed the empty room and obviously unslept-in bed. "Not here, by God! I made sure that he'd head for home."

"Gone to earth somewhere," suggested one of the other men, and the Captain nodded, his pendulous jaw quivering.

"Send out the patrols," he ordered.

"Captain." Lilias moved forward and touched him on the arm. The small eyes between the puffy lids swivelled towards her, and Lilias cast down her own eyes, trying to look suitably abashed. She was beginning to enjoy herself.

"Well, Mrs Pride?"

"Captain, I have been trying to tell you . . . You will find Mr O'Mara in . . . in my room, where, I have to admit, he . . . he has been all night."

The three men goggled at her, then moved as one along the corridor to the only other door which stood open. Patrick, wearing his night-shirt to conceal his bandaged shoulder, was sitting up in Lilias' rumpled bed.

"For God's sake, Lilias," he complained loudly, as she entered in the Captain's wake, "couldn't you head them off? A pretty fluttering this'll cause in the dovecotes of Jamestown."

"I-I'm sorry, but I couldn't prevent them. Captain Marston wouldn't . . . I mean, he seems particularly anxious to see you."

"Well, Marston, what the Hell's the matter?" snapped Patrick. "Here's a God-forsaken hour in the morning to come bothering an honest citizen."

Lilias saw him flinch as he rolled, inadvertently, on to his injured arm, and she moved forward, blocking the militia men's view. "Captain Marston appears to believe that you have been breaking the law," she said.

"Oh? Indeed?" Patrick was now lying nonchalantly

311

against the pillows, his pale face shadowed by the four-poster's curtains. "What is it that I'm supposed to have been doing?"

"You know damn well what you've been doing!" Marston strode nearer the bed, his suspicions by no means allayed. Lilias sat down on its edge, and Patrick's arm came round her, pulling her back against his good shoulder.

"I'm buggered if I know, Marston." He sounded like a man pardonably irritated. "But I'd be glad if you'd enlighten me."

"Night-riding," the captain retorted succinctly, but his confidence was a little shaken.

"Night-riding?" Patrick mocked. "My dear Marston, I'm not as stupid as that, I trust. What? Destroy my own and my neighbours' crops?"

The Captain's flabby cheeks quaked indignantly. "Don't play the innocent with me, O'Mara. All you plantation owners have done it at some time or another, and we all know why."

"Well, not tonight, Marston. At least, not me. I've had other—er—despoiling to do. Night-riding, perhaps, but not the kind you mean."

Marston's little eyes stared once again at Lilias, and his tongue flicked in and out, like a lizard's. One of the other two men sniggered.

"Is that true, Mrs Pride?" the Captain asked.

"Perfectly true," she answered with composure. "Whatever 'night-riding' might be, it has not been indulged in this night by Mr O'Mara."

"You'd swear to that? On oath?"

Lilias hesitated, but only for the fraction of a second. Common sense told her that it was unlikely to come to that. "Of course," she answered steadily.

"We-ell—" Marston continued to look doubtful. It was plain that he was still unconvinced.

A voice sounded in the corridor and one of the men

slipped from the room. He returned after a moment or two to say: "The only horse in the stables hasn't been ridden tonight. It seems we were mistaken, Captain, after all."

"Only one horse?"

"A bay, sir."

The Captain turned back to Patrick. "Where's the roan?"

"I lent her to young Danby," Patrick lied glibly. "His mare has cast a shoe." He trusted devoutly that young Danby, who had not been one of tonight's ride, would have the sense, if asked, to confirm his story.

The Captain grunted. "There was a roan out tonight ... However, it need not have been yours, I suppose. Thompson owns a roan and so does Purley." He hesitated. He was still not sure in his own mind whether he believed Patrick's story or not. There was, of course, one way to make certain: order him to strip and see if he were wounded. But by doing so, he might rob Mrs Marston of a titbit of scandal which would gladden her heart and make her, for a day or two at least, a damn sight easier to live with ... He cleared his throat and came to a decision.

"I ask your pardon, O'Mara. And yours, Mrs Pride. I have to admit that I made a mistake. And now, if you'll permit it, we'll be going. We've wasted enough time here, already. Your servant, ma'am." He leered a little as he bent to kiss Lilias' hand.

"I hope, Marston," Patrick said anxiously, "that we can rely on your, and your men's, discretion?"

"Naturally, my dear O'Mara. Silent as the grave."

"Which means," said Patrick, after Lilias had returned from seeing the Captain and his men clear of the premises, "that he'll tell Mrs Marston just as soon as he gets home, and it will be all over Jamestown by tonight. Your reputation, my dear, is irrevocably lost."

"It was lost, in any case, as soon as I came to work

here," Lilias answered, pouring him some water. When he protested: "You will certainly have no more brandy today," she informed him. "It will only inflame your wound. And perhaps now, I might be permitted to know what you have been up to. 'Night-riding' did Captain Marston call it?"

"Yes. It means that we—the plantation owners—some of us, at least—go out destroying our own and each others' crops."

She stared at him as though he had taken leave of his senses. "B-But why?" she managed to stammer at last.

"We're overproducing." His breath rasped with the effort of speech, and there was a grey tinge about his mouth. "Twenty years ago, tobacco sold at sixpence the pound. Ten years ago, the price had dropped to threepence. Now, it's only twopence the pound. Last year, we petitioned the King to forbid all planting of tobacco for one year, but he refused. So!" He shrugged, an automatic gesture which made him wince with pain. "A few of us decided to take the law into our own hands."

"I'm sorry. I'm stupid, I suppose, but I still don't understand."

"The first rule of economics, my dear; the scarcer a commodity, the higher its price. The simple law of supply and demand."

"But why not simply plant less tobacco?"

He moved his head impatiently against the pillows. "Because not all the planters would agree to do so. There are always those willing to grow rich at the expense of others. While some of us tried to force up the price by planting less, the rest would seize the opportunity to monopolise the market . . . No; the only way is to destroy a part of everyone's crop, whether he favours the scheme or not."

"In short, night-riding. Even though it's illegal?"

"As you say, night-riding. Even though it's damn dangerous and might land us all in prison."

"I see." She saw his look of surprise and, interpreting it correctly, laughed. "Did you expect my good Puritan soul to be shocked?" *Does it shock your good Puritan soul?* Priam had said that to her once, long, long ago. She went on quickly: "I've seen too much and grown too long in the tooth for that."

"How old are you?" His tone, for the first time, was interested, curious.

"Thirty-seven," she answered candidly, and it was his turn to laugh.

"You're remarkably honest. But perhaps when a woman looks as you do, she can afford to be." He recalled having once referred to her as a gypsy. He would never call her that today. Her hair was as dark, her eyes as blue, her figure even better than he remembered it. But there was a self-assurance about her, an indefinable serenity that was, paradoxically, very disturbing. His pulse quickened a little as he looked at her, and it had nothing to do with his wound. "Help me back to my room," he commanded. "It's almost daylight. The servants will be astir in a minute."

"If you insist. But where is the point? If, as you say, the news that I am your mistress will be all over Jamestown by this evening, then the servants are bound to hear. And anyway, half of them have put me in your bed already." She deftly removed a pillow from behind his shoulder and urged him down in the bed. "You need a wife to look after you. Why have you never married?"

A picture of Magdalen's face rose in his mind. It was ridiculous, he told himself, as he had told himself a dozen or so times every year of his life, to let a memory stand between him and marriage. And a memory so old, so faded, that it was like a portrait which had been hung too near the sun; the colours had lost their sheen and the details had been robbed of their sharpness. But the truth was that he had never met any woman, apart from Magdalen, whom he had wanted to marry. Twice, during

315

the past four years, he had been on the verge of proposing, each time to the daughter of a good Catholic Maryland family, Maryland being a county where he transacted lucrative business. But each time something had held him back: a pale face and gentle blue eyes, surrounded by an aureole of fair hair...

"I am perfectly happy as I am," he answered Lilias, in a tone intended to rebuff her. But when she seemed totally unabashed by her impertinence, he found himself adding: "My one great regret is my lack of children."

She glanced up sharply, trying to see his face in the shadow of the curtain. "You said that as though you really meant it," she murmured slowly.

"I do mean it. I should not have said it, else. I should dearly love to have had a son."

"Or daughter?"

"Or a daughter, if that had been God's will ... Why are you looking at me like that?"

Lilias twisted her hands together in her lap. Did he not have a right to know that he had a child? Was it not every man's right? And now that Richard was dead, and fate had brought them together like this, should Patrick not be told? Surely everyone needed to know that he had perpetuated his seed, perhaps the only true immortality of the spirit...

Patrick's sound arm moved and his hand touched her wrist. He was staring at her under frowning brows. "What is it?" he asked with unaccustomed gentleness.

It was all that was needed. With the morning star hanging low in the sky beyond the uncurtained window, and with the first stirrings of day blending their enchantment with the night, it was a moment for secrets and confidences.

"You have a child," Lilias told him quietly. "A daughter. She is twelve years old and her name is Morwenna."

Patrick blinked as though she had hit him, unable at

316

first to take in what she had said. "I have a daughter?" he repeated.

Lilias nodded mutely. She watched him while he did calculations in his head and the significance of the twelve years suddenly struck him.

"Your daughter," he said at last, and it was not a question. "Yours and mine."

"Yes. But everyone, including Morwenna herself, thinks that she is Richard's child. She isn't. She was not a month premature as everyone believed. And she looks a lot like you, for anyone who has eyes to see."

"My child. My daughter." He raised his hand and shielded his eyes. "Mother of God ... that night..." There was a long pause which she thought would never end, then, finally: "I'm sorry."

"You have no need to be. I have had great happiness from Morwenna. And Richard adored her ... He always wanted a daughter, you see."

"What is it you call her?" Patrick asked, as though by concentrating on irrelevancies he would give himself more time to understand and accept the greater truth.

"Morwenna. It's the name of a Cornish saint. I thought ... if you ever did find out ... you would approve."

There was another silence, punctuated by the shrilling of the birds as they flew back from their nightly roost. At length, Patrick hoisted himself painfully on to his right elbow.

"You are the mother of my child," he said wonderingly. "All these years and I never knew. Never suspected, never even thought..."

The young girl who had been trained by Lilias to make the beds and sweep upstairs came clattering in, trailing her broom. At this hour, with the sun already fingering the sky beyond the trees, the room should have been empty, Lilias dressed and downstairs, attending to the cooking of the breakfast. The girl stopped abruptly on

317

the threshold, her button mouth agape.

"Oh lawks! Oh ma'am! I'm sorry . . . I thought. . ." Her round eyes took in Patrick lying in Lilias' bed. She swallowed hard and gave an embarrassed giggle. Then she turned bright pink and fled.

"Well," observed Lilias drily, "it seems that the servants won't have to wait for the news until someone goes into Jamestown."

"It doesn't matter." Patrick's voice was curt. "As soon as I am fit enough, we shall be married."

"I—I beg your pardon?"

"Married," Patrick repeated. "You and I. You said yourself that I need a wife, and you are the mother of my child. What better reason could we have?"

"We could love one another," Lilias suggested, anger at this sudden and total assumption of authority over her life at war with her feminine instinct and need for male protection. Woman's eternal dilemma, she thought with a passing smile. She went on: "Besides, you know that I intend returning to England."

"And I shall come with you." He held up a hand. "No, don't speak until you've heard me out. I've been thinking of selling the plantation for some little time. This only hastens my decision. Tobacco growing is hard on the soil. Every seven years or so, you need to plant new land, and the soil of Clontarf is almost exhausted. It had been worked for the best part of three years when I bought it from the previous owner, and fresh land hereabouts is scarce. I've made sufficient money to enable me to live in comfort for the rest of my life, provided it's wisely invested. Marry me, and we'll return to England together. Think of it! London. The court. Pretty clothes. And, if you wished it, Morwenna could come to live with us."

Lilias' determination to refuse him began to waver before the picture he had conjured up. Music, dancing, gaiety: all those things which her starved soul craved,

318

could be hers. And Patrick was the father of her daughter. . .

"Morwenna must never know that she is not Richard's child. She loved him very much, you see."

"She might grow to love me." There was an empty, hungry look in Patrick's eyes. "But until then . . . very well, let her go on believing that Richard Pride was her father. It will be enough just to see and hear her every day. My own flesh and blood . . . I promise you."

"*We* don't love one another," Lilias said again. Love seemed unexpectedly, desperately important.

"Does that matter?" His voice was thin and jagged with weariness. He had lost a lot of blood. "Did you love your first husband? Or Richard Pride? Love is not always ours to command."

She glanced at him, suddenly wary. Was there someone in his life as inaccessible to him as Priam was to her? But he was right. She had married twice before without love; and although her first marriage had been disastrous, her second had brought her great happiness and lasting affection. Moreover, there was already an added bond in the person of Morwenna.

There were other, less worthy but nonetheless practical considerations. Patrick was a wealthy man, and, since the Restoration, Richard's affairs were in sad disarray. And in a society where Regicides were unkindly remembered, this marriage would afford her the protection of a different name.

Was she being too mercenary? Too calculating? Perhaps. But there were her children to think of, and she had never been a sentimental woman. She had always accepted life as it came.

"I must have time to think," she told him, "and you must rest."

But in her heart of hearts, she already knew what her answer would be.

PART FOUR
1664–1670

Therefore the love which us doth bind,
But Fate so enviously debars,
Is the conjunction of the mind,
And opposition of the stars.

Andrew Marvell, 1621–1678

CHAPTER NINETEEN

"You want Morwenna to live with you in London?" Eliot's tone was cold. "May I ask why?" His eyes were like flint.

He had, thought Lilias, all the sanctimoniousness of his father without Richard's sense of the fitness of things. In similar circumstances, Richard would have seen in an instant that he had no right to ask such a question.

"No, you may not," she rapped back sharply, then added: "Morwenna is my daughter, and it is natural that I should want her with me." And realising that she had fallen into the trap of self-justification, she lapsed into furious silence.

She was anxious to be gone, away from Bristol and from the Broad Street house with its ghosts and crowding memories, to the new life which awaited her in London. The long months' journey from Virginia had tired her, even though it had been, according to the ship's Master, an easy voyage. Moreover like many another before her, she had discovered that returning home after a lapse of time was not the entirely pleasant experience to which she had looked forward. On one hand, there were gaps and changes. Regina's death had shaken her more than she would have believed possible; new buildings were mushrooming everywhere in Bristol, from the Llandoger Trow in King Street to the rows of brash houses on Castle Green. On the other hand, however, it was like stepping back into some enchanted fairyland, where everyone had been asleep for a hundred years. Disappointment that all was not exactly as she had left it warred with irritation at an experience more limited than her own. The conflict of emotions, the inconsistency of her feelings, left Lilias worn and fretful.

But it was not only that. If she were honest, she must acknowledge that her marriage to Patrick O'Mara had been a mistake, more so than her first, unlucky marriage to Barnaby Colefax, for she and Barnaby had never really cared for one another. With Patrick it was different. Their wedding night had brought a physical rapture which not only demanded constant satisfaction, but also laid the foundation for love to grow. And it was the resistance which each set up to this intimate and more lasting relationship which caused the sparks to fly and produced the daily friction between them. Looking back over the vista of years, Lilias recognised that from their very first meeting, here, in this house, there had been that same ambivalence between them. Perhaps when they got to London they would be able to go their separate ways, with Morwenna the only link binding them together.

She realised that Eliot was speaking to her again, but the first half of his sentence had been lost in the fog of her straying thoughts. His last words, however, made it plain what it was that he had been saying.

"—but you make no mention of taking *her* to London."

Judith! Lilias' eyes went to the plain, ill-dressed young woman who was occupying Regina's old chair, and she experienced the same surge of guilt which had always afflicted her when confronted by her elder daughter. Why could she not love Judith as she loved Morwenna? But Judith was not a lovable person. She put up barriers between herself and everyone, except Eliot.

She spoke now, scornfully. "Oh, mother would not ask *me* to accompany her and Mr O'Mara to London. She would be ashamed of me, whereas Morwenna will do her credit."

Lilias answered gently: "Judith, you are welcome to come with us, if you should so wish," and hated herself for the happy certainty that her elder daughter would refuse. Judith would never leave Eliot. Her love for him was painfully apparent every time that she glanced in his direction. *Eliot is not God, Judith!* The words echoed back from the distant past. But for Judith, her cousin had always been more than God, the one being in the whole world who meant more to her than herself.

"What would I do in London, that den of iniquity?" Judith's contempt increased. "And who would look after Eliot and Geoffrey?"

"I was hoping that Geoffrey might be persuaded to come with us."

"Well, he would not!" Judith was triumphant. "He hates London. He says that it is the seat of vice incarnate. The King was here last year, at Bath and Bristol. We saw him with our own eyes, with that creature—that half-naked creature—Lady Castlemaine, flaunting herself in the very presence of the Queen. Geoffrey said that he would pray for her soul."

Lilias, remembering the warm, happy-go-lucky baby who had grown into the gentle and tolerant youth, was betrayed into a giggle and a protest. "I can't believe him capable of saying any such thing."

Before Judith's indignation could be given full rein, Eliot interrupted: "It is true. I heard him say so myself. And although I do not altogether like the influence under which Geoffrey has fallen, his sentiments nevertheless do him credit and are ones with which I must agree."

"What influence? What are you talking about?" Lilias asked, disturbed.

"The Society of Friends. The Quakers, as men call them. They have been very active in Bristol for some years."

"Geoffrey has become a Quaker?" Lilias' uneasiness increased. On both sides of the Atlantic, the followers of George Fox were being persecuted with undiluted venom.

"He has not become one of them—as yet. But he and

325

young William Penn correspond regularly, and both find the teachings of the Society much to their taste."

"Young Penn? Admiral Penn's son? How did Geoffrey come to meet with him?"

"It was in London once, when Geoffrey was there on business with old Fothergill. And young Penn has been in Bristol several times accompanying his father and has called upon us here. He has recently returned from France and is studying law at Lincoln's Inn."

"A sober-minded young man," Judith pronounced. "Not like that reprobate, his father."

"That 'reprobate'," said Patrick's voice from the doorway, "is at present risking his life in this war against the Dutch." He strolled forward into the room, his normally sallow skin whipped to a high colour by the autumn winds. Clinging to his arm was Morwenna, her eyes like stars, her dark curls tumbling anyhow about her excited face. Lilias rose from her chair at their entry.

"Did you have a good walk?" she asked.

"Mr O'Mara said that he would hardly recognise Bristol, it has changed so much since the castle has gone. But, oh mother!" Morwenna rushed on. "Is it really true that you want me to come and live with you both in London?"

"Quite true, my darling." Lilias cupped the elfin face in her long thin hands. "When you are older, you will take the place by storm."

Eliot shot out a hand and gripped Morwenna's wrist, pulling her round to face him.

"You're sure you wish to go, Morwenna?" he demanded harshly. "They cannot force you, if you are not willing. I won't let them. Your home is here, with me—and Judith."

"Not willing!" Morwenna stared at him blankly for a second, then burst into peals of laughter. "Of course I'm willing, you silly!" She leant forward and kissed him lightly on his cheek. Then, seeing the stricken look

326

behind his eyes, her happiness momentarily deserted her. "Oh, not because I want to leave you, darling Eliot. Or Judith," she added hastily. "But because—oh, just because!" All the natural buoyancy of her thirteen years reasserted itself, and she did a little jig. "Just think of it! I shall see St Paul's and Westminster Abbey and all the wonderful shops in Cheapside. And the new theatre in Drury Lane. And there will be the people. Perhaps I might even see the King."

"Certainly, you will see the King," Patrick said, watching her every movement, hanging on her every word, as though he could not bear to miss anything she might say or do. "I shall arrange it personally. His Majesty and I were here together in the garrison at Bristol. I have the honour, I hope, to be counted by him as a friend."

Judith snorted in derision, but Morwenna clasped her hands against her breast, her cheeks aglow with delight. In any other child such a gesture might have seemed posed and artificial, but in Morwenna it merely emphasised her naturalness and charm.

Lilias, happening to glance at Eliot, was shocked by what she unexpectedly saw in his face: the love, not of half-brother for half-sister, but that of a man for a woman. A moment later, she saw the consciousness of his own emotion wash over him like a wave and recognised the naked fear which leapt into his eyes and the gesture of repulsion in his involuntarily uplifted hand.

Lilias shivered. The little room was suddenly charged with tension: too much love, too much hate; poor Judith loving Eliot, hating Morwenna; Patrick hungry for an affection not yet his; Eliot, bitterly resenting her because she would take Morwenna away from him, yet terrified by an adoration which he naturally believed to be incestuous. And what was her own share in this welter of emotion? She did not know. Priam, who she believed had betrayed her, who had made a fool of her, was too close to her here. She had been burned once, giving her heart too entirely, and ever since had resisted the temptation to play with fire.

She said to Morwenna: "We shall come for you in the morning, my dearest. Patrick wishes to set out well before noon, so that we can reach Chippenham by nightfall. And now, we must return to our lodgings." She addressed herself once more to Judith. "I am sorry that Geoffrey is from home. You will give him my love ... and my message. You're certain that you—"

"Quite certain." Judith's back was like a ramrod, her words curt to the point of rudeness. But there was also an air of celebration about her. At long last she was going to be rid of Morwenna, for whom Eliot showed such an unnatural affection. She would have her cousin to herself, except for Geoffrey and the little charity-school girl, who only counted in their roles as chaperons. It had been a shock, her mother's return, married to a noted Royalist, an Irishman and, worst of all, a Catholic. But she had soon realised that the situation had its advantages. The thin lips lifted a little at the corners, a faint flush suffused the narrow face, the pale eyes took on something of Morwenna's sparkle.

Lilias, watching her, was startled to see that there could be moments when Judith was almost pretty.

*　　*　　*

Magdalen waved aside the dress of rich, deep-blue velvet which had been Priam's last Christmas gift to her, and instead indicated to her maid that she would wear the oyster-coloured satin.

"And the opal and diamond necklace," she added in her soft, sweet voice. "You can lock away these sapphires and rubies."

The maid hesitated, her earnest country face alive with dismay. She ventured on a mild remonstrance.

"But—but, my lady, you know that his lordship said

328

that while you were in London as how he hoped you'd wear some brighter colours. You know he said those pale dresses made you look . . . look. . . ."

"Ill? Washed out?" Magdalen raised her eyebrows in faint hauteur.

She was forty-one years old in this October of 1664, and the candles on either side of her mirror showed a sprinkling of grey in the fashionably frizzed and curled fair hair. There were wrinkles, too, at the corners of her eyes, and a very slight thickening of the waist. Other than that, Magdalen Chelwood was still very much the same delicate-featured, lissom-figured woman who had enchanted the court of Charles the first some twenty-five years before. But a close observer might have noted a hint of steel about her, alien to that vulnerable creature who had once been Magdalen Prestcott. The disappointments and hardships which she had been forced to endure, above all loving a man who had never loved her, had given her a kind of withdrawn quality which served her as a defence.

She quietened her maid's voluble denials that the Earl had said any such thing with a gesture of her hand. "That's as maybe, Betty, but I shall wear the oyster satin and opals, nonetheless. And then you will brush this frizz of hair into something more dignified and becoming."

Ten minutes later, her white shoulders sloping above the wide lace collar, the candlelight gleaming like water as it rippled over the oyster satin, and the fair hair coaxed by the capable Betty into a smooth but unmodish knot at the nape of her neck, Magdalen surveyed herself in the mirror. Behind her, she saw the door open as Priam and Cressida walked in, and felt that flutter of apprehension which the sight of her husband and younger daughter always aroused in her. Cressie was too like her father, with his quick, acerbic tongue and unpredictable moods. Cassandra had been the one in whom Magdalen had been able to confide, but she was married now—Viscountess

Hartford—and had settled into domesticity to the exclusion of almost all else.

Cressida, on the other hand, seemed to have no inclination for the married state, constantly defying both parents in their wish to see her happily provided for. In spite of the fact that she was twenty-three years old, she still rejected suitor after suitor. Her obstinacy led to friction between herself and Priam, a state of affairs which exacerbated Magdalen's already over-stretched nerves.

"Are you ready, my dear?" Priam picked up his wife's fur-trimmed cloak from the bed and came forward to put it round her shoulders. "Their Majesties begin receiving at half past six and you would not wish to be late." He paused, his eyes suddenly narrowing in anger. "I thought, Magdalen, that we had agreed that you should wear the blue velvet."

Cressida chimed in: "Oh, mother! Why won't you wear something which gives you more colour? These pale dresses make you look like a ghost."

Magdalen's fingers tightened around the sticks of her ivory fan. Why could she never stand up for herself without this desperate sensation of nausea? She answered breathlessly, and with an artificial little laugh: "I don't like bright colours. I never have. And whatever you and your father might say, I don't really think that they suit me."

She glanced half-defiantly, half-apologetically at Priam as she spoke, and saw his face settle into the polite lines of indifference which she had come to dread. Anger welled up in her, only to be replaced by the familiar, agonising self-blame and self-doubt. There had been a time, years ago in Holland, after his return from England, when things had seemed better between them. He had been gentler, displaying more patience, and she had almost persuaded herself for a while that she really enjoyed making love.

330

But the old inhibitions had come crowding back one night, after Priam had returned home after an evening spent at a friend's lodgings. He had been drunk—not convivially so, but coldly, aggressively drunk—and in a mood to have his needs satisfied at once. She had been frightened and outraged by turns, beating him off with her hands and finally resorting to a stream of abuse which had astounded herself and effectively sobered him. She had said things that night that she had not even known she felt. But however much she might afterwards deny their truth both to herself and Priam, pleading the extenuation of fear and anger, something had ended between them. He had never sought her bed again, reverting to his former haunting of the brothels, with which even a sober town like The Hague abounded.

Outwardly, for the sake of the children and Society, they had continued to play the devoted couple; and in the lax atmosphere of the court which surrounded the young King Charles, the Earl's infidelities were only remarkable in that he paid for his pleasures rather than seducing other men's wives or mistresses. But for Magdalen they were torture, for she was no less devoted to her husband than she had ever been.

"Very well, my dear, you must wear what you wish." Priam inclined his head courteously and slipped the long satin cloak about Magdalen's shoulders.

"I still think that you would look better in the dark blue velvet," declared Cressida, but palliated the remark by a kiss on her mother's cheek. "You have such wonderful skin, even now. I shall be happy if mine is only one half as soft at your age."

Magdalen was indignant. "My age, indeed! You'd better look to your own age, miss! Or you may find yourself an old maid."

"Oh, mother! Please! Not now. Not tonight. Tonight I intend to enjoy myself. See who that is at the door, Betty."

Oliver Pride stood bowing in the doorway. "The coach is waiting, my lord, my lady. I would not presume to hurry you in any way, but I should advise an early departure. The crush of traffic about Whitehall is bound to be extremely heavy."

Three pairs of eyes were turned towards him, each with a different expression. Magdalen's were faintly hostile: she did not care for Oliver Pride and, although she could not say why, she did not trust him. Priam's were amused: he found Oliver an excellent secretary and never failed to be entertained by the young man's self-possession. Yet he, too, did not altogether trust someone as devoted to self-interest as Lilias' elder son. Cressida's, by contrast, sparkled with a love which accepted Oliver as much for his faults as for his virtues. Hers was not an uncritical adoration, but it was deep and lasting. It was also one which she was careful to conceal from her parents. She followed them with decorously lowered lids, into the corridor, down the stairs and out to the waiting coach.

★　　★　　★

A mile or so distant, in a slightly less fashionable district than the Strand, Lilias O'Mara was also putting the finishing touches to her face and gown, observed by an admiring Morwenna.

Unlike Magdalen's, Lilias' hair was profusely frizzed and curled into the style so admired by the court gallants. But the pink-and-white complexion extolled by romantics such as Robert Herrick perforce eluded her, and she scorned to apply white lead or stone lime, having witnessed the havoc which these so-called aids to beauty could wreak on delicate skins. She was not, however, above using a concoction of powdered myrrh and white wine, supposed to be a certain cure for wrinkles, or Gervase Markham's famous skin-tonic: a distillation of rosemary, featherfew, violet leaves, nettles, mallows, orgaine and fennel, all added to three gallons of milk. But she did draw the line at a preparation recommended to her by young Mrs Samuel Pepys made from the urine of a puppy.

"I wish I were coming with you," sighed Morwenna, handing her mother the little box containing powdered ash of pig's jaw-bone, and watching as Lilias carefully smeared it over her cheeks.

Lilias looked round and smiled at her fondly. "When you are older, my darling. And when Miss Martingale has coaxed a little more learning into that frivolous head." She turned back once more to the mirror, her hand hovering uncertainly above the silver pot of Indian lakh, wondering whether or not to apply a little redness to cheeks and mouth. In the end, she decided against it, merely biting her lips to heighten their colour, and pressing on two beauty patches, one at the corner of her mouth, the other to draw attention to her eyes. "There," she said, "I think that must do. Jenny, my dress, if you please."

The maid, round and plump as a robin, reverently lifted the swathes of amber satin from the bed and threw them deftly over her mistress's head. The rich colour glowed in the candlelight, seeming to breathe sun and fire.

"Oh, it's lovely!" exclaimed Morwenna, while Jenny twittered her admiration. "There won't be any other lady at Whitehall as beautiful as you."

Lilias laughed, genuinely amused, but flattered also. "Sweetheart, I'm thirty-eight years old. Well past the first blush of my youth, as they say. I am unlikely to turn any heads."

"I wouldn't say that, my dear," drawled Patrick, and she jumped. She had not heard him enter the room.

"Nor would I, papa," declared Morwenna, going to kiss him.

Papa! Now when had he persuaded her to call him

that? Patrick raised a quizzical eyebrow at his wife in the mirror, reading her unquiet thoughts.

"The child could hardly continue to call me Mr O'Mara, my love. And I am her father—after a fashion."

"My stepfather," stated Morwenna happily. "And I love you dearly."

"Cupboard-love, my child," Patrick answered, but there was a light in his eyes which Lilias had not seen before.

It occurred to her that perhaps Morwenna gave her love too easily, that she was one of those people who, however unwittingly, broke hearts. Lilias thought of Eliot and began to feel guilty. Ought she not to tell him the truth? Explain that however little hope there was that his love for Morwenna would ever be returned, it was not incestuous? That they were not the children of the same father?

But such an explanation would involve too much, reveal more of her past life than she was prepared to share, at present, with anyone but Patrick. It would also mean telling Morwenna, and Lilias was not sure that her younger daughter was yet ready or old enough to understand. Morwenna still spoke of Richard with affection.

She became aware of Patrick's eyes upon her, following her thoughts. She signed to Jenny to hand her her cloak.

In the coach, as it lurched and rumbled over the cobbles between the piles of stinking refuse, she was silent, conscious of the pressure of Patrick's thigh against her own. Patrick, too, said nothing, but was equally aware of Lilias' disturbing presence. Their love-making last night had reached a new pitch of intensity, yet, in the cold light of day, the old animosity had returned, the sense of resentment that each was not somebody else.

The press of coaches increased around Charing Cross, the lumbering vehicles sometimes two abreast in the

334

narrow lanes as they converged in a stream on Whitehall. One coach lay on its side in the gutter, its hysterical occupant being soothed by her distracted husband. The O'Maras' coach swayed perilously as it avoided this obstacle, and Lilias was flung against Patrick's shoulder. His arm came around her, holding her close. Then he released her and she moved back into her corner.

*   *   *

More than one curled and perfumed feminine head turned to watch the progress of the Earl of Chelwood as, with his wife and daughter, he made his way through the crowded ante-chambers towards the glittering whirlpool of the banqueting hall. The tall figure in black and silver, the Garter Star shimmering on his breast, was as much an object of interest as he had ever been, particularly to the young girls, whose mothers hastened to draw them out of range of the Earl's evil and pernicious influence. (Adultery was one thing, observed the matrons one to another, but brothels and whoring were quite another.)

The Earl was the more intriguing in that he seemed totally unconscious of the interest he provoked. Or, if he was conscious of it, uninterested in the languishing glances which were sent his way. He was far more concerned to catch the eye of Prince Rupert.

"Chelwood!" The stern, hard-favoured features broke into a smile. "Here's a waste of time! I wouldn't have come, but the King commanded it. I would much rather have spent an evening at home."

Priam smiled. "Playing with your mortars and pestles and crucibles, no doubt."

Rupert's interest in chemistry was a constant source of amusement to his friends, but the Earl did not make the mistake of so many of them in underestimating the Prince's contribution to the rapidly growing interest in the sciences. Many of the finest brains of the age were to be seen at the royal residence in Beech Street, on the Barbican.

"And why not?" Rupert grunted. "It would be preferable to this." The large eyes, haunted by sadness since the disappearance at sea of his brother, Prince Maurice, many years before, suddenly glowed with animation. "You've heard that we've captured Cape Verde?"

Priam nodded. "What with that and the taking of New Amsterdam—New York, as I suppose I must call it now—last summer, the Dutch must be thirsting for our blood. And war not even officially declared!"

Rupert eyed his old friend shrewdly. "You like the Dutch."

"They are a kind people." Priam spoke with unwonted vehemence. "They were very good to me and my family during the years of our exile. As they were good to many English Royalists."

"And as they were good to many of the Regicides," the Prince pointed out drily. "But I, too, regret this war. I lived amongst the Dutch from childhood onwards. It is unfortunate that both nations are so alike, with this inborn passion for trade." He broke off, his eyes narrowed, peering over the heads of the thronging courtiers, an advantage which his great height gave him. "Strange," he murmured, "I could have sworn that I saw someone ... a face from the past..." He glanced sideways at Priam, and then shrugged. "No, no! I must have been mistaken."

Rupert's attention was claimed by the King's dissolute friend, Bab May, with whom the Prince shared a common interest in tennis, so Priam was free to look about him. A little ahead of him, as he approached the banqueting hall, was Sir Edward Hyde, now Earl of Clarendon, his heavy, lugubrious face seamed by worry. He had many enemies at court, chief amongst whom were Castlemaine herself and the Duke of Buckingham.

The Earl's reputation had not been enhanced by the scandal which had involved both his family and the King's, and overshadowed the opening months of the Restoration. His plain, rather pudding-faced daughter, Anne, had somehow or other attracted the attentions of the young Duke of York, and she had announced herself pregnant by James. James, to his credit and despite the tears and tantrums of his mother, had insisted on marrying Anne Hyde and had been loyally backed by the King. But the marriage had not been a success and the Chancellor, as he had foreseen, was unjustly apportioned his share of the blame.

Inside the hall, itself, Priam's eyes were momentarily dazzled. Clustering chandeliers lit the painted ceiling, and the brilliance of three hundred candle-flames was reflected in myriads of jewels. The King was seated on a dais at the far end of the hall, his Queen, the Portuguese Catherine of Braganza, small and dark, at his side. Lady Castlemaine, in a dress of primrose silk which left nothing to the imagination, was flirting with the young Duke of Monmouth, Charles' bastard son by Lucy Walter. But Cressida, always observant, noted that the King barely glanced in Castlemaine's direction: his attention, when he could spare it, was all for his elusive cousin, Frances Stuart.

The slow procession gradually inched its way forward, brought to a halt as each new arrival at the dais made his or her obeisance to Their Majesties. A sense of unrest, almost of unease, which he could not account for, gripped Priam. He felt like an animal scenting some unknown danger. He was short with Bab May when that elegant dandy, having finished his conversation with Prince Rupert, pushed carelessly past on his way to claim the Duke of York's attention. What was wrong with him? Priam wondered. Why did he feel like this? Perhaps it was because he always associated the banqueting hall with that terrible day of the late King's execution.

At last, Magdalen and Cressida were making their curtsies, furling and unfurling like delicate flowers as they sank to the floor and up again. Then it was Priam's turn. He bowed, first to Charles, then to the Queen, who was apt to regard the wicked Earl with misgivings, and would have moved on to obscurity in the chattering crowd. But the King stopped him with an upraised hand.

"Wait, my lord! There is someone here you will wish to meet. Someone to whom we both owe a very great debt." He slewed round in his chair, imperiously holding out his hand, and a woman stepped out of the shadows. "My lord, let me present to you an old acquaintance of yours. Mistress Lilias O'Mara."

CHAPTER TWENTY

The shock of recognition jarred him from head to foot. He struggled to retain his composure, conscious that he was the cynosure of at least a dozen pairs of eyes, Magdalen's and Cressida's amongst them. Lilias, better prepared for their meeting, dropped a curtsey and said as coolly as she could: "I am glad to see you again, my lord."

"Mistress Pride, I—I am your most humble and obedient servant."

The King, who was looking on in cynical enjoyment of the Earl's discomfiture, broke in with: "No, no, my dear Priam, you have it wrong. Not Mistress Pride: Mistress O'Mara. A double pleasure for you. Here is the lady's husband, another old friend. You recall, of course, Captain Patrick O'Mara."

Priam's dumbfounded silence, which boiled into red-hot fury then congealed to an icy rage, was fortunately covered by Magdalen's glad cry of recognition.

"My dear Captain O'Mara! We thought you were dead. We were sure that you had been killed at Drogheda. What—why—where have you been?"

Patrick kissed the slender hand which lay so confidingly in his. "In America, my lady. Virginia. But it's too long a story to tell you now."

"Indeed it is," approved the King, "particularly as I have heard it already. There is nothing so tedious as a tale retold. Except," he added with a laugh, "the account of my own odyssey after Worcester." He smiled at Lilias. "You have our permission to withdraw, Mistress O'Mara. Later I shall claim the honour of your hand for a dance."

Lilias curtseyed once again, reflecting that the years

had robbed Charles Stuart of none of his potent charm. Indeed, they had only added to it, like the lustre on lovingly polished metal. "The honour will be all mine, sire," she said, aware of the darting hatred from Barbara Castlemaine's blue eyes. She laid her hand on Patrick's arm, inclined her head to the Earl and Magdalen and allowed herself to be led away.

Her heart was pounding and she felt as though she were going to faint. She would not have believed that the sight of Priam could have so profound an effect upon her after all these years.

Patrick asked quietly: "Are you all right? Shall I fetch you some wine?"

"Yes—yes, please." She smiled at him gratefully. "It's the heat." Not for a moment did she suspect that he knew she was lying, that he better than anyone knew the cause of her distress.

She sank down on a bench by the wall, oblivious to the curious glances which were directed her way. Her thoughts and feelings were as yet too confused to attempt to set them in order, so she closed her eyes, trying to let her mind go blank.

A voice said: "Pardon me, ma'am. You must please forgive me if you are not feeling well, but I had to speak to you. So you are Oliver's mama."

Lilias opened her eyes to see a young woman standing before her. A plain girl, was her first thought, but a second glance quickly revised that opinion. Not beautiful in the strict sense of the word perhaps, but with large expressive eyes and a face full of vitality and character.

"I-I'm sorry," Lilias faltered. "You're. . .?"

"Cressida Lithgow. The Earl of Chelwood is my father, and your son, Oliver, is his secretary."

"Of course." Lilias rose to her feet. "You must forgive me, but we have only been in England just over a month, and so much has happened that I am still bewildered."

"I understand. But please, you must call upon us and

see your son. I know Oliver will be anxious to greet you."
Lilias raised her eyebrows at that, and Cressida laughed.
"Well, perhaps that was an exaggeration," she amended
frankly, "but he will certainly wish to see you."

"And I to see him. Thank you, Lady Cressida. I shall
avail myself of your very kind invitation."

"Soon," Cressida urged, as she began to move away.
"I must go now, I am afraid. My sister, Lady Hartford,
is beckoning to me.'

But as she made her way to Cassandra's side, Cressida's thoughts were racing. The look on Priam's face
when he had first set eyes on Lilias had not escaped his
younger daughter, nor had the fact that the beautiful Mrs
O'Mara bore a strong resemblance to that Dutch girl of
long ago. Was it possible that Oliver's mother was the
mystery woman in her father's life? It would explain his
interest in Oliver, Cressida decided.

Lilias, meanwhile, had resumed her seat and again
closed her eyes, wishing that Patrick would hurry with
the wine. A glass was thrust into her hand and a voice
commanded roughly: "Drink this! And then I must talk
to you." For the second time in ten minutes, Lilias
opened startled eyes, and this time found herself staring
up at Priam.

*   *   *

The room was small and ill-heated, especially after the
warmth of the banqueting hall, but at least it was quiet.
Lilias had no idea where she was in that maze of a palace,
having followed Priam through several ante-chambers
and along corridors which seemed to twist and turn their
way on for ever. But at last he had thrown open the door
of this little room, where a solitary wall-sconce flung a
puddle of light, and a few logs burned fitfully in a corner
grate.

"Now," he said, turning on her savagely, "what are
you doing, married to that man?"

341

The words, no less than the violence with which they were uttered, took her aback. She did not know what she had expected of this indiscreet tête-à-tête, but certainly not such a question. She blinked stupidly at the Earl for a moment or two, then answered with an anger to match his own: "And pray, my lord, what has that to do with you?"

He took a step towards her, his face so terrible that she recoiled against the wall. His hands shot out, gripping her shoulders, crushing, bruising.

"It has everything to do with me. I ask you again: how came you to marry Patrick O'Mara?"

There was a movement behind him, and a voice said icily: "I'll thank you, my lord, to unhand my wife." Patrick stood just inside the doorway, his face as full of anger and violence as Priam's own.

The Earl released Lilias and whirled about. He seemed almost pleased, she thought, to see her husband.

"Your wife!" His hands clenched and unclenched by his sides. "What right have you to her? You, who stopped me from having her! Do you know what my life has been like, these past twenty years? It has been Hell! 'A lord's great kitchen without a fire in't.' Tourneur knew what he was talking of when he described Hell like that . . . no warmth, no light . . . You, with your fine talk and your high-flown morality, you ruined my life! Prating about my duty towards Magdalen and the children! And all because you were—are, for aught I know—in love with my wife yourself."

Patrick had gone very pale but he met the Earl's eyes steadily. It was at Lilias that he found it hard to look.

"My admiration for Lady Chelwood harmed nobody but myself," he answered, as he had answered once before. "She never knew of it, certainly never returned it. You, on the other hand, my lord, would have caused nothing but misery and suffering, not only to your own family, but to Lilias also."

342

"How dare you—?" Priam was beginning, but Lilias suddenly stepped between them, glancing from one man to the other.

"Let me understand this properly, if you please, since I am so closely concerned." She turned to Priam. "That night, in Bristol, when you didn't come . . . when you let me think. . ."

"When I let you believe that it was because I didn't want to?" He took a step towards her, then stopped. "Didn't want to! God in Heaven! It was because your husband—" he fairly spat the word at Patrick "—refused to cover for me; to keep my absence a secret from the Prince. Oh, not because I was breaking the rules—he'd covered for me before, a score of times, and I for him—but because he knew that I loved you. He preached to me of the misery I should cause my family. And why? Because he had fallen in love with Magdalen. But as to my harming you, the thought did not so much as enter his head. He hated you for the trouble you had caused when you smuggled Richard Pride out of the city; because Trooper Trenchard was flogged for his negligence. But he disliked you before that. He disliked everything about you. He once described you to me as a gypsy."

"Is this true?" Lilias asked slowly, looking at Patrick. "Oh, not that you called me a gypsy! I should be a fool if I didn't know that you disliked me in those days. But that you prevented my lord coming to see me that night? Because you were in love with his wife?"

"Yes, it's true." Patrick raised his head in challenge to conceal the reluctance with which the admission was wrung from him. Seeing Magdalen again tonight had brought with it the certainty that for years he had nourished nothing more than a dream, an image deliberately fostered to disguise from himself the real reason for his unwillingness to marry: the memory of a warm kitchen, of a black-haired girl trying to escape him, of his naked body bearing hers to the ground ... When he had first seen Lilias again after all those years, in the large, shabby room at Clontarf, the sudden leap of his heart should have warned him of the truth. But he had grown so used to the pretence, to enshrining Magdalen's image as perfection, that the warning had been ruthlessly suppressed. Indeed, it was only now, when he had walked in and seen her with the Earl, that he had been forced to acknowledge the truth. He was in love with his wife. And what a moment for enlightenment, he thought self-mockingly: the moment when Lilias realised that the Earl had always loved her, and that he, Patrick O'Mara, was the one who had come between them.

"I see." Lilias took a deep breath. For the present, she felt as though she never wanted to see either man again. She had to be alone; she had to have time to think. Without a further word to either one of them, she left the room, finding her way by sheer, blind instinct, back to the brilliantly lighted banqueting hall.

*　　*　　*

Her jewels were locked away and her gown lay carefully folded in one of the big cedar-wood chests. Her hair was brushed until it shone, and Jenny had at last retired for the night. But still Lilias made no move to get into bed, sitting on the window-seat, listening to the distant cry of the night-watchman as he called the small hours of the morning.

She and Patrick had not spoken on the way home, and having assured herself that Morwenna was peacefully asleep, Lilias had retired to her room. A deep sense of resentment against both the Earl and Patrick welled up inside her: resentment against Priam for not having trusted her enough to tell her the truth, and resentment against her husband for having interfered unwarrantably in her affairs.

The latch clicked and Patrick came in. She got up,

344

leaning her back against the wall.

"Don't touch me!" she said. The words sounded trite, even to her own ears, but she meant them with all her heart.

Patrick, however, ignored them, coming further into the room. He, too, was confused and in need of comfort. "I'm your husband," he asserted harshly.

The well-worn phrase irritated her more than anything else he might have said. It laid a claim on her which she was no longer sure that he had the right to make.

"Yes, you're my husband," she retorted angrily. "But do you think that I would have married you, had I known the truth?"

"What truth? That I prevented you from wrecking another woman's marriage? A woman, moreover, who was deeply in love with her husband. Did the pair of you once think of her?"

"What need had we to think of her while she had a watch-dog such as you? Busying yourself on her behalf! Playing God! Could you not leave it to our own two consciences?"

Patrick came closer. "It *was* the Earl's conscience, my love, which prevented him coming to you that night. Do you imagine that any words of mine could have turned him from his purpose, had he himself not felt that it was wrong?"

"I see! So the two of you decided *my* fate, *my* destiny, while I remained in ignorance. You sicken me, the pair of you! Richard Pride was worth both of you put together."

She tried to push past him to the bed, but he put out a hand to stop her, catching the neck of her shift and ripping it from her shoulders. The sight of her naked body inflamed him in a way he would once have deemed impossible. Her pale skin, her full, rounded breasts, the abundance of black hair, as yet untouched by grey, were the very opposite of that chaste, Madonna-like image which he had cherished all these years in his heart. How

345

could he have so deluded himself that he was the same romantic person he had been before the events of Drogheda?

He wanted Lilias, but she turned on him, spitting like a cat, clawing at him with her nails. She was normally such a calm woman that this display was all the more shocking. But it was exciting, too. She scratched his cheek, drawing blood, and he grabbed both her wrists in one of his hands, dealing her a stinging blow with the other.

This assault upon her person only enraged Lilias still more. She kicked and tried to wrench herself free of that cruel grasp. Finally, she bit his hand. With a roar like a maddened bull, he pushed her down on to the bed, tearing her night-shift still further...

"Mama? Are you all right?" Morwenna, a pale ghost in her bed-gown, was just visible over Patrick's shoulder. She was staring stupidly; then Lilias saw her eyes widen, blinking away the rags of sleep, as she began to understand the real meaning of the scene before her. "I-I'm sorry," she gulped, and melted away into the darkness.

For a moment or two, Patrick lay still. Then, without a word, he got up, pulled his night-robe around him and followed Morwenna from the room. Lilias stayed where she was, one arm flung across her eyes. And for the first time since Richard's death, she wept.

★   ★   ★

There was a cold wind. Little frets and eddies worried the surface of the Thames. Water welled and sucked among the fringe of reeds, and a sudden whip of foam marked the passage of a boat.

Cressida stood among the winter-bare trees at the bottom of her father's garden and wished that she were at Westovers, away from the bustle and eternal clamour of the London streets. Oliver was so much more accessible when they were at home. Here, he was constantly in attendance upon the Earl, and the Strand house seemed lonely without him.

She moved restlessly, snapping a twig from its branch and twirling it absent-mindedly in her fingers. She stepped on a frozen puddle and watched the spider's web of cracks appear. And for the thousandth time she asked herself what it was about Oliver Pride that made her love him so?

She glanced up and saw him coming towards her, down the long path between the frost-bitten shrubs. He was muffled in his cloak to keep out the cold and carried one of her fur-lined wraps in his hand.

"I saw you from the window, my lady, and brought you this," he said, holding the wrap ready to put about her shoulders. "You should not be out in this chill wind with only that thin cloak for protection." He smiled and her knees felt weak.

She was touched by this concern for her welfare, but replied as off-handedly as she could: "Thank you, you are very kind, although you should not have taken the trouble. I am perfectly warm, I assure you. My mother will tell you that I have the constitution of a working horse."

"It was no trouble." Her apparent indifference did not deceive him for an instant. He knew he had only to lift his little finger and she was his.

The knowledge gave him a sense of power but, being Oliver, power was of no interest to him unless he could use it to his advantage. He looked at her dispassionately. She was not beautiful, but she was attractive, nonetheless. And she had a warm, loving, giving nature, far too good for him, as he would be the first to admit. But, for some inexplicable reason, she loved him, and he was fond of her. A pity, therefore, that she was not her father's sole heir, and her financial prospects that much less alluring than those of a certain Miss Tabitha Smallwood, the only child of a wealthy merchant, who had shown a flattering interest in Oliver ever since Lilias and Patrick had been respectably established among the friends and confidants of the King.

Oliver sighed regretfully. Cressida had so much to offer him; position, breeding and an intelligent, humorous mind; all those things, in short, which Miss Tabitha Smallwood lacked, except a greater fortune. And Oliver, true descendant of generations of Bristolians, knew just how important money was. If only she did not have an older sister! If only she were the Earl's sole heir. . .

These profitless cogitations were interrupted by one of the servants, who came to inform Mr Pride that his mother and sister had called to see him and were awaiting him in the library.

Oliver's first thought on seeing his mother was that she was ill. There were dark circles beneath her eyes, and they had the over-brilliance caused by too little sleep. But in answer to his polite enquiry, Lilias strenuously denied any suggestion of ill-health.

"A little tired, perhaps." She smiled in acknowledgement of his charm, even while her sardonic glance told him that she was not deceived by this lip-service to filial devotion. She knew him only too well.

Oliver offered refreshment. "Unfortunately, the Earl and Countess are from home, visiting Lady Hartford at Chelsea."

"I am perfectly well aware that they are from home," Lilias answered, declining the offer of wine and biscuits. "I should not, otherwise, have called."

During the intervening months, she had carefully avoided Priam as much as possible, according him only the barest civility when they met. She was still unsure of her feelings towards him or, perhaps, frightened of them, she did not know which. As for Patrick, after that first night, he had held aloof, obviously convinced that time would cure all ills.

348

Seeing Oliver's look of surprise at her words, Lilias hurried on: "It is you Morwenna and I have come to visit. As I said, these past months have tired me. Being plunged into a whirl of gaiety at my time of life is unsettling. Balls, masques, the theatre ... My upbringing did not prepare me for so many good things all at once." Oliver looked sceptical and Lilias smiled once more: he must draw his own conclusions. "So I am going home to Bristol for a few weeks and taking Morwenna with me. Patrick insists that, in the spring, she be presented at court, and the poor child will need to build up her strength before then."

Oliver looked shrewdly from his mother to his unnaturally subdued young sister, and reflected that Lilias was not as good a liar as she would wish. There was something amiss between her and that Irish husband of hers, or else he was very much mistaken. However, it was no business of his, and he observed mildly: "Eliot and Judith will be glad to see you, I imagine."

Lilias, suspecting him of irony, frowned, but Oliver met her eyes with a glance of limpid innocence. "When do you travel?" he asked.

"We set out tomorrow, if the weather holds. Otherwise, as soon as maybe. We shall be back in time for the masked ball at Vauxhall Gardens. Do we look to see you there?"

"Oh, I think not. Such things are not for me." Oliver kissed his mother and sister dutifully. "Give my kindest remembrances to Eliot and to Judith. And for pity's sake, mother, see if you can knock some sense into Geoffrey's head and wean him away from these Quakers."

*   *   *

Geoffrey Pride paused within the shelter of St Nicholas' Gate, his ears strained for any sound of the militia or the Watch.

349

Since the Conventicle Act of the preceding year, any religious meeting attended by four or more people and not in accordance with the practices of the Church of England carried with it heavy penalties, the greatest of which was transportation for seven years. And whenever he came to one of these clandestine meetings held in Denzil Hollister's house, Geoffrey always felt sick with apprehension. He was not brave, and only the burning conviction that he must be free to worship God in any way he chose gave him the courage to go on. But as he knocked on the door of the tall, narrow house in The Shambles, his legs were shaking with fear.

Denzil Hollister himself let the young man in, ushering Geoffrey into a shadowy room off the little parlour, where five or six other men were already at prayer. As he entered, Joseph Leach rose from his seat and came towards his friend, his earnest young face radiating pleasure.

"Peace be unto thee, Geoffrey."

"And to thee, Joseph."

They clasped hands, neither removing his hat, for George Fox had decreed it unnecessary to uncover the head. As God dwelt within each man and was manifested by the Inner Light, where a True Believer was, there was the Risen Christ. There was, therefore, no need for the outward trappings of vestments or Cross, of priest or minister. Every man was the Holy Ark of the Covenant of the Lord.

Geoffrey sat beside his friend, eyes closed, emptying his mind until that still, small voice should speak to him, even as it had spoken to Moses out of the burning bush; that still, small voice of love and hope and sanity in a world which seemed irrevocably given into the hands of Mammon.

They waited in silence until one of their number should feel moved to testify. And, suddenly, it was

350

Geoffrey who was impelled to his feet, his face alight with the intensity of his passion.

"Friends, I am a sinner who has been redeemed by the blood of the Lord Jesus Christ, given for me in atonement. When He was scourged on the orders of Pontius Pilate and crowned with thorns, when He was nailed to the Cross on the hill which men call Golgotha, then did He offer Himself up for the sins of the world. But the world has rejected Him, brethren. It has turned its face from Him and trodden the Primrose Path into chaos and darkness, vanity and destruction. My brothers! It is for us, now, to make the atonement with our suffering, with our lives if need be, and to lead our fellows back into the paths of glory and light."

He had barely had time to resume his seat, when someone hammered urgently on the street door. Denzil Hollister went to let in this unexpected visitor and, a moment later, Pring Taylor burst into the room in great alarm.

"Friends! The Watch is on its way with orders to arrest you all. Leave here quickly! Return at once to your own homes!"

But it was too late. Already the sound of heavy feet could be heard, mounting the stairs. Next moment, the captain of the Watch loomed in the doorway, a hand resting suggestively on the short sword which he wore at his waist.

"No bother, Mr Hollister, if you please. We don't want the good citizens of this fair city of ours disturbed by any undue commotion."

"We lift our hands against no man," Joseph Leach said quietly. "We do not believe in violence, friend."

"Turning the other cheek, eh?" grinned the captain. "Well, that's your prerogative, young Leach. But I warn you! The magistrates of Bristol believe in Old Testament justice. This way, gentlemen, if you please."

★   ★   ★

Lilias, seated in Regina's old chair, which had been grudgingly surrendered to her by Judith—"no doubt on account of my advanced age," she reflected with wry amusement—regarded Eliot and her daughter in some perturbation.

"Isn't this a somewhat sudden decision, my dear Eliot?" she asked.

"I have always been extremely fond of Judith," he answered steadily. "Is it so unnatural that we should want to get married?"

Judith's radiant face supplied the answer to this question, but Eliot, Lilias was sure, did not share in her conviction. He was still head over heels in love with Morwenna. She recalled the look on his face when he had come home two evenings ago, weary after the long day's work, to find herself and Morwenna ensconced in their old, familiar places in the kitchen. Morwenna, who had been quiet and withdrawn since that night she had walked in on Patrick and Lilias, had no sooner set foot in the Broad Street house than she had begun, once again, to blossom. The innocence of childhood, which was inevitably slipping away from her, had been miraculously restored. She had flitted with little cries of pleasure from room to room and insisted on rummaging in the attic until she found Clarabelle, her old wooden doll, and the ball of coloured thread which Lilias had once bought for her in the market. Even Judith's hostility had melted a little before her half-sister's pleasure in seeing her again. But this thaw had been brief, as Judith took stock of Lilias' and Morwenna's clothes.

The low-cut bodices, the billowing skirts, combined with the heads of frothing curls, had provoked horrified gasps of astonishment and disapproval. They had also caused Eliot to frown and mutter austerely about perverted influences and the flesh-pots of London. But he could not remain immune to Morwenna's charm, and there was no doubt that the new styles suited her. She

352

had always been pretty, even in the old days, with her demurely smooth hair and plain grey dresses. Now, however, she was beautiful: not with her mother's disturbing, exotic beauty, but with her own ethereal radiance. The coloured silks—amber, green and rich, dark red—enhanced the blue of her sparkling eyes and set off to perfection the almost black hair. From the first moment of seeing her again, Eliot knew himself lost: he could no longer deny to himself that he was in love with his own half-sister.

Morwenna, unaware of his true feelings for her and too young to guess, flirted outrageously with him, as she had always done, as all young girls innocently flirted with fathers and uncles and brothers. Lilias realised that it had been a mistake to bring her. The Morwenna who was rapidly growing to maturity in London would have been more instinctive, and acted less irresponsibly. Lilias, desperately sorry for her stepson, was once more a prey to guilt that he should be so tormented.

What she had not foreseen was that he would propose to Judith as a refuge from his turbulent emotions. Lilias twisted her lace-bordered handkerchief between her hands and asked: "You're sure of this? Both of you?" But the question was intended only for Eliot.

"Yes, I'm sure," he answered levelly. "All we need now, my dear Lilias, is your permission. We hope to be married before you and Morwenna return to London."

What was she doing? Lilias wondered. What crime was she committing by not telling him the truth? What unhappiness was she storing up for Judith? Barnaby's child! Poor Barnaby! She had failed him, too, in the moment when he had most needed her.

"Of—of course you have my permission," she stammered. "Judith is her own woman now. I just wished to assure myself that you are both of one mind."

"Well, I think it's romantic," declared Morwenna, rising from her stool in an uprush of fir-green velvet, and embracing Eliot and Judith with her loving arms. "I shall wear the new blue silk that Papa Patrick gave me, and shock poor old Parson Pentecost by being Judith's maid-of-honour."

"It will be a very quiet wedding," Judith said repressively. "And Parson Pentecost will not be able to officiate. You know very well, Morwenna, that the infamous Act of Uniformity deprived all Dissenting clergy of their livings."

Morwenna knew no such thing, and her high spirits were momentarily dashed. But a wedding was a wedding, however quiet it might be, and she had every intention of enjoying herself.

A knock on the street door sent Judith to see who it could be, while Eliot raised his brows in surprise at a caller so late in the evening. A moment later, Judith reappeared, looking frightened.

"Geoffrey has been arrested," she whispered tragically. "He was taken at a Quaker conventicle at Denzil Hollister's house, and has been locked up with the others in New Gate."

CHAPTER TWENTY-ONE

It was even worse than she had expected. The stench made her retch, and the turnkey, shuffling ahead of her, the light from his lantern moving like some ghostly will-o'-the-wisp, turned every now and then to direct her where to place her feet. The narrow passageway was littered with piles of human excrement, verminous straw and rat droppings. It was also dangerously slippery with damp from the oozing walls. They passed a locked cell where someone was moaning gently, and another where a woman shrieked and raved, banging her head against the bars. The gaoler remained impervious. Such sights and sounds were a part of his daily life, so common that he had long ceased to notice them.

Geoffrey and his friends had been put into the common cell, a larger room than the others, with a beaten-earth floor and a little light, which fingered its pallid way through a grating set high in a corner of one wall. The smell here was even worse than outside in the passageway, and Lilias' senses began to swim.

"'Ere y' are, then," grunted her guide. "'E'll be 'ere, some'eres about. Pride!" he added, raising his voice. "Yer mother's 'ere t' see you. Call us, missus, when ye're ready t' go. I bain't far away." And the turnkey departed, taking his lantern with him, leaving Lilias blinking in almost total darkness.

"Over here, mother," Geoffrey said out of the gloom.

She edged her way towards him, guided by his voice. An emaciated hand grabbed at her skirt, and a hoarse voice whispered: "A drink, missus, fer the love o' God!" Lilias jumped and twitched her skirt from the clutching hands. Someone gave a shrill cackle of laughter, and Joseph Leach cried: "Peace, my friends and brothers!"

Lilias stumbled and nearly fell over a man who was lying in his own filth, chained to the wall. A pair of strong, young arms reached out and caught her, and she found herself forced down on to a stone bench, beside her son. She was trembling violently, and it took a moment or two and the warmth of Geoffrey's clasp for her to recover her composure.

"Geoffrey," she said urgently, as soon as she was able, "for Heaven's sake, child, why will you not give your promised word and let me take you out of here, on bail?"

"We are not allowed to swear oaths, mother," he answered calmly. "It is forbidden by the Society. And I could not promise not to attend another conventicle before the day of my trial. Thou knowest that. Don't worry, dearest. The Lord will give me strength to endure all my tribulations bravely."

"How do you know that the Lord will give you strength?" she cried in exasperation. "In my experience, He usually helps those who help themselves. Geoffrey! Do you realise that you can be transported? Have you the remotest idea what life in the American colonies is like as a transported criminal? There is one thing to be thankful for. You are very young—not yet eighteen—and it is your first offence. The judge will surely be lenient."

"That depends, Mistress Pride," said Joseph Leach from Geoffrey's other side—and Lilias thought how natural it seemed to be called by that name here in Bristol. "It depends on who the judge is and whether or not he is in league with the Mayor and aldermen."

Lilias' heart gave a sickening lurch. She had lived in the city too long not to understand Joseph's meaning. Nevertheless, to make doubly sure, she asked: "Do the city fathers still take their share of the profits?"

"The money for every tenth convict sold in the American colonies goes into the aldermen's pockets."

"But the authorities—" Lilias protested feebly.

"The authorities, ma'am, wink at the practice, because

the city fathers help to increase the trade. Sometimes legally, but more often than not illegally, they threaten some poor wretch with hanging, and then offer him 'clemency' in the form of transportation. So where transportation is the correct penalty—even though it should be evoked only for a second or third offence—what chance have we, dost thou think, of being spared?"

"Oh, dear God!" cried Lilias, but Geoffrey reproved her gently.

"Mother, thou knowest it is a sin to take the name of the Lord, thy God, in vain. That is why we are forbidden to swear any oaths."

A sudden vision of the court at Whitehall sprang into Lilias' mind: a place where every sort of profanity and blasphemy, picturesque or downright crude, was not only laughed at, but actively encouraged. Her recent life seemed shallow and empty when contrasted with the bravery of these simple men.

But the thought of the court suggested a plan of action to her. Of course! She and Morwenna would return to London at once, and she would ask for an immediate audience with the King.

"I owe you my life," Charles had said to her, soon after she had returned with Patrick from America. "For your sake, I would have granted a pardon even to your former husband, if you had not been too proud to ask. Never hesitate to petition me for any favour. All those who helped me in those dark days after Worcester will always hold a special place in my heart."

Relief overwhelmed her. What a fool she had been not to think of this solution in the first place and save herself and the others a sleepless night. But Geoffrey, though gentler, was in many ways his father's son. If he knew of her intention, he would forbid it. Sweet Heaven! How these men of principle loved to make martyrs of themselves! Could they not see, as women did, that life was too short for all unnecessary suffering?

So it would be better to say nothing to him of her plan. He must think what he liked about her apparently unfeeling departure for London. She leaned forward and kissed him on the cheek. Then she rose and stumbled her way back to the iron-barred door, hammering on it and calling for the gaoler.

*　　*　　*

Lilias found London in the grip of snow, the March winds snarling between the chimney-pots and rushing through the canyons of the streets. Patrick had left, along with many others, for Hampton Court, where the King was to take up residence for the rest of the month. Charles himself, however, had not yet gone, having remained behind for the christening of the Duke of York's second daughter, the Princess Anne. Lilias, ignoring protocol and all usual procedures, went straight to Bab May. An hour later, she was ushered into a small oak-panelled room, where the King was just finishing his supper.

She was vaguely surprised to discover him eating alone, and spared a thought in passing for Barbara Palmer. It was common knowledge that Charles, good-natured and easy-going as he was, was tiring of Castlemaine's rapacity. It was also common knowledge that he was head over ears in love with Frances Stuart, but that the lady held him determinedly at arm's length.

The King rose from the table and waved away the two serving-men and the page, who was standing by the door looking extremely bored. As Lilias rose from her curtsey, Charles gave her his hand to kiss.

"And what can I do for you, Mistress O'Mara?" he enquired. "Bab gave me to understand that the matter was urgent."

"It's my son, sire. My younger son. He has been arrested at Bristol for attending a conventicle of Quakers, and I very much fear that he will be transported." And she repeated what Joseph Leach had told her about the Bristol city fathers.

A smile touched Charles' lips as he resumed his seat at the table and motioned her into a chair on the opposite side. With his own hands, he poured wine and pushed the glass towards her. Petulantly, Lilias put it to one side.

"Your Majesty—!"

"My dear Mrs O'Mara! Your son is not going to be spirited away to Virginia while you sit and drink a glass of wine with me. So! Nothing changes in Bristol, it seems; at least, not the nature of its inhabitants." He invited her to smile with him, but seeing her anxious frown, leant forward and took her hands in his. "Believe me, my dear, I have always been opposed to the Conventicle Act. If I had my way, all my subjects— Catholics, Protestants, Jews—should have the freedom to worship as they chose. Three years ago, I asked Parliament to dispense with all penal laws concerning religion. The Members refused and retaliated with this same pernicious Act which we have just been discussing. I dared not oppose them as my father tried to do. I have not the least desire in the world to go on my travels yet again. However," he went on, silencing Lilias as she opened her mouth to speak, "I can, on occasions, exercise my Royal Prerogative of Mercy. And I can offer my protection to a few. Whatever penalties are inflicted upon Catholics in general, no man dares lift his hand against Father Huddleston, the priest who aided me during my flight to France. Rest assured, therefore, that first thing in the morning orders will be issued for the release of your son and his friends. It is the least I can do for you, who also helped me in those days after Worcester."

Lilias blinked back tears of gratitude, knowing how much the King disliked women who cried. She raised his hand once again to her lips and kissed it fervently.

"Your Majesty is more than gracious. I do not know how to express my thanks."

"Oh come, Mistress O'Mara! I cannot believe you mean that." Charles' voice was no longer serious but had resumed its light, bantering tone. Lilias, lifting her eyes to his, saw them mocking her. "For a man such as myself, my dear, there is always a way in which a beautiful woman can show her gratitude." He got up, strolled round the table and, before she could protest, jerked her up and into his arms. He stood looking at her for a moment or two, then his mouth came down, hard, on hers.

"I have been wanting to do that again," he said, "for fourteen years, ever since that evening at Abbot's Leigh, when a very bold young fellow named William Jackson wished that he could make love to you. Do you remember?"

Lilias laughed shakily. "When a woman has been kissed by her King, she is hardly likely to forget."

"Ah . . . You disappoint me. I had hoped that it was the memory of the man that you treasured."

The swarthy face split into a grin and the lean body pressed against hers, leaving her in no doubt of his desire. She felt her own body begin to respond, and part of her would have yielded, if only for the pleasure of being made love to by such an experienced man. But something held her back, some part of her which belonged to Patrick and to Priam and had yet to be resolved between them. She felt that she could not complicate her life still further by any involvement with the King. And it said much for Charles' character, she reflected later, that her refusal in no way imperilled his promise concerning her son.

The King, feeling her resistance, at once released her and stepped back with a disappointed laugh. He was displeased, but a moment later he remarked in his usual laconic fashion: "I have never known so much spurning of my famous charms. I must really be losing my touch."

"Your Majesty," Lilias said breathlessly, "has been too kind—"

"I would have been kinder," the King interrupted mournfully.

But Lilias went on: "For your promised intervention on behalf of my son, I am most grateful. . ." Her voice tailed off, and she looked at him imploringly. The trouble with Charles Stuart was that he was man first and King second. It did not always make life easier for the women who attracted his attention.

He nodded a rather abrupt dismissal. Lilias curtseyed once more and backed from the room. With her hand on the door-handle, the King called out: "Mistress O'Mara!"

"Sire?" She glanced towards him, apprehensive.

He was lolling in his chair, his eyes narrowed, his long fingers drumming restlessly on the table. Suddenly, his good-humour was restored and he smiled. "If ever you should change your mind, I should be happy if you would let me know."

*   *   *

Bab May was waiting for her in the ante-room to show her straight out the way she had come in: through a curtained door in one corner of the room and down a discreet staircase which avoided the public halls and galleries. But as Lilias turned to follow him, the main double-doors to the room were thrown open and Priam entered between the bowing footmen.

"Bab!" he exclaimed. "I'm glad you're here. I've just been with Clarendon. Is it true that we are now officially at war with the Dutch?"

"Perfectly true, I believe. But I don't think that I'd disturb His Majesty just now." Bab winked. "He's expecting Castlemaine."

Priam swore briefly. "I'll leave it then. All the same—"

His eyes alighted on Lilias and the sentence was never finished. "Mrs O'Mara! What are you doing here?" he demanded, forgetting his manners in a sudden upsurge of uneasiness and surprise.

"I have had an audience with His Majesty," Lilias answered steadily, but vouchsafing no further information.

"Oh ... I see." He was plainly at a loss.

A smile quirked the corners of Bab May's lips. He had never before seen Chelwood discomposed in a lady's presence. Usually, the Earl was embarrassingly indifferent to the opposite sex. But there was plainly something here, something Bab did not understand but which he was only too eager to help along. He did not like Magdalen Chelwood, with her prunes-and-prisms airs and her obvious disapproval of himself. He would be pleased to serve her a back-handed turn.

"I was just escorting Mrs O'Mara to her carriage, Priam. But, perhaps now that you are here, and as it seems that you are acquainted with the lady, you would be good enough to perform the office for me. Her carriage is waiting for her at the Holbein Gate." He waved one elegant, beautifully manicured hand towards the curtained door. "Use the King's private stair, if you would."

Priam bowed stiffly. "If Mrs O'Mara is willing to accept my escort, I shall, of course, be only too happy to oblige."

"Thank you," Lilias answered, and was annoyed to hear how breathless she sounded.

It was cold outside, a few early stars spangling the chill blue dusk. The buildings of the palace reared all around them, etched like shadows against the still grey scene. A flight of birds winged silently to roost.

"I must speak to you," he said, detaining her as she would have entered the waiting carriage. "I have scarcely seen you since that night last autumn."

362

"Untrue, my lord, and you know it. We have danced together at least half a dozen times. We have acted together in a masque. We have watched a pageant on the Thames, side-by-side in the royal barge."

"And always surrounded by a host of people! Watched by my wife and your husband ... Where is O'Mara now?"

"Gone to Hampton Court, in anticipation of the King's arrival there tomorrow."

"And you are to join him?"

"No. He believes me to be in Bristol. Family affairs brought me back to London in a hurry. My younger son is a Quaker and has been arrested."

"Ah! I understand. And the King has promised to intervene." Priam's voice grew rougher and his grip on her elbow tightened. "What did he ask in return, Lilias?"

"What you might expect, my lord. But my refusal was accepted."

"You did refuse, then!" His tone was vibrant with relief.

"Did you imagine that I should do otherwise, when I am in love with another man?"

He swung her full round to face him. "Who are you in love with, Lilias? For God's sake, don't tell me it's O'Mara!"

"Would it be so strange for me to be in love with my own husband?"

"It would be more than he deserved."

"Was what he did so terrible? He saved your marriage. And your family."

"My marriage was never the same afterwards, Lilias. Perhaps it would have been kinder to Magdalen had I declared my love for you then. It would have saved her...." Saved her what? Years of vain hope and self-torture? Yes, but would it not also have robbed her of the good times they had had together? Seeing their daughters growing up; sharing a common interest in their future. And yet: "O'Mara did not do it for that reason," he told her fiercely. "He spared no thought either for you or me, only for Magdalen. He wasn't prompted by what he believed to be right or wrong, but only by what he thought best for her."

"Not an ignoble motive. And if I had, all those years ago, gone with you, become your mistress, I should never have married Richard. There would be no Oliver, no Geoffrey . . . no Morwenna," she added, realising that her daughter's existence, too, had depended upon the path her life had taken because she believed that Priam did not love her. And yet, deep down, anger against Patrick and the part that he had played still smouldered, fanned into flame by the closeness of Priam's body and his eyes looking pleadingly into hers.

For she loved Priam. When she had seen him in the ante-chamber this evening, she had no longer had any doubts. The years had rolled back and she had stood once again in the parlour of the Broad Street house—perhaps being there so recently had made her understand her own feelings more clearly—loving him, wanting him with every fibre of her being. The time between had vanished like snow after rain. She had been devoted to Richard, but as a mother to her child, because he had needed and depended upon her. She felt a strong sexual attraction to Patrick O'Mara, whom she had married for mutual convenience and because he was Morwenna's father. But Priam she loved as she had always loved him, simply because he was himself.

"Let me come home with you tonight." Priam was holding her as though he would never let her go. She could feel every contour of his body.

"Your wife. . ."

"Thinks I am in attendance upon the King, here at Whitehall. But you heard Bab May. Charles has Castlemaine with him and will have no need of any of his

364

gentlemen until the morning."

"There's my daughter. . ." Still she made half-hearted excuses when every inclination screamed at her to give in.

"She will go to bed. She need know no more than that you have invited an old friend for supper. And I shall leave before daylight. His Majesty will be astir early if he is to make a royal progress to Hampton Court. Say that I may come."

It was no use fighting any longer. She did not even argue that the servants would be bound to know. She did not care if the whole world knew. She wanted him as desperately as he wanted her. She kissed him, the first time she had known the feel of his lips since that terrifying night in Southwark.

"Yes, come home with me, my darling," she said.

★   ★   ★

The summer of that year, 1665, was one of the hottest that anyone could remember. The flies swarmed in their hundreds about the piles of festering rubbish in the narrow overhung streets. There was no rain to sluice the gutters, and the drains were fouled with excrement. Rats slunk in and out of the crowded houses unpursued; cats were overcome by the heat. John Evelyn once more set pen to paper, as he had done so often in the past, to complain of the polluted London air.

But at court, other matters occupied the mind. A new instrument, the guitar, was all the rage; Jan Roettiers was commissioned by the King to paint Frances Stuart as Britannia, so that her likeness could adorn the new coins; there was talk of a revolutionary style in waistcoats, now fashionable at the French court, and Charles wrote bitterly to his sister, Minette, bemoaning the fact that his order for half a dozen had not yet arrived. And on June the second, while the relentless sun continued to pour down, turning the capital into a bowl of molten fire, news was received of a naval victory over the Dutch off Lowestoft.

For the next few days, London resounded to the sound of distant gunfire as the English ships moved south chasing the remnants of the shattered Dutch fleet. Total strangers stopped to shake one another warmly by the hand; fireworks were ordered in St James's Park; and, in medieval fashion, free wine was to be had in the conduits. But one man resolutely refused to join in the general celebrations.

"We embarked upon this war, Mistress O'Mara," Samuel Pepys said earnestly to Lilias, "in our usual haphazard way: totally unprepared and ill-equipped. Our ships are manned almost entirely by pressed men, and such do not make the best of sailors."

He had caught up with her during the fashionable hour of the promenade in St James's Park, near one of the oyster booths, where Lilias had paused for refreshment. Pepys' round, pleasant face was unusually grave, which Lilias found disturbing. This naturally cheerful man had been appointed Clerk of the Acts to the Navy Board, and was generally considered one of the "coming" men. Lilias always listened to his opinions with respect, and his conviction that this victory off Lowestoft would prove to be hollow, was unnerving.

More unnerving, however, were his final words as they parted near the Cockpit.

"And I very much fear that there is plague in the city, Mistress O'Mara. As I came along Drury Lane this morning, I noticed three doors marked with red crosses."

As always at any mention of the plague, Lilias' thoughts winged back to the war and Hannah. And beyond that again, to her father, whose death had really been the turning point of her life. Only that morning, she had received a letter from Judith to say that she and Eliot had at last been married in St Nicholas' Church. Poor

Judith! How she must have hated being married in a church. The wedding had twice been postponed in the hope that Parson Pentecost might be able to officiate; but the Five Mile Act of earlier this year had forbidden the Dissenting and dispossessed clergy to go within that distance of a borough town.

Lilias sighed. On the surface, life was happier, things were easier, people more contented; but underneath nothing had changed. Tyranny begat tyranny, and so the chain went on, unbroken, from generation to generation. . .

"And why is the lovely Mrs O'Mara so pensive this morning?" asked a mocking voice, and Lilias turned to find her elder son at her elbow.

"Oliver! I didn't see you."

"You were too deep in thought, my dear mother. And sombre thoughts at that, judging by your expression. You know Lady Cressida Lithgow, I believe?"

Lilias glanced curiously at Priam's daughter and smiled, holding out her hand. "We have met once or twice, on more formal occasions."

But there was no answering smile. Cressida looked tired. There were dark circles under her eyes as though she had not slept, and Lilias had the sudden suspicion that she had been crying. Had she heard anything about Lilias and her father? Surely not! In the three months since she had become the Earl's mistress, they had been discreet to the point, on occasions, of self-denial; a ridiculous situation, as Priam had pointed out, at a court where self-denial was a cardinal sin. No, Cressida's unhappiness was to do with Oliver. Lilias could recognise the cruel sense of elation which he wore like a second skin. She remembered it from his childhood, when he had scored over Judith or Eliot.

And, as an echo to her thought, came Judith's name. "So Judith and Eliot are married at last," Oliver was saying. "I received a letter today. Poor Eliot!"

"Why 'poor Eliot'?" Lilias was inexplicably annoyed, even though it had been her own reaction to the news.

Oliver shrugged, turning towards the silent Cressida. "Judith is my plain sister," he observed unnecessarily. "Morwenna is my pretty one." He added challengingly, looking once more at his mother: "I trust Geoffrey is keeping out of trouble? We can hardly expect the King to extricate him and his Quaker friends a second time."

"Afraid that he will bring disgrace on you, Oliver?" Lilias asked sardonically, and her son had the grace to blush.

"Not at all. I hope that I am capable of advancing by my own merits. And now if you'll excuse us, mother, I see my lord Rochester and I want a word with him. Lady Cressida. . ."

The girl inclined her head in Lilias' direction as they moved away, but still she did not speak. "She's in love with him," Lilias thought uneasily. Well, at least Oliver showed no signs of being in love with her, that was something to be thankful for. Lilias could not imagine Priam approving of such a match.

She was late. Her encounters, first with Samuel Pepys and then with Oliver, had delayed her. She quickened her steps as much as she dared in that glaring heat, hurrying past the pit which had once housed King James' menagerie, past the bowling-green and along a path which led to one of the secluded arbours with which the park conveniently abounded. Priam was waiting for her, grim with impatience.

"I thought you weren't coming, or had forgotten," he said.

"Forgotten!"

She was in his arms, her lips locked fast on his. He murmured endearments against her hair as he drew her back into the shadows, forcing her down beside him on the rustic bench. He undid the laces of her bodice and slid one hand inside, cupping her breast.

368

"This is madness," she managed to breathe at last. "In broad daylight."

"I haven't seen you for nearly a week. It drives me crazy when I'm not with you. The thought of you with O'Mara."

"I've told you, you have no need to be jealous. I was never in love with him. And ... such as there was between us is over ... has been over for almost a year."

"Yet he is devoted to your daughter."

"Morwenna ... Yes. He's ... very fond of her."

Priam moved restlessly. "I must see you again soon. Magdalen is in attendance upon the Queen for the rest of the week. Cressida is going to stay with Cassandra for a day or two, and I can get rid of Oliver on some pretext or other. Send him to Westovers on some trumped-up errand. Can you get away tomorrow afternoon? Come by river and I'll meet you at the water-stairs."

"Oh my love ... I don't know. I'm not certain, but I'll try. I'll ... I'll think up a story that will satisfy Patrick."

He forced up her chin to make her look at him. "Why is such deception necessary if he doesn't care what you do?"

"I didn't say that." She gave a little laugh. "He is as moral in his way as ever Richard was."

His hand tightened about her breast, hurting her, and she bit back a cry of pain. "Don't make the mistake of thinking that I'm not moral where you are concerned, my love."

"Do you love me?" How stupid, how womanlike to demand reassurance after all the proof he had given her during the past three months. But the idea was so new to her, after the long, arid years of disbelief, that she could not resist the temptation to hear him say it.

He smiled, and the harsh features, whose natural lines had been deepened by deprivation and suffering, relaxed into a tenderness which few people were ever privileged to see: his daughters when they were young, perhaps;

Magdalen, before her reticence had built an impenetrable barrier between them.

"You know I do," he said.

Lilias pressed her burning face against his shoulder, wanting him now, this very minute, with the same intensity of passion she had felt as a girl of nineteen. She was hardly aware of voices from the path, outside.

"'E came this way, my lady, I saw 'im, not 'alf an hour ago. Taking refuge from the 'eat, I daresay, in one of the alcoves."

A gardener giving someone directions . . .

A shadow fell across the arbour floor. Magdalen's breathless voice said: "Priam!"

They both sprang up, Lilias fumbling with her bodice, feeling naked and ashamed, seeing herself suddenly through the other woman's eyes, her shining idyll reduced to something tawdry.

But Magdalen seemed hardly to be aware of Lilias. Her face was white and she clutched at her husband's sleeve.

"Priam, thank Heaven I've found you. Cressida said you might be here. You must come at once. Hartford has just sent word. Cassie is very ill. Oh, dear God, Priam! He thinks it might be plague!"

CHAPTER TWENTY-TWO

When Lilias returned from Ireland with her husband and daughter in the August of 1666, she had not seen Priam for over a year, not since that June day when his elder daughter had fallen an early victim to the outbreak of plague which had scourged London with devastating results for more than three months.

It had been one of the worst visitations that the capital could remember, and old men, searching their memories for a comparison, gave up the attempt in despair. It was the Black Death all over again, declared the pessimists, as, by the end of July, the pest-houses were full to overflowing. The streets were deserted, except for the plague-nurses: those flocks of carrion-crows whose reward for taking care of the stricken was the plundering of the corpse. And many were the hideous tales of people strangled or smothered who might otherwise have survived, for the sake of a wedding ring or a gold locket.

As more and more foot-high red crosses appeared on doors, with the superscription *Lord Have Mercy Upon Us*, more and more desperate remedies were tried. Bonfires were lit all along the banks of the Thames because smoke was believed to be an antidote to the infection. By the same token, it was thought that smoking tobacco was beneficial, and one Eton schoolboy was flogged for refusing to obey the Headmaster's injunction to provide himself with a pipe. July the twelfth was appointed as a day of penitence and prayer. Then all the dogs and cats were slaughtered, as there seemed to be some basis for the theory that domestic pets were carriers of the disease. Finally, it was suggested by a doctor that syphilis was a powerful counteraction to bubonic plague, and the brothels of Lutener's Lane,

Hatton Garden and Dog Yard were packed to the doors, the most poxy of the prostitutes being in constant demand.

The King had withdrawn to Hampton Court; the law courts extended the long vacation to Martinmas; and Members of Parliament suddenly discovered a pressing need to attend to affairs on their estates. The grieving Countess of Chelwood and her surviving daughter were despatched, under the protection of Oliver Pride, to Westovers. And the O'Maras had gone to Ireland, also, ostensibly, to escape the plague. Only Lilias and Patrick knew that the truth was other than it seemed.

*   *   *

The news of Lady Hartford's death had been conveyed to Lilias in a hastily scrawled note from the Earl, then, for some weeks after that, there had, naturally enough, been silence.

Lilias had been glad of the respite from Priam's company, glad to come to terms with those feelings of guilt which Magdalen's sudden appearance had inspired. The sense of shame, of shabbiness, which had filled her had forced her to realise that she would always make an uneasy mistress. Her natural inclination to indulge her body, which she had first recognised on that night when Barnaby had come to her room, was stifled by her Puritan upbringing. She needed respectability: she was happier as a wife than a kept woman. But her overwhelming love for Priam, all the stronger for having been so long dormant, would not let her rest. She wanted him at any price, even at the price of her self-respect.

So when, after the service of intercession on July the twelfth at St Paul's, Priam pressed another note into her hand, she felt only a wild elation. Unable to wait until reaching home, she opened the slip of paper as soon as she had entered the carriage. She failed to notice Patrick, who had not accompanied her to the service—his

Catholicism had grown more militant of late—seated in the opposite corner. It was only when the note was twitched from her grasp that she became aware of his presence, and by then it was too late.

Patrick read aloud: "My Heart, tonight, if you can, and come by river. I shall await you, as usual, by the water-steps. Your own, ever-loving Priam."

"I—I didn't see you," Lilias faltered stupidly, taking the paper between nerveless fingers as her husband handed it back to her.

"Apparently not," Patrick answered drily, and was silent for the remainder of the short journey home.

But once inside the house, as Lilias would have made for the stairs and the solitude of her own room, Patrick barred her way, pushing open the door of his ground-floor study and motioning her inside.

"In here," he commanded grimly.

She hesitated, but his hand tugged painfully on her wrist and his eyes, when she steeled herself to meet them, were like flint. One of the maidservants came up from the kitchens and looked, puzzled, towards her master and mistress.

"Unless you wish to make a scene before the girl," whispered Patrick, and again indicated the open door with a jerk of his head.

Lilias went into the study. The little book-lined room was dark, the shutters shut against the heat and the danger of infection. Patrick closed the door and leaned his shoulders against it.

"Well?" she asked, in a voice which was a trifle unsteady.

"No, not well, Lilias," was the icy response. "Ever since I first set eyes on you, you have been making a fool of me."

The accusation seemed to her so unwarranted that she gasped, her courage returning on a surge of anger.

"When, pray, did I ever make a fool of you before?"

"When you smuggled Richard Pride out of Bristol, and poor Trenchard was flogged because you bewitched him with that smile of yours."

"One instance!" she taunted him, angrier still. "My sole concern was to get Richard safely away. I did not even know that you were the officer of the guard that day."

"Perhaps not. And it doesn't matter now." He moved away from the door, and there was something purposeful about the set of his shoulders that filled her with apprehension. She retreated to the other side of his desk. "But this is different," he went on. "You know that I am your husband and that you are wilfully betraying me with another man."

"And you knew that I loved him when you married me," she retorted with spirit. "Who better?"

"It doesn't alter the fact, my love, that you married me." He came to stand opposite her, on the other side of the desk. *"Thou shalt not commit adultery.* In case you had forgotten, one of the Ten Commandments. You are my wife and I expect fidelity from you."

She was now thoroughly angry and her bosom heaved with temper. "You! To talk about fidelity! You, who have cherished lecherous thoughts of another man's wife for Heaven knows how many years! You, who raped me when I was married to Richard Pride! You're a hypocrite, Patrick O'Mara!"

His anger now matched her own. He came round the desk, seizing her by the shoulders.

"You're my wife," he hissed again, "in the eyes of the Church and of the law. You need a whip taken to you, my girl, and if I had one handy, I'd make you smart. You're not playing me false with Lord High-and-Mighty Chelwood. You may be in love with that whoremaster, that frequenter of brothels, but your body belongs to me."

"No!" She struggled to be free, but the movement

374

only enraged him further. She recognised the look on his face as the one she had seen all those years ago, in the Broad Street kitchen. "Please, Patrick! No!"

"Only the Earl, is that it? Only he is good enough to touch Lilias O'Mara. Well, my dear, you're about to find out that you are mistaken. You reminded me just now that I once raped you. And what I did once, my love, I can do again."

* * *

Later that night, he had come into her bedroom. There was no apology in his manner, no gentleness, no tenderness which might have mitigated the brutality with which he had used her earlier. Yet, lurking at the back of his eyes there had been something: some desperate plea for affection which had reminded her, oddly, of Barnaby. And so she had listened to what he had to say, stony-faced, but nonetheless she had listened.

"We are going to Ireland, you and Morwenna and I. I always meant to settle there some day and buy back my old home if I could."

"The King may not give you permission to go," Lilias had said woodenly, to hide the mounting panic in her breast. She could not bear the thought of being hundreds of miles from Priam when she had only just found him again.

"I have already broached the matter to His Majesty," Patrick answered. "He knows that, as a practising Catholic, I am under ever increasing pressure here. Restrictions against Catholics and Dissenters alike are daily growing more rigorous. Soon, it will be impossible for anyone not of the Church of England to hold office, particularly close to the King. Even the Queen cannot hear Mass nowadays unmolested. And with the plague so rife, no one will think it strange if we choose this moment to leave London."

"And if I refuse to go? If I quit this house tonight and place myself under the Earl's protection?"

Patrick laughed shortly. "Even today, my dear, deserting a husband to live openly with another man is still condemned: a social solecism which could wreck not only the woman's reputation, but also the man's. Having a lover is reputable enough, but it must be played as a game. Love must never be taken too seriously. But in your case, I am not afraid of your doing any such thing. You see, I should immediately tell Morwenna the truth. At least, no, not quite the truth. After all, there were no witnesses to that meeting of ours in Bristol. Only we know for certain that what happened between us was forced upon you unwillingly."

"You wouldn't dare!" Anger wrecked her precarious calm, and she leaned forward, pummelling him with her fists. "You'd lie, to keep me chained to you?"

He pinioned her back against the pillows, advancing his face to within an inch or two of hers.

"Yes. To keep Morwenna."

The fight went out of Lilias. She lay quiet, looking up at him. "Does she mean that much to you, Patrick?"

"She means everything," he answered simply.

"And if I come with you to Ireland, you'll let her go on thinking that Richard was her father? You will not try to persuade her to your religion?"

He smiled ironically. "My dear, my religion is the same as yours. I am neither a Muslim nor a Jew. It is just that we worship in different ways. But rest easy. Morwenna shall not learn the truth from me. She shall continue to believe that Richard Pride was her father. As for her 'religion', as you call it, that is her own affair. I have always thought it a personal decision, whatever the priests might say. But my promise to you, Lilias, is dependent upon yours to me. You will not see the Earl of Chelwood again, as a lover."

She closed her eyes for a moment. The nightly rumbling of the plague-carts over the cobbles, the distant shouts of "Bring out your dead!" reminded her vividly of

376

the night that Hannah died. How young she had been then! How simple and uncomplicated life had seemed. Could she give Patrick her promise never again to lie in Priam's arms, never again to feel his body close to hers? For Morwenna's sake she must. And not only for Morwenna's sake. She recalled Magdalen's distraught face, with its curiously vulnerable, girlish quality and remembered, too, that Magdalen had just lost a child.

She opened her eyes and said: "Very well, Patrick, you have my promise."

* * *

On their way to Ireland, they had stayed for a week in Bristol, before embarking on *The Bristol Queen*. Judith had obviously been happy, running the Broad Street house with two young charity girls to aid her. Eliot, too, seemed to have found a kind of contentment, although the sight of Morwenna growing into womanhood and looking older than her fourteen years had plainly jolted him. She had lost the faintly coltish look of a year ago. Her breasts were rounder, her hips fuller: a woman ready for childbearing. But there had been an element of resignation in Eliot's affection for her, a coming to terms with his feelings, an acceptance that here was something he could never have. He was even fond of Judith, Lilias thought, in a detached, undemonstrative way.

Lilias herself had been deeply unhappy, hating the house with its constant reminders of the past. Once again, Patrick O'Mara had come between herself and Priam. She swore that she would never forgive him, yet she secretly acknowledged the justice of his actions; she told herself that she hated him, resolutely denying that this was far from the truth.

The year they had spent in Ireland had been balm to neither of their spirits. Patrick had bought back his boyhood home from its present owner, but discovered, as Lilias could have told him, that it was impossible to recapture the past. The place was not the same: too many changes had been made in the name of repair and some of the land had been sold to pay for the alterations. After six months, Patrick had got rid of it to the highest bidder and they had moved to a new home near Waterford. But Morwenna had not been happy, missing the gay life she had grown used to in London, and finding it difficult to settle in a restricted country society. As for Lilias, she had said little, appearing to be the most contented of the three. She did not resist Patrick when he wished to make love, returning to the old armed neutrality of the early days of their marriage.

At the end of April, however, Patrick announced his intention of returning to England. Morwenna, recovering from a severe spring fever which had left her weak, flung her arms about his neck and burst into tears of happiness.

"Truly, Papa? May we go back to London?"

"If you wish it, sweetheart," Patrick had said, stroking her hair and looking down at the bent head with such tenderness that Lilias knew her sacrifice had been worthwhile.

They arrived back in London at the beginning of August to take possession of a comfortable house near the Temple, and to find all London ringing with the news of Prince Rupert's naval victory off North Foreland, over the Dutch Admiral, De Ruyter, and his fleet. As for the gossip in the gilded salons and the wooded pleasances of Vauxhall, it was much the same as it had been a year before. Nothing had changed: Castlemaine continued to hold precarious sway as the King's *maîtresse-en-titre*, but only because Frances Stuart had still not succumbed to the lures which Charles threw in her way. The King himself welcomed the O'Maras with undisguised pleasure, and within a week Lilias was once again caught up in a whirl of gaiety.

On the last night of August, she attended the theatre in

378

Drury Lane to see a performance of *Macbeth*. This sombre tragedy had been enlivened with singing witches and a harlequinade; but the King, who dropped in briefly before going on elsewhere, had another interest in the production.

"What did you say the girl's name is, my lord?" he demanded of the Earl of Rochester.

"Eleanor Gwynne, sire. Known to her friends as Nellie. She used to sell oranges here, until she was promoted to the boards."

"Can she act?"

"As to that, sire, opinions differ," the young man drawled. "But opinion is unanimous that she has by far the most shapely legs in London."

"And how old is this paragon?" sneered Castlemaine angrily.

Rochester's smile was malicious. "About fifteen years old, or so I believe. An age you and I, dear Bab, have long since forgotten."

Lilias reflected sadly that she, too, had long since forgotten what it was like to be fifteen, a fact which was underlined by the appearance of Oliver during an interval in one of the neighbouring boxes. Lilias, quitting the royal box on the arm of Sir Peterborough Sedley, thought that her elder son looked flushed and excited.

A moment later, she was startled by the approach of Lady Cressida Lithgow, who requested a word with her in private. Sir Peterborough gallantly conducted both ladies to a bench by the wall, bowed and politely withdrew.

When he had gone, there was an awkward silence, which Lilias filled with a halting enquiry after the health of the Earl and Countess, and belated condolences on the death of Lady Cassandra. Cressida, answering almost at random, seemed strangely ill-at-ease.

Suddenly, she turned to Lilias, evidently having made up her mind to speak.

"Mrs O'Mara, I . . . I want you to know that I am going to marry Oliver. I feel you should be told."

Lilias blinked at her. The chattering voices, the flaring candlelight, the hush of silks and the laughter all about her receded. "M-marry Oliver?" she stammered.

"Yes. I also think that you should know that my parents disapprove. In fact, they have forbidden it. But I am of age, and they cannot prevent me. It grieves me to go against their wishes, but Oliver and I leave secretly, for the Border, in the morning."

"A runaway marriage?" Lilias laid her hand impulsively on the younger woman's arm. "Oh, my dear, don't! And if your parents disapprove of the match, they probably have good reasons. Oliver—" Lilias hesitated, uncomfortably aware of her own ambivalent feelings towards her first-born son. "Does he love you?" she finished lamely.

"No. I am not deluded on that score. He would never have married me if Cassie hadn't died. You see, I now inherit everything. Papa cannot disinherit me, even should he wish to. It is something to do with the entail. I don't understand these matters, but Oliver has studied it thoroughly."

Oliver's mother felt sure that he had. "But if you know that he is marrying you for your money," Lilias urged, "why do you wish to marry him?"

"Because I love him." The direct eyes looked at her from under straight dark brows, so like Priam's. "I can't explain why I love him. These things . . . just happen. But I know that I can't live without him and that is all that matters. I am very like my father, you know." Again the candid gaze. "And I have seen what marrying someone he does not love has done to him. It's torn him apart, and I don't intend that that should happen to me." Cressida stood up, smiling down at Lilias. "Please don't look so concerned. As long as Oliver gets what he wants, he will make me a faithful husband. Probably a good one.

He is only dangerous when he's foiled." She took a deep breath. "I feel better now that I have told you. Will you wish me happiness?"

"Oh, my dear, with all my heart. But don't you think . . .? Shouldn't your parents be told?"

"Later, when I'm married. When they can do nothing, they will accept it. But I cannot face the scenes and the recriminations. And perhaps father would try to stop me by force. No, believe me, Mrs O'Mara, it's better this way. When we meet again, I shall be your daughter-in-law. Good-bye."

With a last, sweet smile, Cressida was gone, and Sir Peterborough Sedley was standing in her place, proffering Lilias his arm.

"My dear ma'am, I think we must be swift if we do not wish to miss the harlequinade."

But Lilias saw nothing of the harlequinade, nor of the rest of the play. Duty struggled with a natural disinclination to interfere in two young lives. Surely Cressida, who was no schoolroom miss, must know by now what she wanted out of life. And if it was Oliver, what right had Lilias to gainsay her? Furthermore, Cressida's belief that Oliver would make her a satisfactory and faithful husband was probably sound; his tantrums had always arisen from being thwarted. Give him what he wanted, and no one could be kinder.

Yet surely Priam had the right to know that his daughter was planning to elope? And Cressida, rather foolishly, had not bound Lilias to secrecy on that score. Supposing it was Morwenna, and Priam failed to inform her of what he knew?

The audience was clapping, the actors were taking their bow, the King and his party had long since departed and it was getting extremely late. Lilias realised with a start that the hours had sped by without her knowing. If she was to warn Priam in time to prevent the runaways, she must go at once, even though it was nearly midnight ...

She stepped into her carriage and directed the coachman to the Strand.

*   *   *

Priam looked older, more careworn. There were lines seaming the thin features which she had not seen before. He had not gone to bed, and came into the library, overlooking the garden, with a hasty tread. Both hands were held out in greeting.

"Lilias! My dear!" He would have taken her in his arms, but she held him off, remembering her promise to Patrick.

"No! Please, no! I gave my word not to see you alone. Don't make it harder for me, I beg of you. I've come only because I must, to tell you that Cressida is planning to run away tomorrow morning early, with Oliver. They will be making for the Border and a Scottish wedding."

He stared at her for a moment, trying to assimilate her words, coming as they did hard on the shock of her unexpected visit. His agonising disappointment at her opening words was swallowed up in this further anguish.

"Please wait," he said, and went from the room.

Lilias sank on to a chair, overcome by sudden fatigue. Beyond the undrawn curtains was the garden she had grown to know so well during those stolen months of happiness last year: the bone-bleached path, the lacy boughs of ash, the gleam of the river through the bushes, corpse-like under the midnight sky.

Priam returned. "They've gone," he said, and his tone was expressionless.

"But ..." Lilias was on her feet. "It was Lady Cressida herself who told me that they were leaving tomorrow morning. Not three hours since, at the play."

The Earl rubbed his hand wearily across his forehead. "Apparently she returned about half past ten, while Magdalen and I were still from home. One of the servants

382

saw her go out again half an hour later, wearing her travelling cloak. Some of her clothes are missing. Most of Oliver's, too."

"He was there, tonight, at the theatre," Lilias said thoughtfully. "I saw him. And he must have seen Cressida speak to me. If she told him what she'd done, he wouldn't wait until tomorrow. He would guess that I might come to you. I'm sorry. I should not have delayed. Will you go after them?"

Priam shook his head slowly. "No. She has made her choice . . . and he is your son."

Lilias smiled wanly. "More important, he is Richard Pride's son. I know you never liked him, but Richard was a very good man."

"Yes . . . we must hope for the best. Thank you for coming . . . Lilias!" He half-stumbled towards her. "My darling . . ."

"Priam, no! I have promised Patrick . . . Don't look like that! There is something you don't—can't—understand. I must go now."

She brushed past him, down the long hall, tears blinding her eyes, and out to her carriage waiting in the street.

★　★　★

Lilias awoke next morning, Saturday, September the first, to a sense of foreboding and to see Patrick, fully clothed, standing at the bottom of her bed. She sat up, pushing the tousled hair out of her eyes, and stared at him stupidly.

"Patrick? Are we due to pay a morning call?"

He ignored her question, and his voice when he spoke was shaking with anger.

"Williams tells me that he drove you to the Strand last night, and that you were in that man's house for more than half an hour. Do you deny it?"

"No . . . no, of course I don't deny it, but. . . ."

"No, how could you? You fool! Did you think that the

truth wouldn't come out, when you took my own carriage and my coachman?"

"It wasn't like that. Please let me explain!"

But his fury was consuming him like a fire. Always, always, she had brought him nothing but trouble! It was easy to forget at this moment that she had saved his life by her silence, and that later her prompt and courageous action had saved him from a Virginia prison. All he could think of was that she had again betrayed him with the Earl.

"You couldn't stay away from him, could you? You slut! You whore! Holy Mother of God! You've only been back in London a couple of weeks, and you're crawling into his bed already!"

"Patrick, will you listen to me? Please!"

"No, I'll not listen to any more of your black Protestant lies! I warned you what would happen if you did this to me again. And, by God, Lilias, I'll keep my word."

"Not Morwenna! No, not like this!" Not in the white heat of his anger! She scrambled out of bed as he turned to go, running after him, imploring. "Patrick! For pity's sake, listen!"

He swung on his heel, dealing her a blow across the face which sent her reeling.

"Don't come near me, nor mention my daughter's name. God! What a mother to have for my only child." He was breathing hard, but a little of the anger died in his eyes as Lilias, picking herself up from the floor, came at him with a murderous gleam in her own. He caught her easily around the waist and threw her back on to the bed.

"You've always had spirit, I'll say that for you. And I owe you something. I'll not tell Morwenna until tonight, when I've had a chance to think matters over. But meantime I've urgent business in the city. I'm off to see my lawyer. That at least won't wait."

CHAPTER TWENTY-THREE

Lilias passed a miserable day waiting for Patrick to return, not daring to leave the house. Jenny was sent to Lady Dearing's with a note begging her to excuse Mrs O'Mara's absence from her rout that evening on the score of a very severe headache. And it was not, thought Lilias, that much of a lie. By dinner time, her temples were throbbing.

Morwenna, anxious, begged her mother to lie down. "You look ill, darling. I'll bathe your forehead with lavender water."

But Lilias refused to leave her vigil by the withdrawing-room window, which commanded a view of the street. She must speak to Patrick as soon as he came in, before he carried out his threat and sent for Morwenna. She must make him listen to her and understand why she had visited Priam.

By supper time, however, Patrick had still not returned and soon after, Morwenna retired to bed. Lilias breathed more easily. He would hardly rouse the child from sleep. At least, she had a little more time. . .

At midnight, to the accompaniment of a rising wind which prowled among the roof-tops, Lilias, too, went to bed. Patrick had evidently decided to stay at a friend's house for the night, perhaps working himself into a better frame of mind. Thankfully, she let Jenny undress her and brush out her hair. Then she slid gratefully between the cool linen sheets and fell asleep to the noise of the gusting wind. . .

Suddenly, she was awake. Someone was in her room.

"Patrick—?" she began, but Morwenna's voice answered: "It's only me, mother."

"What is it, sweetheart? What's wrong? Are you feeling ill?"

"No. It was the glow which woke me. Come and look. There seems to be a fire somewhere in the city."

"Really!" Lilias climbed out of bed, half-amused, half-irritated. In a city where more than three-quarters of the buildings were made of wood, fires were not that uncommon.

Nevertheless, when she peered from between the open shutters, the blaze did appear to be of more than ordinary proportions, fanned into life by the relentless wind.

"How far away do you think it is?" Morwenna sounded worried.

"Oh, a mile or so. I'm no judge of distances. Inside the walls, at any rate. Now, don't fret, my darling. The Mayor and aldermen will have been informed by this time. It's probably well under control already. Go back to bed and go to sleep. All the excitement will be over by the morning."

★   ★   ★

Patrick had spent an equally miserable evening and restless night. His decision not to return home had been, as Lilias guessed, a desire to think things out more calmly.

His visit to his lawyer's and the making of certain alterations to his will had assuaged his anger. By the time he had eaten a belated dinner at The Dolphin in Seething Lane, he was already regretting his impulsive action. Well, he reflected, picking his teeth and ignoring the coy advances of a lady dining alone in the corner, he could alter his will again any day he chose. He would stay at The Dolphin tonight and go home to hear Lilias' explanation in the morning.

He was now convinced that there must be an explanation. She would surely not have gone to visit the Earl so openly had there not been: it would have occurred to her that Williams might mention the fact to his master. And she had not denied the accusation, had not appeared flustered or guilty. He had allowed his sense of betrayal to override his better judgement. Tomorrow, therefore, he would listen to what Lilias had to say. But for now, still labouring as he was under a certain amount of suspicion and a lingering sense of grievance, he would do better to stay away from her, or else they would merely find themselves quarrelling again.

The beds at The Dolphin were comfortable, and though the shutters of his room were buffeted angrily by the wind, he was too exhausted by the emotions of the day to lie awake for long.

He was awakened in the morning by the chambermaid, who brought him his shaving water, but had forgotten his warm, spiced ale.

"I'm sorry, sir, I'm sure, but we're all at sixes and sevens. There's a terrible fire, sir; somewhere around Pudding Lane, the master reckons. It's been burning since the small hours and they say it's spreading terrible quick. A lot of people have lost their homes already. It's this wind, sir, the master says."

Patrick got out of bed and looked out of the window. The columns of smoke and the belching flames could be seen quite clearly. At the door of a house opposite, he recognised Samuel Pepys and called to him.

"It looks bad, Master Pepys."

Pepys glanced up and nodded. "Bad enough, I should say. I saw a glow in the sky early this morning, but went back to sleep. I thought the fire would have been out by now." He frowned, shielding his eyes with his hand as he stared once again towards the burning heart of the city. "I shall take a look. If it's as bad as it seems, I must go at once to Whitehall and inform the King."

"If you'll wait a moment," Patrick shouted, "I'll come with you."

By the time that the two men, walking as quickly as

they could in view of the fact that they were hampered by a constant flow of refugees, reached the vicinity of Pudding Lane, it was obvious that the fire was out of control. Sparks, carried by the wind, had ignited the hay and fodder bales at the Star Inn on Fish Street Hill. The ship-chandlers' stores in Thames Street were well ablaze, their stock of oil, hemp, tallow and spirits turned into a raging inferno. Stacks of sea-coal and timber along the wharves had also caught fire.

The Mayor and several of the aldermen were already on the scene, but seemed undecided what to do. Patrick and Samuel Pepys glanced at one another, appalled.

"Why don't they blow up some of the houses in the path of the fire?" asked Patrick. "They must create an open space."

Pepys nodded. "Yes. Somewhere where the flames cannot get a hold."

He bustled away to speak to the Mayor, but came back a few minutes later, his round, good-natured face creased with anger.

"They won't do it. They say they can't be responsible for the destruction of property. Property, sir! Property! It's the new Golden Calf of the age."

"Then His Majesty must be persuaded to give the order," Patrick said grimly.

Pepys sucked his teeth. "You're right. I'll go to Whitehall immediately. By river, I think. I shouldn't stay here, O'Mara. You're in danger of being roasted alive."

By midday, chaos reigned. London's only two fire-engines had been rendered useless. The one from St Bride's had failed even to start, its quarterly maintenance of cleaning and oiling having been consistently neglected. The one from Clerkenwell had been surrounded and so jostled by the interested spectators that it had been accidentally toppled into the river. The fire-fighters themselves, using hooks and hand-squirts, were hampered by the intense heat and the narrowness of the streets. There was little help to be had, either, from the majority of the citizens, who were more concerned with saving their belongings than actually fighting the flames.

Patrick, in his shirt sleeves, his face blackened by smoke, was one of the few who were in the thick of things; and when Pepys returned midway through the afternoon with orders from the King for the demolition of the houses, he hardly recognised his companion of the morning.

"For God's sake, go home, Mr O'Mara," he urged. "Your wife will be wondering what has become of you."

Lilias! Patrick had almost forgotten the circumstances under which they had parted all those long hours ago. All at once, he wanted to see her urgently, to hear what she had to say; to reassure himself that she had after all kept her promise to him. And tomorrow, he would visit his lawyer again and undo the mischief which he had done yesterday.

He nodded briefly at Pepys. "You're right. She will be worried. And I can do no more here; the fire has too firm a hold to be quenched by water. Only gunpowder will do the trick now."

He turned to go, away from the heat and the dust and the roaring flames. A scared-faced girl darted out of an alleyway and laid her hand on his sleeve.

"Oh sir! Please help! Please! My mistress is trapped ..." She paused, gasping for breath, one hand pressed to her side.

"Trapped? Where?"

"In a house near St Paul's. Oh sir, St Paul's is burning something dreadful. And all the houses round about. My mistress is trapped in an upstairs room and we can't seem to get to her, nohow."

"Lead the way," Patrick ordered. Then, as they dodged between already smouldering buildings, he asked: "Who is your mistress?"

"The Countess of Chelwood, sir. Oh please! Do hurry!" she added, as Patrick stopped to stare at her in surprise.

"But surely the Countess lives in the Strand," he protested, quickening his steps in response to her words.

"She's been visiting an old servant who used to be in her father's employ. She came this morning, to see if the old lady was safe. And now she's caught and we can't . . . Oh please, sir, can you do something?"

"What about the old lady?"

"We got her out, but my lady went back to try to save the old woman's dog. She managed to drop the poor creature from an upstairs window, but then the stairs gave way . . . Here we are, sir. There she is! Look!"

The smoke was thick, and the fire-fighters were clearing the area around the doomed church as quickly as possible. A burly man loomed in front of Patrick and endeavoured to bar his path.

"You can't come this way, sir. The whole street will catch in a moment. There's no more we can do."

Patrick brushed him aside. "You fool! There's a woman trapped up there. Can't you hear her shouting? Look, man! Behind you!"

The veil of smoke was torn aside for a moment by another gust of wind, and in the house immediately facing him, he saw Magdalen, clinging to the stanchion of a second storey window. He pushed past the burly man and ran for the open door.

The girl had been right. The narrow, twisting staircase was alight, the wisps and curls of flame already turning to a steady blaze. But for the present, the floor of the upper storey held firm. If only there were some way he could mount. . .

The baluster was still intact. It had a solid base, with fluted wooden pillars supporting the hand-rail. As a window buckled inwards, letting in a blast of smoke-laden air, Patrick set his feet in two of the spaces between the pillars and began to climb sideways, like a crab.

It was a race to beat the flames. The wood was warping and scorching under his tortured fingers, and as he swung himself over the rail on to the tiny, first-floor landing, the banister went up with a roar. He moved instinctively, with the celerity of a cat, leaping through the open doorway of the room. As he did so, the floor boards gave way behind him, and he knew that at any moment the floor on which he was standing would follow suit.

Magdalen was in the window embrasure, and turned huge, terrified eyes upon him as he crossed the room.

"I'll have to lower you through the window, my lady," Patrick said. He picked her up bodily as he spoke, and shouted down to the burly man, who was still hovering reluctantly below. "I'm going to lower the lady as far as I can. You and the girl must try to catch her."

Like most houses, the upper storey hung clear of the rest of the building, leering drunkenly out over the street. There was nothing to break Magdalen's fall if they failed to catch her . . . but he had no time to think of that.

"You'll soon be safe," he reassured Magdalen cheerfully; but, looking at her, he was afraid that she was going to faint. "Come, my lady, there's nothing to fear. This isn't the first time that you and I have got the better of a fire. Remember Westovers, the night of the battle of Lansdown?"

She made a pathetic attempt to smile. Flames were now licking at the lintel of the door and the heat was almost overpowering.

The window, even opened to its farthest extent, was narrow. Magdalen, fortunately, still retained her girlish figure, but it was not easy for her to wriggle through and sit on the broad stone sill. She managed it somehow while the precious seconds ticked by, and Patrick could hear the flames leaping and crackling towards him. He held

391

Magdalen under her arms and straddled his feet. Cautiously, she inched her way to the edge of the sill, then thrust herself forward and dropped. . .

His body jerked as he took her weight. At the same moment, the floor gave way beneath him and he heard Magdalen scream as she slipped from his grasp. He thought stupidly, disbelievingly: "It began in fire: it is ending in fire." Then he plummeted downwards into the flames.

★   ★   ★

London was still smouldering on the day of Patrick O'Mara's funeral. The charred remains of once proud buildings pointed crumbling and blackened fingers at the sky. St Paul's, which had boasted the longest nave in Europe, was a derelict shell, the Fishmongers' Hall a ruin. Familiar streets were a faceless desert, well-known thoroughfares a wasteland of ashes. And all that was left of homes blown up to contain the fire was a swathe of featureless rubble.

The King and the Duke of York had worked as hard as the meanest of their subjects, standing for hours ankle-deep in water, passing buckets and directing hoses. For four days, the pitiless wind had carried sparks and what Pepys described as "fire-drops" to start new fires beyond the medieval walls. These, however, had been quickly dealt with; but a week later, the area around Cripplegate still glowed with a lingering heat.

The stench was appalling as sewers disgorged their bubbling contents, and the smell of burning clung to skin and hair and clothes. The homeless were encamped in tents at Moorfields, and the King himself rode out on the Wednesday evening to distribute bread and cheese and beer. He was cheered to the echo, and even the unpopular Duke of York was given a rousing reception as men recalled how he had brought up the militia to fight the flames. And while James had helped the soldiers with

392

hooks and ropes and axes, Charles had ridden from place to place with a satchelful of guineas, distributing them to anyone who was willing to lend a hand.

Already, the King was busy with plans for the rebuilding of the city. The new London was to be more beautiful than Carthage or Troy; and to that end, Charles had summoned a bevy of experts to Whitehall, including the Savilian Professor of Astronomy, Doctor Christopher Wren.

It was one of these meetings which prevented the King from attending Patrick's funeral; but he sent strict instructions that the Catholic rites were to be performed undisturbed, on pain of his greatest displeasure.

Lilias, her black dress and heavily plumed hat making her appear unusually pale, was escorted throughout by the Earl of Chelwood, who had been chosen by Charles as his deputy. But the meeting was painful: both knew that this was good-bye.

As the carriage lurched and jolted over the cobbles to the silent and darkened house near the Temple, Lilias asked in a low voice: "How is Lady Chelwood?"

Priam did not look at her, but she saw his hand clench against his knee. "The doctors say that she will never walk again. She fell in such a way..."

"What will you do now? Go back to Westovers?"

"Yes. She loves it there. And I shall sell the house in the Strand, although not yet. Not until Cressida returns."

"You've heard nothing of them?"

"No. Nor you?"

"Nothing ... It will be a terrible shock for your daughter."

He did not answer. The September rain, needed so desperately a week before, danced and tapped on the roof of the carriage. After a moment or two, Lilias resumed: "I haven't thanked you yet for ... for helping to recover the body."

393

"In God's name, don't thank me! It was the least I could do ... there wasn't much ... to recover..."

"No." Lilias shivered, and unexpectedly started to cry. At once, Priam's arms were about her, folding her against his breast, soothing her as he would a child. But when she made a movement to free herself, he let her go.

"You understand ..." His voice was constricted. "There can be nothing further between us as long as Magdalen lives. I owe her that much. And him." The Earl tried to smile, but failed. "Strange, how he has always come between us, no less now that he is dead than when he was living."

Lilias nodded, not trusting herself to speak. A few moments later, when the Earl's carriage stopped outside her door, she thanked him in the polite, stilted phrases that she might have used to a stranger. His hand, as he assisted her to alight, closed tightly over hers, and he lifted it to his lips.

"Good-bye, Lilias. Think of me sometimes—" His voice broke and he blindly re-entered the coach, rasping out an order. Lilias stood on the steps, heedless of the rain, and watched until the carriage had lumbered out of sight.

*   *   *

The contents of Patrick's new will were broken to her, the day after the funeral, by the apologetic lawyer. Mr Harrogate was thin and bent, a badly made question-mark of a man. He stood in the middle of Lilias' parlour, cracking his knuckles with embarrassment.

"I can assure you, my dear Mrs O'Mara," he mumbled, a little warmth creeping into his dry-as-dust voice as he looked at Lilias in open admiration, "that I did my best to persuade your late husband not to do anything rash. He was—er—plainly upset. A—er—domestic disagreement, I apprehend, such as disturbs the—er—tenor of even the happiest household. Ah, hmmm! Precisely!

394

So foolish, as I pointed out to him, to—er—take steps before the temper has had time to cool. Dear me, yes! Dear me! Dear me, yes!"

"Mr Harrogate," Lilias said, curbing her impatience, "what is it that you are trying to tell me? That Patrick altered his will?"

"Last Saturday morning. The day before he died. Which—er—goes to prove my point. I am convinced that had not fate intervened as it did, Monday would have seen him again in my office, ordering me to destroy the new in favour of the old. Under which, of course, you were the sole beneficiary."

"And now?" prompted Lilias, fear slithering coldly across her skin.

The lawyer cleared his throat once more, reluctantly unrolled the will and began to read. All of Patrick's fortune, amassed during his years as a planter in Virginia and increased by profitable speculation since his return to London, was left in its entirety to "my only child, Morwenna O'Mara, known as Morwenna Pride."

"But why?" Morwenna demanded tearfully of her mother, after Mr Harrogate had tittuped away in his incongruously high-heeled shoes, still shaking his head and lamenting the obstinacy of his clients. "Why should Papa leave me all his money? And why did he call me his 'only child'? I am not really his daughter."

Lilias took her hand and made Morwenna sit beside her on the window-seat. It was almost dark, but the candles had not been lit, and the rain-washed sky was still threaded with light, as pale and transparent as gossamer. Every now and then the wrack of cloud would lift, to show the faint sickle of a moon.

"What I am going to tell you, my darling, won't be easy for me to say or for you to hear. But I think you are old enough now to understand. . .."

And Morwenna, shocked and disturbed though she was, forced into a new identity with the realisation that

Patrick O'Mara, and not Richard Pride, was her father, did try to understand. But it would take her time, as Lilias realised, fully to come to terms with the idea. Fortunately, she was too young yet, too dependent upon Lilias, to question her mother's actions.

"If I had told the truth about what happened that night," Lilias urged, "Patrick would surely have been hanged, once he had been recaptured."

And Morwenna nodded her acceptance. But in years to come, might she not wonder if her mother had done right to withhold the truth from those most nearly concerned? However worthy her motive?

"You won't leave me? You won't go away and live somewhere else?" Morwenna cried in alarm, holding tightly to Lilias' hand. "It won't make any difference that the money is mine and not yours. I don't want it, anyway! Promise me that you'll stay with me!"

"Of course I shall stay with you," Lilias said, putting her arms around this most beloved of all her children and cradling her against her breast.

But later that night, after Morwenna had gone to bed, Lilias forced herself to face the future, stretching bleak and uninviting before her. She had nothing. She was as penniless as on that day, long ago, when her father died. She was her daughter's pensioner, dependent upon Morwenna for the roof over her head, the clothes on her back. And while such a situation did not matter now— except in terms of pride—it might in the years ahead.

Morwenna, on her visits to court, had already attracted more than her fair share of attention. Soon, prospective husbands would be clamouring for her hand; and although, initially, an ardent suitor might accept the idea of a dependent mother-in-law, it would be a prospect which could not but pall. She would, in time, become a burden to Morwenna. The idea was chilling, a situation fraught with danger and offering nothing but the promise of degradation. . .

396

There was still her share in the soap-works, left her by Richard. Things had not been easy for Eliot in the six years since the Restoration, which had restored not only the monarchy, but also the sovereign's right of seizure and monopoly. Lilias had been more than content, since her marriage to Patrick, to forgo whatever small income it brought her, making it over to Judith, partly as a sop to her conscience. But now, she could no longer afford to do so.

Lilias rose from the window-seat at last, lit the candle which had been left beside her by the faithful Jenny, and went slowly towards the door. She felt suddenly old and tired. She wanted to go to bed and never wake up. But in a day or two she must go to Bristol and confront Eliot and Judith with the truth.

★   ★   ★

She had been prepared for anger, but not this sullen bitterness that turned Eliot into a total stranger. She had expected resentment on his father's behalf, but he had scarcely mentioned Richard. From the first moment of her revelation, Eliot's thoughts had been only for himself.

Lilias had chosen her moment with care, giving some trumped-up reason for her visit when she had arrived the previous day, and waiting until now, when Judith and Geoffrey had gone to bed, and the calm of a Sunday night flooded the house.

"A moment, please, Eliot," she had said, when he would have followed Judith to their room, "there is something about which I must talk to you."

They had all spent the evening in the kitchen, with its familiar, friendly smells, its solid, reassuring shapes of range and water-barrel and store-cupboards. It had evoked so many memories—of Regina and Hannah, of Barnaby and Mollie Hanks, and, above all, of Richard—that it had made what she had to say so much more difficult. But, somehow, the story had come stumbling out, while Eliot, politely attentive at first, had gradually frozen into immobility. For a while, after she finished speaking, he said nothing, simply sitting and staring ahead of him. Then, abruptly, the flood-gates of his fury had opened.

"You knew—you always knew—that Morwenna was not my half-sister!" He got out of his chair and went to stand behind it, gripping the back until his knuckles stood out, bone-white, threatening to split the skin. "What is more, you have always known how I felt about Morwenna. I've seen it in your eyes, and I've been ashamed. *I* have been ashamed!" He struck his chest with his fist. "You let me torture myself for years with the belief that what I felt for her was unclean! Incestuous! When all the while you knew that there was no bond of blood between us." Tears glistened on his lashes, and he flung away from her into a corner of the room, where it was dark, out of the circle of candlelight and the warm, flickering glow of the fire. Somewhere in Tower Lane, a horse neighed and stamped, and a late returning reveller called out a greeting to his neighbour. The Watchman's melancholy voice told the hour, and a coach rattled by, over the cobbles. In the distance, a door slammed shut.

Eliot returned to stand once more behind his chair. His face had fallen into bluish folds, and Lilias noticed the evening's stubble shadowing his firm, square chin. Never had he looked more like Hannah, staring at her with malevolent eyes.

His next words came in a rush. "I've loved Morwenna since she was a baby. Adored her! Not as a brother loves his sister; at least, not since she was small. I've been in love with her for years and hated myself for it. I've tried to atone, to do penance. I've prayed to God to forgive me, to deliver me from my sin! When all the time I was not the one who needed forgiveness. It was you! You with your lying and deceit. Oh, dear Heaven!" And he covered his face with his hands.

Lilias endeavoured to speak calmly. "Eliot, what good would it have done you to know that Morwenna is not your half-sister? She was too young to return your love, even had she wished to. And, dear Eliot, believe me when I tell you that she has never thought of you in that way, and never will. You have Judith. And Judith has always loved you."

"Judith!" His tone was scathing, lacerated by his pain. "What's Judith to me? I would never have married her had I thought that there was a chance for me with Morwenna. And how do I know—how do *you* know?— that there might not have been that chance?"

"Eliot, I give you my word. . ."

"Your word! And what is that worth, pray?"

"I did what I thought was best." But her words mocked her. How many of life's worst disasters were caused by doing what one thought was best? She was right: Morwenna would never have loved Eliot in the way that he loved her. She would never have married him. But would it not have been kinder to Eliot to let him find out the truth for himself? And what of Judith? What trouble had she stored up for her first-born, when she had allowed Eliot to marry her, without saying the necessary word?

Lilias lay back in her chair, emotionally exhausted. She had made a mess not only of her own life, but of Eliot's and Judith's also. But not, please God, of Morwenna's. She was young and resilient, and because her memories of Richard had grown faint, was already adapting to the idea of Patrick O'Mara having been her father.

But Lilias' most pressing problem was still not resolved. Taking her courage in both hands, she admitted to Eliot why she had come to Bristol, why she had been forced at last to tell him the truth. His response was shattering: the soap-works was teetering on the edge of bankruptcy.

"We had intended, Judith and I, to ask you for help, now that you were a wealthy widow." His laugh was bitter. "But it would seem that we are all out of luck."

So she was still Morwenna's pensioner; there was no independence, however slight, to be gained from what Richard had left her. The silence of the house closed round her. Eliot, quiet at last, stared into the fire, looking as though he were suffering the tortures of the damned. Lilias could not bear to watch him. She closed her eyes and let her mind drift back to earlier, happier times. . .

She was standing in the front parlour of this very house, and a young man was looking at her through half-shut lids, a swarthy young man, but with such charm of manner and such a heart-melting smile, that she did not realise until much later that he was ugly. . .

The scene blurred and shifted like water. She was standing now in a different room, but the same eyes still caressed her, the same charm still lapped her about with its warmth. And the King's voice said plaintively: "If ever you should change your mind, I should be happy if you would let me know."

CHAPTER TWENTY-FOUR

The bed was empty of anyone save herself, only the dented pillow and the soft valley in the goose-feather mattress showing where Charles had lain. The sheets were cold: he must have left her early this morning, or, perhaps, even late last night, to seek other satisfactions with which to pleasure his insatiable body.

Lilias stretched, then slid out of bed, padding softly across the room to a mirror, which reflected the day's first wash of light. Sunshine edged across the floor between the folds of damask, curtaining the windows. It was going to be another glorious day.

She regarded herself thoughtfully in the mirror, her image drowned in the rippling glass like Ophelia in her tree-haunted stream. She stood on tip-toe, tautening her stomach muscles and twisting from side to side, narrowing her eyes in an effort to persuade herself that she was still sixteen. Then she laughed and gave it up. She was, in this May of 1670, nearly forty-four years old: the skin of throat and hands testified to that fact, and the black hair which cascaded across her shoulders was, if one looked closely, threaded with grey.

She sighed and went back to bed. It would be some while yet before a maid brought her hot spiced wine, before she could rise and dress and leave Whitehall Palace to make the necessary preparations to accompany the King to Dover.

Lilias tried to sleep again, but could not; so she lay, hands linked behind her head, thinking back over the past four years. Charles had been delighted at her surrender, coming as it had at a time when his feelings had been scarred by Frances Stuart's marriage to the Duke of Richmond. For a while, the newly-weds had been forbidden the court. But, finally, Charles had relented, and his good-nature had been amply rewarded, the gossips declared, the new Duchess bestowing her favours where plain Frances Stuart had not.

Castlemaine, now Duchess of Cleveland, had to face the fact that she was now only one of many. The actresses Moll Davis and Nell Gwynne had been brought to court; and although Moll's star was quickly on the wane, Nellie's was still in the ascendant. The birth of her son in February had established her permanently in the King's affections.

During the past twelve months, Lilias had found herself more and more Charles' confidante, lending a sympathetic ear to his troubles rather than comforting his body with her own. She had listened to him and soothed him during his conscience-stricken dismissal of Clarendon and his elevation of those five men whose surname initials made up the word Cabal. She had shared his shame and anger when the Dutch, in the sort of exploit which had hitherto been the prerogative of the English, had sailed up the Medway to Chatham and captured the flagship, *The Royal Charles*. Above all, she had let him talk endlessly about his yearning to embrace the Catholic faith and his love of the Church of Rome.

"What should I do without you?" he had asked last night, lying with his head against her shoulder, drowsy after making love.

"You could talk to Her Majesty," Lilias had suggested, tracing the line of his cheekbone with her fingers. "The Queen is a very able woman."

"But so plain. Poor Catherine. I should never have married her. Never been seduced by the Portuguese promise of Bombay and Tangier—and those three hundred thousand pounds in cash. But I won't divorce her, whatever Buckingham and the rest advise. I won't send her back in disgrace to her own country. I'm not like my famed—or infamous—ancestor, Henry the

402

eighth." He had lain quiet for a while, then asked her on a sudden spurt of laughter: "Do you know what my latest nickname is?"

"Old Rowley, after that stallion you keep in your stables at Newmarket. But I didn't think Your Majesty knew."

"One of the Queen's ladies was telling another about it the other day, as I happened to be passing the door."

"So you eavesdropped."

"Naturally. And when her friend had gone, I went in and proved to her that the nickname was justly deserved." He had chuckled unashamedly at the recollection, then turned over and gone to sleep. He had not disturbed her again.

No; her hold on him was beginning to weaken. Indeed, after the first eager flush of his triumph, it had never been strong. She was four years older than he, and his taste had always run to younger women. The relationship between them was really forged by that bond which drew Charles to all those who had helped him in the years of his adversity. In her case, being a beautiful woman, it was natural that he should have wished to sleep with her, an ambition for so long thwarted by time and circumstance and distance. But once he had achieved his aim, desire had quickly faded for them both.

But he had been more than generous with jewels and money. She was financially independent of Morwenna. She need never be a burden to the daughter she loved so much.

Morwenna ... Patrick's child. Patrick, who, like Barnaby, she could never think of without regret. Of her three husbands, Richard was the only one whose ghost did not return to haunt her. Of Priam, she would not let herself think at all.

He came rarely to London these days, and when he did, she kept out of his way. Magdalen was a permanent invalid, never leaving Westovers, nursed by the devoted

403

Cressida. The runaways had returned a few weeks after their marriage, defiant but happy. Even Oliver seemed to have mellowed, now that he had got what he wanted. Priam found him invaluable in the running of the estate, devoted to the interests of everything that would one day be his. It was through Oliver and her daughter-in-law that Lilias received the news of Westovers—and of that unhappy, childless house in Broad Street.

Lilias sat up in bed, hugging her drawn-up knees. She did not want to think of Eliot and Judith. About them, she felt guiltiest of all. . .

The maid came in with her wine and left it beside the bed. Soon, someone would be coming to lead her out of the palace and down the water-steps to the King's waiting barge. And after a few hours' rest at home, she would be on the road to Dover, to welcome the King's sister, Minette.

*　　*　　*

Dover was crowded to suffocation for the signing of the treaty between England and France: a military and political alliance, ostensibly negotiated by Buckingham. But there were secret undercurrents, she was certain, which Lilias could not quite determine. Charles was playing some deep game of his own; she guessed that there was a treaty within a treaty, whose terms were known only to himself, his sister and the King of France.

The little town was so crammed that many of the French nobles and officials in the Duchess of Orleans' entourage were forced to camp outside the city walls. The royal party was housed in the ancient castle on the cliffs, while Lilias and Morwenna found themselves lodged in a house near the harbour, thoughtfully rented for them in advance by the King.

"Then I may slip away and see you in comfort, whenever I want," Charles had toid Lilias, affectionately pressing her hands.

404

But his sparkling eyes told her that, for the next few days at least, he would want no other company than that of his sister, the only woman whom, in his whole life, he had truly and disinterestedly adored. There was, too, an added attraction in the person of one of Minette's ladies-in-waiting, a voluptuous young Bretonne, Louise de Kéroualle.

Lilias first noticed Louise at the great ball given in Minette's honour, and smiled wryly to herself. It might be the baby-faced Duke of Monmouth who was hovering solicitously about Mademoiselle de Kéroualle, but it was Charles who sent her the covert glances calculated to arouse her desire. Lilias, dancing with Prince Rupert and recalling more hazardous days in Bristol, noted how the girl's pale cheeks flushed each time her eyes encountered those of the King.

As the dance ended, Rupert escorted Lilias to a seat and offered to fetch her refreshment.

"It's hot in here," he said dourly. "Bloody hot." Always the same blunt Rupert. "All this nonsense. Waste of time."

He glanced about him disparagingly, condemning the frivolities of the court. He had put on weight, which counteracted the effect of his great height, but he was still an imposing figure. He had never been an easy man to like, and his natural taciturnity had increased after Maurice's death. The Prince's body might be here, its presence commanded by the King, but his heart was in his laboratory, among his burners and crucibles. He had perfected gunpowder, invented the process known as etching, and discovered a way to make droplets of glass which would not break, even when struck by a hammer. And Lilias, whose knowledge of scientific matters was as limited as any other woman's, found it hard to engage his attention. She was relieved when he moved away to procure her a glass of wine.

"Mother!" She glanced up to see Morwenna in a glow

405

from dancing. The dark hair was a riot of curls, the rose satin and lace of her dress complementing the white skin to perfection. "Mother, this is the Comte de St Amand. Lucien de St Amand. The Duchess of Orleans introduced him to me herself."

Lilias transferred her gaze to her daughter's cavalier. A smiling, fresh-faced youth bowed low over her outstretched hand.

"I can see now, madame, where the so beautiful Miss O'Mara gets her looks."

It had been one of the stipulations of Patrick's mischievous will that his daughter should take his name, but Lilias could never hear it applied to Morwenna, even after all these years, without it sounding strange.

"Miss—? Yes; yes, of course, my daughter . . . You are very gallant, comte, but I am afraid that such a comparison is likening winter to spring." Her eyes mocked him. *Let me hear you wriggle out of that, Monsieur le Comte!*

The young man did so with ease and an answering gleam of amusement which immediately endeared him to Lilias.

"Not winter, madame. Not even autumn. Late summer, which is the best of all seasons."

Lilias laughed and rose, tapping him on the arm with her fan. "You have an extremely agile tongue for so youthful a gentleman. A born flatterer. Ah! I see Prince Rupert returning. I beg you will excuse me. Take care of my daughter for me, comte." And she had no doubt, from the look on his face, that he was more than eager to do so.

The Prince claimed his partner again and handed her a glass, his face more lugubrious than ever.

"I've been talking to Sir William Penn," he announced, as she gratefully sipped her wine. "He's been in Bristol, and then went on to Bath. He tells me that Chelwood's wife is sick and not expected to recover."

* * *

406

He stared into the face where all pain had been smoothed away, the flesh already falling back from the bones in the pale anonymity of death.

"Magdalen," he whispered.

Cressida's hand slid into his. "She can't hear you, father. Mother is dead."

Dead. He had never before realised the finality of that word, like a door closing and the key turning in the lock. There were so many things he ought to have said to her, so many things he ought to have done. Now, it was too late for any of them. Magdalen was beyond his reach and his power to hurt her any more.

Oliver said, from Priam's other side: "Come away, my lord, and leave her to the women. They must lay her out. There is nothing more that you can do."

"Oliver's right, father." Cressida's voice was choked by sobs, her eyes, in the candlelight, brilliant with unshed tears. "Come downstairs to the library and rest for a while. I've ordered a fire to be lit."

The library was dim, full of leaping shadows and unquiet ghosts. The Earl's portrait, which had once so irritated Patrick O'Mara, still hung over the fireplace, depicting a much younger, less careworn man. Priam glanced at it, then looked away. He had no wish to be reminded of his youth.

He longed to feel more grief, to weep silently, as Cressida was doing within the shelter of her husband's arms. What a strange marriage that was, yet Cressida seemed content, and Oliver showed unexpected moments of affection. Had Magdalen been content with the few small crumbs of comfort which had come her way? And Oliver was unlikely to fall in love with another woman; Cressida would be spared that ultimate betrayal. Priam shivered and moved nearer to the fire.

A face seemed to form in its molten heart. Lilias! He was free to marry her at last.

The thought dismayed him. How could he even

407

contemplate such a thing, with Magdalen's body, not yet cold, lying upstairs? But he had never been one for hypocrisy or self-delusion. Lilias had been the guiding star of his life ever since he had first seen her, pregnant and laying about her with a broom-handle, twenty-seven years ago, on the Frome Bridge. In all the vicissitudes of their lives since then—the misunderstandings, the separations, their few brief months of happiness—she had never been out of his thoughts. She had been his first thought on waking, his last on going to bed at night. Nothing that had happened, that she had said or done, had made the slightest difference; not even now, when he knew her to be the mistress of the King.

"You mustn't grieve, father." Cressida's hand pressed his. "Mother has suffered so much pain. And she's with Cassie now."

Priam looked into his daughter's face and envied her her simple faith. To Cressida, death was like going from one room to another. To him, it was an unknown darkness. He was not even sure of life after death.

I am the Resurrection and the Life. He that believeth in me, though he were dead, yet shall he live . . . The words of St John's Gospel mocked him; words uttered nearly two thousand years before by a Jewish carpenter in Galilee. How could he be sure that they meant anything, had, indeed, ever been said?

But his love for Lilias, that was something he knew and understood, something he could hold on to. Was that blasphemous? Perhaps; he only knew it was the truth. He was not young any more, but he still felt for Lilias a passion which seemed to melt his very bones. Whatever years were left to them, they should spend together. In a month or two, when he had acknowledged convention by a decent interval of mourning, he would go to London and find her. And then he would bring her home.

★   ★   ★

The chill of the September day struck through the walls of St Mary Redcliffe, William Canynge's gift to his native city two hundred years before. "The fairest parish church in England," Queen Elizabeth had called it; but today, it was sombre and forbidding as Admiral Sir William Penn was lowered into his grave.

Lilias had travelled to Bristol for the admiral's funeral, feeling that it was the last respect she could pay to Richard's friend. She had also received a letter from Eliot, saying that he and Judith had urgent business which they wished to discuss.

She had arrived feeling tired and dispirited. The journey had taken three days over roads whose pot-holes had jolted and bumped her every inch of the way. This time, Morwenna did not accompany her mother, preferring to remain in London under the chaperonage of old Lady Tremayne. Lucien St Amand had returned to the English court on a protracted and apparently aimless visit.

"But," old Lady Tremayne had cackled, nudging Lilias in the ribs, "not quite so aimless as it seems, my dear. He will make a match of it with your little one, I think, if his parents can be brought to agree. A great match for Morwenna. The St Amands are one of the oldest families in France."

She did not add—did not need to add—that Morwenna's antecedents were mixed; that her parentage had been the subject of a minor scandal; that she was either the daughter of a Regicide or the bastard of an Irish adventurer, whom her mother had later married. And who was Lilias O'Mara? The child of a Cornish parson, elevated by time and events beyond her deserts.

As well as being despondent, Lilias was also lonely. Her relationship with the King had come to an end, as she had always known it must, but sooner than she had expected. For this, the reappearance of Louise de Kéroualle had been responsible. Three weeks after

409

returning to France, the Duchess of Orleans had died very suddenly. Charles, mad with grief, and listening to rumours of poison, had declared his intention of renouncing the Treaty of Dover. King Louis, to placate his cousin, and being apprised of Charles' attentions to Mademoiselle de Kéroualle, had ordered Louise back to England. Charles, for the present, had eyes for nobody else.

So Lilias had been glad of an excuse to leave the court. Unlike Castlemaine and Nell Gwynne, she did not feel threatened by Louise de Kéroualle; the little Bretonne had only brought her inevitably brief time as Charles' mistress to a premature close.

"It was too late when you came to me," the King had said, kissing her a fond farewell. "We should have been lovers years ago."

His parting gifts had been lavish, in appreciation of the fact that she neither screamed nor shouted nor abused him like a fishwife, accepting her dismissal with dignity. If he suspected that she did not really care, he refused to admit it, in deference to his pride.

The atmosphere of the Broad Street house did nothing to lift Lilias' spirits. She was in the depths of despair because she had received no word from Priam. She had hoped, as the months wore on after Magdalen's death, to have either a letter or a visit from him. But he had remained silent. Did he despise her so much for becoming the mistress of the King? Was it all over between them?

She was worried by Judith's appearance: thin to the point of emaciation, her face aged by bitterness and disappointment. Eliot, too, looked older than his twenty-seven years. All through supper, on that first evening of her visit, Lilias noticed how they avoided one another's eyes.

After he had pronounced the final grace and pushed back his plate, Eliot said baldly to Lilias: "Judith and I are going to America."

"You mean—to settle?" She was startled. It was an event she had not foreseen.

"To make a fresh start." Eliot's voice was harsh and Lilias saw Judith wince. She put out a hand and covered one of her daughter's. It lay passive, like a dead thing, under hers.

Eliot went on: "We are going to Massachusetts, to Boston. I believe you have acquaintances there."

"Elizabeth and Makepeace Farleigh. I know that they would be most happy to do anything in their power for ... for your father's son. They thought the world of Richard ... But, Eliot, are you sure about this? New England is a long way away."

"The farther the better." It was Judith who spoke, in a flat, colourless voice. All the spirit seemed to have been knocked out of her as the longed-for marriage to Eliot had turned to dust and ashes in her mouth. "Anywhere," she added with a tinge of animation, "would be better than here."

Eliot nodded. "We are agreed that there are too many memories here. We have talked it over very carefully. We need a new country, a new world, a new beginning. We must put the past behind us. Geoffrey has agreed to come with us."

"Geoffrey? Will he be happy?" Lilias felt a sudden twist of the heart as she remembered a small soft body embracing her knees, and a pair of dove-like eyes raised trustfully to hers. She realised with a stab of conscience that she had lost touch with her older children during the past ten years.

"He wants to come. To travel with us, at least. It's true that persecution of the Society is as great—perhaps greater—in Massachusetts than it is here in England. But he can go south to Providence, to Roger Williams, who believes in toleration for all sorts and conditions of men. William Penn is also talking of going to America,

411

especially since his arrest and imprisonment. He talks—a little wildly, I think—of founding a Quaker settlement there. A city of brotherly love. If that happened, Geoffrey would certainly join him."

"Where is Geoffrey? I should like to speak to him."

"At a meeting ... We don't enquire. Then if the authorities ask us, we can say with truth that we know nothing."

Lilias sighed. "Is he as committed to the Society as ever?"

"More so, since his meeting with George Fox. Fox married the Widow Fell last year, here at the Friends' Meeting House in Broadmead ... We shan't sail until next spring; it would be foolish to risk a winter crossing. But I need your authority to sell the house and the soap-works. You will, of course, receive your share."

Lilias shook her head. "No, I don't need it, not any more." She saw Judith's embarrassment at this oblique reference to her liaison with the King, and hurried on: "The money is all yours, Eliot. Yours and Judith's. No one deserves it more. It will help you to make a fresh start in the colonies. Your father, I know, would have wished it so, as long as Morwenna and I were provided for."

It was the first reference she had made to Morwenna, and Eliot flinched. Lilias glanced at Judith, who sat stony-faced, looking fixedly at the opposite wall. Lilias pushed back her chair and rose.

"Will you be coming to the funeral tomorrow, Eliot? The admiral was your father's friend. I believe, years ago, when your mother was alive, Sir William lent him money when times were hard."

Eliot rose, also. "Geoffrey and I will both be there. And now, you must be tired after your journey. Judith and I will wish you a very good-night."

Thus dismissed, she went up to bed, up the familiar staircase to her old room, which she had shared for so many years with Richard. On a sudden impulse, she mounted yet further, to the attic, in which she had slept with Mollie Hanks. As she raised her candle, shadows leapt from their cobwebbed corners, darting across the floor with its carpet of dust, running over the ceiling and clinging to the walls. Nobody slept here now to dispel the phantoms, born of old memories and things which were past. . .

It was here it had all begun, that night that Barnaby had forced his way into her room, desperate to prove himself a man. The pattern of events had been woven from that thread, linking Barnaby to Hannah and Richard. Twenty-seven years, with their births and deaths, their hopes and fears, and their terrible, irretrievable mistakes. But there had also been moments of joy, brightening the tapestry with gold.

She lowered the candle, sheathing its flame with her hand, and the phantoms slunk back to their corners. It was only a neglected attic. Lilias turned on her heel and went downstairs to her room.

★　　★　　★

The service was over. The body of Sir William Penn had been lowered into its last resting place in the south transept of St Mary Redcliffe, and the congregation began to disperse.

Geoffrey, who had escorted his mother, murmured: "I must speak to William," and darted from her side. A moment later, Lilias saw him, face alight with hero-worship, talking to the elder of the admiral's two sons. The disagreements of the younger William Penn and his father on matters of religion had led to a breach between them; but the quarrel had been patched up before the admiral's death, and William had accompanied his father's body from Wanstead.

Someone touched Lilias on the arm, and she turned to find Joseph Leach beside her.

413

"I have had no chance, Mistress Pride," he said gravely, "to thank thee for thy intervention with the King, and my release from prison, some years back. So I thank thee now."

Lilias inclined her head. She recalled the merry-eyed youth of ten years ago, who had been breaking windows in an excess of zeal for the Restoration. And now, in his place, was this grave, unsmiling young man. Cromwell, Ireton, Sir John Eliot and the rest who had fought for freedom of worship could lie easy in their graves. The Lord of Misrule might reign in Whitehall, but elsewhere the spirit of Puritanism was far from dead. Where Englishmen lived and breathed, it would flourish, and men would fight and suffer for what they believed in. Judith had told her that Joseph Leach had been imprisoned, pilloried and whipped for his beliefs many times during recent years. Only the shadow of the King's protection had saved him from transportation.

Joseph bowed and went on his way, while Lilias looked round for Geoffrey. But he was still deep in conversation with William Penn. He did not need her, had not needed her for years. Eliot and Judith were absorbed in their own unhappiness; and as for Oliver, he had not needed her from the very beginning. And soon, Morwenna would have no more need of her: she would marry Lucien St Amand and go away to France.

As she left, greeted here and there by an old friend, snubbed by others, Lilias glanced behind her at the bulk of the church. She remembered it, crouched in the watery dusk of an April evening, when she and her father had walked wearily into Bristol for the very first time. Tears of self-pity filled her eyes as Eliot assisted her into the coach and ordered its return to Broad Street. It was no good looking back: she must look forward. But to what?

Judith met them at the door. "You have a visitor," she said to her mother, jerking her head in the direction of the parlour. It was obvious by the pugnacious set of her jaw that, whoever it was, she disapproved. Lilias looked at her enquiringly, but got no response. With a tired sigh, she pushed open the parlour door and went inside.

★   ★   ★

Lilias raised her head from Priam's shoulder, where it had been resting for the past two minutes.

"How did you know that I was here?" she asked.

"Oh ... word travels fast when it concerns the King's mistress."

"Ex-mistress. Such as it was, it is over between us ... Priam, do you hate me for that?"

His arms tightened about her and his voice was thick. "I could never hate you. I have loved you from the first moment of seeing you, laying about you with that broom."

They both laughed shakily. After a moment, however, she insisted: "But can you really forgive me for having become Charles' mistress?"

"It hurt ... but I understood. You were lonely ... and Magdalen might have outlived me."

"Yes ... and there was Patrick's will. I couldn't bear the thought of becoming Morwenna's pensioner."

"Is she truly O'Mara's daughter?"

"Oh yes. She looks very much like him, you know. The resemblance is easy to see, once you accept the truth ... What a tangle it all was ... Worse than you know ... But I couldn't live on Morwenna's money."

"Could you live on mine?"

"Be your mistress again, do you mean?"

He pushed back her head until she was looking him full in the eyes. Then he kissed her.

"No, I do not mean that, you beautiful but obtuse and foolish woman. I am asking you to marry me. I want you to be my wife."

The world spun round her. She had enacted this scene

so many times in her dreams, had dismissed it so often as impossible, that, now that it was happening, it did not seem real. It was just another dream which would vanish when she woke, shattering into a thousand pieces...

"Well? Will you marry me, Lilias? Don't keep me in suspense. Not after all these years."

Fragments of memory nudged one another. Barnaby, catching her at the foot of the stairs and urging her frantically: "Marry me! Marry me!" Richard, sitting on the edge of her bed, imploring: "Lilias, I'm asking you to marry me." Patrick, with a wound in his shoulder, telling her: "As soon as I'm fit enough, we shall be married."

Ghostly echoes from the past, holding her silent for a moment longer. Then she smiled, sliding her arms about her lover's neck. And this time, it was with true joy in her heart that she answered: "Yes, oh yes, Priam, my love, I'll marry you."